Advance Praise For

Kiss Tomorrow Goodbye

"Foster skillfully evokes the barely controlled chaos and high-wire camaraderie of the ER, and regales readers with intricate, absorbing accounts of the struggle to stabilize patients under extreme pressure. Alex Randolph is an engaging guide to this scene, and on the way to a riveting climax, his saga gives us a vivid dispatch from the front lines of American medicine. Enthralling ... with real depth and pathos."

—Kirkus Review

"Foster creates emergency room scenes that enable readers to almost smell and taste the fear.... a tale that resonates with real life and includes the bonus of a credible love story."

—ForeWord Review

D1713168

Also by D. Bruce Foster

Twelve Lead Electrocardiography
For ACLS Providers
First Edition
Elsevier Health Sciences

Twelve Lead Electrocardiography
Theory & Interpretation
Second Edition
Springer

D. Bruce Foster

KISS TOMORROW GOODBYE

This book is a work of fiction. Names, characters, places, and incidents are products of the author's imagination, or are used fictitiously. Any resemblance to actual events, locales, or persons, living or dead, is coincidental.

Copyright © 2011 by D. Bruce Foster

All rights reserved.

Visit D. Bruce Foster's website at www.dbrucefoster.com

Macdougall Press

Printed in the United States of America

ISBN-10: 0615493882
ISBN-13: 978-0615493886 (Macdougall Press, LLC)

LCCN: 2011930885

To Jan

ACKNOWLEDGMENTS

I can tell you that every first-time fiction author needs lots of encouragement. This was provided in abundance by my gorgeous, long-suffering, and book-loving wife, who kept me convinced that *Kiss Tomorrow Goodbye* was a worthwhile endeavor during up times and down times. Her encouragement was supplemented by an immeasurable dose of patience during her year-plus sojourn as a writer's widow, and to Jan I offer my thanks and my love.

Two talented people deserve special recognition and thanks for their contributions. First, my editor and friend, Marie Lanser Beck, for her light and gentle hand, superb editorial skills, ever insightful suggestions, unfailing encouragement, and rock-solid advice. It is a far better book for her tireless efforts. I owe her for that.

Second, Ellen Ternes, for her early reading of the manuscript and her sage story line advice. She always had the big picture in mind.

To the extent that Alex Randolph is hip, much credit goes to my daughter, Allison Fortmann, herself a harried thirty-something mother of two, who was immediately able to relate to Penny Murray.

Many first readers are to be thanked for their careful reading and suggestions, including Christopher Lowe, whose comments precipitated a rewrite of the love story; Wendy Scott; Miles and Anna Cole; authors Mary Alice Baumgardner and Sarah Sawyer; physicians Ed Foster, Scott Card, Vickie Ellis, and Kittsey Reihard; George and Downey Dress; and Brian and Jennifer Foster.

My thanks also to Sergeant Billy Price, retired from the Baltimore County Police Department, Arley Scott, Emergency Communications Technician with the Baltimore County Fire Department, and Dr. Larry Rogina, OB-GYN *par excellence*, for their technical advice.

And finally, my thanks to Allen Baumgardner who was the inspiration for the wonderful character of Allen Whitfield (who he does not parallel precisely), and who graciously allowed me to portray his dog, Daniel T. Boone, by his real name.

D. Bruce Foster
September 2011

PROLOGUE

THE GLEAMING WHITE LEXUS PULLED INTO A short gravel driveway just south of the small town of New Freedom, Pennsylvania, looking bizarrely out of place beside a dilapidated clapboard house with peeling white paint. Out of the car climbed four young men. The last to exit—a slender, blond boy dressed in khakis and a polo shirt—anxiously scanned his surroundings as he closed the door.

The boys walked through a short stretch of knee-high grass, stepped onto a crumbling concrete porch, and entered the house. A flimsy spring-loaded screen door clapped loudly behind the last of them, causing the blond boy to start.

He stood just inside the door and allowed his eyes to adjust to the light. Empty pizza boxes and beer cans littered the room. A single bare light bulb glared from the ceiling. The room was devoid of furnishings excepting a threadbare stained sofa, a flat-screen television sitting low on a wooden crate, and a rickety end-table with an overflowing ashtray.

He sank into the sofa and watched with a dry mouth as another boy emptied the contents of a plastic sack onto the end table. *I can still back out,* he told himself. But in his heart he knew that it was too late—the decision was made when he first climbed into the Lexus.

A frisson of anticipation and foreboding rippled through him—anticipation, because after six months of pain and self-denial, he longed for the release of heroin flowing through his veins; foreboding, because he knew that all would be lost the moment the needle punctured his skin, and he loathed himself for it.

This time and this time only, he lied to himself again. *I can be back home tonight and back in class in the morning.*

A wave of guilt washed over him, bringing before his mind unbidden images of his family: the laughing face of his twelve-year-old sister; his mother's benevolent eyes with a deep furrow of worry; his father's hard face, reddened with anger. He didn't want to face any of them tomorrow.

The owner of the rented house handed the blond boy a beer and saw the anxiety written on his face. "Relax," he said. "My girlfriend works in a nursing home. She scarfs up everything I need. I've got nice sterile syringes, sterile water; even sterile cotton balls. And," he added with a grin, holding up a tiny, waxy envelope containing a white powdery substance, "this is really good shit."

The blond boy's remaining will to resist steadily evaporated. He flicked the lighter with his thumb, holding the yellow flame under the spoon until the powder slowly dissolved, then sucked the warm liquid through a tiny, cotton-ball filter into the syringe. Now committed, his pulse quickened as the doubts receded, and the anticipation of intense pleasure grew.

He tied the rubber tourniquet just above his left elbow, careful to leave an end sticking out the top and angled toward him, so that he could grasp it with his teeth and release the tourniquet once the needle had found its mark. Pumping his fist several times until a forearm vein bulged, he winced momentarily as the needle pierced his skin, then slid smoothly into the vein. A flashback of blood appeared in the syringe. Quickly he released the tourniquet with his teeth and carefully leaned back into the sofa so as not to displace the needle.

Licking his lips, he slowly pushed on the plunger until one-quarter of the liquid had been injected, and then paused to assess its power. If it was too strong—after six months of being clean—he could limit the dose to prevent losing consciousness. Ten seconds later his cares fell away, and he began to float into euphoria.

How did I live without this for six months? he wondered, and eagerly pushed the remaining liquid into his veins. Rapidly, he began to float further and further from the dingy room toward darkness. As he gained velocity, for a brief instant he felt a vague flare of panic, then all was black.

CHAPTER ONE

MIDNIGHT PASSED, AND WE WERE thankfully down to just three patients in the department. In a minute, another one of them would be gone.

I hit *PRINT* in the discharge instruction dialogue box, and walked over to the printer to collect the eleven pages of canned computerized instructions and prescription information for *Low Back Strain*. They could only have been written by a lawyer. They're single spaced, if you can believe that; so long and tedious that no one ever reads them except the people who write them.

This is characteristic of the way that we do things in medicine. Documents are written with an eye toward litigation, not communication. A couple of trees a day go down in support of covering our asses with useless paper. I put the discharge papers under the clip in the chart and slid it into the discharge rack.

Tonight I was the only male in the department, a status reflected in the estrogen-laced conversation at the nursing station. Not that I mind estrogen. I'm a big fan of estrogen, in fact. I just have trouble, sometimes, identifying with the subject matter that arises when women gather. Rebecca Franklin and Jen Wilke sat in their blue scrub suits, amiably chatting and leafing through a celebrity magazine.

"Can you believe she had a baby with that jerk?" asked Rebecca. "I think he's creepy. I wouldn't let him touch me."

Jen shuddered. "He *is* creepy! He's cheated on her a zillion times, he beats her up, and she just keeps going back to him. She's an idiot."

~

The triage nurse saw him first—dimly—through the smoked glass of the sliding entrance doors. Two men roughly dragged the limp body by both arms from the front seat of the car, carelessly dropped it on the patio under the lights of the driveway canopy, and leapt back into the car. I barely heard the nurse's cry for help amidst the background noise of the department, but its urgency was unmistakable.

I slipped through the secure triage door and out into the lobby. An excited receptionist stood at her counter, pointing at the sliding glass doors. "Outside!" she exclaimed.

Tiny Lisa Turano knelt on the paved patio over a motionless young male, her hand held over his mouth feeling for air movement. Her pregnant belly brushed the brick pavement. Taillights rapidly receded out the circular drive accompanied by the whine of an accelerating engine and the squeal of rubber on asphalt.

"I don't think he's breathing, Alex!"

My fingers went to his neck, searching for a pulse. A second—two, three, four—passed, and finally a little surge of blood pushed against my finger tips.

"God, his heart rate must be about ten," I said.

Pinching his nostrils and lifting his chin, I placed my mouth over his and blew, the resistance against my breath increasing as his lungs expanded. The smell of alcohol was powerful. We're not really supposed to do this these days. Mouth-to-mouth is forbidden for infection control reasons. We're supposed to use a pocket mask. But I didn't have one in my pocket, and sometimes you have to do what you have to do.

Rebecca and Jen appeared, pushing a gurney. The three females and I struggled to lift the victim's dead weight onto the stretcher, arms flopping off to the side. We raced through the lobby and into the resuscitation room, roughly sliding him onto the table. April Keller strode in a few seconds later, and I now had four nurses in the room.

Under the brilliant light of the surgical lamps, I could see that the boy was maybe late teens in age. He was clean and well-dressed in a turquoise polo shirt and khakis. Curly blond hair fell over his ears, merging with the fine peach fuzz that covered his face. His skin looked like he'd been dipped in a vat of blue dye—*cyanosis*, it's called—from insufficient oxygen in his blood.

All four nurses efficiently went about their work without commands and, for the most part, without words. The room was a frantic blur of motion. Lisa clapped a mask and ventilation bag over his face and began to push air into his lungs. Data began to pop up on the overhead monitor screen. "Heart rate is only eight," called out April. He was near death.

Rebecca handed me a laryngoscope and an endotracheal tube that I would insert into his lungs to restore his breathing. With a final squeeze of the ventilation bag, Lisa stepped aside, the basketball in her pregnant belly bumping my hip as we hurriedly tried to switch places at the head of the bed. With the boy not breathing, I had at most twenty, maybe thirty seconds, to get this done. We were working to save more than simply a life—it was really the boy's brain we were pursuing.

I rapidly slid the curved blade of the scope over his tongue, into his throat, and lifted. His vocal cords immediately popped into view. I gently slid the tube through the cords into the trachea—the main airway into his lungs—and removed the scope.

Lisa's small hands squeezed a ventilation bag attached to the tube. The boy's chest rose. She released the bag, and steamy vapor wafted into the tube as his chest fell with exhalation. I felt a wave of relief wash over me. *Good, I think we're in.* Sometimes you miss, and the tube goes into the esophagus. Then you've got a big problem—you're ventilating stomach instead of lungs. Not helpful.

A pair of feminine hands plugged a little color carbon dioxide indicator into a side port on the endotracheal tube. "We've got yellow," Rebecca announced loudly. The indicator had detected carbon dioxide coming from the boy's lungs and turned yellow. That confirmed that we were in the trachea, not the esophagus.

I placed a stethoscope on each side of his chest and listened: loud, clear breath sounds with each squeeze of the bag. *OK. So far so good.* We had control of his airway and breathing.

His heart rate began to gradually increase as the oxygenation of his heart muscle improved. But he was still in deep trouble. His blood pressure was too low to register on the machine, and so the icon on the monitor screen just displayed a question mark instead of numbers.

I lifted one eyelid. His pupils were constricted—pinpoint in size, really. No diagnostic magic was necessary here. Given his age, the circumstances of his arrival, the respiratory depression, his slow heart rate, and the pinpoint pupils, almost certainly we were dealing with a narcotics overdose.

I glanced at one arm. It bore confirmatory *track marks*—telltale small blemishes over the course of his veins that indicated repeated needle sticks. Heroin had arrived in the countryside.

"OK. I've got a line," Jen announced as she taped the IV into place. "Do you want an amp of Narcan?" We were in luck. The veins of most drug addicts are so scarred that it usually takes multiple attempts to find a vein.

"Just one for now," I said.

Narcan is a powerful narcotics antidote that almost instantly reverses the effects of heroin, allowing the overdose victim to start waking up. If fact, you have to be a little careful with this stuff, because if you give addicts too much Narcan they wake up fully and go into immediate narcotics withdrawal. Then you've got a wild man on your hands. But after two full doses of Narcan, John Doe didn't stir.

We struggled for another twenty minutes to get John Doe's cardiovascular system stabilized. Gradually, all the numbers began to come into line—heart rate, blood pressure, oxygen saturation—all good. But we were now a total of forty minutes into this, and he was still showing no signs of recovering consciousness. I didn't like that. He must have apneic—not breathing—for a very long time.

The ward clerk handed me a lab report. Urine toxicology studies confirmed the presence of a narcotic in his blood. There remained now only one big looming question: had this poor kid fried his brain from lack of oxygen?

At the moment, things weren't looking so good. But only the passage of time would tell whether John Doe would ever wake up and be able to read and write again, or whether he would sleep forever.

"Do we know who this kid is?" I asked.

The girls were pulling off his khakis and started rummaging through his pockets.

"Nothing," said Jen. "No wallet; no nothing."

~

"How many kids were in the car?"

"I don't know for sure," said Lisa. "I think there were two, plus the victim."

"Could you tell their race?"

"I think they were white, but I can't be sure about that either. I was looking out through the smoked-glass doors from triage, and it was dark. I guess I was just focused on the kid," she said.

"How about a make and color on the car?" Sergeant Jack Schmidt was gathering information from Lisa and me, trying to track down an identity on John Doe. It was about 1:30 in the morning. His grizzled face looked tired.

"I don't know, Jack," I said, stretching my back. "I'm pretty sure it was one of the Japanese sport coupes. It was a fairly light color. Might have been light gray, or even white. It had very large rectangular LED taillights."

"OK. Not much to go on, but we'll give it a whirl. I'll let you know if we have any relatives call in looking for a blond-haired kid," he said, closing his notebook.

"This is our second serious overdose in a week," I said.

Jack ran his fingers through his thinning hair. "Yeah, I know. Feel like you're back at Hopkins again?"

~

The sun was shining brightly when I pulled the blinds shut on my bedroom window about 8:45 that morning and finally crawled into bed. Ironically, sometimes when you're extraordinarily tired it can be tough to fall asleep. So I lay there thinking about the good-looking kid in khakis and polo shirt, who now lay comatose in the ICU on a ventilator.

He should have been waking up this morning in a college dorm. If he was lucky enough to make it through this overdose and woke up with a brain, he still faced a continued lifetime struggle with heroin. In truth, I feared it likely that he would never wake again.

Somewhere out there a pair of sleepless parents wondered where their son was.

I think he's gone, I replied softly.

CHAPTER TWO

I GET TESTY BY THE END OF A TWELVE HOUR shift in the ER. My empathy well runs nearly dry, and Mr. Hyde starts bursting out of his chains. It's not taking care of sick people that drains you. The sick ones are easy. It's trying to figure out who is sick and who's not really sick that drives you crazy. Who should I spend ten thousand dollars working up, and who really just needs a brain transplant?

Lurking among the drug-seekers faking illness, the attention-seekers looking for sympathy, the people who really just want a work note to cover their mental health day, the worried well in need of reassurance, and the nervous wrecks having a full-blown panic attack, are a handful of folks each day who have truly serious disease. Finding them is sometimes a little bit like looking for a life raft in an ocean. At the end of the day you wonder which one of them you missed.

With a little bit of luck, I would be out of here in fifteen minutes—before Mr. Hyde wriggled free of his last chain and started pissing off patients. Mr. Hyde likes Grey Goose and tonics. Drinks and dinner with Elizabeth would help calm him down.

It was *Low Back Pain Day* this Saturday in the ER, and I headed in to see my fifth back pain of the day and, hopefully, my last patient—Clayton Buterbaugh, twenty-two years old. Clayton crossed the state line to honor us with a visit because he happened to be in town helping his buddy move into new digs.

Actually, when I checked the computer, Clayton had just happened to be in town with back pain five times in the last three months, despite the fact that his address is thirty miles north of the Mason Dixon line—not five minutes from our larger, friendly-competitor hospital—and we're here on the Maryland side of the border. Today, according to the triage nursing notes, he lost his grip on the sofa he was carrying down the stairs and… well, you can imagine the pain that knifed through his low back.

"Hi Clayton. I'm Dr. Randolph."

Clayton stood leaning on a chair in a sweatshirt with the sleeves cut out, one hand gripping his low back. Tattoos cascaded from shoulder to wrist. His butt crack was just visible above his jeans. He adjusted the bandana tied around his head and winced as he looked up.

"Ya gotta help me, man. I can take a lotta pain, but this really, really hurts."

I asked Clayton a few questions, did my exam, and we got down to business.

"OK, Clayton, you've got myofascial strain of your low back. You're going to have to avoid all heavy lifting for about two weeks, and I'm going to put you on an anti-inflammatory drug, and a muscle relaxant."

"What are ya gonna gimme?"

"Eight hundred milligrams of ibuprofen which you'll take three times a day, and ten milligrams of Flexeril which—"

Clayton cut me off. "That shit is useless."

"What shit?"

"Ibuprofen. I've had that stuff before. It don't do shit."

"What works for you, Clayton?" This was the big question.

"Last time they gave me something that starts with a *P*–Per… Per-something." The *Per-something* Clayton is digging deep to remember is Percocet—oxycodone and Tylenol. Five bucks a pop on the street. Clayton knows the game.

I adopted my best bedside manner. "No Percocet, Clayton. I'll give you some Dolobid."

"I'm allergic to Dolobid. Can't take that stuff."

"What happens when you take Dolobid?"

"Tears my guts up."

"OK, Clayton. Tylenol number three with codeine. That's it. Nothing more."

Clayton glared at me, but recognized that I was onto him and he wasn't going to get any Percocet. Tylenol with codeine, or *T-3's,* as they're known, are a poor cousin to Percocet in narcotic potency and street value, but Clayton decided he had to salvage something from this visit.

He looked at the floor and said, "Just get me the fuck out o' here."

End of negotiation. I walked out of the room back to the nurse's station to finish Clayton's paperwork, while Dr. Jekyll and Mr. Hyde resumed their argument in my head. Jekyll said, *How do you know the kid doesn't have a herniated disc and is really in pain?* Hyde said, *You're an idiot! He knows all the drugs, and he comes across the state line because they've cut him off at York Hospital.* These two guys are at it all the time.

~

Elizabeth sat across our cozy corner table for two, looking her usual slender and immaculate self. She wore a simple white V-neck summer dress that revealed the freckles on her tanned chest. A white linen tablecloth, gleaming white china, and a single white orchid graced the table. Everything was white tonight. Her perfectly manicured fingernails ran through her blond, highlighted hair as we talked.

"Nice that you could get away on time tonight," she said smiling.

I ignored her veiled reference to my chronic tardiness, and smiled back. "I couldn't wait to get here. I skipped out at 7:00 and abandoned six patients to Ben. I think I need a drink."

Elizabeth was a Baltimore girl who rode horses—as opposed to skateboards—in high school. High school for Elizabeth was the Oldfields School near leafy Glencoe in Baltimore County, where, since 1867, rich fathers have been sending their daughters to cuddle up to horses instead of boys. Her maternal grandmother, five times removed, was Lord Calvert's niece or something like that. Her father's heritage really didn't matter because he is Managing Partner at Hamilton, Duncan & Blackstone—one hundred and twenty-five lawyers strong—and we all know that breeding can be overlooked when real money is involved.

After horse high school, Elizabeth moved on to Bryn Mawr, another elite girl's school, and then law school at Columbia. Needless to say, Elizabeth is very well educated, possesses more than a little streak of feminism, and normally does not well tolerate fools or insensitive males, which, of course, begs the question of why we are having dinner together tonight.

"How was your shift, Alex?"

"Busy. The usual mix. Kids with fever; women with abdominal pain; crashing old folks. And today was *Back Pain Day* in the ER."

She frowned. "Why women with abdominal pain? Don't men get abdominal pain too?"

Somewhere in the distant recesses of my brain, a faint alarm began to sound.

"Men get abdominal pain too. They just don't go to the doctor," I said.

Elizabeth slid back in her chair, arms folded and eyebrows raised. She crossed her legs for good measure. I couldn't see her panties during the cross.

"So what's your point, Alex? That women over-utilize the medical care system?"

The Grey Goose was steadily flying into my brain, but I was still sober enough to recognize that I had stumbled into a gender trap of my own making.

"Generally speaking, men have only one piece of apparatus that rises to a level of medical concern in their minds," I said.

Elizabeth's expression softened, and then a faint smile crossed her face. "Very funny, Alex."

Elizabeth and I met at a wedding. Funny how weddings beget weddings, or at least beddings. But in any case, Elizabeth's brother was marrying my best friend John's little sister, if you can follow that relationship—a very sweet girl from Sparks, whose father was a solo accountant.

Managing Partner Hamilton was not thrilled that Hamilton Junior was marrying down. And so, to avoid a socially dangerous church basement reception, he popped for the reception himself at Baltimore Country Club. It didn't take me long to spot Elizabeth among the bridesmaids. We ended up the evening with Elizabeth in bare feet, sitting behind the barn on the fabled sixth hole, sharing a glass of champagne. And, of course, both of us being highly educated overachievers and highly drunk, we found something in common.

CHAPTER THREE

I HAD CHANGED INTO SCRUBS AND WAS striding down the hall from the locker room, past the open door of the Nursing Manager's office, toward the secure ER entrance. I was about to make it on time for the last of my three night shifts. From behind me an annoyed voice rang out through the open door. "Alex, you didn't finish that agenda, and the department meeting is Tuesday!"

Julie Talbot, MSN, emergency department unit manager and my self-appointed guardian angel, had caught me. "I'll work on it tonight," I yelled back. "What are you doing here anyhow? It's Sunday night."

Unit managers have Monday through Friday day jobs, but Julie gets her days mixed up sometimes. Nights too. Occasionally, I get e-mails from her at three o'clock in the morning. She's an incurable workaholic. She keeps my feet to the fire, and usually manages to keep me out of trouble with the administrative types.

I took this job nearly three years ago as chief of emergency medicine at the new Mason-Dixon Regional Medical Center in northern Baltimore County, because I was tired of the academic world. In general, it's filled with insufferably pompous boors whose primary conversational skill is a recitation of the most recent articles they've read in the *New England Journal of Medicine*. Okay, that's not quite fair, but close. They also tend to not hold docs in little rural hospitals in very high esteem.

Apart from medical school and residency, I'd spent three years as an assistant and then associate professor of emergency medicine at Johns Hopkins University, so I'd spent enough time in the hallowed halls of academic medicine. I loved the teaching, but I needed some time outside the ivory tower in the real world.

It's not often that the opportunity arises to build a brand new department from scratch, so the job at Mason-Dixon appealed to me. I would have the opportunity to build my own team and workplace culture. And, it was out in the country near my home—no more dreadful morning commutes into the city in bumper to bumper I-83 morning traffic.

I flashed my security badge at the wall-mounted reader, heard the click of the door lock opening, and entered chaos. It's amazing how quickly your mind takes a snapshot of a situation. I could tell instantly that tonight would stretch on for an eternity.

Pat Cole, the night shift charge nurse, brushed past me and said, "If I were you, I'd just turn around and go right back home." A young woman with a blond ponytail shuffled past the nursing station, pushing an IV pole and clutching her gown together behind her buttocks with one hand in an attempt to salvage some modesty. Three nurses were charting at nursing station computers, and another one was at the Omnicell medication dispenser, pushing buttons to get drugs. From somewhere on the Fast Track side of the department, a symphony of wailing kids was playing. I saw an ambulance crew exit critical care Bed Ten with an empty stretcher, and a Baltimore County cop was leaning against the wall outside Bed Fourteen.

Scott Foreman, whom I'm relieving, looked up at me from his computer station and rolled his eyes while yelling into the phone. "Look, this guy definitely needs a surgeon. It's a big laceration, I think it involves an extensor tendon, and I really need you to come in and do that repair for me." Surgeons love to come in to the ER on Sunday night. Especially during football season.

My eyes went to the big Panasonic flat screen status board hanging from the ceiling of the nursing station. All sixteen beds were filled, and five more patients were in the waiting room. I felt a migraine coming on.

Dr. Lauren Dorfman, who would be my second doc until 1:00 AM, was walking back to her computer terminal, chart in hand. She caught my eye and just shook her head.

Scott put down the phone and looked up. "You are a sight for sore eyes, Alex. Wasn't a bad day until about three o'clock, and then all hell broke loose. It's been like this ever since."

I grabbed a sheet of scratch paper to take notes, and slid a chair up to the computer beside him. Scott started his report. "Sorry, but I've got five patients I've gotta leave you." The next part is a little like a relief air traffic controller standing behind the guy he's relieving and watching traffic flow on the radar screen until he says "I've got it," and then real quick slides into the chair.

"OK. Bed Three is a seven-year-old with fever and sore throat, and she's just waiting on a strep screen.

"Bed Seven is an eighty three-year-old female, Mrs. Finney—very nice lady—with fever, vomiting, and abdominal discomfort for twenty four hours. She's the one I'm most worried about. She's got a temp of a hundred and two. Her blood pressure was only in the nineties when she came in, and her pulse was in the one-twenties, so I think that she's probably septic. White blood cell count is fifteen thousand, and she's got leukocytes in her urine. Lisa is just now hanging antibiotics and the rest of her studies are still pending."

And so it went until Scott finished reporting on all five patients and said, "I'm outta here, Alex. It's all yours." *Thank you, Scott.*

There were six new patients that hadn't been seen yet, but I decided that first I better take a look at Mrs. Finney. Lisa Turano, RN, mother of two—soon to be three—was standing at the bedside punching buttons on the IV pump over her heavy-with-child belly when I walked into the room.

"How's she doing?"

Lisa replied without looking up from the pump. "She just vomited again, and her blood pressure is only in the eighties after a half-liter of saline."

Mrs. Finney was lying quietly with her eyes closed, breathing rapidly; nostrils flaring slightly. A fine sheen of sweat glistened on her forehead. Although her face was lined with fine wrinkles, she had a classically chiseled nose and arched eyebrows. It occurred to me that she must have been a very handsome woman in her day.

Her paper-thin skin was clammy to the touch when I gripped her hand and said softly, "Mrs. Finney?"

In response, her eye lids opened and she wordlessly looked directly at me. A trace of fear flickered across strikingly bright blue eyes, still clear after eighty-three years. The prongs of a plastic nasal oxygen cannula were inserted into each nostril.

"I'm Dr. Randolph. Dr. Foreman has gone home for the evening, and I'll be taking care of you tonight. I understand you haven't been feeling too well the last couple of days."

She shook her head slightly, obviously fatigued by the slightest physical effort, and her eyes closed again. Mrs. Finney was running out of gas.

I glanced up and absorbed the numbers and waveforms on the color monitor screen, giving me a real-time snapshot of how her heart and lungs were coping with the stress of this illness.

Her heart was beating at one hundred twenty-six times a minute—more than two beats a second—at probably the maximum effort level it could sustain after eighty-three years of faithful service. She was breathing rapidly, and the percentage of her blood that was saturated with oxygen—O_2 *sat*, as we call it—was only ninety-one percent instead of the high nineties. With her blood pressure now falling into the eighties, all of the numbers indicated that Mrs. Finney was clearly slipping into shock.

"Lisa, help me to sit her up." We struggled against the dead weight of lifting Mrs. Finney into a sitting position, and I quickly listened to her lungs. They were clear. Just from the exertion of trying to help us, her heart rate jumped to one hundred thirty-eight.

I started running a differential diagnosis through my head as I put my stethoscope on her chest, then gently felt her belly. Fever, vomiting, abdominal discomfort, and now shock. Could be dehydration from a gastrointestinal virus, but she looked too sick for that. Could be a surgical problem like diverticulits or appendicitis, but her belly was soft and not really very tender. She had leukocytes—white blood cells—in her urine, so my bet was urinary sepsis—an infection that started as a simple common bladder infection, but which, in this elderly female, had now spread into her bloodstream.

If I was right, a climactic battle was currently raging within Mrs. Finney between a little unicellular microorganism and Mrs. Finney's overwhelmed defense systems. The bacteria were reproducing faster than she could mobilize antibodies and white blood cells to kill them. She had all the classic signs of septic shock. If we weren't successful in keeping her cardiovascular system going until the antibiotics kicked in, she would die.

"Lisa, let's put her on a non-rebreather oxygen mask, and I'm going to put a central line in her." Lisa replaced the nasal oxygen prongs with a face-mask that would provide Mrs. Finney with one hundred percent oxygen, and then scurried from the room to retrieve the kit that I would use to insert a central venous catheter into Mrs. Finney's chest.

As she reached the doorway, Lisa bumped into Jen Wilke, gently leading a distinguished-looking older gentleman into the room as he slowly made his way with a cane."

"Dr. Randolph, this is Mr. Finney."

I reached out, and his bony hand gripped mine firmly. "Tell you what, Mr. Finney, follow me and let's find a place where we can sit down and talk." We walked slowly down the hall to the family counseling room, where I motioned for him to take a seat. I sat beside him.

"Mr. Finney, your wife is pretty sick." Leaning forward in the chair, elbows on knees, he clasped his hands together around the cane, met my gaze directly and briefly nodded.

"I don't have all of the studies back yet, but at this point it looks like she has an infection of her bloodstream that we call *sepsis*. It probably started in her bladder and spread from there to her blood stream."

They say that people who live together a long time eventually grow to look like each other. Mr. Finney had the same clear blue eyes and aged, but handsome, face as his wife. His thinning white hair was carefully groomed. I could see comprehension in those eyes, so I continued.

"Mr. Finney, I think you should know that this is a pretty serious infection. Mrs. Finney's blood pressure is quite low, and her heartbeat is very rapid. She is showing signs of slipping into shock."

Mr. Finney tapped his cane on the floor several times as he thought about that. After a moment, he said "I think you're telling me that she could die, right?"

I nodded. "Yes, sir."

"And what are the odds?" he asked.

This is always a tricky moment. There's a balance between communicating the seriousness of an illness to family members, yet offering hope and not striking terror in their hearts. Some people are unable to cope with the specter of potential death and quickly change the subject. Others want honest answers to direct questions. Mr. Finney was looking for an honest answer.

"The mortality from sepsis can approach fifty percent," I said quietly.

He held my gaze for several moments then looked off into the distance. "You know," he said, "we've been together for sixty-two years. I was nineteen and she was only seventeen. I thought she was the most beautiful creature I had ever seen." He looked at me again. "I always knew a moment like this would come, but I always thought that it would be somewhere out in the distant future."

~

I slid the roughly four-inch-long needle under Mrs. Finney's collarbone while pulling back on the attached syringe plunger in order to create a vacuum inside the syringe. I was aiming at an invisible point about one inch behind her breastbone, searching for a return of blood that would indicate that the needle tip had penetrated her subclavian vein. The needle went in all the way to the hub without a return of blood. I pulled the needle out almost all the way, and then redirected it a bit more toward her back. This time I was rewarded with a sudden gush of blood into the syringe.

I unscrewed the syringe from the needle and, leaving the needle in place, slid a long, thin, flexible guide-wire through the needle into her superior vena cava—the mother-of-all-veins that returns blood from the upper body to the right side of the heart. I then carefully removed the steel needle, and over the guide-wire threaded the catheter that would give me the information that would, with luck, help to save Mrs. Finney's life.

A central venous catheter gets hooked to a pressure transducer that measures the pressure of blood flowing into the heart and displays the pressure on a monitor screen. We call that a *central venous pressure*, or CVP. It's pretty straight forward. If the pressure of blood flowing into the heart is too low—as it often is in shock—they need more IV fluid. If it's too high, the heart begins to fail under the load, and you have to back off the fluids. The fluid we would use in Mrs. Finney was normal saline—salt water.

Lisa connected the catheter to the transducer, touched a few icons on the monitor screen, and a number popped up. It was three—low. I could push the fluids pretty hard.

"OK, Lisa. Let's start pushing normal saline wide open, and we'll see what happens."

~

By now I had fallen way behind in my share of the ER workload. It had taken almost an hour to deal with Mrs. Finney. Pat Cole was on me as soon as my butt hit the chair at my computer station. She's a forty-two-year-old single mother with two teenagers and she has no problem with being directive. That's why they made her a charge nurse.

"OK, Alex, you need to get goin' here," she said emphatically. "We need to get some of these people out of here. The strep test is back on Bed Three, and that family's been waiting over an hour. And what are you going to do with Bed Twelve? She's back from CT, and she's got diverticulitis. You need to get her admitted. And I've got eight patients backed up in the waiting room."

"Is this why you're a divorcee?" I asked.

"You need guidance, Alex, guidance," she said.

Rebecca Franklin walked up to the station and said, "Alex, you need to come see Mrs. Norris. She's still wheezing up a storm, and her O_2 sat is only in the high eighties. And Bed Five wants a work note." I dropped my pen and put my face in my hands.

My partner, Lauren, who had been valiantly processing patients as fast as she could while I was occupied with Mrs. Finney, walked back into the station.

"I see that you decided to come back to work," Lauren said, smiling.

~

I got rid of three patients, and was typing discharge instructions on a fourth, when I felt a hand on my shoulder. Lisa was standing there in blue scrubs with her belly in my face, so I couldn't help but pat it and ask, "How's your passenger?"

She grinned. "I think there's a soccer game going on in there. There's feet going in all directions. Maybe they missed one on the sonogram and there's really two of them."

Lisa is a very cool girl, with a very well-wired brain. Her husband, Frank, is a detective in the Baltimore City police department. They met in the ER at Hopkins, of course, long before we recruited Lisa to join our happy little band at Mason-Dixon Regional.

She screwed up her face. "We're not doing so well, Alex."

"Who's not doing so well?"

"Mrs. Finney's had three liters of saline in forty minutes, and her blood pressure is only seventy nine.

"What's her CVP?"

"It's up to twelve."

This was not what I had hoped for. Her CVP was about as high as I could push it without throwing Mrs. Finney into heart failure, and she was still in shock. If I didn't get her blood pressure up soon, her major organs were going to start to die. Then we'd be stuck with her kidneys and liver shutting down, and that would certainly be curtains for Mrs. Finney.

"OK. Start her on a norepinephrine drip, and try to get her blood pressure up over ninety."

Norepinephrine would constrict her blood vessels and raise her blood pressure. That would keep blood flowing through the large coronary arteries and keep her heart pumping. But there would be a price to pay. Too much vasoconstriction could potentially reduce blood flow through the smaller arteries to the rest of her body, damaging her other organ systems. This is often the way it is in medicine. You pay your money and you take your chances. I would have to tread a fine line here.

~

By 11:30 PM, the trains dropping off patients at the ER door were running less frequently, and although all the beds were still full, we were down to only two patients who had not yet been seen.

Lauren sighed from her computer terminal and brushed a lock of hair back behind her ear. "Remind me never to work with you again on a Sunday night."

I checked in on Mrs. Finney again. This time, when I touched her shoulder, she turned to me and managed a faint smile. Her oxygen saturation was better and her blood pressure was higher—hovering in the high nineties. Mr. Finney was sitting on the other side of the bed, holding her hand.

"We're not there yet, Mr. Finney, but we've made a little progress in the last hour," I said. "I think we've got a real shot at getting her back to you."

He stood, shuffled his way around the end of the bed and shook my hand. "Thank you," he said simply.

~

Lauren didn't leave until about one 1:45 AM. She's such a trouper. By that time, we were down to eight patients, and I thanked her for staying beyond the end of her scheduled shift.

The blond-haired kid from Friday night had been popping into my head all night long, so finally I picked up the phone and called the

ICU. I asked for whoever was taking care of the John Doe kid with an overdose, and the ward clerk who answered said, "That would be Andrew Price, and Mary Ellen is taking care of him." So, they had a name. They must have found the kid's parents.

"This is Mary Ellen."

"Hi, Mary Ellen. Dr. Randolph. They figured out who that kid was, huh?"

"Yeah. The police found his parents, and they came in yesterday. His mother hasn't left his bedside in twenty four hours. The father looks shell-shocked. Walks around like a zombie. His little sister's been here, too."

"The kid's not doing well?"

"Still comatose on the ventilator. He's unresponsive to pain, and he's got no cranial nerve reflexes. His EEG this morning was flat line. The neurologist ordered another EEG for tomorrow morning. Depending on what that shows, they're thinking of pulling the plug. They'll have to get a second neurologist to see him before they make that decision."

"I was afraid of that. Is he a local?"

"Yeah. His parents live in Parkton. I think his dad's an executive with Black & Decker. Missy up here knows them. They go to her church."

"How old is he?"

"Nineteen."

"Did they know he had a drug problem?"

"Yeah. He's been in rehab twice and had been clean for about six months, 'til this happened."

~

By 5:00 AM my brain was turning to mush. All the wackos come out in the middle of the night. I had had my fill of panic attacks, suicide gestures, intoxicated twenty-five-year-olds with four-letter vocabularies, and stuffy noses who couldn't sleep. Mr. Hyde was getting really agitated. Dr. Jekyll kept reminding him that these people have needs, too.

I discharged the last patient at 5:30. The board was clear. I lay down on a stretcher in Room Fifteen—because it's the most distant from the noise of the nursing station—closed my eyes, and prayed that no one else would come in before the end of my shift at 7:00 AM. Room Fifteen is also, appropriately, the psych room where we put people who need their brains examined.

CHAPTER FOUR

TUESDAY MORNING I CLIMBED INTO MY '95 Jeep Wrangler about 7:15 and headed west on Shepherd Road, through the little hamlet of Monkton, on my way to the monthly Department of Emergency Medicine meeting—better known as the *Doc's Meeting.* It was one of those glorious early October mornings when a bit of smoky-blue mist sits in the hollows, and the colors are all vivid. As I climbed Monkton Hill, out of the lower terrain along the Gunpowder Falls and past harvested corn fields, the sun struck the undulating, evenly-spaced rows of stubble, turning them to ribbons of gold.

Northern Baltimore County is a beautiful place to live. Still mostly farms, its steeply rolling hills are a transition from the Piedmont Plateau into the most northeastern ranges of the Blue Ridge Mountains, another thirty or forty miles north into Pennsylvania. It's a major bedroom community, however, for wealthy Baltimorons, as we call them, so more and more McMansions are sprouting forlornly in the middle of cornfields.

I grew up here, actually. My dad owned a nursery and landscaping business in Sparks—about ten or fifteen miles north of the city—which was still pretty well country in those days.

I slid into the 7-Eleven convenience store in Hereford, grabbed a cup of coffee, and headed north up York Road to the hospital, just off I-83 on Middletown Road.

Getting all the docs together at the same time for a meeting is a near impossibility. Someone is always just getting off a night shift. Somebody else has worked until 1:00 AM and doesn't want to get back out of bed for an eight o'clock meeting. For someone else, it's their day off. Others are on vacation, or away at a continuing medical education meeting someplace—hopefully where it's warm and there's a soft, sandy beach. I'm always amazed that as many people show up for these meetings as do.

We have the meetings in the staff lounge where the coffee pot is located, so the meeting room ends up being a little like Grand Central Station. By 8:05 on this Tuesday, enough people had straggled in that we could get started. Ben Russell stumbled in off his night shift, poured a cup of coffee, and stood in the corner in the certain knowledge that if he sat down he would fall asleep.

Besides Ben and me, four other docs had shown up. The room was packed with five other people, including Julie Talbot, who brings the agendas and documents, and four guests from other hospital departments who had requested time to address our august body. Sometimes we have more guests than docs.

I called the meeting to order.

"OK guys, let's get this show on the road."

I always let the guests speak their piece first, so we can get rid of them and have more oxygen in the room. Three of the four had exciting info about new rules, or audits of compliance with old rules. If you like rules, hospitals are a great place to work.

The fourth was Sam Warren, our congenial physical plant manager.

"Just wanted to let you know," said Sam, "that we're gonna be installing a wif-fi system in the ER next week as a customer service feature for patients and families. We may be in your way a bit with ladders in the hallways, etc., but it should only be a couple of days."

This made Sam very popular, because practically all my staff have an iTouch or smart phone on which they keep software for looking up drugs, so they'd be able to access the web and their e-mail. Sam got whistles, a round of applause, took a bow, and left.

After the guests had their say, we were finally able to wade into the actual agenda which, to Julie's annoyance, I hadn't completed until the day before the meeting. Mark Showalter did the monthly review of all transfers to other institutions—the Feds require this because they don't want us dumping uninsured patients on other hospitals—and all deaths in the ER. He concluded that all transfers were justified, and all deaths were non-preventable.

On to more substantive items. My revised protocol for treating pulmonary embolism—blood clots to the lungs—was approved. Unfortunately, we couldn't use it for a couple of months because it now had to be referred to Pharmacy Committee, Critical Care Committee, and Medical Staff Executive Committee for their approval. Whoever invented committees should be subjected to a dull guillotine. In the meantime, we would just do it informally without the approved sheet of paper.

We next launched into an important subject—namely how to reduce unnecessary radiation exposure to our patient population from CT's, better known as *CAT scans*. These marvelous imaging studies provide an astonishing 3-D view of body parts, but have just two little drawbacks—they carry a lot of radiation and they're expensive.

They're so fast, and so good, that people have started using them at the drop of a hat. They eliminate a lot of diagnostic uncertainty, and they cover your ass—meaning that a CT scan goes a long way to protect you in a court of law—but that's another subject.

Lauren Dorfman, with a voice that sounded like a bullfrog had recently taken up residence in her throat, led the discussion.

"There are two primary groups of immediate concern who are at risk: kids and kidney stones," she croaked. "Kids, of course, because their cells are dividing, and kidney stone patients because they often get so many repeat CT's that their lifetime exposure to radiation can become enormous."

Radiation, of course, is a two-edged sword. It kills cancer cells because they are growing rapidly by cellular division, and radiation has a much bigger effect on cells that are dividing. Unfortunately, every cell in a kid's body is dividing, too, because they're growing, so you don't want too many CT's on your kid—especially to their brains."

Since Lauren had just returned from a conference on ER radiology, I moved that she should draft some guidelines on CT utilization. I called for a show of hands, and Lauren was the sole dissenting vote.

Finally, we reached the last item on the agenda under *Old Business*—namely the response from nursing administration to our proposal to reduce door-to-doctor wait times. A committee had been working on this for three months, co-chaired by Julie and Rick Stapleton, a Duke medical school classmate of mine. Rick didn't make today's meeting because our charming southern boy was at a conference in Hilton Head, no doubt snoring in class in the morning, and soaking up rays and bourbon in the afternoon.

The biggest delay we found in getting patients ready to see the doc was the roughly twenty-minutes-time required for nurses to enter their patient assessment into Samson, the hospital-wide software platform. As is often the case with software, Samson was a one-shoe-fits-all application. It forced ER nurses to do the same extensive patient documentation on simple things, like ankle sprains, as on the most complex of critically ill patients. Very time consuming, very expensive, and very unnecessary.

The committee's recommendation to nursing admin was to modify the software to require only an abbreviated nursing assessment for simple complaints. It would reduce our door-to-doctor time by about twelve to fifteen minutes per patient, we guessed—nothing to sneeze at when you're processing eighty or ninety patients a day. Just as importantly, it would mean a lot more nursing time at the bedside caring for patients, and less time caring for computers.

Julie reported on the response back from Jacquelyn Ford, MSN, MBA, our glamorous Vice President of Patient Services.

"She said 'no.'" Scowls appeared around the room.

Tall, slender and impeccably dressed under her long white clinic coat, Jackie Ford is an Americus Health Systems, Inc. administrative thoroughbred. Americus, the parent corporation of Mason-Dixon Regional, also owns three other hospitals in the Baltimore area. It's a non-profit health system that's very much into integration and visionary strategic planning. They're also into control.

"Of course, they gave our proposal *very* serious consideration," Julie continued sarcastically. "And, of course, they are sooooo happy that we are looking for ways to be more efficient. But, unfortunately, it would be very expensive to modify the software, the other three hospitals are using it, and, as you know, we are committed to full integration across the Americus family of hospitals. Furthermore, it might compromise patient safety, and expose us to greater litigation risks."

Julie sat back in her chair and looked around the room like she was expecting thunder. Scattered curses around the table ionized the air.

"Let me talk to her," I said with a sigh.

Julie smiled. "She hates you."

This was a true statement. Jacquelyn and I are not always on the best of terms. She occasionally senses that I am inadequately respectful of her turf and, moreover, am not always a reliable supporter of Americus goals and objectives.

"I will make every attempt to be charming, courteous, and reasonable," I said.

By 9:30 we were done. We got a unanimous vote in support of the adjournment motion, and the meeting broke up. Julie hung around.

"You know," she said quietly, "they pulled the plug on that narcotics over-dose last night."

"You mean that kid from Friday night?" I asked.

Julie nodded. "The transplant team came about 9:00 PM, and they harvested all his organs."

"Oh, God. Those poor parents. I can't imagine."

"Those pricks who dumped him out should be put up against a wall and shot," she said.

CHAPTER FIVE

TEARS TRICKLED DOWN A PALE FACE FROM red, mascara-smeared eyes.

"I started spotting last night and when I got up this morning the blood just gushed out. I've been having terrible cramps."

Twenty-three-year old Samantha Thompson sat on the edge of the exam table in a huge patient gown that dwarfed her tiny frame. Her feet were up on the table, and her arms hugged her knees to her chest. Long brown hair was pulled back in a ponytail, and she wore tiny silver rings in her ears. Samantha was seventeen weeks pregnant with her first baby, and now she was bleeding. Her husband, Mark, a burly guy in jeans and a plaid work shirt, sat quietly on a folding chair in the corner of the room, leaning forward with a stricken look on his face.

"How much have you bled through the rest of this morning?" I asked.

Samantha's lips drew tight as she mustered up the control to reply. "I've been through about ten pads, and it just keeps running over into my underwear. I had to change my sweatpants. They were soaked."

It was about 10:30 in the morning. That was a lot of blood in just a couple of hours.

"Did you have clots?"

"Yes! They were huge! Am I going to lose my baby?" she whimpered.

"Samantha, I can't answer that question just yet," I said quietly. "I'm going to have to examine you first, but certainly, with this much bleeding, we have to be worried."

With that, Samantha's attempts at control faltered. "We've been trying to have this baby for two years!" she said between sobs.

I glanced down at the chart in my lap to review her vital signs. Her pulse was one hundred and four, and her blood pressure was ninety-six over sixty-eight. Her heart rate was fast—she was a little tachycardic—and although, with her diminutive size, it was possible that she normally had a blood pressure in the nineties, she could also be slipping into shock from blood loss.

I looked up and noted that April had already started an IV of normal saline. Good. April was showing initiative.

April Keller was a relatively new grad from the Associate Degree RN program at Anne Arundel Community College, but she was coming along very nicely as an ER nurse. She was young and a little bit ditsy, but that was OK. Rail thin with bouncy, short, copper-red hair and freckles, her exuberance for life was refreshing.

"April, what do you have that IV running at?" I said with my best grammar.

"Two hundred and fifty cc's an hour."

"OK, give her a bolus of five hundred, and let's get her ready for a pelvic exam. You can buzz me when you're ready."

~

At the central nursing station I recorded Samantha's history, and then wrote orders for lab work, and a type and cross-match for two units of blood. The call buzzer went off for Bed Three, indicating that April was ready for the pelvic exam.

I walked down the hall, briefly rapped on the door and entered. Samantha lay on her back covered with a sheet; feet in the stirrups and knees up. She silently looked up at me with pleading eyes.

"Samantha, slide your bottom down about another six inches," commanded April.

My primary interest in this pelvic exam was to see how heavily Samantha was bleeding, whether her cervix—the little ring-like opening to her uterus—was open or closed, and whether there was any fetal tissue extruding through her cervix. An open cervix, or visible tissue, would indicate that she was, indeed, going to miscarry.

I put on gloves, slid the wheeled exam stool into place at the bottom of the exam table, sat down, and lifted the sheet.

"Alright, Samantha, I need you to make like a frog for me. Let's drop those knees apart. Come on. I know they go further than that." Samantha slowly dropped her knees apart in increments, like a mechanical cog-wheel. She was shaved, as is the current fashion among many younger women.

I plugged the light into the bottom of the clear plastic speculum and smeared it with surgical jelly. Spreading her labia open with my left hand, I placed the speculum at the vaginal introitus—the opening into her vagina. Blood oozed from the introitus, and began to pool on the absorbable pad that April had placed under Samantha's buttocks.

"OK, Samantha, I need you to relax those muscles and just let this thing slide right past." Samantha took a deep breath, and the speculum smoothly slid deep into her vagina.

I opened the jaws of the speculum. More blood poured out, and several large clots slid rapidly over the smooth speculum toward the floor, plopping on my beat-up old loafers, which I wear expressly for this reason. I couldn't see her cervix for all the blood.

After soaking up some of the blood with four or five long cotton-tipped swabs, her cervix finally came into view. It was not good news. Her cervix was open—perhaps two centimeters or more. And projecting through the open cervical canal was a tiny, blood-smeared foot. *Shit.* A steady trickle of blood flowed from beneath the foot. It would be another eight or nine weeks before this fetus would be mature enough to live, and that wasn't going to happen. Right now, the larger concern was making sure that Samantha didn't lose her own life.

The next part is never fun. I decided that Samantha didn't need to know about the foot. Pulling off the gloves, I stood, placed my hand on

Samantha's shoulder, and made eye contact. She looked up apprehensively.

"Samantha, your cervix is open, and it should be closed," I began. "In addition, I can see a piece of tissue pushing through your cervix. I'm sorry, but you are definitely going to lose this pregnancy." Samantha covered her face with both hands and quietly wept again.

"Right now our main concern is that you are bleeding quite heavily. We need to get this fetus out so that your uterus can clamp down and stop the bleeding." In the corner, Mark's leg began to jiggle.

~

I had April move Samantha to Bed Fourteen—a fully monitored procedure room with surgical lighting—in case she started to crash. Right now we were replacing her blood loss with normal saline—salt water—until the lab had blood ready. Then we would switch to packed red blood cells unless her bleeding slowed down dramatically.

I had the ward clerk get Dr. Susan Whitely on the line, today's on-call OB-GYN.

"Hey Susan, Alex. How are you?"

"Good, Alex. What's happening?" she inquired cheerfully. An attending physician cheerfully answering a call from the ER qualifies as abnormal behavior. Attendings don't like us screwing up their day. Susan, on the other hand, is one of those congenitally happy people who act like they're on Prozac all the time, but aren't. She also looks great in a tight pair of jeans, but happens to be married to my brother, Brian, so with her, I have to restrain my lust.

I gave her a quick rundown on the case. Susan and I communicate well.

"What's her name?"

"Samantha Thompson. Do you want a sonogram?"

"No. The baby's not viable. I don't want to waste time if she's bleeding that heavily. I think I'll just take her to the operating room. Start a pitocin drip on her," she ordered. "Hey, are you still seeing Elizabeth?"

"Elizabeth and I are currently in a cease-fire mode, so, yes, I think I am."

"Well, if the truce holds until Friday night, why don't the two of you come by our place for dinner? I'll whip up a pasta and you bring the wine."

I was scheduled to work day shift on Friday, so the thought of dinner with Susan and Brian, after twelve hours in the ER, was already making me long for a Grey Goose and tonic. They have a fairly spectacular waterfront place in Fells Point on Baltimore's Inner Harbor.

"I don't get off until 7:00 on Friday, but if eight o'clock would be OK, I'll check with Elizabeth and e-mail you."

"OK. I'll be down in about ten minutes to see Samantha. I just finished a case."

"Gotcha."

"Ciao."

~

I went back into Bed Fourteen, scanned the monitor, and laid my fingers on Samantha's arm. Her skin was still cool and dry, without sweating, or *diaphoresis*, as we call it. But her pulse was faster, despite the fluids we had given her, indicating that we weren't quite keeping up with the blood loss.

"April, call the blood bank and tell 'em to hurry up that blood. When it comes, I want you to run it wide open. And Dr. Whitely wants a Pitocin drip."

Pitocin is actually a trade name for oxytocin—a dandy little naturally-occurring hormone secreted by the hypothalamus in the brain. Oxytocin plays a major role in stimulating uterine contraction in labor. Hopefully, for Samantha, it would make her uterus contract enough to slow down the bleeding, or maybe even pop out that fetus. Oxytocin's also a favorite of mine because in studies it's been shown to stimulate sexual arousal and bonding in rats and prairie dogs.

~

April had hung the first unit of blood, and appeared at the nursing station looking downcast. "Gosh, if that ever happened to Brad and me, I don't know if I could deal with it," she said forlornly. "It's just so heartbreaking."

Danielle Jones, our retired Army nurse—now on career number two—was charting nearby. She looked up impassively. "What makes you think you're gonna have babies with that mattress salesman, child? Did he ask you to marry him yet?" Older nurses are very protective of younger nurses.

"No," said April, pouting. "But he really doesn't have a choice. I mean, how could he possibly find another girl as charming and devoted as me? Besides, he's going to get promoted to Assistant Manager." And with that, she cracked her gum, flipped her hair, and was gone; cute little hips swaying as she disappeared down the corridor.

I glanced at the big central nursing station slave monitor. Samantha's heart rate was down to one hundred, and, for good measure, her blood pressure was now up to one hundred. Neat coincidence. Maybe we were catching up with the blood loss. I needed to have another conversation with her.

Husband Mark was leaning protectively over Samantha's stretcher, holding her hand, when I walked in.

"Listen guys," I began. "You're losing this baby, and I know how hard that is for you. Dr. Whitely, our OB-GYN, is coming down to see you, and she's going to be taking you to the operating room so we can stop this bleeding. She's a very good obstetrician, and you're going to be in good hands. But there are a couple of things I want you to think about.

"The first is that miscarriages are nature's way of making sure that we have healthy babies." Samantha, with her eyes squeezed shut and her face screwed up tight, fighting back tears, nodded knowingly.

"The second is that you *did* get pregnant," I continued. "That means that you *can* get pregnant, and that's ninety percent of the battle. Remember that about a third of girls who have healthy babies have a miscarriage at some time or another. So let's get you taken care of, Samantha, then you guys can start making babies again."

I don't know if my little speech made them feel any better, but it always makes me feel better. In fact, it's all true.

Susan showed up, and soon, with April's help, was wheeling Samantha past the nursing station toward the OR. I squeezed Samantha's hand as she went by, and she squeezed back.

~

Jack Schmidt appeared at the nursing station in uniform. His big jowls had a little more color in them than usual this morning.

"Hey Jack, how's it going?"

"We found the kids that dumped off Andrew Price," he growled.

"Great. I hope you can put 'em away forever."

"There were three of 'em. One of them's a regular narcotics user, and the other two were your basic idiot teenagers playing with fire. Too much time and money, and no brains."

"So will you charge them?"

Jack scowled. "The state's attorney is looking at it, but I doubt that she will be able to come up with any charges that she can make stick. We'll track back through their sources and try to nail whoever's pushing the heroin into this end of the county. But," he sighed, "odds are we won't get past a low-level middleman."

"Any idea who *is* pushing the stuff?"

Jack sat his ample frame down on the corner of the nursing station counter, his gun belt creaking under the strain.

"Well, sure. You probably know there's been a turf war going on in the city. The old retail distribution system was controlled primarily by loosely organized local gangs—mostly the Crips. But there's a new player in town—a Salvadoran gang called *Mara Salvatrucha.* They also go by *MS-13*. They're a much more disciplined organization. Their leadership is older. Some of them are former soldiers or guerrillas from the civil war in El Salvador. They want the business, and they've been basically killing off their competitors. I'm sure you heard about the killings last week—five Crips; all kneeling; heads down; bang, bang, bang."

"Yeah. It was in all the media."

"Up here, we think it was mostly the Crips that started pushing into the rural market several years ago. If the Salvadorans decide to move in on them, it might get a little bloody up here too. You might be getting more business," he said smiling.

~

I dialed Elizabeth's private number at Hamilton, Duncan & Blackstone. Elizabeth works for daddy's firm, but has her own little fiefdom where she takes care of mostly non-profit clients, like the Walter's Art Gallery, where mummy also serves on the board. This arrangement allows Elizabeth to keep a comfortable distance from too much capitalism on the corporate side of the firm, and allows her to preserve some of her more progressive political views.

"Elizabeth Hamilton."

"Hey, Elizabeth. It's me."

"I *did* recognize your voice."

"Listen, I just ran into Susan and she has invited us to dinner at her place on Friday night."

"You're giving me all of a day and a half's notice that you want to go out with me, and you expect me to drop everything and be at your side?" Elizabeth sometimes feels the need to remind me that she is not at my beck and call.

"Elizabeth, think of it this way. This nice little spontaneous, last-minute invitation is from Susan, not me." A pregnant pause ensued, and I thought I heard a sigh.

"What time, Alex?"

"I get off at seven on Friday, so I could meet you there about eight."

CHAPTER SIX

FRIDAY MORNING ROLLED AROUND, BRINGING with it my last shift for the week. I had a rare weekend off. Rick Stapleton was back from Hilton Head and was now paying his dues. His shift started at 9:00, and he plopped his big frame down in a chair at the second doc's computer terminal.

"Hey Rick, welcome back to Paradise. How was Hilton Head?"

"Great. Good food, pretty women, and plentiful booze," he drawled.

"I meant the conference that we spent precious budgeted dollars sending you to."

"Oh, that. Well, actually it was pretty good. I saw our old buddy from Duke—Charlie Reeder—and he said to say hello."

"Yeah? How's he doing?"

"Second wife. New baby. He's runnin' an ER in Georgia now."

Fran Williams, the day-shift charge nurse, walked up and slid another chart into the *To-Be-Seen* rack. "Keep 'em movin' today, boys. We're short one nurse."

"Who's out?" I asked.

"Joyce. She called off again this morning," Fran said with obvious annoyance.

"Alex, can you step into my office for a moment, please?" I looked up at Julie from my computer station with a quizzical expression, but she offered no explanation. The subject of this little impromptu meeting was obviously not a matter for public discussion.

"Let me finish discharging this patient, and I'll be right there." I printed the discharge instructions, hit the *TO GO* icon on the computer, and, a minute later, exited the ER and walked down the hall to Julie's office. The door was closed, so I rapped twice, then walked in.

Julie's office is about twice as big as mine. That's because this is a unit manager's office—part of administration—and I'm just a doc. But, hey, I never complain about this inequity, because I wouldn't want Julie's job for the world. If I had a bigger office, they might expect me to do more administrative work.

Julie was sitting at her desk. Across from her, in the opposite corner, sat a young woman wearing enormous black sunglasses. Her shoulder-length brown hair appeared still damp from a shower. She wore jeans and a dark-brown leather jacket. It took me a moment to recognize her—Joyce Harbaugh, today's missing day-shift nurse.

Joyce was perhaps early thirties, but had only been a nurse for two years. She was one of those people who I admire, because she had pulled herself up in the world by her bootstraps. For ten years, she had worked full-time as a nurse's aid while taking evening classes—year after year—until she finally achieved her goal of entrance to nursing school. And then, to support herself, she had had no choice financially but to continue working part-time all through nursing school, despite the demands of her studies.

I liked Joyce. She was kind, and had a nurturing personality. But she had developed a little problem with chronic absenteeism. Moreover, she often appeared to have trouble focusing in the ER, so people had learned to keep an eye on her. She had been skating on thin ice with regard to keeping her job. I wondered if today was the day that the guillotine would fall.

"Alex, would you mind taking a look at Joyce's eye?" asked Julie. Hesitantly, Joyce slowly reached up and removed her sunglasses. She looked awful. Her left eye was swollen completely shut, and glowed an angry purplish red. The eyelid bulged out to the edge of her swollen cheek bones. I was afraid that this looked like the result of an enthusiastic love tap.

"What happened here, Joyce?" I asked.

She was slow to respond. "My boyfriend has a problem with drugs and alcohol," she began. "He's a great guy when he's sober, but when he's not, he gets very angry." Joyce looked down at the floor, then looked up at me as if to see if her explanation was sufficient. She was obviously embarrassed.

"So what happened?" I asked again.

"He's back on heroin again," she continued. "He wanted money—a lot of money. He wanted my paycheck. I wouldn't give it to him. He started drinking early last night, and…" she paused and gently touched a hand to her swollen cheek, "he hit me."

"Have you called the police?" A tear trickled down from her open eye, and she briefly shook her head "no."

"OK, Joyce, let's take a look," I said softly. Joyce winced as I gently pried open her swollen eyelids.

"How's your vision in that eye?"

"It's OK," she said.

The globe of her eye appeared intact. I could see no layer of blood in her pupil. There was a subconjuctival hemorrhage—blood under the membrane that covers the white of your eye—but that represented no threat to her vision. Apart from the swelling and discoloration, there appeared to be no significant long-term damage.

"Well, I think your eye is OK, Joyce. Looks to me like the bigger problem is the threat of your boyfriend. What are we going to do about that?"

"I *know* I have to move out," she said, now openly crying, "but I'm scared."

"You're afraid that he will come after you if you leave him?" She nodded silently. "And I'm worried about my daughter."

"You have a daughter?"

Joyce nodded again. "She's seven."

"Has he ever been violent with her?"

"No, but she watches when he beats me up. It's not something a little girl should see. And sometimes he's mean to her."

"OK. We need to put together a plan, here. First we need to call the police. Second, we need to get a protective order. And third, we have to get you out of there. Whose apartment is it?"

"Mine."

"Then maybe we need to have him arrested, and get *him* out of there."

"He'll just be in jail for a day or two, and then he'll come right back," she said, her control faltering. "And if I turn him in to the police..."

I turned to Julie. "Maybe we can get Women In Need up here to see her. She's going to need some help with this."

"I can do that," said Julie. Women In Need is a non-profit skilled at helping women in exactly Joyce's position.

But the truth is that the legal system for protecting threatened women from physical abuse is piss poor. It's always much more reactive than proactive. I hoped to hell that Joyce's fears didn't turn out to be well-founded.

~

Late morning, Sam Warren stopped by to look at moving a built-in base cabinet in Bed Eight in order to create more space for the new ENT chair. Sam's a towering, jovial guy who keeps this place working like a Swiss watch. He's always a soft touch for whatever we need done in the department.

"Hey, Sam!" I said in greeting. "Your wi-fi system is working great. I've had a lot of positive feedback from patients—especially their families. They love it."

"Well, if it's good enough for McDonalds, it's good enough for Mason-Dixon Regional. Only here you wait longer, you pay more, and you can't get a Big Mac or a shake. Gotta give 'em somethin' for their money," he said.

"The staff likes it too. They can access it with their iTouches."

"I didn't hear that, and don't mention it again. That's a bit of a sore spot with administration. I had to assure them that you guys are already working so hard, there's no time to look at porn on the web," he said grinning.

"Sam! I can't believe you said that," Julie chided. "We're all professionals here."

~

All in all, Friday wasn't a bad day, and before I knew it, I was seeing my last patient of the shift—six-year-old Toby Smith. Chubby little Toby was here with grandmom, who was probably late forties, but looked like she'd been ridden pretty hard and put away wet on more than one occasion. Toby's head was shaved, except for a little ponytail in the back, and he had a diamond stud in his left ear. He wore a black tee shirt that said "Mad as Hell… And I ain't gonna take it no more!"

Toby had been coughing for a week. He didn't have a cough, of course, until he came back from his court-mandated custody weekend with his father. Last night, the cough kept grandmom up all night. "Yes," he had a runny nose and, "no, he didn't have no fever."

I did a quick exam on Toby. Apart from the caked snot under his nose, Toby was the picture of health.

"Grandmom, I think Toby has a respiratory virus that he's probably just about over, and I think he's going to be just fine without any medicine."

"I just want an antibiotic so we can get rid of this cough."

"Well, as you probably know, we don't have any drugs that will kill viruses and, unfortunately, an antibiotic just won't help. Antibiotics kill bacteria, but not viruses."

"You mean you ain't gonna give him nothin' for this cough just 'cause we don't have no insurance?"

Mr. Hyde spoke up. *If you give in to that idiot old nag, you'll sacrifice your intellectual honesty, and she'll want an antibiotic again next time Toby has a snotty nose.*

Jekyll responded. *Look, you're not going to win this scientific argument. Just give him some harmless cough medicine and everybody will be happy.*

Jekyll won. "Actually, Grandmom, I'm going to give Toby some cough syrup that's going to allow you both to get some rest tonight. He should be better in a couple of days."

~

I signed out to Bob D'Amelio, and changed into jeans and an oxford. Traffic down I-83 and the Jones Falls expressway into Baltimore is pretty good after 7:00 PM, and, by quarter of eight, I was turning left onto Aliceanna Street in the Fells Point neighborhood of the Inner Harbor.

Baltimore is an old port on the Chesapeake Bay that couldn't make up its mind whether it belonged to the North or the South during the Civil War. Forty years ago, the downtown surrounding the harbor was filled with cavernous old brick warehouses and glorious, but decaying, Federal-style townhouses. Some visionary political leadership and a healthy dose of capitalism turned it into quite a little gem in the late sixties and early seventies. Many of the old buildings were salvaged and turned into hip shops and restaurants.

Susan and Brian bought a circa 1830 brick house in Fells Point, one of the gentrified waterfront neighborhoods, for a very nice price just before the real estate boom hit. They basically gutted it and added lots of glass, granite, and recessed lighting. It's on a tree-lined, cobblestone street about a block from the water, but you can see the harbor from the second floor. It's a very nice place to have dinner on Friday night after work.

They used to build ships in Fells Point. It was famous for producing the *Baltimore Clippers*—fast, topsail schooners that harangued the British during the War of 1812. The shipwrights felt that thirst is a dangerous thing, so Fells Point is also famous for having something like one hundred and twenty pubs. It pretty well rocks on weekend nights.

Susan responded on the intercom to my push of the doorbell, and I heard the click of the door lock opening. I climbed the spiral staircase to the second floor where the kitchen and living space have been located to take advantage of the harbor view.

Susan was standing by the big, black granite island licking her fingers, clad in a pink cotton sweater and jeans, with a white apron tied at the back. She held her arms with sticky fingers wide, and gave me a warm hug and a big smacker on the cheek.

"Hey, Alex. Where's your sparing partner?" she asked brightly.

"She's driving separately from the office. Should be here any minute."

Brian was bringing up his music playlist on an iPod docked in the white bookcases that occupied the length of the east wall, interrupted only by a fireplace in the center. A spectacular view of the harbor filled a solid wall of glass at the far end of the room. A panoply of color from the city lights shimmered across the quiet water.

This has to be one of the coolest rooms in all the world. Susan and Brian's architect friend, John Fallworth, helped them with the interior design. He incorporated a variety of lowered, curvilinear ceiling components with tiny recessed halogen lights that shined like stars in the otherwise cozily dark room. Tightly focused ceiling spotlights highlighted several vivid, contemporary paintings on the exposed-brick west wall.

Mr. Hyde noticed a bottle of Grey Goose sitting in an ice bucket on the island. I picked up the bottle.

"Susan, can I fix you a drink?"

"No, I'll wait until Elizabeth arrives. Go ahead."

"You want a Grey Goose and tonic, Brian?"

He looked up from his iPod. "Yeah, fix me one, too."

I poured the drinks and handed Brian his glass. Miles Davis launched into his first song.

"You must not be flying tomorrow," I said.

"Nope. Off for three days."

Brian flies left seat in a 737 for Southwest Airlines out of BWI. There is a little bit of jealousy here because if I were going to do anything but be a doc, I'd want to fly airplanes. Brian eats, sleeps and breathes flying. He spent six years in the Air Force flying KC-135's before he joined Southwest. With his heavy transport experience, he moved from copilot to the left seat at Southwest in record time.

The doorbell rang, and Elizabeth arrived bearing flowers. She and Susan brushed cheeks, and Brian gave her a hug. He never misses an opportunity to hug a pretty woman. As for me, I got a quick kiss on the lips despite Elizabeth's earlier pique on the telephone.

My end of the bargain with Susan for tonight's dinner was bringing the wine, so I had picked up two bottles of a very nice cabernet at ten dollars a pop. There are so many nice wines available on the market for ten bucks or so, that I have a visceral opposition to twenty-five dollar bottles of wine. My selection for the evening was actually officially approved by *Wine Spectator* as a good, inexpensive cabernet. This helped to assuage my conscience at being a cheapskate.

I uncorked a bottle, poured for both Susan and Elizabeth, and we all clinked glasses

Susan and Elizabeth get on quite well and were soon chatting about their workouts and personal trainers. Susan slid a serving dish onto the island of her own hummus, crowned with a little sprig of sage, and surrounded by stone wheat wafers.

"Don't pig out on that," she said. "Save room for the pasta."

The connection between Susan and younger brother Brian was, of course, my doing. Susan was an OB-GYN resident rotating through the ER at Hopkins. I managed to find a way to introduce them at an outdoor Sunday afternoon jazz concert at Boordy Vineyards up in eastern Baltimore County. He owes me for that.

While the ladies talked about their exercise programs, Brian and I talked about Russian girls on the pro tennis tour. Despite the fact that they're all gorgeous, this is less perverted than it sounds, because we both are actually interested in tennis. In addition to his passion for planting trees, our father loved tennis and had us on the court at an early age. We grew up playing together. By the time Brian was fifteen, he was beating me. He ultimately played number one at Washington College, a nice little Division II school in Chestertown, on Maryland's eastern shore.

We stood together with our drinks on the far side of the room, gazing out over the harbor. "Dad's PSA test came back elevated this morning." I said quietly.

"Is that the prostate cancer test?"

"Yeah. It doesn't mean that he's got cancer, but the higher the test value, the greater the probability."

"How high was it?"

"High enough. They're going to schedule him for a biopsy."

Brian visibly paled. He stared at me for a moment. "Does he know yet?"

"Yeah. He had an appointment with Jack Snyder this afternoon."

"Wow. How's Mom dealing with this?"

"You know how she is. She says, 'Edward, we're just going to face this head-on together.'" Our mother is a very practical woman. She taught elementary school full time for thirty years and still managed to raise three willful kids.

~

Brian himself tossed the salad—not that this is a major feat—but he tossed it with his own version of Caesar dressing made with fresh eggs, crushed garlic, and anchovies. I would never tell him, of course, but he's actually pretty good in the kitchen.

Susan finished tweaking her pesto sauce, folded in the sautéed chicken, and pulled a baguette from the oven. "*Le dîner est servi,*" she announced brightly.

I uncorked a second bottle of cabernet—I didn't know we were having chicken—Brian lit the candles, and we all took our seats. The aroma of fresh bread and pesto sauce was having a decided impact on my central nervous system.

"I'm starving," I said.

"You're always starving," said Elizabeth. "It's that giant tapeworm in your gut."

"He's very fond of Susan's cooking. Hope everybody likes cabernet with chicken," I said, pouring for the ladies. "I didn't bring a white."

"Red's great, said Susan, "I drink it with everything."

There was a pause in the conversation as everyone delicately stuffed pasta in their mouths, followed by the expected accolades for Susan's cooking.

"So, Brian, what are your routes this month?" asked Elizabeth, picking up her wine glass. "Any exciting destinations?"

"Baltimore to Orlando. Orlando to La Guardia. La Guardia to Baltimore. No layovers. Home every night."

"Nice."

"Especially since he gets home in time to cook me dinner," said Susan.

"Is that a good thing?" I asked.

"Of course! Brian's a wonderful cook. And he loves to cook for me, don't you Brian?"

"Baby, I spend most of my idle cockpit hours thinking about menus and you," he said smiling, "—usually without clothes." Susan snorted.

"Speaking of your precious cockpit," she said, "I read a cute little blurb on the internet the other day about an all-female crew on an Air Force C-5A. For your information, *they* don't call it the *cockpit*; they call it the *box-office*." Brian thought that this was hilarious.

"Maybe you could take some lessons from your brother," said Elizabeth, turning, of course, to me.

"What? Flying lessons?"

"Ways in which to communicate your love and devotion, such as cooking me dinner."

"That might fall into the category of being careful what you wish for," I said smiling.

"He's a slow learner, anyhow," offered Brian. "Not very teachable. I've tried with tennis," he said, glancing at me across the table.

"It's the universal affliction of older brothers," I said. "Your victories in tennis are simply my way of quietly protecting my younger brother's fragile ego."

Everyone helped clean up and load the dishwasher. The conversation continued over after-dinner drinks. We moved into the family room, the girls curled up in an overstuffed leather sofa.

"Oh," moaned Susan, laying her head back on the sofa, "I've gotta get up and make Saturday rounds tomorrow. I don't wanna to go to work."

"I have to go in tomorrow, too," Elizabeth commiserated.

"Are you still working full-time?" asked Susan.

"Actually, I'm working a lot more than I want to. Billable time is way off—the economy—so the firm let a bunch of the new associates go, and now I'm having to pick up more of the slack."

"I don't know if that's a good thing or a bad thing," I said.

"What? Me working so much?" asked Elizabeth.

"No. Unemployed lawyers. I'm happy to see them without a paycheck. But if you have too many of them sitting around with nothing to do, they're likely to think up new and creative ways to make our lives miserable."

"Are you talking about all those horrible people who step up to protect the injured public because your state medical board won't police themselves?" Elizabeth asked brusquely.

"Exactly. Those brave defenders of the public welfare who courageously filed a suit against *me* when the medical board failed to pull *my* license," I said. Susan leaned back behind Elizabeth's field of vision, caught my eye, and made a silent "cut it" sign across her throat. Occasionally I have some trouble knowing when to quit.

~

And so it went until a very pleasant evening came to an end.

Susan grasped both of Elizabeth's hands. "Elizabeth, it was great to see you! It's been too long."

We finished saying our goodnights, and I walked Elizabeth to her car. The air was warm for mid-October, and I could hear tree frogs, even here in the city.

"Susan and Brian are very nice people, Alex. One would never guess they're related to you." Elizabeth's claws are sharp.

"I am blessed. Great folks for a last minute get together, despite the blood relationship," I said.

"Don't push your luck, Alex. We could have lots of spontaneous evenings together if I were just a little higher on your priority list." Elizabeth and I have been working on this for three years. She thinks my progress in relationship priorities is slow.

We reached the car and I opened her door. Elizabeth slid behind the wheel. I didn't get an invitation for a nightcap at her place.

"See you tomorrow night?" I asked. "You want to go to dinner before or after the concert?

"Before. I'm a little short on sleep this week."

"OK. I'll pick you up about 5:30."

Elizabeth turned the ignition key, offered a brief kiss through the open window, and pulled away.

CHAPTER SEVEN

WHEN I OPENED MY EYES ABOUT 8:00 AM, the sun was shining brightly through the east window of my bedroom, bathing the white-washed walls in gold. I threw back the covers and padded over to the window. The two sugar maples at the rear of the house, separated by a solitary blue-green spruce, had now turned crimson pink.

Beyond was a pasture with lush fall grass, bordered by a black board fence. Two thoroughbreds, owned by Sally Horn—the young lady that boards her horses here—grazed beside the stream that bisects the twenty acre pasture. Sunlight danced on the water, creating a lazily meandering ribbon of brilliant white. A single giant sycamore rose from the bank on the far side of the stream, its massive and stately white branches lifting toward a cloudless, azure sky.

To the left sat a bank-barn with a high stone foundation and red metal roof. The first floor held six horse stalls and a loafing area. Above were two hay mows and my most prized possession—a blue New Holland B 3040 tractor with front-end loader and a brush hog on the rear.

This thirty-five acre farm, just east of Monkton, in the district known as *My Lady's Manor*, was my major life investment to date, and probably forever. It was my insurance against an early retirement and descent into the ranks of the idle rich in the British Virgins.

I'm told that Charles Calvert the 3rd generously gifted the original ten thousand acres of My Lady's Manor to his fourth wife, Margaret, in 1713. Today the general area is populated by what locals sometimes call the *Manor crowd*—descendants of old money who like chasing foxes on horses. In fact, the Manor is steeplechase country, where *nouveaux riche* who erect boundaries that prevent a herd of horses from galloping across their properties are frowned upon and risk social isolation. Amazingly, despite being an easy commute to Baltimore, it's still pretty rural, dotted with a quilt-work of manicured horse farms, and a slew of grand old brick and stone houses.

The landed gentry here are afflicted with a touch of political schizophrenia. Staunch free-market Republicans convert to fire-breathing proponents of strict land-use regulation whenever a local farmer decides to cash in to a developer. The dames of the great farms form conservation coalitions, and lobby legislators for more laws.

I was standing in one of four bedrooms of this farm's 1823 brick house. It was chilly. Heating this old house costs a fortune, and I refuse to turn the heat on until it's as close to November as possible. I took a hot and leisurely Saturday morning shower, stepped into a pair of fleece-lined slippers, and took the curving, sneaky staircase down from my bedroom into the kitchen

Maggie was at the foot of the stairs, wagging her tail and looking up expectantly for a scratch behind the ears. She's an affectionate golden retriever who is useless for defending the property. She even makes friends with the groundhogs that dig holes in the pasture, risking the fragile legs of Sally's thoroughbreds. Sally keeps a twenty-two rifle in the barn, and plinks them if they're out when she's feeding the horses.

With a lot of practice, I have disciplined myself to load up my coffee maker and punch the buttons on the timer before I go to bed. Sometimes, if I hit the snooze button, the distant whine of the grinder is a more effective inducement to climb out of bed than my alarm clock. So, the coffee was ready. Makes me feel like I have servants, or maybe a wife. I poured a cup and wandered over to the laptop on the countertop.

I've gotten in the habit of checking my Google calendar first thing each morning, just in case I have forgotten some important obligation for the day, like going to work. Google told me that boyhood-friend-John and I were scheduled for a tennis match at Hereford High School at two this afternoon. And I had even remembered to note tonight's dinner and concert at the Meyerhoff with Elizabeth. This led to a brief panic attack when I realized that I didn't have dinner reservations. I made a mental note to call Sammy's Trattoria later in the day.

Restoring this house has been the most fun you can have with your clothes on, although it's a little short in immediate gratification. I purchased the place from Mr. and Mrs. Stuart Robinson, an elderly couple who both ended up in a nursing home and needed dough. It was hard for them to give it up, and my heart went out to them. We had the settlement at the nursing home.

Fortunately, none of the owners in the last hundred years had the money to renovate it, so all the original random-width pine floors and wide window casements were still intact. Nobody had laid down new, narrow oak floors in the 1920's. Many of the windows still had hand-blown glass in the panes.

I decided early on that, apart from the bathrooms and some recessed lighting, my only concession to modernity would be the kitchen. The cabinets were done in solid recessed-panel cherry, which added to my budget overruns. I chose a tobacco and midnight-blue quartz composite for the countertops. The saleslady convinced me that quartz held up better than granite, and was more stain resistant. I couldn't be sure at the time whether my decision was based on fact, or cleavage.

Above the cabinets, I had a bulkhead constructed that projects out over the countertops. It contains the tiny recessed lights that I love in Susan and Brian's place. The bulkhead and counter then turn ninety degrees and continue out into the room, where they serve to separate the kitchen space from the family room beyond. Not that I had a family, but, hey, you never know. Someday there might be a little woman and kids.

The centerpiece of the family room is a huge, original walk-in fireplace that was used for cooking in the old days. I can see the fireplace from my gourmet kitchen when I'm busy cooking up instant oatmeal. On the far wall, a pair of French doors open onto a stone patio, which sits on a knoll above the pasture.

This was all still a work in progress. I had become friends with Tim Rutledge, a small local contractor and the husband of Cathy Rutledge, our ER clinical coordinator. He gave me great deals in return for letting him do the work on his own timetable, when business was slow. Although sometimes it seemed like the construction would never end, this arrangement had the advantage of spreading out cash flow requirements a bit.

There was a knock on the entrance door to the mudroom off the kitchen, and I heard the door push open.

"Good morning!" sang out a female voice. That would be Ruth Hollens. Ruth is a seventy-something widow who is my contracted mother-in-residence. I originally hired Ruth to clean once a week, but from the very beginning it was clear to her that I was in need of much more expansive services. These services include close monitoring of my diet, sleeping habits, relationships, and how I look when I go out. Ruth always insists on a copy of my schedule so she can be certain not to come in and wake me after night shifts, or at least, that's the stated rationale.

I lit a fire to warm the room, poured another cup of coffee, and caught up on some e-mail. My mother had a question about prostate cancer. My sister, Anne, of course, was worried and had essentially the same questions. I got one over-the-top estimate, for repainting the exterior of the house, that would not fly. There were a bunch of hospital-related e-mails from Julie and others. I decided to answer them later. Meanwhile Ruth busied herself tidying up the kitchen, loading the dishwasher, and gently inquiring as to my plans for the weekend.

"What a gorgeous morning!" she said cheerfully. "How did you sleep last night?"

"Great. I had dinner with Susan and Brian last night."

"They are such a sweet couple."

"They're lovely people."

"Do you need any clothes pressed for this weekend?"

"No, Ruth. I'm going to a concert tonight, but I'm wearing the navy suit. I haven't worn it for a while, so it should be fine."

"I'll check it. What time are you leaving?"

"Well, I'll have to be out of here by about five o'clock."

"Oh, you must be going out to eat before the concert."

"Yep."

"Did you make reservations?"

"No, Ruth. I have to remember to do that later today as soon as Sammy's Trattoria is open."

"I'll remind you after lunch."

I could tell that my evasive answers had not yet provided Ruth with the critical piece of information for which she was searching. She resorted to a more direct approach.

"Are you going with that woman?"

That woman was Elizabeth. Elizabeth and Ruth had so far failed to bond.

"Yeah. I'm picking up Elizabeth at five-thirty."

"That woman doesn't want children. You need children in this house," she said flatly.

"We're not getting married, Ruth. We're just going to dinner and a concert."

"I'll have some lunch ready for you at one o'clock. Don't forget you're playing tennis with John at two." I don't know how she remembers all this stuff.

I heard the crunch of tires on gravel and looked out the east window. Sally Horn's red pickup truck pulled up to the barn. A young woman climbed out wearing tight jeans, a beige sweater, and a stained, lavender down vest.

Sally's got long legs and a really spectacular little butt. Most of the time she smells like horses, which I find kind of strangely attractive. Must be some sort of pheromones. Anyhow, she shows up twice a day to feed her horses, and I get to watch her climb out of her truck. The monthly boarding fee covers the payments on my New Holland. That's the definition of a win-win.

By the end of coffee, I was mulling over how I wanted to spend the rest of the morning—pay bills, paint crown molding, or start cutting firewood for the winter? Cutting firewood won, mainly because it was a beautiful day, and it gave me the opportunity to climb onto my New Holland and use the front-end loader for hauling firewood back to the house from the three acres of woods on the north side of the property. I waved to Sally as I walked out to the barn. She was gracefully forking horse shit in the loafing area.

~

After Ruth's lunch of tomato soup, a grilled tuna melt, and a glass of milk, I climbed into the Wrangler and headed out for Hereford High School about quarter to two. The air had warmed up nicely, and it was about seventy degrees.

John Adams—no relation to John Quincy—has been my best friend since grade school. He lived a mile and a half from my house; well within bicycle range. Our parents were good communicators, so we tended to get grounded at the same time when trouble arose. In our teens, John worked with Brian and me on my dad's landscaping crews in the summertime, so, of course, he played tennis with us, too.

Grown-up John is an electrical engineer for Westinghouse, who travels all over the world working on radar sites, but mostly in the Middle East. He speaks three languages, including English, French and Arabic. I can speak a little French, but learning Arabic I consider to be a huge intellectual feat.

John spent a semester abroad during college at the Sorbonne in Paris, where he met Annick Devereux, a fetching and feisty little thing from Aix en Provence, whom he eventually married. So, I don't give him too much credit for speaking French. His motivation was very high. Annick teaches undergrad French at Johns Hopkins.

We're pretty well matched in tennis. John has a wicked one-handed crosscourt backhand, but I have an edge with my serve. Most sets end up six-four, or in a tie breaker.

John pulled into the parking lot right behind me. He's a big guy—six-three and probably two hundred pounds—with close-cropped, slate-gray hair. It's very funny to see he and Annick together. She's probably five-two, and maybe breaks a hundred pounds. I've often wondered how they physically arrange things when they hook up.

"Wow. What a great afternoon for tennis, huh?" he enthused.

"We better enjoy it. It'll probably be one of the last warm days this year."

We grabbed our bags and walked toward the courts, overlooking a narrow steep valley and distant woods alive with color. I could see the Hereford cross-county course winding across the far hillside. It's a brutal course that has made the Hereford team state champions for years.

"What have you been up to the last couple of weeks?" I asked.

"Just got back from Bahrain last week. I'll be heading out to Jordan next week." Annick has had to adjust to a lot of travel on John's part, but she was a pretty independent woman, and it seemed to be working OK for them.

"Hey, Annick's a little late this month," he said with a grin, looking over at me.

I saw his grin and got the message. "No shit! You did a home pregnancy test?"

"Yup," he nodded.

"And it was positive?"

"Nice little blue line," he said, measuring with a thumb and index finger.

I punched him in the arm and gave him a high-five. "You dog, you! Firin' real bullets! And she's such a nice little girl!"

"Wildcat," he corrected.

John ran me ragged with crosscourt rallies, and then forehand rifle shots down the line on weak returns. I managed to hold my serves, and we reached a tie breaker. I lost seven-three.

"OK. I just didn't have the heart to beat a new papa," I said as we clasped hands across the net, drenched in sweat.

~

When I stepped out of the shower and walked back into my bedroom, I noticed my navy blue suit hanging from the door to the walk-in closet, creases sharp. A fresh white shirt hung behind it. That reminded me that I was having dinner in roughly an hour. *Oh shit, I don't have reservations.* I walked over to the bureau to grab my cell phone, and saw a message taped on the mirror. "I made reservations for Sammy's at six PM for two. Ruth."

~

My Wrangler doesn't have the requisite elegance for transporting high-born young ladies to dinner and a show, so two years ago I broke down and bought a used little black Miata, which I was now driving down I-83. I got it for under twenty grand. My Miata is a quite serviceable little sports car—if not in the BMW or Mercedes class—and at least spares Elizabeth the embarrassment of pulling up to the Meyerhoff in a rusted Jeep. This is important, because the Meyerhoff Symphony Hall is the home of the Baltimore Symphony Orchestra, which, of course, is another of Elizabeth's star-studded clients.

Tonight, the BSO was doing a symphonic tribute to American jazz with Wynton Marsalis as the guest performer and narrator. I was actually looking forward to this concert.

I pulled into the driveway of Elizabeth's modest Roland Park mansion shortly before 5:30 and blew the horn. No, actually I got out of the car. Elizabeth was ready when I rapped on the side door, and was tying the knot on a silk scarf around her neck.

"Hi," she said brightly. So far so good, compared to our last parting.

I stood behind her and held the storm door open as she closed and locked the main door.

"You look terrific," I said, hoping to extend my good luck. This was a true, if somewhat gratuitous, statement. Elizabeth has impeccable taste, and the face and body to go with it. Tonight she was wearing a form-fitting, ankle-length, silk dress, probably worth more than my Miata. I could see the soft roundness of her buttocks as she bent over to find the key hole.

"Stop staring at my butt," she said as I heard the lock turn. "You'll be drooling on your suit, and I need you to be presentable." I don't know how she knew.

~

We arrived at Sammy's, and the hostess didn't have a blank look on her face when I said we had reservations for two at 6:00.

"Right this way, Dr. Randolph," she said, and we headed off toward our table.

"I'm impressed that you actually remembered to make reservations," said Elizabeth over her shoulder. We ordered drinks and looked over the menu.

"I am starved tonight," began Elizabeth. "I was rushing around all day, getting a thousand little errands done, and I worked out with Charles at two o'clock. I haven't had a thing to eat all day."

Charles was Elizabeth's buff personal trainer, with blond hair down to his ears and nothing else in-between. He and Elizabeth get on famously. She tells him what a jerk I am, and he bitches about his special friend, Matt.

Elizabeth's pinot noir arrived along with my Grey Goose and tonic.

"Mmmmm," she said. "Listen to this. Doesn't this sound fabulous? Fresh Italian sausage and fresh broccoli rabe, sautéed with extra virgin olive oil and roasted garlic."

"You forgot. I'm a Republican. Republican's don't eat broccoli."

"That's going to be my appetizer, and I'm going to have Papardelle Alfredo for my entrée," she said decisively.

The Papardelle Alfredo actually sounded pretty good—an alfedo sauce with jumbo shrimp and lump crab meat. But since I'd already had fish-out-of-a-can for lunch, I settled on red meat—a seared peppercorn filet with gorgonzola cheese, shallots and mushrooms.

Elizabeth started digging into the bread, tore off a piece, and dipped it into a little plate of olive oil.

"Did you play tennis with John today?"

"Yes. He beat me in a tie-breaker, seven-three."

"Oooooo," she frowned. "Is your ego a little bruised tonight?"

"Actually, no. I told John I didn't have the heart to beat a new papa."

Elizabeth's eyes popped open.

"What?" she exclaimed.

"Apparently the little blue line was positive this morning."

Now her mouth dropped open. "No! You're kidding!" she squealed.

"He looked like a little kid when he told me."

"Wow!" Then she frowned. "How are they going to deal with all his traveling with a little one around?"

"I think it will be pretty tough; maybe worse for John than Annick. He loves traveling, and it's a great job, but he misses Annick when he's away, and now with a kiddo in the oven..."

"Well, at least with her teaching job she should be able to continue working almost right up to when she delivers."

"John says she's thinking about quitting after the baby comes."

Elizabeth stared at her plate for a moment. She looked up and sighed. "I don't know if I could do that," she said quietly.

We walked the three short blocks to the Meyerhoff, and Elizabeth flashed her VIP pass at the ticket taker. He waved us through, and we walked up the stairs to the terrace box reserved for important guests.

"Behave yourself tonight, Alex," she whispered emphatically as we walked down the short flight of stairs into the box.

This is the point in the evening when she needed me to be presentable. So I checked my suit for drool, did my duty shaking hands and making charming comments, and, in general, did my best to enhance the public image of Hamilton, Duncan & Blackstone.

Elizabeth worked the box; touching shoulders, kissing cheeks, and making herself visible to clients and potential clients.

She grasped the hand of a perfectly coiffed, gray-haired matron whose shrink-wrapped face suggested one too many encounters with one of my plastic surgery brethren.

"Mrs. Roth, so nice to see you!"

"Elizabeth, darling, you look ravishing in that dress. Who is this gorgeous man?"

"Mrs. Roth," said Elizabeth, placing her hand on my shoulder, "I'd like you to meet Dr. Alex Randolph."

"Oh, is he that marvelous heart surgeon?"

"I hope to be one day," I said smiling. This earned me a kick from Elizabeth.

~

The concert was terrific. Elizabeth and I held hands in the dark box, and she even rested her head on my shoulder during *Stardust*. Later, when we pulled into her driveway, she leaned toward me and softly asked, "Would you like to come in for a nightcap, Dr. Randolph?"

"I'd like nothing more, Counselor."

Standing in the kitchen, she poured two Grey Goose and tonics. This was unusual behavior for Elizabeth as she typically doesn't drink vodka. She raised her glass in a toast. "To that marvelous heart surgeon," she giggled.

Then she placed her drink on the counter in front of me, turned, and slowly pulled the black dress up and over her head until her round buttocks came into view, followed by the delicate curvature of her spine.

My mouth got dry, my mental processes starting drifting south, and a deformity appeared in my slacks. With arms extended over her head, she deftly tossed the dress on the floor in a heap, then turned to face me, shook out her hair, and smiled. She wore nothing else.

CHAPTER EIGHT

I TOOK A TWO-HOUR NAP ON WEDNESDAY afternoon and got up about 4:00 PM. Most of the time, I'm able to sleep pretty well during these pre-shift naps. They help enormously in making it through the night.

Eating before my 7:00 PM shift is not usually a gourmet experience. I keep some individually-wrapped steaks in the freezer, and occasionally I'll sear one in a cast iron skillet and cook some home fries. But most of the time I fix some variation on breakfast, because I like it, and it's quick and easy.

Tonight, I pulled out a couple of frozen waffles and five or six strips of bacon. The waffles went into the toaster, and the bacon into the microwave. I smothered the waffles with butter and maple syrup, sat down on a stool at the island, picked up my cell phone, and touched the icon for my parents' house.

"Hello?"

"Hey, Mom. How are you?"

"Life is always good, Alex. Are you eating?"

"Yes."

"I thought so."

"Waffles and bacon. Did Dad have his biopsy today?"

"He did."

"Is he requiring a lot of nursing care?" In truth, a prostate biopsy is not that big a deal—just a couple of needle sticks in the prostate. My dad, however, was not likely to waste this opportunity for secondary gain.

"As you know, your father has not had a lot of practice dealing with pain, and he seems quite incapacitated at the moment. Fortunately he's never been through a pregnancy. He's laying on the couch with his feet propped up on the arm rest, moaning." I laughed. Sympathy is hard to come by from a practical woman.

"Has he had any pain medicine?"

"He just took a Per… Per-something."

"That's Percocet, Mom. Did you know they're worth five bucks a pop on the street?"

"Well, he's definitely not getting any more of those at that price."

"OK, Mom. Tell him I said hello, and to keep a stiff upper lip."

"I think a stiff bourbon would do him more good."

"Catch you later, Mom."

"See you, honey."

~

All the shifts change at 7:00 PM. Cathy Rutledge walked up to me before she left for the day, accompanied by a pretty young woman who I did not recognize.

Cathy is our clinical coordinator, who is second in command after Julie Talbot, does most of the nursing education, and orients the new hires. She's a little brunette who's a crackerjack nurse. Besides that, Cathy is a pretty hot mid-forties mom with two kids in college. She loves tequila.

Cathy is married to my friend, Tim Rutledge, the local contractor who does most of the construction work on my house. They're very fun people. We've had lots of great parties at their house in the woods on Corbett Road.

"Dr. Randolph, have you met Penny yet?" This had to be the new hire for the open nursing position.

"No I haven't." I stuck my hand out and said, "Hi Penny. I'm Alex Randolph."

She grasped my hand firmly and looked me directly in the eyes. "I'm Penny Murray, Dr. Randolph."

"Penny, you're coming to us from Sinai, right?"

"Yes."

And, if I remember correctly, you used to work ICU at Hopkins."

"Yes. Actually, Pediatric ICU."

"Welcome. We like old ICU nurses, or at least ex-ICU nurses."

"I prefer to think of myself as 'ex'," she said with a wide smile. This was an obviously intelligent girl. She appreciated my humor.

~

Lisa walked into the nursing station as fast as her pregnant anatomy would allow.

"I don't like what's going on in Bed Fourteen, Alex. You need to go in there," she said emphatically.

"What's the matter?"

"There's a Hispanic guy in there with a big laceration on his arm, and a stab wound in his left chest. I just took him back there from triage, and there's three other rough-looking guys in there with him that barged through the triage door. I told them they need to wait in the waiting room, but they won't leave. I'm going to call security."

"Is he breathing OK?"

"Yeah." Lisa picked up the phone, and I headed toward Bed Fourteen.

Two dark-skinned guys in ski parkas stood like sentries on either side of the patient bed, hands in their jacket pockets. A third stood off in a corner staring at me impassively. All three silently watched as I walked toward the young male in the bed, holding a big absorbent dressing soaked with blood over the back of his left forearm. I quickly decided that the better part of valor was not to confront the three standing males.

"I'm Dr. Randolph." The patient looked at me without speaking, his pock-marked face hard and expressionless. "What's your name?"

"Julio," he replied slowly.

He was obviously breathing quietly with no respiratory distress, and his skin color was good. I dropped my fingers to his wrist and felt a strong pulse in the eighties or nineties. His skin was warm and dry.

"Julio, let's take a look at your chest."

He lifted both arms over his head, still holding the blood-soaked pad in place with his right hand, and I pulled his open shirt to the side, revealing a dressing taped on three sides that had obviously been placed by Lisa in triage. I could see both sides of his chest rising and falling equally as he quietly breathed. So far, no evidence of shock, or collapse of a lung.

Lisa walked back into the room. "The chest wound is not sucking," she said quietly, and began hooking Julio up to the monitor.

"Move!" she commanded, as she reached up to punch buttons on the monitor. The male on the left side of the bed stumbled back two feet, glaring at the little brunette with a big belly that encroached on his space. Hyde thought that this was hilarious.

I put on a pair of gloves and peeled away the tape. Julio's dark eyes followed my hands. A half-inch, vertical slit was visible on the far left side of his chest, near the lower ribs. A trickle of dried blood wound down over the side of his belly. There was no active bleeding, and it was not sucking air. It had to be a knife wound. I put on my stethoscope, listened to his heart, then had him lean forward and pulled his shirt up. His breath sounds were loud and clear. I glanced up at the monitor and saw that his oxygen saturation was ninety eight percent—also normal. The knife had probably not penetrated into his lungs.

"What happened here, Julio?" I asked.

"I fell through a glass door," he said in a bored voice with a heavy Spanish accent. *And my name is Che Guevara.*

I heard the exam room door open and saw both standing males at the bedside stiffen. The one behind Lisa moved the hand in his right pocket, and I saw a half-inch round bulge appear in the parka. Mike Szymanski, our head of security, stuck his flat-topped head through the door and started to walk in.

"Get him out of here," said Julio quietly.

We were outnumbered in this little confrontation, and, I suspected, outgunned. I stared straight into Julio's eyes and said, "Mike, I think we're OK in here."

"You sure?" Mike was Special Forces in Iraq in another life, and he would not back down easily. Leaving his brothers alone with the enemy was not in his blood. I raised my hand to wave him off.

"Yeah, you can hang around outside, but we're OK for now." Mike surveyed the room, hesitated, then backed out, leaving the door ajar.

I re-taped the dressing over the chest wound and began to examine his arm. There was a clean, linear, horizontal wound across the back of his mid forearm. It appeared confined to the subcutaneous tissue. There was no obvious damage to tendons. I had Julio put his wrist and hand through range of motion, and everything worked. I then tested the sensation in his fingers and hand with normal results.

Somebody has obviously inflicted some damage on Julio, but it appeared that both the forearm and chest wound were superficial. Julio had probably raised his arms in a defensive posture, when a roundhouse slash of a knife caught the back of his forearm. A thrust had caught the left side of his chest, but the knife had probably slid along a rib under the skin, and not penetrated the chest cavity. The attacker was right handed. I wondered if he was still alive.

Julio spoke. "You've got ten minutes to get these cuts sewed up."

I looked up and stared at him again, our eyes locked for a long moment. I would not soon forget those eyes—black and cold as death, without mercy or remorse. In the background Hyde was getting agitated—royally pissed, actually. *Tell that asshole to go fuck himself!* The room was quiet.

"Get me a suture tray, Lisa," I said finally, "with lidocaine and four-oh nylon."

I put interrupted sutures in the chest wound, and used a running stitch on the long forearm cut to save time. We were obviously not going to get any diagnostic imaging studies. Before we could clean his skin and dress the wounds, Julio threw the bloody drapes on the floor and stood.

"*Vamos,*" he said. One of his goons threw him his ski parka, another roughly shoved open the door, and the four of them strode out of the room, Julio's short frame surrounded by the three bodyguards.

An astonished clerk, waiting outside the door with her little computer registration cart, stood wide-eyed and mouth agape as she watched them walk briskly down the hall to the exit door. Mike Szymanski stood near her, his eyes searching my face as if asking for permission to engage. I shook my head. The goon closest to Mike kept the bulge in his jacket pocket pointed at Mike the whole way down the hall. As soon as they turned a corner, Mike followed them anyhow.

Behind me, I heard Lisa let out a long breath. "I don't know who those guys were, but I don't want to see them again," she said quietly.

"I think we may have just had a cordial little introduction to *Mara Salvatrucha*," I said. Three minutes later we could hear the faint siren of the first arriving Baltimore County police car.

CHAPTER NINE

FRIDAY WAS FINALLY MY SCHEDULED MEETING with Jacquelyn Ford. I was working day shift, so I would have to skip out of the department for twenty or thirty minutes and leave Bob D'Amelio by himself. It had taken about five e-mail exchanges with Jacquelyn's secretary to find an appointment time with Ms. Ford that was convenient. I interpreted this difficulty as Jacquelyn's way of communicating whose time was more important, and where I fell in the pecking order of things. I was challenging Jacquelyn's decision on modifying Samson, and she was setting the stage for our encounter.

About nine o'clock I also suddenly remembered, in a panic, that today was Elizabeth's birthday. I was not well prepared—no card; no flowers; no gift. Birthday dinner was at 8:00 at the Oregon Grille in Hunt Valley. I would have about forty-five minutes between the end of my shift and dinner to salvage this relationship. The drive-time alone would take nearly thirty minutes. Today was not going well so far.

I saw a bunch of routine cases, and about ten got a call from Jack Snyder, Dad's urologist. My heart skipped a beat for a moment. I picked up the phone.

"Jack?"

"Hey, Alex. I got your dad's biopsy report back this morning."

"How's it look?"

"Well, I don't think it's too bad. The biopsies were positive for well-differentiated peripheral adenocarcinoma, but the Gleason score is only four, and the tumor foci are small. There's a little bit of controversy over the management of these tumors, but here at Hopkins we're not treating these. We're just using active surveillance. The ten year mortality is less than ten percent. I think he'll do fine without treatment. If his cancer starts progressing, we've got lots of treatment options."

I gave a little sigh of relief, even though I had basically expected good news. This was a little revelation for me. We never realize the emotional importance of the unconditional love residing in parents until confronted with a potential loss, even at nearly forty years of age.

"That's a relief, Jack. I appreciate your call. I'll let my sibs know. Will you be talking to Dad?"

"Yeah, I'm going to give him a call now and follow up with him in the office next week."

"Great. Thanks."

"Bye."

I grabbed my cell phone and quickly texted Anne and Brian. Anne, especially, would be royally pissed if I didn't let her know right away. I would hear back almost immediately from her, for sure, but I was falling behind in seeing patients and just couldn't talk to her at the moment.

Anne had an early marriage that didn't work out too well. She was a very successful investment counselor who lived in Federal Hill and worked for T. Rowe Price, but she was still a little girl as far as my parents were concerned. She had a rough time when her marriage went south. The emotional connection with my parents, especially my father, was her salvation.

~

Eleven o'clock rolled around. I apologized to Bob for having to leave, and walked to the administrative offices on the third floor in the west wing of the hospital. Gwen Reynolds flashed me a bright smile as I walked into the expansive receptionist's foyer.

"Hi, Dr. Randolph!" Gwen likes me. If I'm late with some

document or another that has to go up the administrative chain, she always calls to remind me. I also get subtle little warnings when the ER shows up in somebody's administrative crosshairs. She's like my little mole buried in the upstairs offices. I always feel smug about that.

"Have a seat, Dr. Randolph," she said cheerfully. "Ms. Ford will be right with you."

This delay was to be expected—part of setting the mood for the meeting. I sat in the plush wing chair in the waiting area and absently picked up a copy of *U+Me* magazine.

I was just getting into *Ten Hot Hollywood Bodies* when Jackie came briskly striding out of her office.

"Dr. Randolph," she said as she firmly gripped my hand. "I'm so sorry to keep you waiting. Come on in." This, of course, was also not a good sign. When an administrator whom you know well calls you by your formal title, it's tantamount to a declaration of war.

Jackie walked ahead of me, carefully placing one high-heeled foot directly in front of the other, in a Heidi Klum runway walk that I was certain she had been practicing since age twelve. I couldn't see her hips sway because she was wearing her usual starched, white, knee-length clinic jacket. Lord knows why, because there's no vomit or blood up here requiring protection for your black silk dress with an elegant white floral pattern.

Jackie motioned to a chair. I took a seat in front of her wide mahogany desk, where not a scrap of paper marred its gleaming surface. I have never been able to figure out how people function without stacks of paper in chronological order on their desk.

The room was closer in size to an auditorium than an office, and, of course, was elegantly appointed. There was a sofa, coffee table, and several armchairs, all in carefully coordinated muted tan and coffee colors. Several table lamps with burgundy shades warmly lit the room. The carpet was definitely plush enough to screw on, without getting carpet burns.

Jackie sat down, placed her elbows on the armrests of her executive chair, clasped her hands together, and smiled.

"Well, Dr. Randolph, I think you are here to discuss your

committee's excellent work on reducing door-to-physician times."

"I am, Jacquelyn. And we both know that you don't like it."

"On the contrary, Dr. Randolph," she replied, raising one eyebrow. "I think your concern with not keeping the public waiting is to be commended. But there are larger issues with which the hospital must be concerned."

I decided to start by making the business case. Administrators are interested in money.

"You know, of course," I said, "that a fairly minor modification of the Samson software would cut door-to-doctor times by maybe twelve to fifteen minutes. And you also know that short door-to-doctor times win you patient satisfaction and greater market share." Market share is something administrators understand.

"Dr. Randolph, our Trustees have charged us with the task of achieving meaningful integration across the Americus family of hospitals. In the overall scheme of things, the necessity of this integration occasionally means that the well-intentioned proposals of individual departments must take a back seat. We are determined that Samson is going to be used in a uniform fashion across the spectrum, and that all Americus hospitals and departments are going to adopt the same policies." Jackie gives pretty good speeches.

"Jacquelyn, you know that that's not the trend in business? You know that in big business there is renewed emphasis on allowing individual operating entities to adapt to local circumstances and business needs; to give them the freedom to innovate and succeed?" I was very pleased with this last line—made me feel like a Wharton School professor.

"That may be the case, Dr. Randolph, but the desire of our Trustees has been very clearly expressed," she said firmly.

I decided to try one more line of reasoning.

"Jacquelyn, what about the tremendous waste of nursing time? Ten minutes of unnecessary computer documentation times eighty patients a day. Do you know the clinical impact of having eight hundred more minutes a day for nurses to be at the bedside taking care of patients rather than computers?

"Dr. Randolph," she sighed, "we all wish that we had more time to spend with patients. But the documentation demands of this litigious medical environment are here to stay."

This was going nowhere fast. I had one last card in my hand that I really didn't want to play, but Jacquelyn was such a pompous bitch that I couldn't resist.

"You know, Jackie," I said, switching to the familiar, "I think that you should talk with Ed Simpson about this." She stared at me, absently twirling her wedding ring.

Edward Simpson, MD, retired general surgeon, was the Americus Vice President of Medical Affairs, and a completely untrustworthy asshole. Ostensibly his job was to represent the views and needs of the medical staff. But Ed had long ago gone over to the dark side, because that was from whence came his paycheck. There wasn't a doc on the staff who would confide in him. He was also technically my boss.

The key here, however, was that Jackie was fucking Ed, and I knew it. How I found out was a completely serendipitous thing. A month earlier, my sister, Anne, and I had walked from her townhouse on Federal Hill to have dinner at the Inner Harbor Hyatt, where, lo and behold, I spotted our lovely administrative couple snuggling in a corner booth, followed by a hand-in-hand trip to the elevator. This was not an arrangement of which the Trustees would likely approve.

I played my card. Jekyll gave out a low moan.

"One of these evenings when the two of you are having dinner together at the Inner Harbor Hyatt," I continued quietly, looking her directly in the eyes, "you should ask Ed if he doesn't think there is some room for local innovation in the Americus family of hospitals."

The color slowly drained from Jackie's face. She swallowed hard and sat there staring at me. I smiled back. Her right knee started to jiggle under the desk. A long moment passed.

Finally, she gathered herself together and spoke. "All right. Fair enough, Dr. Randolph. I'll discuss it with him." The color had returned to her face and was now headed in a crimson direction.

I stood and reached my hand out across the desk. "Thanks, Jackie. I really appreciate your open mind on this issue." And with that, I headed back to work.

Gwen waved "bye" as I crossed the foyer. Hyde chuckled quietly all the way back to the department. He's usually careful not to gloat too much because Jekyll gets on his case, especially after such a shameless exhibition of blatant moral depravity on my part.

~

I was typing discharge instructions for an ankle fracture when Julie walked up to my computer station and plunked her butt on the counter.

"Well, how did it go?" she asked.

I looked up and smiled. "Actually, I think Jackie approached this very rationally. I think she might have actually seen some merit in our position, and she is going to give it some serious thought."

Julie gave me an incredulous scowl, shook her head, and walked away. "I'll believe it when I see it," she said over her shoulder.

~

There were two notes at my station that said, "Your sister called." My cell phone was lying on the counter, making little beeping sounds, and I saw a text message from Anne—"CALL ME!" There was going to be no putting this off. My sister was a very tenacious woman. I dialed her direct line at T. Rowe Price. Anne picked up the line.

"Why didn't you call me?"

"I was with a woman on the verge of having a cardiac arrest," I explained. "Besides, it's all really good news, so nothing lost."

"Well you could at the very least be concerned about giving me gray hair."

"Listen, Dad's cancer has such a good prognosis that they're not even going to treat it. They're just going to watch it. He'll be out there playing tennis for at least another ten years."

"And what then?" she asked, like this was a death sentence.

"If the cancer begins to spread, there's a dozen treatment options that will give him another ten or twenty years."

"Well, he's not likely to live *that* long." There was no satisfying this woman.

"Anne, tell you what. You meet me tomorrow at noon for lunch and I'll tell you everything. We'll meet halfway—at Paoli's in Towson."

"You better be on time."

"Okay, okay. I said I'll be there."

"Bye." The explosion of her phone hitting the cradle ruptured my eardrum. My life today was filled with over-achieving women who were feeling very assertive, and the day was only half over. In fact, the worst was likely yet to come.

~

I gave Rick the briefest report that I could get away with on a couple of patients that I had left over. He looked at me and drawled, "You've got a date with a thoroughbred filly, don't you?"

"I do, and I'm likely to get bucked off if I don't get out o' here."

"Hey, that reminds me. Did you ever hear that joke about rodeo sex?"

"Later, Rick."

~

By the time I grabbed a card at CVS, and a bunch of roses on sale at Wegman's supermarket for $10.99, I was fifteen minutes late. Traffic at Hunt Valley is not good on Friday nights. I scratched the price tag off the flowers' cellophane wrapper with my thumbnail at a stoplight. It took me two more minutes and a near rear-end collision to find a pen in the glove compartment to sign the card. I walked into the elegant Oregon Grille with a smile, and my flowers and card, twenty-three minutes late. Elizabeth was not impressed.

"Glad you could make it," she said with crossed arms and legs. This conversation already had a familiar ring to it.

"I'm really sorry, Elizabeth. I had a couple of leftover patients I just couldn't get rid of," I said with the lamest of lies.

"Perhaps the solution would have been to schedule yourself *off* on the night of my birthday," she suggested. My response to this would have required another somewhat broader lie, but fortunately, at that very moment, an angel arrived in the form of a cute little server in very tight black pants, who asked with a smile if she could get me a cocktail.

I wanted to kiss her.

"I'll take two," I said.

"I've already got one," said Elizabeth.

"Actually, I'll take just one, but make it a double Grey Goose and tonic."

"Certainly, sir," she said with her heavenly smile.

We passed a very quiet dinner of Coriander Crusted Long Island Duck and Colorado Lamb Loin. No one ordered dessert or coffee. Finally, Elizabeth stood and spoke.

"Well, Alex, thank you very much for a lovely birthday dinner. Good night." Elizabeth usually gets right to the point. It was perhaps fortunate that we drove separately. She left the flowers and card on the table. So did I. But I also left the angel a very nice tip.

I was surprised to hear myself whistling as I walked through the parking lot to the car. Maybe everything happens for a reason. I suddenly realized that I hadn't called my parents yet, and today my dad had been diagnosed with cancer.

CHAPTER TEN

JULIE WAS ON ME FIRST THING WHEN I CAME IN AT 9:00 on Monday morning. She was sitting on the counter beside my computer station.

"What did you do to Jacquelyn, crawl under the desk between her legs?" she asked.

"I never touched her legs."

"I got a call from her this morning. She wants me to put together an outline of all the steps we want to modify in Samson."

"I told you she saw the merits of our case."

"You're lying. There's something wrong here. She hates you. She would never agree to this."

"Maybe she wants to kiss and make up with you after your last performance evaluation."

"I'm still on a sixty day action plan!"

"There you go, now you can take some action."

"You're holding out on me, Alex," she warned, crossing her arms. "If you don't tell me what's going on here, I swear I'll never save your ass again." *What is it about me and insistent women?.*

"Jackie just thought the better part of discretion was to cooperate with us," I said.

"Oh, so it's *Jackie* now?"

"Okay, okay." Julie was completely trustworthy and unfailingly discrete. We had stood, back-to-back, for three years fighting department battles, and Julie had paid a price for that. I decided there was no way I was going to avoid telling her the truth. Actually, after all the hell that Jackie had put Julie through with her last rotten performance evaluation, Julie deserved to hear the truth.

"Jackie has been involved in a little indiscretion with Ed Simpson."

She jumped up off the counter.

"You didn't! You blackmailed her?"

"Shhhh." I looked around to see who else was listening. "Not exactly."

"She's fucking that jerk? Oh, that is *too* funny!"

~

I went into Bed Six to see a kid that fell off a jungle gym during recess. Both parents were with him, displaying concerned faces. Both were well-dressed; dad in a pinstripe suit and mom in skirt and blouse. She had some sort of ID badge on her sweater.

"Hi. I'm Dr. Randolph." I shook hands with mom and dad. "What happened today?"

Mom spoke up, looking over at five-year-old Tyler, who was punching buttons on some sort of electronic game with both thumbs. "Well, Tyler was playing on the monkey bars at school and fell and hit his head pretty hard. I think he was pretty high." I presumed that this was not a reference to Tyler sniffing glue, or popping PCPs.

She looked over at Tyler again, and said, "Tyler, were you far up on the monkey bars? Did you fall a long way, honey?" Tyler shrugged and kept punching buttons.

"Well, anyhow," she said, "he hit his head and complained to the school nurse of a bad headache, so she called us. She thinks he needs a CAT scan. We just want to be on the safe side."

I sat down on the exam table beside Tyler. "You look like you're pretty good with that game, Tyler." He looked up at me with a smile, and nodded.

"Tyler, what game were you playing on the monkey bars?"

"Pirates," he said.

"And were you a pirate, or a good guy?"

"I was Peter Pan, and Matthew was Captain Hook."

"Were you up very high on the ship?"

"We were up in the sails."

"So Captain Hook must have knocked you down." He nodded.

"Did you hit your head when you fell?" He shrugged again.

"Do you have a headache right now?" Another shrug. Well, so far it was pretty clear that Tyler was alert and oriented, and if he had a headache, it at least didn't appear to be bothering him too much.

I looked over at mom and dad. "Did anybody tell you that he was knocked out, or said that he lost consciousness?"

"No. We don't know that," said dad. That at least meant that a loss of consciousness was improbable, or someone would have reported it. If there was no loss of consciousness, the probability of a serious head injury fell to less than one in a hundred.

"Has he had any nausea or vomiting?"

Mom handled this one. "Tyler, do you feel sick on your stomach? Tell the doctor if you feel sick." Tyler shrugged once more.

"OK, Peter Pan, let's take a look at you." I did my exam, checking his scalp for a goose egg, his eardrums and behind his ears for bruising that might indicate a basilar skull fracture, checked his pupils, and checked his nose for leaking cerebrospinal fluid. All were negative. A quick check of the rest of his body revealed no bruises, or pain to palpation.

"Well, folks, everything looks really good," I announced. "Tyler has a normal physical examination. I can't find any bumps on his head, and there's no evidence of a skull fracture. We're going to let him go home, and we'll give you a check list of things to watch for, but I don't think we need to worry too much."

Silence.

Finally dad spoke up. "You're not going to do a CAT scan?"

"You know," I said, "in the old days, Tyler might have gotten a CAT scan. But we've grown more and more concerned over the years about the amount of radiation from a CAT scan, so we're trying not to do them, especially on kids, unless we really have pretty strong evidence of a serious head injury."

"Well, we'd much rather be on the safe side," said mom emphatically. I could sense Hyde getting agitated in the background.

"I understand. The issue, Mom, is that radiation damages dividing cells more than cells that are not dividing. Because kids are growing, their cells are constantly dividing, so they are more susceptible to radiation injury than adults. The radiation involved in a CAT scan is actually equal to several hundred chest x-rays. On examination, Tyler currently has no clear evidence of a head injury. So, I am really very reluctant to expose his brain to radiation without a more clear indication."

"Well, we're just not interested in taking these kinds of chances with our son's life," dad said formally. "We'll seek care elsewhere. Thank you for your time, Doctor."

Mom and dad stood and started gathering up their things, protectively putting on Tyler's coat, ski cap, and gloves. This patient encounter was clearly over. *Why didn't you just tell them they're idiots?* asked Hyde.

I wanted to tell them that too many CT's might make Tyler a dunce, quite apart from the increase in lifetime cancer risks. But mom and dad clearly saw the world only in black and white, and I was afraid that if I went too far with demonizing CT's, these two would refuse a CT in the future when Tyler really needed one. *You're gonna have to take one for the gipper*, said Jekyll.

"If you folks will hang on for just a second, I'll get your paperwork done, and have the nurse in here with your discharge papers in just a couple of minutes."

Silence. *You are such a wimp*, said Hyde.

I slid into my chair at the computer station and looked over at Lauren, today's second doc. "Well, so much for my patient satisfaction scores today."

"Have you been acting like an arrogant asshole again?" she asked.

Joyce Harbaugh caught me at the coffee pot in the break room near the end of the shift. There was still a trace of discoloration around her left eye. Joyce had been functioning pretty well in the last week. She seemed to have renewed vigor and interest in her work. I was happy to see that.

"I wanted to thank you for your help a week or two ago," she said quietly. "Things are better now."

"Did you get a protective order?"

"Yes. Actually, he's in jail right now."

"For how long?"

"I don't know. Probably not very long, but at least, for now, he's gone, and I'm sleeping better. I hope that some time in jail will make him think twice about violating the restraining order."

"I hope so, too, Joyce." She turned to leave the room.

"Joyce," I called after her. She stopped and looked at me.

"You've been doing a good job in the last week."

"Thanks," she said smiling.

CHAPTER ELEVEN

JACK SCHMIDT STOPPED BY TO GIVE US AN update on the Julio incident. Jack, Julie, Mike Szymanski, and I gathered in the break room and poured coffee.

Jack started off. "We tracked down the tag number that you got off their car," he said looking at Mike. "It was stolen, so that's a dead end. But we did find the car, and it's been dusted for prints. We also found blood, interestingly, on both the front and back seats. That's still being tested." He looked around the room while he let this piece of information settle in. Now he had everyone's attention.

"But here's the really interesting news. A hiker found the body of an African-American male in Gunpowder Falls three days ago, just below the Prettyboy Dam spillway. He was shot in both kneecaps and castrated." Julie made a yuck face.

"We found blood on the concrete side wall of the road that runs across the dam. Looks like he was tossed over the side and down the spillway. The coroner says he was probably still alive when he went down the spillway, because the cause of death was drowning." Jack looked around the room and smiled. "You know, that spillway is a hundred and fifty feet high."

"Good Lord," said Julie, placing her hand over her eyes.

"Friendly folks, eh? We're running DNA tests on the blood we found on the wall, too," Jack continued. "It's probably the victim's, but you never know—might be some of Julio's there, too. We got Julio's DNA from the bloody drapes in Bed Fourteen."

"You think the two are connected?" asked Mike Szymanski.

"This victim didn't look like your average born-and-bred-on-the-Manor resident. We're pretty sure he was a Crip, from the way he was dressed and from his tattoos. Julio, on the other hand, is almost certainly Salvadoran, and, as you know, there's a real war going on these days between MS-13 and the Crips. Another Crip was killed in the city last week."

"Oh my God!" said Julie. "Sharon told me that while Julio was here there was a nervous looking black guy walking around the waiting room, who looked like he was checking out the place. He never registered. And he left before Julio and his guys walked out. What if he was a Crip and these other guys were MS-13?"

Everybody looked at her in silence.

"Who is Sharon?" asked Jack.

"The registration clerk out front," offered Mike.

"Why are they *up* here?" moaned Julie.

"I don't know," replied Jack, running his fingers through his graying hair. "Two obvious possibilities come to mind. The first is that they are coming up here when they're wounded and are using Mason-Dixon. instead of a city hospital, because it's way the hell out in the boondocks. That way they can get out of here before the police arrive."

"Yeah, there was no way we were going to hold onto them until you guys arrived. We never even got them registered," I said. "But in fact, it was still pretty close. Your guys got here about three minutes late."

"The other possibility," continued Jack, "is that the northern part of the county is the drug turf they're now fighting over, and this is just where the action is."

"OK, well how are we going to get the police here faster?" asked Julie, leaning forward in her chair and slashing the air with her ballpoint pen for emphasis.

"That's a big problem," sighed Jack. "Precinct Seven is only budgeted for one cruiser for the whole northern part of the county. I've already spoken with Captain Louis about increasing patrols up here, but it doesn't look promising."

Sergeant Schmidt left the informal briefing, and Julie, Mike, and I looked at each other. Our little incident with Julio had scared the bejesus out of the staff. We had an obvious security problem.

"Well, folks, where do we go from here?" I asked.

"Stan Robinson has a formal meeting scheduled for Thursday morning to discuss security," said Julie. "You need to be there, too."

The brazenness of Julio was frightening. Julie's report of a black guy casing the joint only made me worry more about one of these idiots doing something stupid in the ER.

"I'm going to talk with Frank Turano," I said. "I need to know more about the players here."

"Lisa's husband?"

"Yeah. He's a Baltimore City homicide detective. He and Lisa met at Hopkins before we came up here. We used to hang out together in the old days. He'll know something about these guys."

~

I walked back into the ER and grabbed the first chart in the rack. I was looking up the nursing assessment in the computer, when Sam Warren, our popular physical plant manager, walked up to the nursing station. His skin was ashen. Sweat dripped off his nose onto a chart sitting on the counter. He leaned on the counter with one hand and was clutching his chest with the other. Cathy Rutledge and Penny Murray stood nearby reviewing a policy manual. Penny's orientation period was almost over.

I stood. "Sam? You don't look so good!" I walked around the counter, grabbing Cathy and Penny. "Ladies, I think Sam needs a bed."

We led Sam across the hallway to the empty Bed Six. "Are you having chest pain?" I asked, as we eased him back on the bed. He nodded, eyes closed; his face a mask of pain.

"We need a twelve-lead EKG in here," I yelled out through the open door to the ward clerk. Cathy slipped nasal oxygen on his face and started connecting him to the monitor. Penny tied a tourniquet around his arm and began probing for a vein. I put my fingers on his wrist as I began asking questions. His skin was wet and cold. From the low amplitude of his pulse, I guessed his blood pressure was well under one hundred, but his heart rate was fast—maybe a hundred and ten or twenty.

"Sam, when did you start having pain?"

"About fifteen minutes ago," he said with an effort, eyes still closed.

"Where is your pain?" Sam ran his hand up his sternum, and on up into his neck.

"What does it feel like?"

"Like somebody's blowing a balloon up inside my chest," he said. "You got your penknife on you Doc? Maybe you can pop that balloon," he joked weakly.

I carefully leaned him forward so I wouldn't disrupt Penny's IV attempt, and listened to his lungs. They were clear. I leaned him back again and listened to his heart. The rate was fast, with a sound like a horse galloping, that indicated developing heart failure.

Joyce Harbaugh arrived—pushing an EKG machine—looked up, and saw who was in the bed. "On my God! Sam!"

I glanced up at the monitor, which was now displaying data. Sam's heart rhythm was regular, but fast–one hundred and eighteen. His first blood pressure came up at eighty-eight over fifty-six. He sure as hell looked like he was having the big one—a major heart attack. I would know in just a second.

Joyce's machine whirred and spit out a strip of paper. She ripped the electrocardiogram off the machine and handed it to me. It looked awful. I needed only a glance to see that Sam was indeed having a heart attack—a *myocardial infarction*—and it was huge.

"OK guys, we've got a big anterior MI here," I announced. "Let's get moving. I need four baby aspirin and a bolus of heparin. And let's start with four milligrams of morphine and try to get his pain under control."

There are actually only two major arteries that come off the aorta and feed the muscle of the heart with fresh, oxygenated blood. The bigger of the two—the left main artery—immediately splits in two itself, and supplies about two thirds of the heart. If the left main gets obstructed so that the blood supply to two thirds of the heart muscle is cut off, the game is over. All that heart muscle just dies—hence the slang name *widow-maker* for the left main artery. From the tombstone-elevation of Sam's ST segments all the way across his EKG tracing, that was Sam's bad luck, and he was on his way out.

I had a bunch of nurses in the room now, and people started scurrying to get a second IV started and to get the necessary drugs from the Omnicell drug dispenser.

I stuck my head out the door and yelled to the ward clerk, "Get me St. Joe's cardiology on the line. And we're gonna need a helicopter!"

There was basically only one opportunity to save Sam's life: he had to get to a cardiac cath laboratory before his heart muscle died and get that artery reopened. We had about a ninety minute window to get that accomplished, *if* he didn't die first from ventricular fibrillation, a form of cardiac arrest with a high probability in a heart attack this big.

Saint Joseph's Hospital in Towson was the closest facility with a cath lab and open-heart surgery. I needed to get Sam there pronto.

I spoke with the cardiologist who quickly accepted the patient. CISCOM, the Maryland emergency communications center, was in the process of dispatching the helicopter. It would be roughly twenty minutes before its arrival.

I walked back to the bedside. Penny was injecting the heparin into the IV line. "He's still having a lot of pain, Dr. Randolph," she said. Penny's formality struck me. She was still new enough that she didn't feel comfortable calling me Alex.

I looked at his blood pressure on the monitor—eighty-six over fifty-four. He was still in a lot of pain after the first small dose of morphine. But morphine drops the blood pressure, and Sam was already on the edge of a cliff. In fact, he was in the early stages of cardiogenic shock. I wanted to relieve his pain, but I had to be careful.

"OK, Penny. Let's give him just small doses of two milligrams of morphine at a time, and we'll see how it goes with his blood pressure."

It was time to let Sam know what was going on. That was going to be made more difficult by the fact that I knew Sam well and he was one of us.

I looked down at him, and our eyes met.

"Sam, you're having a heart attack," I said simply.

"I figured that, Doc."

"The good news is that you had it here in the hospital, and you're alive. The bad news is that it looks pretty big on your EKG. We need to get you out of here to St. Joes so they can open that clogged artery with a catheter and a balloon, and get this heart attack reversed before it does a lot of damage to your heart muscle." Sam would be lucky if they could open the artery with a balloon or stent. If it was the left main artery that was blocked, as I suspected, he might have to have emergency open-heart bypass surgery. "I've got a helicopter enroute."

"Hey Doc, I trust you," he said. "I'm in the best of hands." I hoped to God that these hands were good enough.

~

Fifteen minutes later Sam's family arrived. His wife, Tricia, sat in a folding chair at the bedside holding his hand. Skinny, sixteen-year-old Amy Warren, the apple of her father's eye, leaned on the rail on the other side of the bed in jeans with a ripped knee. She wore big hoop ear rings, and displayed more cleavage than was explicable for a tiny girl. I had explained Sam's condition to them. Tricia maintained her composure, but I could see in her face that the fear was consuming her.

Sam was more comfortable at the moment, and he was making small talk about Amy's volleyball team, clearly trying hard to put his terrified family at ease. His blood pressure was holding in the mid-eighties. Not great, but so far so good under the circumstances. Another five minutes and he'd be loaded on a helicopter. I stood in the room wrapping up my notes on the chart.

Sam was telling his wife to check on the salt in their water softener, when I heard his sentence trail off into a moan. Pandemonium broke out. Tricia gasped and jumped to her feet, her folding chair clattering to the floor behind her. I heard Amy scream "Daddy?" A second later the monitor began to clang insistently.

I knew what it was even before I looked at the monitor. A quick glance confirmed it. *Shit.* His heart rhythm had degenerated into ventricular fibrillation—a sort of electrical short circuit in which current goes in all directions randomly over the heart muscle, turning it into a quivering mass of useless muscle with no coordinated pumping action. It's fatal.

By the time I reached the bedside, Penny was already placing the paddles of the defibrillator on Sam's chest. He was unconscious, of course, with a few erratic breaths. She punched a button on the paddles, and I heard the warning tone of the defibrillator rise to a crescendo as the machine charged. April grabbed Tricia and Amy, and herded them from the room.

Penny looked up at me, and I nodded. "Clear! Clear! Clear!," she announced loudly three times. Everyone stepped back from the bed. Penny pushed the discharge button on the paddles. Sam's body jerked from the shock, his arms flying up in the air. Penny stepped back, and we all looked up at the monitor expectantly. It took two or three seconds for the electronics to settle down. For another two seconds the tracing was flat, and then we saw return of the first heartbeat, and then a second, and then a third.

But it was not to be. A premature heartbeat struck on the green tracing, and was immediately followed by the uncoordinated, squiggly line of another episode of ventricular fibrillation. Penny hit the button and charged the machine again. Sam's body convulsed with a second shock. We again waited. Seconds passed. This time—nothing. The line remained flat, and the monitor warning bell clanged ominously

"OK, let's get on his chest," I said. The room was filled with people responding to the *Code Blue.* Bob Dalton, the day's orderly, stepped forward and began delivering rapid, crisp compressions to Sam's chest.

"He needs an epi," I ordered. Penny had already reached into the code cart drawer for the drug, and inserted the syringe of one milligram of epinephrine into the IV line. April handed me the laryngoscope and a tube, and I was able to quickly intubate him without difficulty. Jill from respiratory therapy slid to the head of the bed, attached the ventilation bag, and started to push air into Sam's lungs.

We worked Sam that day for forty more minutes, briefly getting a heart rhythm back once, but in the end, he died. We let Tricia back into the room as we worked him. She stood on one side of the bed, holding Sam's hand as the chest compressions continued. It's often very therapeutic for a family member to feel like they were there with their loved one when they passed on. From time to time, Tricia would bend down and whisper something in Sam's ear. Amy stood back several steps behind her mother, hugging her arms to her chest, tears streaming down her face in disbelief. Sam was forty-nine years old. Amy was his and Tricia's only child.

~

I sat at my station, absently completing the paperwork that would be the last vestiges of Sam's life. The profound intimacy expressed by Trish during Sam's dying moments struck me. Perhaps it was the reminder that I had no such equivalent relationship in my own life.

Penny Murray was walking by the nursing station, gathering supplies to restock the room. I lay down the pen that I was using to sign Sam's death certificate, and watched her. I had worked with Penny on a couple of very emergent cases now, and the quickness of her mind impressed me. She always seemed to be one step ahead of the circumstances; anticipating what was going to happen, and prepared to address it.

She was quiet; well spoken. She never seemed to be very involved in the idle chit-chat around the nursing station. But, my God, she was lovely. Slender, with shoulder-length, blond hair—always in a ponytail—a square face with a wide soft mouth, a straight nose, and delicately arched eyebrows above deep luminescent green eyes. From what I could tell, she wore virtually no makeup. My eyes had been drawn to her left hand when she had placed the paddles on Sam's chest. She wore two rings—a diamond and a wedding band. Out there, someplace, was a very lucky man named Murray.

~

I pulled into the little shopping center on the corner of York and Mount Carmel Road on my way home, and grabbed a pizza for dinner. Maggie greeted me with tail wagging when I walked through the door, but the house seemed empty. I am very used to death, and it rarely bothers me, but I had been thinking about Sam all the way home. He was only ten years older than me. At the end, he was surrounded by a small family that adored him. Somehow the thought of a family for me always seemed somewhere out in the distant future—maybe when I grew up. I didn't know how, or when, that might ever happen. It pretty clearly wasn't going to happen with Elizabeth. Tonight, I felt very much alone. I put my dishes in the sink, scratched Maggie behind the ears, turned out the lights, and went to bed.

~

I almost never go to the funerals of patients, but this one was different. Sam was a friend more than a patient. There were a ton of hospital people there, with standing room only in the back of the little church on Middletown Road. It was a dreary November day with a cold drizzle. After the service I stood at the graveside beside Julie, under a shared umbrella, as the minister led a chorus of *Amazing Grace*. Outside the periphery of the small crowd, I spotted Penny Murray standing alone.

CHAPTER TWELVE

I MET FRANK TURANO, LISA'S HUSBAND, AT AN old hangout—the City Lights bar on Calvert Street downtown. I ordered my usual, and Frank had a Heineken.

"Your wife thinks there may be a whole soccer team in her belly," I said.

"You know," replied Frank, leaning forward, "this one just might be a boy. She's never gotten beat around like this before." Frank had a pair of little princesses at home, and he was dying for a boy.

"You mean you guys don't know what you're having?"

"Nope. We like the surprise. Makes the big day more exciting," he said with a crooked smile on his handsome, but slightly lopsided, face. He had some faint scars that gave him a mildly dangerous look.

Frank took a hit in the face from a baseball bat wielded by a Crip gang member—maybe five years ago. I was in the ER the night he came in. His face was a tribute to the plastics guys at Hopkins. I never knew for sure, but I think he outlived the gang member. That's how I knew that Frank was the right guy to tell me about the Crips. I hoped that he knew something about Mara Salvatruca, too.

"Lisa told you about our little encounter with the Salvadorans last week?"

"Yeah."

"God, your wife's got balls. You should have seen her shove that goon out of the way."

"That's why I don't fool around," smiled Frank.

"You know about the other guy they found in the Gunpowder? The one they think was a Crip?"

"I looked at the body myself. He was a Crip, alright. I recognized him from the street."

"I need to know about these guys, Frank," I said earnestly. "Are they nuts? Are they rational? Do I have to worry about them having a war right in the middle of my ER?"

Frank looked at me for a long time. Finally he spoke.

"Alex, remember all that stuff you learned in Catholic school? All the rules of life? Empathy for your fellow man; taking care of the other guy; fair play; honesty; all that stuff—the stuff that holds the social fabric of civilization together? He paused. "Forget it. Doesn't apply to these guys—either gang. No empathy. No pity. Utter, complete, naked brutality," he said slowly.

"That doesn't mean that there are no rules of sorts," he continued. "The Crips are pretty loyal to their own. The bond is their hatred of the other gangs. But they're not smart. They're not organized. No strategic planning. Half of the time they're messed up on dope. They do stuff on the spur of the moment.

"The Salvadorans, on the other hand, are far more dangerous. Their leadership is older, and they're much better organized."

"That's because the founders were veterans of the Salvadoran civil war?" I asked.

"Yeah. These guys are in it for the money and the power. They've got more military-style discipline. They do stuff for a reason. But they are pitiless."

"So who do I have to worry about in my ER?"

"I don't think the Salvadorans are a big risk for war in your ER. They're bold and brutal, but they don't take unnecessary risks. If they show up, just stay calm and get them out of there. You handled them well last week.

"The Crips, on the other hand," continued Frank, "are less predictable. They're young. They're emotional. They go off at the drop of a hat, particularly if they've just shot up. If you have trouble from one of them it's gonna be a kid who's out to make his mark. You can recognize most of them. They often wear blue athletic clothes and, you know, jeans with the crotch around their ankles. And they always have a blue bandanna tied around their head, or their neck."

We finished our drinks, reminiscing about the old days when I was at Hopkins. I shook Frank's hand and left a ten on the table. City Lights drinks are a very good value.

Frank stood and hesitated. "One more thing, Alex," he said making eye contact. "Next time one of those bastards shows up in your ER, I'd be very grateful if you'd keep Lisa out of that room. I know that sounds paranoid, but sometimes Lisa doesn't think about these guys being bigger than she is."

"I'll do it, Frank. I won't forget."

~

Eight people sat around the conference table the next morning at Stan Robinson's ad-hoc security meeting. Stanley Ward Robinson is an Americus VP of Health Systems, and the Chief Operating Officer of Mason-Dixon Regional Medical Center. He has a handlebar moustache and a fondness for bow ties. Besides having the enormous ego that is requisite for all Americus officers, he's actually not a bad guy.

I sat between Julie and Mike Szymanski. Stan Robinson sat directly across from me, decked out in his trademark gold and navy blue striped bow tie, and a button-down, blue oxford. He was flanked by Jack Schmidt on his right and Larry Kline, the Assistant Director of Physical Plant, on his left. It should have been Sam, but he wasn't with us anymore. I was glad to see that Jack Schmidt had been invited

Jackie Ford sat at the end of the table, wearing her designer black-frame glasses. This was the first time I had seen Jackie since our meeting. It would be interesting to see how she handled the interaction. Gwen Reynolds sat at the other end of the table as secretary to the committee, and began to pass out agendas.

"I want you all to know," began Stan, "that we are taking this Julio incident very seriously, and that the safety of our employees is of prime concern to Americus." We sat through the predictable preliminaries as he continued, and finally, Stan turned the meeting over to Mike Szymanski.

"As you can see from the agenda," said Mike, "there are about three major steps that we've outlined that will be taken immediately to improve our security in the ER. And I want you to know that I'm certainly open to any additional ideas that you all have.

"The first, and most important," continued Mike, "is that we're installing a security station in the waiting area, right next to the reception desk. There will be a guard stationed there twenty-four hours a day.

"Second, we're installing a panic button at the triage station, under the counter, that is directly connected to the Baltimore County Police dispatch center. When this button is pushed, a patrol car will automatically be dispatched to the hospital. The dispatch center will then make a follow-up phone call to the ER to ascertain the conditions, and to cancel any false alarms."

Julie raised her hand, and Mike nodded to her. "How long will it take the patrol car to get here?" she asked emphatically. Mike looked over at Sergeant Schmidt.

"That depends," said Jack, "on the location of the northern sector patrol car at the time of the call, and whether that car is tied up on another call or not. If the northern sector car is unavailable, another car from Precinct Seven will have to be dispatched."

"So it could," said Julie, "be as long as fifteen or twenty minutes?"

"Yes, maam, I'm afraid so." Julie slumped back in her chair and frowned. "That's a long time," she said.

Stan took this as his cue to jump in. "I've spoken with Captain Louis of Precinct Seven, and tried to emphasize to him how important it is to the safety of the citizens of his precinct to have another car added in the northern sector. And I have also spoken with County Executive Benchoff about the necessity to allocate more resources to the northern end of the county. Americus is one of the county's biggest employers, and I'm certain that he will see the wisdom of providing adequate protection for Mason-Dixon."

Jack Schmidt looked down.

Ain't gonna happen, Stan, I said to myself. *Not with just one little Julio incident. The votes are in the southern part of the county, as is all of the crime.*

Mike moved on. "The third thing we are doing is installing new surveillance cameras in the waiting area itself and outside at the ER entrance. Larry, do you have a timetable for these folks on your construction?"

Larry was unaccustomed to participating in meetings with all the bigwhigs. He began softly and tentatively. "Well, we hope to begin in about a week to ten days on construction of the security station. Construction will take about a week, so maybe somewhere between two, or two and a half weeks, we'll be done. Another company is installing the security cameras and the panic button. That should all be up and running in about ten days."

"I should tell you," interjected Mike, "that we have to hire another two guards to be able to provide twenty-four hour coverage in the ER, and that is likely to take two weeks, at least. It could be the longest lead-time item. In the meantime, you can dial the security office anytime at extension five-one-seven-seven, and I also have sent all of you an e-mail with the number of my cell phone, which I carry all the time."

"There's one more thing," said Stan, once again taking control of the meeting in his booming voice. "I've spoken with Jacquelyn, and we're going to limit the number of visitors accompanying patients at the bedside to one, unless it's a pair of parents, in which case we'll let two back. That will prevent another incident like we had with Julio."

Brilliant, Stan, I thought, looking over at Julie who was silently shaking her head. Now we've adopted all the common sense of the TSA. No doubt, had Julio's guys known of this little rule, they would have quietly taken their seats in the waiting room. Perhaps we should also ban baby bottles and sippy cups to ensure that no liquid explosives are transported into the ER. Next time Mom comes in with three toddlers in tow, we'll let her know that two of them will have to have a seat in the waiting room.

After some more discussion about less important measures, the meeting broke up. I stood and pushed my chair in, looking over toward Jacquelyn. I caught her eye and flashed a big smile. She beamed back, poised as ever. Julie and I walked back to the ER together.

"Of course, neither Stan nor Jacquelyn ever mentioned their little one visitor per patient rule to you?" I asked.

"Of course not. I'm not senior administration. I don't have the intellect to deal with such weighty decisions."

"Maybe I should have another talk with Jackie."

"No! Let me deal with it. I'll fix it. Even Jackie's not that dense."

We walked on a little further in silence.

"Well, at least I give Stan some credit for actually committing some bucks to this," Julie said.

"But unarmed rent-a-cops aren't much of a deterrent," I replied, "and the action will be pretty much over before the cops get here. We're gonna be pretty much on our own."

"Maybe they won't be back," she said halfheartedly.

"Maybe," I said.

Events would prove our hopes to be wishful thinking.

CHAPTER THIRTEEN

IT WAS CRISP AND BRIGHT WITH A COATING OF thick frost on the still-green fall grass when I locked the door and walked to my Jeep at six-thirty on Thanksgiving morning. Overhead, I could hear the caw of a crow echo through the stillness of my little valley. I was on my way to work a half-shift in the ER until 1:00 PM. The docs often split holiday shifts so that everyone has an opportunity to spend at least a half-day of the holiday with their families. I would head to my parents' house in Sparks after work for Thanksgiving dinner.

I hadn't spoken to Elizabeth in three weeks. Neither of us had picked up the phone to make the first call. Maybe that was because we didn't have much to say. Still, we were unfinished business, and at some point we would make contact. I didn't know how I would feel, what would happen, or what I would say.

Elizabeth had Thanksgiving with my family last year, and, of course, it takes only one year to establish tradition for family holidays. My mother would have a place set for her. It was inconsiderate of me not to let her know that Elizabeth wouldn't be there, but I hadn't felt like talking about it. I resolved to give her a call on my cell phone after I left work and tell her to set one less place.

Holiday mornings are usually slow in the ER, and today was no exception. Goes to show you how urgent are most ER visits.

I had only one patient in the works—a thirty-two-year-old mother of two with abdominal pain named Linda Baird. Linda was a frequent flier. I counted ten previous visits in the computer for Linda over the past two years for abdominal pain. I had seen her myself on three of those occasions. She had ended up having six abdominal CT's, which should have been enough to make her glow in the dark.

Each visit was pretty much the same. She always complained of intense abdominal pain and a couple of episodes of vomiting, yet her belly exam was never very impressive. She never had fever, or an elevated white blood cell count, and her chemistries were always normal.

Apart from a history of mild hypertension, she otherwise seemed to be in good health except for some psych issues and a history of two past seizures. Linda was apparently bipolar—that's manic-depressive. She was seeing a psychiatrist and was maintained on Zoloft. Sometimes she complained of some numbness and tingling in her extremities, which probably fit with her psych history. She usually got pain meds and anti-nausea meds, and was then signed out as chronic abdominal pain and anxiety.

I had ordered the usual lab work, but decided to try to avoid a CT today because the odds were very high that it was again going to be negative, and the poor woman had already had enough radiation. I gave her some IV Demerol for pain and eight milligrams of Zofran for the nausea and vomiting.

I went back into the darkened room to see if she had gotten some relief with the Demerol and Zofran. She was lying on her side with her back to the door, curled up in a ball, covered with one of our thin, white blankets, which are a poor defense against the frigid temperatures that usually prevail in the ER.

"Hey Linda, how are you feeling?" I said, placing my hand on her hip. She rolled over and looked up at me with a strained look on her face.

"A little better, but it still hurts," she said softly. Despite Linda's psychiatric history, she never really seemed crazy to me, and I sensed that her pain was real.

"Let me feel your belly again." She squared up her hips, then pulled the blanket down, and her gown up. I palpated her belly again, and each place I pressed I looked up at her and said, "Tender there?" Each time she shook her head "no".

"OK. I'll have the nurse give you some more pain medicine, and we'll wait and see what your lab work shows." I turned to leave the room, but hesitated and went back in.

"Linda, do these episodes always seem to occur around the time of your periods?"

"Not during my periods, but maybe in the week or so before my periods."

"Have you seen an OB-GYN about this pain? Did they ever discuss endometriosis as a possibility?"

"Yes. I've seen Dr. Lombardi, and he says I don't have endometriosis."

"OK." I scratched my head, walked back to the nursing station, and ordered some more Demerol.

In a rare moment of extraordinary self-discipline, I decided that while things were slow and I was waiting for lab work, I would clean out the inbox on the desk in my little office just off the ER. I grabbed the oldest papers on the bottom half of the pile and took it back to my computer station.

Most of the stuff was quickly allocated to the trash can. I opened an inter-office envelope from Deborah Strong, RN, our Quality Assurance Manager. It was a letter with a little post-it attached that said "Dr. Randolph, FYI. Deborah". I unfolded the letter and began reading.

Stanley W. Robinson
COO Mason-Dixon Regional Medical Center
1238 Middletown Road
Parkton, Maryland 21120

Dear Mr. Robinson:

My wife and I have long been highly satisfied with the excellent services rendered to our family by your staff at Mason-Dixon Regional. However, we recently had an experience at your hospital of which you should be aware that I hope is not repeated with another family.

We brought our six-year-old son, Tyler, to your emergency department on November 14 after a bad fall off the monkey bars at his school. The school called us and said that he had hit his head and had a bad headache. The school nurse advised that we take him to the hospital and have a CAT scan of his head to make certain that he didn't have bleeding into his brain.

The registration clerk and the nurses were very cordial and efficient. We were seen promptly by Dr. Alexander Randolph. Dr. Randolph engaged is some verbal games with our son, but never seemed to take his injury seriously.

Because we had been advised by a medical professional on the scene to have a CAT scan, and because we are all aware of the recent stories in the media where head-injured patients have died after <u>not</u> receiving a CAT scan, we were naturally anxious that Tyler have a thorough examination. We asked for a CAT scan to be done, and Dr. Randolph became obstinate and refused.

Of course, we took Tyler to another hospital where they immediately performed a CAT scan and made a diagnosis of a concussion. He was off school for two days. Fortunately, Tyler is now doing fine, but no thanks to Dr. Randolph.

We hope that this issue with Dr. Randolph will be addressed, and that no family will again have to endure his cavalier attitude. Moreover, we are now faced with two hospital bills in order to ensure quality care for our son where there should only have been one. We would like to be able to continue to utilize the resources of Mason-Dixon Regional, but feel in all fairness that this issue must be first properly addressed.

Sincerely,

Ralph D. Fowler

I sighed. *Well, there goes my smiley face from administration for the month.* Hyde was jumping up and down in the background with a red face, cursing about the world being full of idiots. Jekyll told him to put a lid on it. This is the nature of humanity. You can't make all the people happy all the time. It's an occupational hazard.

Mr. Fowler would probably get his bill waived by the hospital. In point of fact, no one would ever convince Mr. Fowler that his son had received appropriate care, and Deborah would undoubtedly decide that the best course of action was to essentially pay him off and be done with it. It was not surprising that someone else, faced with an already unhappy family, had consented to do a CT of poor Tyler's head But the fact that there was no hospitalization proved the absence of a significant head injury.

My little reverie was interrupted by Stacey throwing Linda Baird's lab work down in front of me. As expected, both her complete blood count and her chemistries were again normal. Her urine was clean too. I looked again at her vital signs. No fever. Her blood pressure was up a little, and her heart rate was slightly fast, but that could all be due to the pain and anxiety. As usual, nothing here to hang your hat on.

I accessed the computer, completed her discharge papers, and wrote yet another prescription for Vicodin. I was concerned about the quantity of narcotic pain medication prescriptions she had received in the last two years. With her psychiatric history and chronic abdominal pain, she was a prime candidate for prescription narcotics addiction.

I walked to her room to have the discharge conversation.

"Linda, I have all your lab work back, and it's all normal again, as usual. Are you feeling better after some more pain meds?"

"It still hurts, but it's definitely better," she said genuinely. "I need to get home. I have ten people coming for dinner." There was something here that just didn't quite add up. Linda just didn't appear to me to be either a drug seeker or a nut case. Somewhere in the back of my brain there was a Google search going on for a thread that could tie this together. I couldn't quite bring the thread to the surface.

"I tell you what, Linda, I want to take a look at something, and I'll be right back."

I walked back to the nursing station, frustrated. My brain was trying to find something, but I didn't know what it was. I sat down at the computer and accessed *eMedicine.* I typed "abdominal pain" into the search engine and began to scroll down through the entries. All the usual diagnoses that had been ruled out, on one of Linda's visits or the other, flashed by—appendicitis, irritable bowel syndrome, pancreatitis, cholecystitis, etc., etc. On page three I hit it. *Porphyria.* That's what I was trying to bring to the front of my poor brain—a rare hereditary disorder caused by an enzyme deficiency in the synthesis of heme. It affects primarily the nervous system, producing sensations of abdominal pain, often vomiting, paresthesias or funny feelings in the skin, psychiatric disturbances, and often high blood pressure and a rapid heart rate.

A very simple test would rule it in or out. I ordered a spot urinary porphobilinogen, and asked Linda's nurse to tell her that I wanted just one more test on her urine before she left.

Thirty minutes later, Stacey laid the test result in front me.

"Well what do you know? Bingo!" I said to no one in particular. It was positive. Linda had acute intermittent porphyria. She wasn't crazy after all. Even her psych symptoms were probably due to the porphyria. I wondered what Ralph Fowler would have to say about this. I needed to tell Linda. The poor girl would probably be immensely relieved to learn that she wasn't nuts. Jekyll gave me a pat on the shoulder. *You're a good boy, Alex*, he said.

~

I dialed my mother as I was pulling out of the parking lot, and let her know that Elizabeth wouldn't be making it today.

"Oh dear! I hope she's not sick!"

"No, Mom. It's probably my fault. I'll tell you about it when I get there."

I grew up in an 1890's white, clapboard farmhouse with a red metal roof on Sparks Road, not far from the Gunpowder Falls. As the family was growing, my father built a matching addition. Behind the house were twenty-five acres upon which he had built his nursery and landscaping business, with lots of financial bootstrapping, and the brawn of him and his two boys. My sister pretty well skated on the brawn part, although she was pretty good in the cab of a skid steer.

My mother grew up in Baltimore County, but chose to go to school at William and Mary in Virginia, where she met my father. He followed her back to Maryland after school and used his horticulture degree to find a job in landscaping. She taught English in the Baltimore County school system. Seven years and a couple of kids later, they bought this place, and he started his own business. My father had pretty clear ideas about the value of a work ethic, so my brother Brian and I got pretty lean and calloused in the summertime working with his crew.

I pulled into the gravel driveway and entered the house through the back mudroom door. Everyone else was already there. The place smelled fabulously. My mouth immediately began to salivate.

I walked into the kitchen, searching for something edible. My father had already started carving the turkey, so I was able to snatch a small slice and stuff it in my mouth.

"Dad! You're on your feet!" I said.

"No choice," he growled. "Around here it's pretty close to a Darwinian environment—survival of the fittest."

"Leave that turkey alone, Alex," admonished my mother, holding out her cheek for a kiss while carrying a casserole dish of something in two gloved-hands into the dining room.

Susan was whipping potatoes, clad in a white apron. I distracted her with a kiss on the cheek and stuck my index finger into the potatoes. The beaters caught the edge of my finger. I gave a yelp and stuck my finger in my mouth. "Serves you right, bad boy," she said smiling.

My sister Anne was watching from the other side of the kitchen, stirring a saucepan. “There better not be any blood in those potatoes,” she warned. “I don’t do well with blood.”

I grabbed a hand towel off the oven door handle and snapped her on the butt. “You’re such a hard-ass. You need to develop a more empathetic personality.”

“Yeah, well just take a look at the beasts I had to grow up with. I was tortured. I’m lucky I’m not in therapy.”

Brian walked over and handed me a glass of red wine. “Here. You look like you could use some pain relief.” I dipped my finger in the glass and sucked on it again.

“So, what’s the story with your girlfriend, brother? She figure out what a beast you are, too?” Anne graciously continued. Everyone’s head turned in my direction. The room got quiet.

This was not a question a concerned sister asked in front of an entire family audience. I raised the glass to my lips and took a gulp.

“She… didn’t like my choice of birthday flowers,” I said.

“Let me guess,” Anne replied. “They were delivered late, they came from the grocery store, and they cost under ten bucks.”

“Actually,” I said, “they were eleven sixty-one with tax.”

~

Everyone held hands around the table while my father offered grace, which was a custom that I assumed was older than me. He was gracious enough to thank the Lord for all his family, not just his wife. And with that, it was finally time to eat.

The outcome of the meal was a foregone conclusion, with obligatory moans and groans around the table after the last fork had found its final resting place.

Everyone started carrying dishes into the kitchen. As they all retired into the living room with coffee, Anne caught me in a corner of the kitchen.

“OK, so tell me,” she said looking up at me, “what really happened with Elizabeth?”

“We can’t get it to click, Anne. Sometimes we have just wonderful evenings, but it’s never totally easy; relaxed; comfortable. And, you know, she's just not usually on my mind. I forget from one day to the next when we're going out, special days—you know the story. Your little guess was closer to the mark than you could have imagined. I screwed up her birthday dinner and we haven't talked in three weeks."

"So who *is* on your mind?" she asked.

I hesitated. "Nobody, really," I lied.

CHAPTER FOURTEEN

SATURDAY, AFTER THANKSGIVING, THE ER WAS packed. This is usually the case after a holiday when doctor's offices are closed. It was a cold, rainy day. It seemed that every elderly person in the community had medically crashed right after making it through the Thanksgiving holiday. Maybe they feel that after the major family gathering of the year is a good time to finally give it up.

Compounding the glut was the fact that we had six admitted patients still sitting in the ER, awaiting transfer to the inpatient floors. This has become an issue in most American hospitals, as procedural steps become more complex in our never-ending quest for safety and accountability.

Rooms have to be cleaned and disinfected for infection control reasons. The responsible ER nurse has to give a detailed and complete verbal report to the accepting nurse on the floor. All the transfer paperwork has to be complete. The stars have to be aligned. Things have to be quiet enough on the receiving inpatient unit that the accepting nurse can take a half-hour out to process the admitted patient. That means that at change of shift, or meal times, it's nearly impossible to get an inpatient floor to accept a new admission from the ER.

And, of course, the admitted patients are the sickest, so they are very resource-intensive and require a huge portion of the ER staff's time. We functionally become an ICU, leaving less time for us to process all the new arrivals. The net result is often something close to gridlock in the ER. Of course, no one but *us* sees this as a safety issue.

I walked into Bed Six. Eighty-eight-year-old William Stonesifer lay motionless with his eyes closed and his mouth open, the head of his bed elevated at a forty-five degree angle. Beside his bed sat a wrinkled, little old woman who looked like she probably weighed all of eighty pounds. Her head was permanently cocked to one side from a deformity of her spine, and bobbed rhythmically with a minor tremor. She clutched a cane. Mr. Stonesifer had been transferred to the ER from a local nursing home.

The transfer sheet from the nursing home said that Mr. Stonesifer had been sent to the ER because of decreased responsiveness, a low-grade fever, and low oxygen saturations.

I shook Mrs. Stonesifer's frail hand, and she smiled. I always look at an elderly couple like this and wonder what they were like when they were twenty and immortal, with the hormones raging and a lifetime of dreams ahead of them.

The records showed that Mr. Stonesifer had been in the nursing home for three years. He was initially admitted with advanced Parkinson's disease and dementia, by which time he was unable to recognize his family members. He had been bedridden and in diapers the whole time.

Within a year of his nursing home stay, he was unable to swallow without choking, and so somebody had put a PEG tube in him—a tube that goes through a small abdominal incision directly into the stomach. It was through this tube that he had been fed and watered for nearly two years. His list of diagnoses was a mile long: hypertension, kidney failure, congestive heart failure, etc., etc.

"Mr. Stonesifer?" I said loudly. No response. His face had the frozen-mask appearance of advanced Parkinson's disease. He was breathing quietly through an open mouth; his mucous membranes dry as bone and his tongue like a piece of dried beef jerky. The monitor over his head said that his oxygen saturation was only eighty-nine percent, despite three liters of oxygen through his nasal cannula.

I listened to his heart. He had a loud murmur—a whooshing sound—that came from a tight aortic valve that had calcified and lost its flexibility. He belly was soft and unremarkable, except for the PEG tube protruding from his upper abdomen. Fran Williams was walking by, and I grabbed her to help me lift him up so I could listen to his lungs. He was as rigid as a corpse, and we struggled to get his body to bend. Actually he was breathing so shallowly that when I listened I couldn't hear much anyhow.

I told Mrs. Stonesifer that I would be right back, and walked to the nursing station to check her husband's lab work and chest x-ray. These had been ordered an hour and a half earlier when he first entered the department by Danielle Jones, Mr. Stonesifer's primary nurse. Most ERs these days give nurses the authority to order preliminary studies in order to save time.

The findings were no surprise. A large, white patch of pneumonia glared from Mr. Stonesifer's right lower lung field on the plasma screen monitor. *Pneumonia is the old person's best friend*, goes one of the oldest medical aphorisms, and the thought occurred to me that it was never more apt than in the case of William Stonesifer.

There hadn't been anybody home in Mr. Stonesifer's brain for more than four years. He had lain in a nursing home—bedridden in diapers, soiling himself, unable to eat or drink, and robbed of all dignity—for at least three years. The response of our society had been to stick an artificial tube through his abdominal wall to feed and water him like a plant.

At some point in time in the last thirty years or so, Americans had decided that death was an unnatural occurrence, and that all we had to do for the Mr. Stonesifers of this world was to uncover the right diagnosis and fix the problem.

Forty or fifty years ago, when he stopped eating and drinking, he would have slipped into kidney failure, fallen asleep, and died—a very peaceful way to go. In Mr. Stonesifer's case, I would guess that society probably spent in the neighborhood of maybe four hundred and fifty or five hundred thousand dollars over the last three or four years, prolonging his dying as opposed to prolonging his life.

I checked the packet of papers forwarded from the nursing home. I could find no *living will*, as people call it—a document that expresses a patient's desires as to how much end-of-life medical intervention they want.

I walked back into Bed Six, pulled up a chair beside Mrs. Stonesifer, and sat down.

"Mrs. Stonesifer," I said leaning forward, "I think we've found the cause of your husband's fever and low oxygen levels. He has pneumonia. It's a pretty big pneumonia. His oxygen levels are pretty low. He's not suffering, as you can see, but I think you should know that in Mr. Stonesifer's condition, this could well be a fatal illness."

I paused to assess her reaction. She was silent, but still composed.

"If we were to work hard to save him, we might have to put a tube into his lungs and place him on a ventilator to breathe for him. Do you understand what that is?"

Mrs. Stonesifer, as best she could, given her deformity, nodded her head silently.

"Did you and your husband ever have a conversation about whether or not he wanted to be put on life-support equipment if he was very sick?

She looked over at Mr. Stonesifer. "Not exactly," she said. Her voice had a tremulous quality that matched the rhythm of her head tremor. "But, you know, he was an engineer—a very precise man." She spoke slowly and carefully, trying to make her words clear despite the difficulty with her speech.

"He couldn't stand it when things weren't working perfectly. And as we got older, he used to say when this old body breaks, just throw it on the junk heap." She hesitated in her reverie and looked up at me. "I don't think he would like being on one of those machines."

"Well," I continued, "we have some decisions to make. And they are really more philosophical decisions than medical decisions. I think by now you realize that Mr. Stonesifer is never going to get better in terms of his function and mental status?" She closed her eyes and nodded again.

"There are a couple of different ways we could approach this. The first is that we could do everything possible to save your husband's life—antibiotics, oxygen, drugs to keep his blood pressure up, and maybe put him on a ventilator in the intensive care unit.

"A second approach would be to give him IVs and antibiotics, but not place him on any life-support equipment.

"The third approach would be to decide that it is really time to finally allow Mr. Stonesifer to die. In that case we would do nothing. We could actually send him back to the nursing home and simply keep him as comfortable as possible. Have you ever heard that old saying that pneumonia is an old person's best friend?"

"Yes," she said, "I have heard that."

"So, Mrs. Stonesifer, we will go in whatever direction that you decide."

"I understand the choices, Dr. Randolph. I don't think I would like him on a ventilator. But I have to talk with our daughter. She lives in Dallas."

My heart sank at this. I have rarely had out-of-town children opt for anything but everything. Perhaps it's the guilt at not being close to their parents in their later years; near the end of life. The one's that live close by—those who have witnessed the suffering and the indignities, and participated in the care—are much more likely to decide on a sensible end to life.

"Would you like us to help you get her on the phone?"

"Please."

"OK. You wait here, and I'll have the nurse bring a portable phone to you and help you make the call."

I asked Danielle to help Mrs. Stonesifer make her call, and grabbed the next patient chart out of the rack. Fifteen minutes later I walked back into Mr. Stonesifer's room and sat down again.

"Were you able to reach your daughter?"

"Yes."

"OK. Good. What did you guys decide?"

"Well, Diane says that she just can't stand the thought of not doing everything possible to help her daddy."

"Does that include the ICU and a ventilator, Mrs. Stonesifer?"

"Yes."

"Is she flying in?"

"Diane has a very important job in Texas. She travels all over the world, you know, seeing clients. It's very hard for her to get away. But she's going to try to come in next weekend."

"OK, Mrs. Stonesifer. We'll do everything we can for your husband."

And so, this is the way that our society manages to spend eighty cents of every health care dollar on the last year of life.

~

By Sunday morning the low pressure area that had brought us rain and wind the day before was up around Halifax, and the sun was shining in the mid-Atlantic. I decided to go to church. I only make it maybe once a month. Between Saturday night shifts and Sunday day shifts, there are usually only one or two Sunday mornings a month that are open.

I carry a little ambivalence about my occasional forays into the sanctuary, perhaps even more so these days when idiots with beards are running around blowing up the world in the name of God.

The big buzz phrase in medicine that is constantly pounded into our heads these days is *evidence-based.* This phrase is supposed to encourage us to rigorously base all of our medical practice on reproducible scientific studies published in the literature, rather than on experience, intuition, or tradition.

Hard evidence is a little hard to come by in spiritual matters, of course, so you might think that by training it's a little more difficult for a doc to believe. But God, like pregnancy, is or isn't, so your only other choice is non-belief. I find non-belief to be just as difficult as belief, and perhaps just as much an act of faith. You have to believe that the staggering complexity of the human body was solely due to chance, and I find that almost inconceivable.

So, despite my ambivalence, I am somehow drawn to the church enough that I feel the need to periodically make that connection and pay a visit to St. John's. Maybe I'm still looking for answers.

I climbed the steps to the ornate mahogany doors of the sanctuary and slipped into a rear pew. St. John's is in the heart of My Lady's Manor. A rear pew is a good place from which to observe the culture of the Manor, as well as the ideal spot for a quick exit. It was a chilly, early winter day, so everyone came in wrapped up. Harvey Mays and his wife, Claire, walked in past my pew without noticing me, and took their place about a third of the way back the sanctuary on the right side.

Harvey is Chief of Medicine at Mason-Dixon. He's an endocrinologist by training, who actually held an endowed chair at the University of Maryland before being recruited to Mason-Dixon. I was never sure why he vacated his chair for our little country hospital, but I was glad he was there.

Tall, with a thick head of graying hair and big, bushy eyebrows, Harvey came from one of the oldest families on the Manor. He still has the ancestral home—a two hundred and fifty acre farm anchored by a stone manor house with towering chimneys. Despite having been born into more money that he could ever spend, Harvey is every inch a gentleman, as well as one of the smartest guys I've ever met. He's an old-school, Renaissance man who I always thought would have been an intellectual peer of Sir William Osler, had he been born a hundred years or so earlier.

Claire Mays was the perfect mate for Harvey—a quiet and gracious woman who was still rather stunning in her early sixties.

The sanctuary gradually filled, populated with Burberry tweeds and cashmere, and a scattering of jeans on younger folks. People greeted each other vivaciously, and had the little kids shake hands with the adults.

Out of the corner of my eye I glimpsed a tall and elegant young woman walk by. She had flowing auburn hair, and was wearing a form-fitting long black coat with a brilliant, red wool scarf around her neck. Her narrow hips were unconcealed by the coat, and they swayed gracefully to the rhythm of her long stride. There was something vaguely familiar about her, but I couldn't place her, until she turned to enter a pew eight or nine rows ahead of me. I caught the profile of Sally Horn's face and her familiar hoop earrings.

Wow. I had never seen Sally dressed, or dressed up, I should say. I doubted that she smelled like a horse this morning. Now I understood why those hips looked so familiar—I had been reverently watching them sway across my barnyard for eight or nine months.

A blast from the pipe organ broke my reverie, and I stood and fumbled for the page of the first hymn. *I wonder if Sally likes chili and a cold Corona?*

~

Sally didn't disappoint me. She showed up at four o'clock that afternoon, as usual, in those lovely jeans to feed the thoroughbreds. I took a bit of a risk and whipped up a Crockpot of chili, starting with something out of a can and doctoring it up a bit. If she said no, I'd still have something for supper. I had a pan of ready-to-bake cornbread in the freezer, and pulled it out.

After observing *Sally Two* at church, I didn't want to give *Sally One* an excuse to refuse my invitation for chili because she couldn't possibly enter my house without going home and cleaning up. So I rummaged around in the laundry room and pulled out the dirtiest jeans I could find. I put on a denim shirt and my ragged down vest, pulled on my mucked-up Wellington boots, and headed outside.

The timing of this had to be just right so that it looked like a spur-of-the-moment invitation for chili and a beer, not a date. That was a bit too risky, given our financial relationship. I didn't want to screw things up if she and I didn't click. I figured she'd be here for at least an hour—possibly two. About forty-five minutes after her arrival, I walked out to the barn, waved to Sally, and fired up the New Holland. Sally typically forks all the manure into a pile just outside the loafing area.

Every couple of weeks I push it outside into a bigger pile with the front-end loader. So, today was the day.

Sally was finishing brushing down the horses when I put the tractor away and walked over to the stall, folding my arms across the top of the stall door. Brushing down two horses generates a lot of body heat, so she had stripped down to her plaid flannel work shirt.

My timing was impeccable. She was bent over, with the gelding's left hind leg gripped between her lean thighs, cleaning out his hoof with a pick. Her frayed jeans fit her magnificent little butt like a glove. I didn't think she had heard me walk up, so I watched appreciatively for a few moments before I spoke.

"Pedicure time, huh?" I said. Startled, Sally let out a yell and jumped, dropping the leg, whose hoof landed squarely on her left foot. This was followed by a second expletive, and then she began hopping around on one foot exclaiming, "Oh shit, shit, shit." So far, so good.

~

When we arrived in the ER, both smelling like horses, I commandeered an empty bed and expedited an x-ray of Sally's bruised and swollen foot. Nobody said much, but I saw plenty of raised eyebrows as the staff transparently speculated on who was this woman, what was the relationship, and why did we smell like that? I ignored them.

The x-ray, thankfully, showed only a fractured third toe, which I buddy-taped to the second toe. But her whole forefoot was black and blue, and about twice normal size.

~

When we returned from the hospital, I put Sally's arm around my shoulder and my arm around her waist. She hopped in through the kitchen door on her good foot. So far, this was the highlight of the evening. I led her to the leather armchair facing the fireplace, and pulled the ottoman into place. She winced as she lowered herself into the chair. Gently, I lifted her leg onto the ottoman. The place smelled of burned chili. I rushed to turn off the Crockpot.

"Jeez, I am really sorry, Sally," I said.

"It's not your fault, Alex. I shouldn't be such a scaredy-cat," she replied graciously. "And you've taken such good care of me. I've just got to figure out how to get these horses taken care of for a few days until I can hobble around on this foot again."

"Look, Sally, I can do it," I said, perching on the arm of the big leather chair "The timing may be off a little, compared to what they're used to, but they'll get fed twice every day, and I can keep the stalls clean. It's the least I can do."

"Oh, that's very sweet of you Alex," she smiled, touching my arm. "But you are such a busy person. Are you sure you want to do that?"

"Please, Sally. It'll make me feel a lot better."

"OK, Alex," she said skeptically, "if you insist. But if you have any problems, you call me, OK?"

"Sure."

"A half bale of hay each, and one and a half scoops of grain each twice a day."

"Got it."

"And you don't have to brush 'em down. They can just go dirty for a while."

"Right."

"Could you do me another favor?" she asked. "Could you hand me my cell phone in my jacket pocket over there, so I can call my father to come and get me?"

Mr. Horn showed up fifteen minutes later to claim his daughter. His wife drove him over so he could drive Sally's pickup truck home to her apartment. She hopped back out through the kitchen door again with her arm around daddy's shoulder. I held her truck door open while Mr. Horn helped her into the truck, then waved goodnight in the glare of the headlights as the two vehicles drove off. Not exactly the way I had planned for this evening to end.

CHAPTER FIFTEEN

I HATE TO START THE DAY WITHOUT A SHOWER. I can't seem to get going. Good thing I wasn't born in the 1800's. Nevertheless, it didn't make sense for me to take a shower, go out and feed the horses, and then take another shower. So Monday morning I set the alarm fifteen minutes early, climbed out of bed into the clothes I had especially worn for Sally, and walked out in the pre-dawn darkness to the barn.

Soft neighs broke the stillness as I approached, until finally the dark outlines of the horses appeared like apparitions. I ran one hand down the neck of the gelding, and with the other caressed the mare's nose. Soft lips nuzzled my hand, searching for carrots. The scents seemed to be more intense in the dark—fresh hay, the sweetness of grain—all mixed with horse flesh.

I threw a half bale of hay into each end of the hay rack, and threw a total of three large scoops of grain into the long wooden feed trough—half at each end to keep the fighting over food to a minimum. I wouldn't have to water them because the loafing area was open to the pasture, and they could drink from the stream.

There's something about keeping company with large animals that soothes the soul and makes you feel a little more grounded. Perhaps it's that there is no pretense in the relationship. In any case, I walked back to the house thinking that this wasn't such a bad way to start the day.

On the horizon to the east, the inky blackness of night perceptibly lightened, transitioning to gray.

I realized as I jumped in the shower, however, that I hadn't really allowed enough time for my morning chores. Ten minutes late, I burst through the secure ER door, and hurried to my computer station.

"Late night last night?" asked Lauren, who I was relieving.

"Early morning," I replied.

"Well, good for you!" she said.

Lauren thinks she's got men pegged. She probably does. She lives with three of them. Lauren is married to Richard Dorfman, a urologist at Sinai. They've got two boys in college. She only works half time, but she's got the commitment of a full-timer. Whenever there's a staffing crunch, I can always count on Lauren to jump in. Lauren says she's the token Jew on the ER staff, and also claims to be the only Republican in her synagogue.

~

I could hear a sobbing child in triage. A few minutes later Fran Williams slid a chart into the new patient rack. Fran is a mid-fifties grandmother of three who is never without a pair of reading glasses slung around her neck. She usually works triage and functions as day-shift charge nurse because she's got experience up the wazoo, and she's no-nonsense.

"You should see this darling little boy in Fourteen!" she squealed. "He's so adorable! Poor little thing has a dog bite on his face—left cheek. He and the dog were going for the dog food at the same time. He's gonna need stitches. Dog's shots are up-to-date."

I walked into Fourteen. Penny Murray was already in the room, setting up a suture tray. Mom was standing by the bed, tears in her eyes, holding two-year-old Cameron in her arms, trying her best, without success, to console him. Sweat plastered his thick brown curls to his flushed face. Between endless wails, his lower lip quivered as he sucked in little gasps of air. Terrified, his head swiveled from side to side as he searched for threats from the strangers in the room in blue uniforms. Blood smeared the left side of his face.

I introduced myself to mom, and, without touching him, tried to get a look at Cameron's wound. At each approach, he whipped his head away from me.

"It's OK baby. It's OK. He's not going to hurt you," mom pleaded. "He just needs to see your boo-boo." She finally got Cameron to lay his head on her shoulder with the wound up for about two seconds. That was enough.

It looked like a single canine tooth had grazed his cheek, creating a triangular flap laceration about an inch long. Mom said the dog had snapped at him, but hadn't latched on. I would have to lift up the flap, carefully irrigate the wound with saline to reduce the chances of infection, and then close the wound with a fine suture material to minimize scarring. I didn't have a prayer in the world of getting that done properly with Cameron awake. We would have to sedate him to get the job done, and now the task was to have a discussion with mom.

You should try having a conversation, sometime, with a mother holding a screaming, injured toddler in her arms. Makes you feel irrelevant. I started in.

"Mom, this really isn't too bad a wound. We're going to be able to close that and have a pretty nice little scar." Mom cooed to Cameron and said, "It's alright, baby. It's alright."

"But as you can imagine, doing a nice job of sewing up that cut on his face, with him crying and moving all over the place, is almost impossible. I think we probably should talk about putting him to sleep for this." Mom nodded briefly in my direction, and then returned her attention to Cameron, adjusting him and rocking back and forth. The wailing was deafening.

"We use a drug called ketamine that will put Cameron in a kind of twilight sleep," I said loudly. "Makes him very spacey. He might not even close his eyes, but he'll be very quiet." Cameron caught a quick breath and let out another major wail.

"Ketamine is a very safe drug," I continued. "They use it in Africa when there's only a surgeon, but no anesthesiologist, because it's so safe." Mom brushed Cameron's curls out of his eyes and kissed his bloodless right cheek.

"But like all anesthesia, there are some risks. The biggest one is that he might vomit while he's asleep and breathe in his vomitus, but that doesn't happen very often, and we'll be prepared if it does."

"Shhh, shhh, shhh, shhh," said mom.

"So, what do you think, Mom? Do you have any questions?"

"Cameron, Cameron, it's all right, baby."

"Mom?"

Mom looked over at me with a blank look on her face for a moment, and then said, "I'm sorry. Just do what you have to do." And so, that was the completion of the informed consent process, except for the signing of the paperwork.

Rebecca came in to help with setting up for what we euphemistically call *conscious sedation.* It should be called *unconscious sedation*, because, in fact, we put them all out cold. This little euphemism is an outgrowth of the turf war between anesthesiologists and other physicians who need to have people asleep briefly for procedures.

Putting people to sleep, of course, is the business of anesthesiologists, so they usually put up fierce resistance when other departments want to use anesthesia drugs. Early on, we used to use drugs that sedated you, but didn't put you to sleep—hence the phrase *conscious sedation.* Over the years, we gradually moved to drugs in the ER that, like ketamine, induce an unconscious state, and the anesthesiologists functionally lost the battle. But we still call it *conscious sedation* in an effort to stay off the anesthesiologists' radar screens.

We're very careful with this stuff, because you don't want a kid with a little cut to die from putting him to sleep. So we hook them up to lots of monitoring equipment and have lots of staff standing by when we do this. Then, every case is retrospectively reviewed by our quality assurance committee. Jill Brown was here from respiratory therapy, and she would take care of Cameron's airway. Penny and Rebecca would take care of everything else.

We usually let the parents stay in the room if they want to, but mom was not up to witnessing the torture and the blood. She elected to vacate to the waiting room while we got Cameron's cut fixed.

Penny took Cameron from mom's arms, and the screaming intensified. Mom ran from the room, sobbing.

"OK, what's he weigh?" I asked.

"Ten kilos," replied Penny.

I quickly calculated the dosages of ketamine and atropine, which Rebecca drew up in a syringe.

"Everybody ready?" Nods all around "OK, let's go."

While Penny continued to cradle Cameron in her arms, Rebecca pinched Cameron's thigh, plunged in the syringe, and the shot was over before Cameron knew what was happening. I put on sterile gloves and stood with my hands folded, waiting for the ketamine to take effect, which wouldn't be long. It's incredibly fast acting. Two to three minutes after an intramuscular injection, Cameron would be out cold.

The girls lay Cameron down on the procedure table. Rebecca began attaching the monitoring equipment. From the head of the bed Penny leaned close over the child's face, one hand caressing his good cheek, the other stroking his forehead. Wisps of blond hair fell over her face. Cameron continued to sob. Suddenly, above the sobbing, I could hear soft singing. It was Penny. She was singing to the kid. "Hush little baby, don't say a word..."

Slowly the sobs subsided, and still I could hear the soft, pure notes. I stood and stared. I had never heard a nurse sing to a child before. For some reason the tenderness and intimacy of the act just overwhelmed me. I was stunned.

I don't know how long I stood there, but it must have been a while. Rebecca's voice broke through and I heard her say softly, "I think he's ready now, Dr. Randolph." I felt my face flush, and I quickly turned my back to the girls and busied myself arranging instruments on the tray.

~

We slid past eleven o'clock, and the ER was getting packed. Nobody could even find a moment to go pee. Lisa, with not a lot of room left in her growing belly, had apparently held it as long as she could, because she suddenly jumped up from her computer terminal and announced, "That's it. I'm going to go pee now, if anybody cares."

I heard the phone ring and Stacey yelled across the nursing station, "Dr. Randolph, Sergeant Schmidt on five-one-three-one for you."

I picked up the phone. "Jack?"

"Hey, Doc. How ya doin'?"

"Good, Jack."

"I wanted to call you first thing. I just got the blood tests back from the crime lab. We found two different blood types on that wall above the dam, and, whaddya know, the same two blood types in the car. One matches the victim we found in the Gunpowder Falls. The other matches Julio." He paused. "We've just issued a warrant for his arrest for murder."

"Wow. In whose name?"

"Julio Carlos Ramirez. We found a match on the fingerprints in the car with an old assault charge against Ramirez. He's Salvadoran, all right. Entered the U.S. on a student visa in 2003, and then Immigration lost track of him. He skipped bond on the assault charge and disappeared. Almost certainly he's MS-13, and he may be quite high up in the leadership.

"You guys need to be careful if he shows up again," Jack continued. "He's obviously very dangerous. If he checks in, just quietly process him as normal, and call us. He's likely to be armed. We probably wouldn't try to arrest him until he walked out the door. Keep him there as long as you can, but don't endanger the staff by acting too far out of the ordinary."

"I understand."

"I've finally persuaded Captain Louis that, at least temporarily, we need to have two cars in the northern end of the county. Hopefully that will improve our response time if something happens. It won't last forever, but at least for a while we should be able to do a little better."

"Are you going to let Mike Szymanski know?"

"Yeah, I'm going to call him next."

"Jack, I know you're trying very hard to take care of us. I really appreciate it."

"You're welcome, Doc. If we can nail Ramirez, we'll all sleep a lot better."

I punched the end button, and then dialed Julie's office extension.

"This is Julie."

"Julie, this is Alex. We need to talk."

CHAPTER SIXTEEN

AFTER SEVERAL DAYS I BEGAN TO LOOK forward to my twice-daily encounters with the thoroughbreds. I actually brushed down the two of them one evening. Following Sally's example, I started carrying carrots in my pockets, and they were soon trying to push their soft noses into the too-small space, searching for their little treat. This is hard on your pockets, and within several days the stitching on my old barn coat was tearing.

I also got better at the timing of the morning chores, denying my staff the coveted opportunity to dig at their boss about being late for work.

Sally called several times over the next couple of days to find out how things were going. I tried to figure out exactly what that meant. I wasn't sure if it was concern for her babies, because she missed her contact with them, or because she wanted to chat with me. I preferred the latter interpretation, but, hey, it doesn't hurt to fantasize once in a while. In truth, so far my attempts to explore a mutually satisfactory adult relationship with Sally had been disastrous.

My thoughts turned to Elizabeth. We had still not made contact. I wondered how she was feeling about all of this. I really didn't know whether she felt relief or regret. For my part, I was surprised that so far I hadn't felt a huge sense of loss, and I still felt no compulsion to call her. I probably missed the sex more than anything, but I have been told that testosterone and estrogen alone are not the best basis for a relationship. They're a good start, however.

Ruth had noticed the absence of Elizabeth in my weekly plans, and her questions had nibbled around the edges of whether things were off or not. But so far, I hadn't given her the satisfaction of a formal declaration that it was over.

Today I worked the 5:00 PM to 1:00 AM shift. Jack Schmidt's call had serious implications for the safety of the staff, so I showered and headed in an hour before my shift to talk with Julie and Mike Szymanski.

The three of us gathered in the hospital café for our impromptu meeting. I ordered a burger and a chocolate shake. The burgers aren't so great, but the café has the best milkshakes around.

I filled Julie in on the gist of Jack's call, and she shook her head.

"This is *very* scary," she said emphatically. "This is real stuff! I can't believe this is happening!"

"Odds are, Julie, that we'll never see Julio again," said Mike. "Don't panic. We're going to take every precaution. Julio's got no quarrel with us."

"Yes, but what if they try to arrest him and he runs back inside the ER and we have a big shootout?" she said, pounding her ballpoint pen on the table.

"Julie, my darling," I said between hamburger bites, "some things are within our control and some things aren't. Our job is to do the best we can to protect the staff, and the rest is out of our hands. We need to figure out how to give them some clear guidelines as to what to do if he ever shows up again. Somehow we have to do that without producing mass panic among the staff, and without inducing such fear that they all freeze up and create a lot of suspicion in Julio's mind. We need to give the cops time to get here."

Julie sighed. "Actually, I'm thinking that we might be better off not even mentioning it to the staff. If we talk to them about it, they'll telegraph to Julio, for sure, that something's wrong. The staff might be safer without having to put on an act."

"And then, if something did happen and we hadn't prepped the staff, the lawyers would have a field day," chimed in Mike.

"Screw the lawyers," said Julie. "If something happens, they're going to have a field day no matter what we do, God forbid."

There was a long pause in the conversation as everyone tried to think through this little conundrum. I took this as an opportunity for a couple more bites of shoe leather.

"We could just give them general guidelines about remaining calm and reporting suspicious activity immediately to security," offered Mike. "Or, punching the police call button in triage immediately if there's anything that looks truly dangerous. The doors into the ER are all secure and require a badge to enter."

"Yeah, but we saw the first time that those secure doors don't mean shit," replied Julie. "They didn't keep Julio's goons from barging through with him. But I think you may be right about giving them guidelines without specifically mentioning Julio. They don't need to know the gruesome details about his last victim."

"The only problem with that," I said, loudly sucking my milkshake dry, "is that we need somebody to punch that button *immediately* if they lay eyes on Julio. How about if we just say that the cops are interested in Julio, and if they see him they should punch the button, but just continue to process him normally? We don't have to tell them that he's wanted for murder and will cut your balls off if he doesn't like you."

"You're right," sighed Julie resignedly. "We have a staff meeting early next week and that's what I'll tell them."

"I wish I had my nine millimeter," said Mike wistfully.

"We could shoot him with ketamine darts," I said. "That's what they use on large animals wandering around the city."

"I wonder if we should tell them about the Crips, too, just in case they start showing up?" Mike mused.

"Let's keep it simple for now," replied Julie. "We haven't seen any of those guys yet, and I'm going to have enough trouble with staff paranoia as it is. When will the construction be finished on the security station?"

"Larry Kline says he'll have it wrapped up in two or three more days," replied Mike.

~

I walked back to the ER with Julie to begin my shift.

"You know, I've worked with Joyce a couple of times in the last ten days," I said. "She's been doing OK."

"You're not the first person to tell me that," said Julie. "She hasn't missed any more shifts either. Maybe the boyfriend has been the whole problem."

"Let's hope so."

~

The evening rush was beginning to taper off when I heard Medic 60 dispatched for a head injury. Fifteen minutes later I was seeing a young woman with a urinary tract infection, when Fran Williams, tonight's charge nurse, stuck her head through the door and said, "Excuse me, Dr. Randolph, but I think we need you in Fifteen." That was my cue to make haste for the trauma room.

I walked into Fifteen just as Patty Friedman and her crew from Medic 60 shoved their stretcher through the big doors.

"Dr. Randolph," Patty said breathlessly, "this woman was conscious and alert until about two minutes ago—as we were pulling up—and now she looks like she's going down the tubes. She's completely unresponsive, and her airway is *not* great. She was in an altercation with her boyfriend, and he apparently shoved her. She fell and hit her head on one of those old iron heating radiators. Her daughter called 911."

The crew hurriedly unstrapped the victim from the stretcher. Fran, Rebecca and I grabbed one side of the trauma board and, on the count of three, six of us slid her onto the trauma table.

"Oh, NOOO!" I heard Fran moan. "It's Joyce!"

Joyce Harbaugh lay strapped to the immobilization board—unconscious—with a protective cervical collar around her neck, and her head wrapped in bloody bandages like a gruesome turban. A combination of snoring and gurgling sounds emanated from her throat.

"Get me an airway! And let's have suction over here," I barked.

Someone handed me a plastic curved airway. I tried to insert it, but the jaw was clenched tight. Joyce's tongue was obstructing her airway, and her color was turning dusky blue.

I needed to relax those jaw muscles so I could open her airway. The best way to do that was with succinylcholine or *sux* as we call it, a fast acting curare-like drug that would paralyze every muscle in Joyce's body, relaxing her jaws.

"Get me some sux! And some lidocaine. Has she got a line?"

"Yes," answered Patty, "an eighteen in her right antecube."

"OK. Let's try to bag her until I can get her intubated." With little success, I held the mask tight to her face while Fran squeezed the bag, but her chest really wasn't rising. Data started popping up on the screen, and her oxygen saturations were already down in the low-eighties. Poor Joyce's brain was now suffering injury from hypoxia—low oxygen levels—on top of the traumatic injury.

Without warning, greenish-brown fluid erupted into the clear plastic face mask like a geyser, as Joyce violently emptied the contents of her stomach.

"Get her on her side!" I yelled. Three people tilted the immobilization board onto its side so that gravity would drain the vomitus from Joyce's airway.

"Suction!" Someone handed me the large, rigid suction catheter attached to a vacuum, but I couldn't get it through the clenched teeth. Joyce was now dark blue.

Rebecca crashed through the door with a vial of succinylcholine in her hand, and began to draw it up in a syringe. "How much sux?" she asked.

"A hundred. But seventy-five of lidocaine first. Actually, forget the lidocaine. We don't have time." Rebecca inserted the syringe of sux into the IV line and pushed on the plunger. "OK. One hundred of sux in," she announced.

"O2 sat is only sixty-four," called out Fran.

It seemed an eternity, but just thirty seconds later, Joyce's jaw gradually relaxed as the paralytic took effect. I quickly inserted the plastic airway, and then, as best I could, suctioned the vomitus from Joyce's airway. "OK. Try to bag her."

I moved to the head of the bed, with laryngoscope and tube in hand, and waited as the team attempted to manually ventilate Joyce with the bag-valve-mask. Slowly, her oxygen saturation began to rise into the seventies, and then the low eighties. But there it stopped. We couldn't get her any higher than eighty-four.

"OK. That's as high as she's going to go. Let me in."

The crew moved aside. I stepped in at the head of the bed and inserted the scope. There was still a large pool of vomitus in her pharynx. I couldn't see the cords, but I tried to slip the tube in blindly, right under the epiglottis, and when we squeezed the bag, condensation vapor wafted into the tube.

"I think we're in," I said with relief. I connected the end-tidal CO_2 monitor cable to the tube and looked up at the screen—a nice waveform with a CO_2 of sixty; confirmation that we were in the trachea. The oxygen saturation icon read "ninety-two." There was no doubt that Joyce had aspirated some of her own vomitus into her lungs. That would likely lead to a pneumonia. But that would have to be dealt with later. For now, at least, her airway was secure and her oxygen levels were coming up.

"OK, get her out of here to CT." The team frantically gathered up the cables, connected Joyce to a portable monitor, and were gone in two minutes.

Patty and her ambulance crew were still in the room, gathering up their equipment and cleaning the stretcher.

"Patty, did she have an initial period of unconsciousness when she first hit the radiator?" I asked.

"I don't know for sure," Dr. Randolph, "but I think so. She was awake when we got there. The boyfriend was gone, but the little daughter was there, bless her heart, and she told me that her mom was asleep for a little while. You know, she's got finger-mark bruises around her neck underneath that collar?"

"That prick needs to be put away for a long time."

I was almost certain what the CT was going to show as the result of the loving attention of Joyce's boyfriend. Joyce had been knocked out, regained consciousness, and then suddenly lost consciousness again just as she arrived at the hospital. This was the classic presentation of an epidural hematoma—a bleed into the layer of tissue that lines the inside of the skull—typically caused by a skull fracture.

The patient has an initial concussion, wakes up, and then, as the blood rapidly collects and compresses the brain, loses consciousness again. The collection of blood grows rapidly because it's usually escaping from torn arteries that are pumping under pressure. In Joyce's case, it had happened with frightening speed. If she were to survive, she would need emergency neurosurgery to stop the bleeding, evacuate the pool of blood, and relieve the pressure. We didn't do that here at little Mason-Dixon Regional.

I walked back to the nursing station. "Stacey, get me Shock Trauma on the line, and I need a helicopter."

Ten minutes later, Joyce was back in the room—Fran and Rebecca stripping off her clothes, and inserting a urinary catheter into her bladder.

I lifted both eyelids and checked Joyce's pupils. The left one was now dilated—an ominous sign. The pressure was rising so high in her brain that the third cranial nerve to her pupil was being compressed and becoming dysfunctional.

"OK, let's get an amp of mannitol into her." Mannitol is an osmotic diuretic that would hopefully reduce the swelling in Joyce's brain, and perhaps somewhat reduce the pressure. At best, it would do nothing more than buy us a little time.

I continued my exam, pulled open the Velcro cervical collar, and glanced at her neck. Several linear, horizontal bruises were present on both sides. It takes a lot of force to make marks like that. I wondered how long Joyce had struggled for air, with his fingers wrapped around her neck, before she was thrown to the floor.

The ward clerk stuck her head around the door. "Dr. Ching on five-three-one-five." That would be Nathan Ching, tonight's radiologist. I picked up a phone and punched the blinking button.

"Nathan, this is Alex."

"Joyce Harbaugh. She's got a big two by three centimeter epidural, Alex. Depressed left occipito-parietal skull fracture. There's a one centimeter midline shift, and I'm worried that she's brewing a subfalcine herniation. Her cervical spine looks fine."

"OK, Nathan. Thanks for the quick report. She's got a blown left pupil, now. You know, this is one of our ER nurses?"

"You're kidding."

"I only wish I was, Nathan."

"Best of luck to her."

Joyce Harbaugh's entire life had been a struggle. And she had been winning against a lot of odds—until tonight.

~

Rebecca and I walked out through the ambulance bay doors behind the flight crew on their way to the helipad.

We stood silently as we watched the crew load Joyce into the blue and white ship. The doors closed and the rotor blades started to turn as the whine of the turbines accelerated. Rebecca's hair whipped in the wind from the rotor wash, and the tears streamed horizontally from her eyes.

LifeNet 6-1 lifted off, slowly rotated into the wind, and gathered speed. The aircraft turned south, and we watched until the blinking red aviation lights disappeared in the night sky.

"Goodbye, Joyce," Rebecca said softly.

~

I was suddenly struck with an overwhelming urge for a cigarette. This occasionally happens after stressful major cases or procedures. Mr. Hyde is fond of tobacco smoke, and sometimes becomes quite insistent. One of Patty's crewmembers was standing beside his ambulance, smoking. I walked over and bummed one, lit it, and inhaled.

A little after midnight I got a call from John Shiley, the neurosurgeon on-duty at Shock Trauma at the University of Maryland.

"Well, we evacuated the hematoma. But her intracranial pressures are still pretty high—she's got a lot of edema. I don't know how she's going to do. We'll just have to wait and see."

So much for protective orders.

CHAPTER SEVENTEEN

THE MORNING WAS FILLED WITH KIDS WITH snotty noses and fevers. The nice thing about daycare is that it's a very efficient way of infecting all the toddlers with the same virus at the same time, so we can just get it all over with in a couple of weeks. It was early December and that time of year.

About nine o'clock, I picked up the next chart for yet another kid with a fever and runny nose.

"If I see one more kid with a fever and snot bubbling out of his nose, you may have to tie me down, call Crisis, and put me in the nut house," I said to Ben.

"Are we gonna have to forcibly commit you, or are you going to go peaceably and voluntarily?" he asked.

"I'll sign any papers they put in front of me," I said. "How long do you think they'll keep me?"

"I'd say it'll take 'em about six hours to figure out that you're way too sick for our psych ward, and then they'll send you back down to the ER."

Five-year-old Ryan Butler, I noted in the chart as I walked down the hall, had a temperature of one-oh-two point eight.

Ryan's mother was a pretty young woman, dressed in a matching jogging outfit with a gold choker around her neck, carefully painted nails, and bright lipstick. She was cradling Ryan, who appeared to be asleep, in her arms as she sat. She smiled and gripped my hand firmly when I introduced myself.

"Hi, Dr. Randolph. I'm Kelly," she said brightly. Despite her assertive social skills, I could see concern in her eyes.

"When did Ryan get sick, Kelly?" I asked, sitting on the exam table.

"He was fine when he went to bed last night, but about 2:00 AM I heard him crying, and when I went into his room he was burning up with fever. So I gave him some Tylenol and called our family doctor. She told me to alternate Tylenol and Motrin. I have an appointment for 11:00 AM, but he just looks so *sick.* I didn't think I should wait."

"What was the highest temp you saw last night?"

"One-oh-three point six."

"How does he look sick to you?"

"Well, he's just so lethargic. I can't keep him awake."

"Has he had any other symptoms? Cough; runny nose; vomiting; diarrhea?"

"Maybe a little runny nose late yesterday. Nothing else."

"He has a good health history? No serious illness or injuries?"

"Nothing. He's been great."

"And all his baby shots are up-to-date?"

"Yup."

"OK, let's take a look. Can you put him up here on the exam table for me?"

Kelly stood with some effort under the burden of Ryan's weight and laid him on the exam table. One arm flopped to the side as she moved him. He didn't stir. I didn't like that.

"Kelly, can you wake him for me please?" I asked. "Better that he sees his mom rather than the doctor when he first wakes up."

Kelly brushed Ryan's hair back from his forehead and in a soft song-song voice said, "Ryan, wake up honey. The doctor's here to see you. Ryan, wake up, baby. Come on, Ryan, wake up. Ryan?" Nothing. No response. Kelly looked up at me.

Kids are often dead to the world when they fall asleep, but this was the middle of the day—mid morning—and not nap time for a five-old-

old. I began to wonder if Ryan could have been rapidly slipping into a coma over the last couple of hours. If so, that was very bad news.

I quickly raised both of Ryan's eyelids. His pupils were both equal in size, and they both constricted when exposed to room light. That was good, at least. I grasped the back of Ryan's head with both hands and gently tried to flex his neck forward. Ryan's face briefly grimaced, but he didn't wake up. His neck was stiff as a board. His torso actually started to lift off the table. This was not good.

Ryan had nuchal rigidity, an almost certain sign of bacterial meningitis—a deadly infection of the tissues and cerebrospinal fluid that cover the brain and spinal cord. And from all evidence, it was galloping along at such a frightening speed that this could well be a fatal illness. In less than twelve hours from onset of his fever, Ryan was essentially already comatose. When it goes this fast, the prognosis is terrible—over half of these kids die, even with the best of treatment.

"You said Ryan had all his baby shots?"

"Yes, every one of them."

"Kelly, excuse me for just a moment, please. I'll be right back," I said.

I quickly walked back to the nursing station and found Pat Cole and Jen Wilke at the station.

"Ladies, I need this kid out of Bed Three and into a monitored bed *now*. I need an IV, and get set up for a lumbar puncture. I'm gonna tap him. Get all the blood work when you start the IV, including two blood cultures, and let's get one more nurse in here. This kid's gonna die."

I quickly consulted the computer for Ryan's weight—seventeen kilos—and did the calculations. "Jen get me seven milligrams of dexamethasone and one point two five grams of Rocephin. Give the dexamethasone first." The girls started scrambling.

I had to finish my exam on Ryan, but things were going to start happening very fast, and I had to let Ryan's poor mother know what the hell was going on. Pat Cole and I got back to Ryan's room at about the same time.

"Kelly, Pat's going to take Ryan to another room where we can hook him up to some monitoring equipment," I said. And with that, Pat had scooped Ryan up in her arms and was gone. Kelly turned white, and a look of barely controlled terror came over her face. I pulled out a chair for her, then sat myself on the foot step of the exam table.

"Kelly," I began, "Ryan has a high fever, and we're having trouble waking him. More importantly, when I tried to flex his neck it was very rigid. We call that *nuchal rigidity*—it's very often a sign of meningitis. Are you familiar with the term *meningitis*?" Kelly closed her eyes, bit her lower lip and nodded.

"I can't prove it yet, but I'm very concerned. We're going to immediately do a lumbar puncture—people call that a spinal tap—but even before we do that, we're going to start him on some powerful antibiotics through his veins."

Kelly closed her eyes again, took a deep breath, and then said, "This is very serious, isn't it?"

"Yes," I said simply. A single tear trickled silently down her cheek.

"I need to call my husband," she said, as she struggled to maintain her composure and began to rummage through her purse for her cell phone.

"If you can't find it and need to use this phone," I said pointing toward the wall-mounted telephone in her room, "just dial nine to get an outside line. Doesn't matter if it's long distance. I'm going to go be with Ryan now. We're going to need you to sign some papers giving us permission to do a spinal tap—we really don't have any choice in this. Do you have any questions?" She shook her head "no."

"You will be welcome to come in the room and be with Ryan as soon as you're done with your calls. Pat will come and get you." Kelly nodded, and I left the room.

Ryan lay prostrate and comatose under the glare of the lights in Bed Sixteen, our resuscitation room. Pat was starting an IV in Ryan's right arm. Jen was hanging the Rocephin and connecting the tubing to a pump. April, never one to miss out on the action, was in the room and was connecting Ryan to all the monitoring equipment.

"Everyone in this room needs a mask," I said. Let's limit the staff that come in here to you three." If this was what I thought it was, we needed to minimize the number of nurses who were directly exposed.

"Has he stirred for you guys?"

"No," said Pat. "When I stuck him for the IV he didn't flinch."

While the girls worked, I quickly completed the rest of my physical examination. I pulled off Ryan's little brown cords, and a matchbox car fell out of his pants pocket. I took a quick look at his legs and found another ominous sign: several round little hemorrhages beneath the skin on his lower legs. These are often found when meningitis is caused by a very nasty bacteria called *neisseria meningitidis.* That was going to be my bet. I would be shocked if the lumbar puncture wasn't positive for these little round agents of death.

"OK. I've got a line," said Pat.

"Let's get that dexamethasone and Rocephin going," I said. "April, let's get him rolled up in a ball for this tap."

I pulled a mask over my nose, donned sterile gloves, and began organizing the stuff on my lumbar puncture tray. I would first anesthetize Ryan's skin between about the third and fourth lumbar vertebrae in his back, and then would insert a long needle between the vertebrae until I entered the space surrounding his spinal cord that contained cerebrospinal fluid, or *CSF,* as we call it. I would then drain two to three milliliters successively into four numbered sterile test tubes which would be rushed to the lab for analysis. That analysis would tell the story. We'd know with certainty whether or not Ryan Butler had acute bacterial meningitis.

April rolled Ryan onto his side, grasped his shoulders and legs, and pulled him into the fetal position, opening up the spaces between his vertebrae.

I was in a hurry and Ryan was comatose, so I decided to skip the local anesthetic. I prepped his skin with betadine antiseptic and then carefully felt with my index finger for the opening between his vertebrae. I inserted the needle and began to slowly push, trying to sense the moment when the needle popped through the dural membrane into the subarachnoid space that contained the CSF.

At about two centimeters, the needle abruptly stopped. I had hit bone. I withdrew the needle, redirected it slightly more toward his head, and pushed again. This time I hit no solid structures. I sensed a tiny change in resistance and thought I might have popped through the membrane. Withdrawing the stylet from the needle, I watched and waited for a drop of fluid to appear. A second later fluid began to drip from the hub of the needle.

I watched fluid slowly accumulate, drop by drop, in the bottom of the test tube. CSF is normally crystal clear—like the purest water. Gradually, the fluid collected in the bottom of the tube until there was enough for me to be able to assess its characteristics. I held it up to the light. There was no pleasant surprise. I couldn't see through it. The fluid was cloudy, and it had an ugly yellowish cast. Ryan Butler had bacterial meningitis, and it was rapidly killing him.

Whether Ryan would survive this illness, or not, was, at best, a coin toss. And if he did survive, there was always the question of how much neurologic injury he would have suffered, and whether there would be permanent neurologic disability that he and his parents would have to cope with for the rest of their lives.

~

The lab knew that this case was hot and jumped right on the CSF analysis. Within twenty minutes Stacey handed me a preliminary report on the CSF. The bad news was all there in black and white. There were a zillion white blood cells and tons of gram negative diplococci bacteria seen in the fluid on gram stain. This confirmed that neisseria meningitidis was the most likely organism. I sighed and made a mental note to congratulate the lab on their turnaround time.

Stacey got Peter Horsham on the line for me from the Division of Pediatric Infectious Disease at Hopkins. I knew Pete from my Hopkins days, and he quickly accepted Ryan in transfer. Now that I had real, objective information, and I knew where Ryan was headed, it was time to sit down with Kelly Butler.

When the adrenalin is pumping and you're doing what you're trained to do, it's often pretty easy to keep a lid on the emotions and avoid thinking too much about the real-life human consequences of what's happening. Indeed, you can't think about them. It slows you down and clouds your brain. Sitting down with the parents, however, is a different story. You can't avoid it. The human consequences are stark, raw, real, and in your face.

~

Mr. Butler had evidently arrived, so I had Pat put the two of them in the family counseling room. I took one more swig of my cold coffee and walked down the hall.

As I walked into the room, both parents immediately looked up at me expectantly, their eyes searching my face for clues as to what I was going to tell them. I shook hands with Mr. Butler and sat down in the armchair opposite their couch, instinctively leaning forward, as I always seem to do, to try and establish some sort of emotional connection with the family for the dreadful conversation to come. The hardest part is always getting started.

"Mr. Butler," I began.

"Please, call me John."

"John, I'm sure Kelly has told you that we were unable to get Ryan to wake up. He had a stiff neck that, along with the fever, made us very concerned that he might have meningitis. So we immediately began him on some powerful antibiotics and did a spinal tap." He looked at me as if to say, "Yes? Well?" This was it. I couldn't delay the bad news any longer.

"I have the lab work back now, and it confirms that Ryan does, indeed, have meningitis." Kelly put her face in her hands, and John sat rigid, like a condemned man. I could see that John's computer was going into overload and that his processing was cruising toward a halt.

"Well… what does this mean?" he asked. A sad voice in the back of my head said, *It means that your son is probably gonna die.*

"It means," I continued, "that Ryan is very, very sick, and that he's going to need very specialized care if he's to survive."

"You mean he could… die?" John said, hopelessly bewildered. Kelly reached out for his hand.

"John, we certainly hope not. Your wife used excellent judgment this morning in bringing him directly to the hospital when she sensed that something wasn't right." I wanted to help alleviate the guilt that would almost certainly plague poor Kelly Butler for years, as each day she asked herself, *why didn't I take Ryan to the hospital earlier*?

"We were able to quickly diagnose the problem," I continued, "and we got antibiotics going at the earliest possible moment. And now we're going to transfer him to Dr. Peter Horsham at Johns Hopkins, one of the best pediatric infectious disease specialists in the country."

John Butler looked at me with a blank look on his face and blinked. This was clearly the most information that he was going to be able to process at the moment. Informing him of the cold mortality statistics would have to come later.

I placed two calls. One was to the hospital infection control nurse who would manage antibiotic prophylaxis on all the staff who had been in Ryan's room. The other was to the county health department. They would need to contact every family that had a child in Ryan's kindergarten class, and then make a decision about which close contacts to treat and which not to treat. This can be a tough call sometimes, although, in general, the Centers for Disease Control does not recommend treatment of all regular classmates. This is information that you could care less about, unless your kid was in that class.

ER's leave no time for reflection and are no repository for human sentiment. The room in which Ryan was diagnosed with a life-threatening, dreadful illness was torn down, disinfected, and, before his bed was cold, was occupied by a forklift driver with a dislocated finger. Five minutes later I was yanking on his finger to reduce the dislocation.

~

About 3:00 PM, April quietly appeared at the nursing station in street clothes. I looked up from my computer station. Mascara smeared her freckled face, and her swollen eyes glowed red.

I stood. "April, what's wrong?"

She scrunched her eyes shut in an effort to hold back the tears, and then sobbed. "It's just so awful! I don't think Joyce is going to make it."

Pat Cole rose out of her chair and hugged April to her chest.

"I just left there. The doctor told her mother that he wasn't very hopeful. And poor Emily just doesn't understand. She looks so afraid!"

"Emily is her daughter?" I asked.

"Yes! She's only seven."

~

I arrived at home after dark and pulled on my barnyard clothes and jacket. As I walked to the barn, the horses whinnied their usual soft greeting in the crisp December night air. The visceral emotional connection with the horses and the simplicity of these chores were becoming important to me. They helped sweep the cobwebs out of my mind. I was beginning to understand why people did this sort of thing day in and day out. I wondered what I would do after Sally came back.

CHAPTER EIGHTEEN

JULIE WANDERED INTO THE NURSING STATION Friday morning and leaned on the counter.

"So what do you want for Christmas?" she asked.

"For Christmas?"

"Yeah. It's budget time. What's on your wish list besides an eighteen-year-old blond?"

"You know what I'd really like?"

"What?"

"One of those video laryngoscopes."

"You mean the ones that are about thirty grand?"

"Yeah. Those."

"OK. I've got a quote someplace in my files. What else?"

"I'd like a really good ultrasound machine for FAST exams."

"Oh. They're only about sixty grand."

"Yeah. So far we're under a hundred grand, right?"

"Right. Considering that our capital budget last year was twenty-five grand, should be a piece of cake."

~

Victoria Sanchez, twenty-three-years-old, was the next patient in line. The tracking board said "abdominal pain." Victoria was about as wide as she was tall. She had two chubby babies in her lap. A wiry male sat in the corner in a work shirt that bore a logo with a tree and a shovel. I said, “Hi. I’m Dr. Randolph. Tell me what the problem is today.” She smiled. So far we were communicating really well. My Spanish sucks and her English was no better.

But, we have a nifty solution to these communication issues. We put the wall phone in the room on speaker-phone, dial up this company that has translators standing by for everything from Spanish to Mandarin, and voila... a little *ménage a trois*. It takes a little longer than conversing in English, but it works really well. I started asking questions.

It turned out that Victoria had been having episodes of pain in the right upper quadrant of her belly off and on for about two months. Sometimes she feels it in her back. Sometimes she throws up with the pain. It lasts a couple of hours and fades away. Last night, after dinner, she had another episode, but this time it didn’t go away. She’s still having a little pain.

One of the little mnemonics you learn in medical school is “fair, fat, fertile, and forty”. This is a description of the classic patient with gallbladder disease. Well, Victoria only met two of these criteria, but I was pretty sure that she still had gallbladder disease. We re-arranged the kids to dad’s lap, and I palpated her belly. She was still a little tender in the right upper quadrant, but I wasn’t too impressed with her level of pain. She still smiled.

I decided to go right for pay dirt, ordered a gallbladder sonogram and some blood work, and moved on to the next patient.

~

I saw three more patients: two twenty-somethings with flu and a very urgent paper cut to the index finger. Not everyone has the same understanding of the word *emergency*. Stacey Dorsey, our ward clerk for the day, shoved Victoria’s sonogram report in front of me.

“Her blood work is back, too,” she said.

Victoria’s report described a gallbladder full of stones. I checked her blood work. It was normal. I re-examined her belly, which was no longer tender. She had never had a fever. All of this meant that her pain was the result of spasm of her gallbladder, or *biliary colic*, as we call it.

This was good and bad news for Victoria. The good news was that the attack was over, and Victoria didn't need emergency surgery to remove her gallbladder—it could be scheduled electively. The bad news was that Victoria had no health insurance and probably couldn't *get* scheduled for elective surgery. That might require a trip back to Mexico. The hospital, of course, would never get paid for Victoria's ER visit today.

The other option was that Victoria could wait until a stone lodged in her common bile duct and she turned yellow with jaundice. That would convert her into an emergency category. The hospital and on-call surgeon would then be required by law to care for her until the emergent condition was over, including taking her gallbladder out. She would get billed, of course, but the hospital and surgeon would never be able to collect.

Victoria, undoubtedly, would not be applying for state Medicaid coverage for the poor because she was probably an illegal alien. Besides, her husband—or significant other—had a job, and she therefore probably wouldn't qualify for public assistance anyhow.

If you have no insurance and you have an emergency, you're in good shape, thanks to a little 1986 law called COBRA/EMTALA. The feds require emergency departments to take all comers, regardless of ability to pay. Of course, all those non-paying people mean that hospitals have to raise fees for everyone else who *does* pay in order to break even. On the other hand, if you have a medical condition that's *not* an emergency and you have no insurance, you're basically screwed. This is how our system works.

I discharged Victoria and gave her the name and telephone number of a couple of surgeons with whom she could follow up for removal of her gallbladder. Of course, that would never happen.

~

"I've got a very sweet old lady in Bed Five," said Jen as she slipped a new chart into the rack, "who smiles brightly and doesn't speak a word of English."

"So what language does she speak?" I asked.

"Italian. And she's here with her American daughter-in-law who doesn't speak a word of Italian."

My second non-English speaker of the day. "OK, well, why don't you just get that translator service on the line again? Let me know when you've got 'em and I'll be in."

"No need. Penny's in there talking with her."

"Penny?"

"Yeah. She speaks Italian."

"Penny speaks Italian?"

"Yeah."

I gave her a quizzical look, grabbed the chart, and walked toward Bed Five. When I entered the room, Penny was in the midst of an animated conversation with Mrs. Fiorenza. I stood for a few moments and listened to the musical rhythms of the conversation. It was amazing. Penny was absolutely fluent. I couldn't tell any difference between her speech patterns and those of Mrs. Fiorenza's. I speak a little French, but I couldn't speak French like Penny was speaking Italian.

Penny turned, saw me, and smiled. She raised her palm toward me, then said to Mrs. Fiorenza, "*Beh, qui è il Dr. Randolph.*"

My paranoid personality translated that to something like, "And here's the SOB now."

I couldn't possibly relate to you the detail of the conversation over the next ten minutes because I don't speak Italian, but the gist of it was that Mrs. Fiorenza had a cough, low grade fever, and nasal congestion. It turned out to be nothing more complicated than the common cold. I told Mrs. Fiorenza—through my translator—that she was going to be fine, and that I'd give her some cough medicine that would help her to sleep better for the next few nights.

"*Arrivederci,*" I waved in closing, using the only Italian word in my vocabulary besides *ciao*. I walked back toward the nursing station beside Penny, staring at her.

"Where did you learn to speak Italian like that?"

"I lived in Naples for three years when I was in middle school."

"What were you doing in Naples?"

"I'm a military brat. Couldn't you tell?" she asked, her luminescent eyes glowing mischievously. "My father's in the Navy."

"Still, how did you get so fluent? American kids usually live on base and go to American schools."

"My father insisted we live off base, and he made us go to Italian schools." This was not the usual pattern of things. I began to suspect that Penny came from a not-so-average family.

"What does your father do?"

"Well, he started off as a pilot, but now he has a desk job."

"And what is that?" I asked.

"He's the Superintendant of the Naval Academy."

~

Toward the end of the day I heard an overhead page, "Dr. Randolph, Dr. Horsham on five-one-three-zero." That would be Pete getting back to me about Ryan Butler.

"Hey, Pete. Alex."

"Hi, Alex. I wanted to let you know that Ryan Butler died this morning."

"I'm not surprised."

"He never regained consciousness. The organism *was* neisseria meningitidis, by the way. By the middle of the afternoon on Monday he started to get shocky. We put an ICP catheter in him, and his intracranial pressures just kept rising. He went down the tubes pretty fast."

"How's the family doing? His father wasn't processing very well when he was here."

"I guess as well as you can do when you lose a kid. The father's still in a daze. It's gonna take him a while. The mother comprehends, but she's devastated of course. She asked me if it would have made any difference if she had gotten him to the hospital earlier."

"What did you tell her?"

"I told her that in these fulminant cases it often doesn't matter what you do, or when, they still die."

"Was Ryan their only kid?"

"Yes."

"OK, Pete. Thanks for calling."

"You're welcome. By the way I was looking over your records and I noticed that you guys had the antibiotics going fifteen minutes after arrival. That's fast. You did a good job."

"Thanks, Pete. I really appreciate you mentioning that. I'll let the staff know what you had to say."

"See you, Alex."

"So long, Pete."

~

As I walked down the hall on my way out, a little after 7:00, Julie's office door was open and the lights were on. I poked my head in to say goodnight. "What are you doing still here?" I asked.

Julie looked up from her desk. "Come in," she said quietly. "Sit down." I obeyed and sat in the chair adjacent to her desk.

She looked me in the eyes. "I just got a text from April. Joyce died about thirty minutes ago." I stared back at her silently.

"Did you know that Joyce was the first of her family to ever go to college?" she asked.

CHAPTER NINETEEN

SATURDAY MORNING WAS THE FIRST TIME IN A week that I had heard the crunch of Sally's tires on gravel as her truck pulled in. I pulled on my jacket, grabbed my coffee cup, and headed out to greet her. I was going through the door when I decided that it might be nice to bring her a cup, too. I thought she took it with just cream.

I headed back out the door again with a steaming mug in each hand, spilling coffee as I tried to kick the door shut. Sally had opened the door of her truck, swung both legs out, and was gingerly descending onto the foot with the broken toe. Instead of her usual jeans, she was wearing a pair of baggy beige cords and had a big fluffy slipper on her left foot. Her auburn hair was down and glinted in the sun. She waved when she saw me coming.

"It's nice to see that blue truck in my driveway again," I said, handing her a mug. "I think you take it with just cream."

"You're still trying to kiss up to me," she said with a grin, shaking out her hair. *Well, maybe just a little more than that.*

"No, I just hate to throw away good coffee."

"But you *did* remember that I take it with just cream. So today you get a smiley face for that one." I was genuinely happy to see Sally back.

"So have you bonded with Robert E. Lee and Abigail?" she asked, looking over at the two of them standing with their heads over the fence.

"Truth is, I've come to look forward to my little twice a day ritual with those animals."

"It's nice, isn't it?" she said softly, looking back at me.

"They're great listeners. And better yet, they rarely disagree with me," I smiled. "How's the foot?"

"The pain is much better. It still aches if I'm up on it too long, but it's getting better rapidly now. I think another week or so and it's going to be pretty good."

"I've already fed the horses this morning. And it would be very good for my soul to do that for another week," I suggested.

"I don't think I could go another week without going stark raving mad."

"Then how about if we split the therapeutic value of these chores—at least until your foot gets better? I'll do the morning and you do the evening. And the hay will be the tough part for you, so I'll just throw enough in the racks in the morning to last them all day."

She squinted her eyes and looked up at me with mock seriousness. "You drive a very hard bargain, Dr. Randolph."

~

I love the way the house smells by Saturday afternoon. Ruth was busy all day cleaning, polishing, vacuuming, and doing laundry. I don't know what the stuff is that she cleans with, but the house smells so fresh by the end of the day that you'd think you were living in the pristine out-of-doors.

I could tell that she had something on her mind, and I suspected that I knew what it was.

"Are you going out tonight?" she asked cheerfully. "Do you need anything?"

"Yes. As a matter of fact, I'm headed over to Cathy and Tim Rutledge's for a holiday party this evening. But no, I don't think I need anything."

"Oh, is that just for hospital people?"

"I don't think so. I think there will be a lot of their other friends there, too."

"So, people will be bringing spouses and dates?"

"Yes, I imagine so, but probably not together."

"What time do you have to leave?"

"Oh, around eight o'clock or so."

"So you don't have to pick up anybody?"

"Nope."

I heard Ruth let out a little satisfied sigh.

~

I stepped out of the shower, toweled off, and walked over to the dresser. I pulled open the underwear drawer, and there, lying on top of my clean boxers, was a wispy, pink thing with strings and a short crotch about two inches wide. I grinned to myself and picked them up. Ruth had obviously found them somewhere and didn't know what to do with them. Given that they were Elizabeth's, I was shocked that she hadn't found a pair of scissors and slashed them to ribbons. But then again, maybe she wasn't so sure that they were Elizabeth's. At that thought, I collapsed on the bed with laughter so loud that Maggie came trotting into the room with her tail wagging to make sure everything was OK.

~

The cars were lined up along Corbett Road for fifty yards on either side of Cathy and Tim's driveway. I pulled onto the grass at the edge of the road and walked back the driveway toward the house, carrying my little gift of a bottle of Grey Goose. Self-serving, I know. But booze for a party of this size can set you back a couple of house payments.

The house was tucked among mature trees at the edge of a wood. Warm light spilled from the tall windows, and the whole house, with its gables and dormers, softly glowed from several spotlights on the lawn. It looked like a shot from *Architectural Digest.* Tim was fairly anal about how his house looked.

I entered, without knocking, amidst a low roar of conversation.

The place was packed with people. Candles were everywhere. Somewhere in the background, I could hear Jason Mraz. I made my way from the foyer, down the hall, and into the kitchen where I knew there would be ice and glasses. I knew most of the people here, including my sibs and close friends, who had become part of Cathy and Tim's extended family of friends.

John and Annick were standing by the island talking with Brian and Susan. It was the first time I had seen Annick since John announced her pregnancy on the tennis courts, and I noted the first little hint of a belly on her tiny frame. She looked up and spotted me.

"Alex! *Salut*!" She reached up to me, and we kissed on both cheeks. I looked down at her belly and said, "What do we have growing here?"

Her eyes sparkled, and she said with mock seriousness, "I am not sure. Maybe I need to see *un médecin*. Every week it grows a little bigger."

"It could be a disease you caught from your husband," I said. "You know he travels to a lot of exotic places."

"Yes. But, you know, he is never home. So perhaps I caught it someplace else?" she said looking over at John. This girl was a riot. She reached around his waist and gave John a hug to soften the blow.

I poured myself a light Grey Goose with a liberal amount of tonic water and squeezed in a lime. I would have to keep a lid on it tonight because I didn't have a designated driver. It would not do for the Chief of Emergency Medicine at Mason-Dixon to be written up for a DUI in the *North County News* next week. Not good for one's career path, although Jackie Ford would absolutely love it.

I looked around the room and caught a glimpse of Penny Murray standing talking with Rebecca Franklin and her boyfriend, Peter. Rebecca and Peter live in Bolton Hill, a gentrified section of Baltimore near the University of Baltimore. He just finished law school and is a lackey at Drummond, Porter & Kaplan, the chief rival of Hamilton, Duncan & Blackstone in the Baltimore law market.

But my eyes were drawn to Penny. I had never seen Penny out of a scrub suit. The pony tail was gone. Her wavy, blond hair was down and shimmered in the subdued light. She wore a form-fitting, white shirt that followed the gentle curve of her narrow hips. The first couple of buttons were discretely undone. It was tucked into a pair of low cut jeans. A gorgeous round little butt curved out from her spine. I could see long, dangling earrings, and a matching short necklace of small blue stones, when she periodically brushed her hair back behind her ear. It was a lovely package.

She appeared to be alone. I subconsciously looked around the room for an unfamiliar guy who might be her husband, but found no one that fit. In the back of my mind, Jekyll was having a hissy fit. *My God, man, where is your brain? This is a married woman!*

I mentally whacked myself in the head a couple of times, turned to find a conversation partner, and ran smack into Elizabeth, about four inches from my face. She was close enough that I could detect her familiar, delicate scent. Our eyes met, and for once in my life I was at a complete loss for words. Bizarrely, the image of Elizabeth's pink panties popped into my head. *Oh, my. This is becoming a complicated evening.*

"Hello, Alex," she said, smiling.

"Hello, Elizabeth." We looked at each other for a long moment. And then she was gone. I took a deep breath.

Anne appeared and walked over to me.

"That was a short *tête a tête* with Elizabeth," she said.

"Yeah. I didn't expect that. I was speechless."

"Is that the first time you've seen her since the birthday celebration?"

"Yeah."

"How did it feel?"

"Bizarre. I could smell her. In one way, it would have seemed perfectly natural to just put my arm around her waist and pull her in, but yet it wasn't."

"Life is complex," she smiled. "I saw Eric two weeks ago, walking into a restaurant," she continued, referring to her ex. "It was like I should have waved so he could see where I was sitting. And then, he walked to another table, kissed the woman sitting there on the cheek, and sat down.

"Ooooh," I said. "And how did *you* feel?"

"It was interesting. For an instant, my heart sank. And then for the first time, I thought, *you know what? I hope Eric is able to give her his heart, whoever she is.*" I gave Anne a hug. I love my sister. She's a wonderful woman. Eric was an idiot.

Ben ambled up to us, glass in hand.

"Hey, Ben. Do you know my sister, Anne?"

"No, but it would be my pleasure," he said in that amiable, rumbling voice.

"Well, I'm not going to introduce her to you because you're a dangerous predator."

"I can take care of myself, thank you," said Anne, and reached out her hand. "Ben, it's nice to meet you. Actually, I feel like I know you because I've heard Alex talk about you so many times."

"Well you just remember that it's all lies," he said smiling.

"There's a kernel of truth in every creditable lie," I said.

~

Cathy was standing talking with Lisa and Frank. I walked over and gave Cathy a hug. Lisa got a kiss because I couldn't get close enough for a hug. Her belly was now nearly as big as the rest of her put together, and she was standing holding her back with one hand.

"Oh, I need to get this kid *out*!!" she moaned.

"Hang in there, baby," said Frank. "Another two weeks and you'll have gin in that glass instead of coke."

"Have Frank drive you back and forth over some railroad tracks on the way home. That might get things going," I suggested.

"An orgasm!" said Cathy. "You need an orgasm. Gets the oxytocin flowing."

Frank hopped right on that one. "That can be arranged."

"Oh God, Cathy. That's what got me into this in the first place," Lisa said laughing.

I was having a good time. As is always the case with Cathy and Tim's parties, it was a nice group of people and an interesting mix. I talked with Tim and his friend Rich Copenhaver for a while. Rich is a realtor who sells the occasional spec houses that Tim builds. They both moaned and groaned about the real estate market. Actually, I think that Tim and Cathy were having a pretty tough time of it financially in the last year with the depressed construction industry, not to mention two boys in college—one a freshman; the other a senior. I was personally glad that they had still popped for their holiday party.

~

I refilled my glass with one more light Grey Goose and tonic and vowed to switch to plain tonic water for the rest of the night. *Maybe I should get some food in my stomach.*

I turned to walk to the hors d'oeuvres table and bumped into Penny Murray, spilling my drink onto her shirt and jeans.

"Oh, gosh, Penny, I'm sorry." I looked around for napkins or a towel and spotted a roll of paper towels on the counter. I tore off a section, contemplated wiping off her jeans, and thought better of it. I handed her the paper towel. I was definitely on a roll with women the last couple of weeks.

"It's OK, Alex," she said wiping down the leg of her jeans. "You know, it is really hot in here. An ice-tonic bath was perfect. Was there some Grey Goose in that, too?" That was the first time that I had heard Penny call me by my first name.

"Not as much as I would have liked."

"Well, you better get yourself another drink. I think I got the benefit of most of that one," she said smiling.

For the second time tonight, I found myself at a loss for words—unexpectedly face to face with a lovely woman. Under normal circumstances, I knew exactly what I would have wanted to say to Penny, but it would have been a wholly inappropriate conversation with a married woman, as Jekyll was currently reminding me in a very loud voice in the back of my head. I decided that shop talk was relatively safe.

"I'm glad to see you were off tonight," I said.

"I am having so much fun! This is a whole new group of people for me. It was really nice of Cathy to invite me."

"Penny, I have to tell you that we are really happy to have you at

Mason-Dixon. You're a really good nurse," I said genuinely. *Not only that, but you are gorgeous.*

I looked around the room, reflexively searching for Elizabeth—old habit. I didn't see her and wondered if she had gone. I looked back at Penny.

"Do you remember little Cameron with the dog bite?" I said.

"Yes."

"Do you remember singing to him while we were waiting for him to go to sleep?"

She smiled and nodded.

"You know what I thought? I thought, 'Penny Murray is the closest thing on earth I've ever seen to a real angel.'" *Oh shit. I can't believe I just said that.*

Penny looked in my eyes for a long time, as if searching for the meaning of my words. She didn't smile. Finally, she simply said quietly, "Thank you, Alex."

I could feel the steam rising. This was getting away from me fast. I needed an exit. I looked around the room again. There was no one else standing close by to bring into the conversation. Penny came to the rescue.

"I just love this song," she said. In the background, I could hear that the music had shuffled to an old Andrea Bocelli album.

"*Nessun Dorma*?" I asked.

"Yes!" she said. "You know it! *Nessun Dorma–None shall sleep.*"

"I love it, too," I said. "It's incredibly moving, even if you don't speak Italian. But I know nothing about it."

"It's from Puccini's opera, *Turandot.* Did you know that if you were a suitor and couldn't answer Princess Turandot's three riddles, she would cut your head off?"

"I think I used to date her."

Penny giggled. Her green eyes sparkled.

"No, silly," she said, punching me in the arm, "that was a hundred and fifty years ago!"

I looked at her quizzically. "How do you know all this stuff? Because you lived in Italy?"

"No. I was a fine arts major in college."

"A fine arts major? You went to college before nursing school?" This girl was full of surprises.

"I didn't go to nursing school until later."

"Where did you go to college?"

"Notre Dame, here in Baltimore."

"So when did you decide to go to nursing school?"

Penny paused. She looked off in the distance for a moment as if deciding whether or not to answer this question, and then looked back at me.

"My husband was in the Navy," she said quietly. "He was a SEAL. He was wounded in Iraq and transferred to Bethesda Naval Hospital. It was a serious wound. I sat by his bed in ICU for five days before he finally turned around, and I watched the nurses care for him day and night. I thought they were angels. I decided that's what I wanted to do."

"And he recovered?"

Penny nodded. "He returned to duty six months later."

"So, then you went to nursing school?"

"I went through an accelerated program at Notre Dame for students who already had degrees. It only took three semesters."

I stared at her. Penny was a most remarkable woman. In the background, Jekyll's rational admonitions had turned to howls. This chick was screwing up my head.

CHAPTER TWENTY

MONDAY MORNING, WHEN I WALKED IN, ALL the nurses were in Bed Sixteen for the monthly staff meeting. This was less erotic than it sounds—they were all erect, standing on the floor. The software changes in Samson were finished, and today we were going live with the new shorter documentation procedures. Julie had been training staff for the last two weeks. It would be interesting to see how much faster the work flowed. I hoped to hell it made a significant difference after all the work, open warfare, and political blackmail that had gone into this.

The new security station in the lobby was to open today, and the police call buttons in the security station and triage had been tested and were functional. Admin had also added a *Code Brown* to all the other color codes that were announced over the hospital PA system to indicate cardiac arrests, fires, disasters, and bomb threats. *Code Brown* indicated "Armed Suspect In Building." I figured that this one would empty the building faster than *Code Red* for fire.

Julie would be instructing the staff in all the new security procedures, as well as making specific mention of Julio and the interest of Baltimore County's Finest in his whereabouts. It would be interesting to see whether or not this freaked out the staff. By the end of the day, I'd have a pretty good indication from the scuttlebutt around the nursing station.

I was a little on edge this morning. I had spent most of the weekend trying unsuccessfully to banish Penny Murray from my thoughts. I couldn't be sure what she was feeling during our conversation on Saturday night, but I was almost certain that she had felt the same connection that I had. The intensity of my feelings had caught me off guard. I had never been involved with a married woman before, and didn't plan to be now. Nevertheless, I was a little frightened by what might pass between us the next time our eyes met. To my relief, Penny was off today.

It was a fairly quiet morning for a Monday. Mondays are usually the worst, after a weekend of physician's offices being closed. The staff was noticeably subdued in the wake of Joyce's death. Voices were quiet and faces strained as each personally coped with the realities of death of one of their own close contemporaries—the first such occurrence for many younger members of the staff, including myself.

I saw a bubbly little eight-month-old who had fallen off the couch and hit his head on a carpeted floor. I love the way babies connect with you. He just lay there and stared directly into my eyes the whole time that I was examining him. It's very interesting how they zero in on your eyes as the entry point to the relationship at such an early age. I'm always amazed at the intimacy of the experience.

Julie appeared at the nursing station after she had wrapped up the meeting.

"Well, how did it go?" I asked.

She shrugged her shoulders. "Maybe it's been long enough since Julio that fears are fading, but they didn't seem that worked up when I told them to punch that button if Julio shows his face again. I think they also feel that everybody is doing everything they can to improve security, so we'll see, but I think they're OK with it."

About 10:00 AM Stan Robinson showed up with his administrative entourage and tried to have a little ceremony to celebrate the opening of the security station. This was an opportunity to demonstrate the concerned and caring nature of the administration, which Stan couldn't pass up. Nobody showed much interest, and most of the staff missed Stan's little speech, which he nevertheless delivered with gusto to the bemused interest of the patient family members in the waiting room.

By mid-afternoon, I thought that I could see a difference in patient flow. The charts were hitting the rack faster after registration. Volume was picking up, but things seemed to be flowing pretty well.

I looked over at Lynn Saylor. “I think these changes to Samson are going to work.”

“I do too. I’m not sitting around today waiting for patients to get through triage.”

It’s a small world. Lynn actually went to Washington College with my brother Brian—although I didn’t know her at the time—and then went on to medical school at Brown University. She had wanted to come back to Maryland, and I hired her right out of an emergency medicine residency at Beth Israel Deaconess in Boston about a year and a half ago. She’s a very smart girl.

Lynn was still single, although I couldn’t imagine why. She said she hadn’t found her dream boy yet. A striking brunette who’s tall and athletic, she’s a wicked volleyball player. More than once I had been on the receiving end of her spikes, and they were painful. I think most of the potential Mr. Rights found her a little intimidating.

Jen Wilke was in triage today. She walked up and slid another chart into the to-be-seen rack. Cheerful, confident, and amply endowed, Jen’s a late thirties mother of four elementary school kids. She lives on two hundred and fifty acres with her kids, dairy farmer husband, and one hundred and fifty Holstein cows. She works here full time. I don’t know how she finds enough hours in a day to do it all.

“There’s an ankle sprain for you,” she said. “I just love this! I got him entered and through triage in five minutes! He got in a tussle with a cow, and she showed him who’s boss.” This was a good sign. Jen liked our modification of Samson.

By 6:00 PM the evening rush had hit us like a tsunami. Every room was full, and they began to back up into the waiting room. I knew we would pay for the slow morning.

The next patient name on the tracker board had an entry beside it that said "Abscess." As I walked into Bed Fourteen, I could see the problem even before I introduced myself. Nineteen-year-old Jeremy Sanders' left arm was swollen to about twice its normal size at the bend of the elbow, and it glowed like the end of ET's finger. I could see the red color streaking up the inner aspect of his arm towards his axilla, commonly known as the arm pit. I looked for the vital signs on the chart and noted that his temp was one hundred point four.

"That looks like it hurts," I said.

Jeremy said nothing.

"How long has your arm been this way?" Jeremy was slow to reply. His mother, seated in a folding chair beside his bed, picked up and answered.

"I don't know for sure. I think maybe just in the last thirty-six hours or so."

"Jeremy?" I said.

"Yeah, maybe. Since Saturday morning." Jeremy's sullen face showed little emotion, and he didn't look at me as he spoke.

"Jeremy has a problem with heroin," his mother said. "I think he shot up on Friday night."

"Is that so, Jeremy?" I inquired. He nodded.

"Have you been having shaking chills, Jeremy?" He nodded again.

"Any vomiting?"

"Once," he replied.

I pulled a pair of gloves from the wall dispenser and gently began to palpate the tissue around the abscess. I could feel a firm area under my fingers all around the periphery of the abscess, extending from over the middle of his upper arm, all the way down into his mid-forearm. As I moved toward the center it got softer, and there was an angry purplish area in the center that looked as though the abscess might break through the skin.

"Jeremy," I said looking up at him, "this is an abscess—an infection under the skin. It's growing very fast. You have a large cavity filled with pus in the center, and that's going to have to be drained."

"What do you mean?" he asked apprehensively, looking up at me for the first time. "You mean a knife?"

"Yes. We're going to put your skin to sleep first—and maybe we'll actually put *you* to sleep—but we will have to make an incision and allow all that pus to drain out of there."

The abscess was huge. It endangered vital structures in Jeremy's elbow. He was going to need hospitalization and IV antibiotics. It would be best to let the surgeon who would admit him drain the abscess.

"I'm going to page our surgeon on call, Jeremy, and have him come take a look at you. You're probably going to need to be in the hospital for a couple of days." Jeremy looked down at his arm and said nothing. I turned to leave the room, and his mother spoke up.

"Doctor? May I have a word with you?"

We walked outside the room and stood in the hall. Jeremy's mother was a well-kept woman with thick, black hair streaked with gray. A white turtleneck was tucked into her jeans beneath a black faux leather jacket. Her face looked like she had been tired for years.

"Jeremy needs help," she began, with a deep, throaty voice.

"How long has he been on heroin?"

"Probably two and a half years. He dropped out of high school three months before graduation and left home. Thank God, probably, because at least he wasn't around the two younger kids. But he just moves from place to place, staying with his friends. By the time he left home he had stolen everything he could lay his hands on around the house." She lost her composure and faltered for a moment. I could see the anguish in her eyes. "Dr. Randolph, he even stole from his *grandparents*!"

"Has he ever been in rehab?"

"Once. We put him in that place over in Harford County for six weeks. My husband sold his pickup truck to pay for it. It was fifteen thousand dollars." This was an all too familiar story.

"Has he been arrested?"

"Yes, for shoplifting. He was in jail once for sixty days. Can we please do something to help him now that he's going into the hospital?"

"Mrs. Sanders, I hate to ask this question, but the reality is that it has a big bearing on what we can do for Jeremy with regard to getting him into rehab again. Does he have any health insurance?"

She squeezed her eyes shut, and shook her head "no." "He lost his insurance when he left home and turned nineteen."

"And I assume that he doesn't have a job?" She shook her head again.

"And he probably hasn't applied for Medicaid either?"

"I don't think so."

"Mrs. Sanders, we'll get Social Services involved and do everything we can to see if there isn't a way to get Jeremy some help. But I have to tell you that under these circumstances it will be tough."

I squeezed her hand. She thanked me and walked back into Jeremy's room. Unfortunately, I had the strong impression that Mrs. Sanders was much more interested in help than Jeremy. In that case, insurance isn't the issue.

Drug rehab is almost never successful unless the patients themselves want it badly—*very* badly. And unfortunately that often doesn't happen until they completely crash and burn—often taking their extended families with them. Jeremy didn't look to me like he was ready to take personal responsibility for his own life.

"Stacey, who's the surgeon on call today?"

"Dr. Broddick."

Great. Broddick was a dick, no pun intended. It was dinnertime, and he would for sure give me a raft of shit about coming in, especially for a drug addict with a self-inflicted infection and no insurance. I was not in the mood for his bullshit.

"Would you please get him on the line for me?"

Five minutes later Stacey announced, "I've got Dr. Broddick on five-three-one-three.

"Bob?"

"Yeah."

"This is Alex Randolph in the ER. How are you?"

"Fine."

"I've got a kid here with a great big antecubital abscess extending from mid-forearm to mid-biceps. He's got a fever and lymphangitis all the way up to his axilla. He probably got it from shooting up heroin.

He's going to need this thing drained, and then he's going to need a couple of days of IV antibiotics."

"And you can't do that?"

"I could drain it. That's not the issue. The issue is that it probably should be done by the surgeon who's going to be taking care of him in the hospital."

"I don't see why this is such a big deal. Why don't you just open him and then admit him to the medical service."

"Bob, it's a *surgical* problem. This is a very big abscess, and it's endangering some vital structures. It needs to be taken care of by a surgeon."

"You know how many of these kids I end up taking care of, and none of them have insurance, and I don't get squat for any of them? And then they all come back with complications?"

"Bob, are you the surgeon on call?"

"Of course I'm the surgeon on call."

"Well, I tell you what. You've got twenty minutes to get your sorry ass in here. If I don't see your ugly face in twenty minutes, I can assure you that my next call will be placed to the Chief of Surgery, and that I will do everything in my power to make sure that you never do another case in your life at Mason-Dixon Regional."

CHAPTER TWENTY-ONE

THE FUNERAL WASN'T HELD UNTIL Wednesday. Because this was a homicide case, it took five days for the coroner to finish his work before the body was released for burial. I slipped into a back pew of Faith Methodist Church in Shrewsbury, as *Rock of Ages* played on an electronic organ.

The family was gathered in the first few rows of the sanctuary—tears quietly streaming from the puffy eyes of a few of the younger women; Kleenexes in abundance. Most of the men sat uncomfortably, as if looking for escape. Dress for the occasion was clean sport shirts and zip-up nylon jackets. One older man wore an ill-fitting green suit with an open white shirt. Apart from the minister, I was the only man in the sanctuary wearing a tie. Kids bounced around on pews, and mothers leaned over to shush them.

A heavy, middle-aged woman limped past my pew with the aid of a cane. She held the hand of a slender little girl with long, brown hair held back by white barrettes. I wondered if this was Emily and her grandmother. They walked slowly down the aisle to the casket, and paused for a long moment. The woman whispered something in the little girl's ear, then, with some difficulty, leaned forward and gently kissed the forehead of the body. After another moment, they turned together and walked to the front pew. One of the younger men jumped up and helped the older woman to take her seat.

Most of the off-duty ER staff were here—sitting in clusters—scattered among the sparse congregation. I could see April's copper hair glinting from the third row, just behind the family. April and Joyce were classmates in nursing school.

The minister rose, arms extended, and the organist finished the last bar. "Dearly beloved," he began, "we are gathered here today to celebrate before God, the life of his servant, Joyce Harbaugh, our beloved daughter, sister, mother, and friend; and to others, a compassionate nurse who ministered selflessly to their needs. We are also here to commend Joyce to God's keeping, and to comfort all who mourn, knowing of God's promise that dying in Christ, we may rise in Christ to life eternal..."

Twenty minutes later the eulogy of Joyce Harbaugh's life was over, and the casket was closed. I wondered where the piece of shit was who put her here. His sentence should have included sitting in this congregation today.

This was the second Mason-Dixon Regional Medical Center funeral in as many months. I hoped that they didn't come in threes.

CHAPTER TWENTY-TWO

AFTER THE WEDNESDAY FUNERAL, I WAS BACK on days Thursday and Friday. I still had not seen Penny, but my emotions were cooling down and I felt a little more under control. An affair would be a grand way to screw up my life, and probably Penny's too. I was gradually settling into the conviction that I was never going to let things get away from me like that again. Still, she continued to creep into my thoughts with disturbing frequency.

Julie showed up at the nursing station carrying a printout of some sort, and laid it down on the counter in front of me.

"Look at this," she said, bending over beside me. "I've only got three full days worth of data, but in those three days we've cut eight minutes off the average door-to-doctor time." She triumphantly stood erect, put her hands on her hips, and said, "What do you think of that?"

"Nice," I said, pouring over the figures.

"*And*, the staff is still getting used to the system. I bet once they're fluent we'll be up to twelve or thirteen minutes!" It's nice when a plan comes together.

"What do you bet me that Jackie jumps right on this and adopts it as her own?" I asked.

"I don't care what she does… just so she leaves us alone."

~

Lisa was working today. It was her last shift before she left for maternity leave. I saw her walk slowly back to the nursing station, legs wide apart. I smiled as I watched her. She looked up and saw me smiling.

"Don't give me that look. I'd like to see you make a trip down this hall with a medicine ball wedged between your legs," she said.

I couldn't help it. I laughed out loud. She carefully lowered herself onto a chair and exhaled, blowing wisps of hair out of her face, then looked over at me.

"I hope I'm in here one day when you come in with a massive kidney stone, writhing and whimpering on the bed," she said. Now I was convulsing with laughter.

"I told Penny on Saturday night, be glad you got it over with at two. This eternal quest for a boy is killing me."

I almost choked.

"Two? Penny's got kids?"

"Yeah. Two of 'em. A girl six and a boy three. So she's in good shape—one of each."

~

About four o'clock I walked into Bed Six to see a back pain. An African-American male with a little goatee and a blue bandana around his head—maybe early thirties—was lying on his right side moaning and cursing. I could see several teeth missing when he grimaced. He wore a Dallas Cowboys jersey. I looked down at his chart and was surprised to see that he was only twenty-one. His name was Jawara Reynolds.

There were two other guys in the room. One had a bruised right eye that was almost swollen shut. He stood leaning back against the sink, looking sullen, with his hands tucked in a blue, hooded sweatshirt. The third guy was big. He stood protectively over the bed, a black stocking covering his hair and a blue bandana tied around his neck. Three days of stubble on his face was bisected by a long, white scar across his left cheek. He stared at me expressionless as I entered the room. All three wore jeans with crotches below their knees. I hate to be a profiler, but these guys were not locals. I would have bet the farm that they were Crips. I paged back through the chart to the demographics page and saw a listed address in Timonium. That didn't sound right.

"Jawara, I'm Dr. Randolph. What's the problem today?"

"I fell down… a fucking flight of stairs," he moaned, holding his breath between phrases. I caught a strong whiff of alcohol.

"And where are you hurt?"

"My back, man, my fucking back! How many times do I have to tell you?"

"Show me."

"Right over my shoulder blade!"

"Which shoulder blade?"

"This one over here," said his tall companion in a deep voice, pointing to Jawara's left shoulder.

"Let's get this shirt up," I said, and began pulling up the Cowboys jersey.

"Watch it, man! That fuckin' hurts!" he screamed.

"Careful with my brother, Dude," said the big one.

"Tell you what, guys," I said, standing up straight, "why don't *you* pull the shirt up?"

"Come on, brother, let the man look at you," said the shorter one.

Amidst much cursing, they finally got Jawara's shirt up above his shoulder blades. A wide, six-inch welt with a lot of swelling and dark discoloration ran diagonally across Jawara's left scapula. I didn't need to touch it to see if it was tender. I took the opportunity to listen to his lungs with my stethoscope, and they were clear with good breath sounds

"Where else are you hurt, Jawara?"

"That's it, man. I *told* you, it's my *shoulder*." I tried to get a look at Jawara's head, extremities, and belly to see if he had other injuries from his alleged fall down the stairs, but he was having none of it.

"Don't touch me, man! I'm tellin' ya, get your fuckin' hands off o' me!"

Jawara was obviously trashed, and I needed to defuse this before things started to get out of hand. That meant just leaving him alone for a while.

"OK, Jawara. We're going to get an x-ray of your shoulder blade and chest, and then I'll be back." People who fall down a flight of stairs have other injuries—at least bruises here and there, incurred as they tumble down. This looked more like the work of a Louisville Slugger than a fall down the stairs.

~

Sandy Lucas, the radiology tech, walked up to the nursing station, rolled her eyes, and said, "The x-rays are up on Bed Six. They're not great, but they're the best that I could do. Don't ask me to do any more films on *that* guy."

I walked over to the PACS screen on the wall and pulled up Jawara's images. There was a little motion artifact, but that didn't obscure the problem. He had a clean diagonal fracture across his lower shoulder blade, or scapula. The glenoid fossa on the shoulder blade that provides the socket for the ball of the humerus was uninjured. His chest film was otherwise clear with no underlying evidence of pulmonary injury or a rib fracture.

The lower part of the scapula kind of free floats on muscle and it's very hard to fracture. Usually it takes a direct blow of enormous force. My Louisville Slugger theory was looking better all the time.

To my great reluctance, I punched out a prescription for the narcotic Percocet for pain, as well as a referral to the orthopedic surgeons for follow-up. No surgery would be required. We could treat Jawara with a simple sling and swathe, and he would heal in about six weeks.

I walked back to the room thinking about the piece of shit to whom I was providing the most polite customer service we could muster. I could still picture the peach fuzz on Andrew Price's face under the glare of the surgical lights, his brain gone, courtesy of the Crips and their efficient market distribution of heroin. Poor Joyce Harbaugh and Jeremy Sanders were additional collateral damage. I wasn't in a very magnanimous mood.

Jekyll reminded me that I really didn't know if Jawara was a Crip, and furthermore, I needed to be careful about pre-judging him.

Hyde, on the other hand, presented me with a whole series of options regarding how we could relieve Jawara of his pain on a permanent basis. I personally favored his idea of a couple hundred milligrams of succinylcholine IV. That would give Jawara about three minutes to think about the significance of his life's work while he lay there, paralyzed and unable to take a breath, before finally lapsing into unconsciousness.

Jekyll was horrified and appalled that I would participate in this fantasy with Hyde. Sometimes I remember reading *Lord of the Flies* in college, and I think about how short the distance may really be between someone like Jawara and myself.

I took Pat Cole in the room with me to help get Jawara into the sling and swathe. Pat was a good choice. She's a divorced single mother of two kids in high school. Successfully raising two teenagers by yourself pretty well requires the discipline of a drill sergeant. She was not likely to be intimidated by Jawara Reynolds.

"Jawara, you have a broken scapula, also called your shoulder blade," I began. "It's going to take about six weeks to heal. But since we can't put your chest in a cast, the next best thing is a sling and swathe to immobilize it. Then Pat's going to give you some Percocet to take home for pain."

Pat approached and gently began to lift Jawara's arm to get the sling around his elbow. "Watch it cunt!" he screamed. "You're fuckin' killin' me!"

Pat dropped the elbow instantly, prompting another scream out of Jawara. The two males standing near the bedside took a step forward. I started to move between the big one and Pat, but she held out her hand to stop them. They hesitated and then reluctantly stepped back. Slowly she placed both hands on the stretcher and leaned forward until she was six inches from Jawara's face. Her voice was quiet.

"If I hear that word one more time out of your rotten little mouth, you can forget the Percocet. Understand? You'll get *nothing* for pain. Do you hear me? *Nothing*. You'll go home on Tylenol and squirm around on the couch, blubbering like a baby, for the next six weeks. Got it? One more time," she said, holding up her index finger, "that's all it will take."

Jawara glared at her ominously, breathing rapidly. With great difficulty and amidst another round of cursing, but without either the "F" or the "C" word, we got Jawara into the sling and swathe, and got him and his crew out of there.

~

I asked Stacey to get Jack Schmidt on the line for me.

"Hi, Jack. Alex Randolph."

"How ya doin', Doc."

"Did you find that prick yet that bashed in Joyce's head?"

"Yeah. He's not that bright. We found him at his cousin's house. Now he's got bigger problems than heroin. He's got a little homicide charge to deal with."

"Can they put him away forever?"

"Not likely, unfortunately. He'll be indicted for second degree murder—ten to thirty years."

"I vote for thirty."

"Me, too."

"Jack, can you do me a favor?"

"Sure."

"See what you can find out in your little computers about a Jawara Reynolds at an address of 2020 Northwood Drive in Timonium. Birth date four-seventeen-eighty-nine. Social security number 419-22-6843.

"You got a problem with this guy?"

"No. He's gone. But I'm betting that you'll find that he doesn't exist. I think he's a Crip that got whacked with a baseball bat."

"Give me a day. I'll get back to you."

~

Thankfully, the place was packed. We were in the middle of the *Five O' Clock Rush*, and I was seeing patients as fast as I could without being rude, and hopefully, without screwing up. This was a good thing, because Lisa's casual mention of Penny's kids had hit me like a ton of bricks. The distraction of the workload was helpful. It had never occurred to me that Penny might have children. I needed to forget this woman.

CHAPTER TWENTY-THREE

I GOT TO WORK FRIDAY MORNING ABOUT fifteen minutes early for my nine AM shift, poured a cup of coffee, and sat down in Julie's office. She was banging away on her computer.

"I've got a question," I said.

"What's that?" she asked, continuing her typing.

"I haven't seen any signs in the department saying only one visitor per room. How did you head that one off with Jacquelyn?"

"Simple. I told her that the changes to Samson were working, and that if she got rid of Stan's visitor restrictions, I'd make sure she got full credit for our reduction in door-to-doctor times."

"How does your husband stand you?"

"What?"

"How does your husband stand you? You're so disgustingly competent."

~

I walked into the ER. Bob D'Amelio had started at 7:00 AM, and the tracker board was already displaying nine patients. The day was heating up fast.

"What have you been doing for the last two hours?" I said. "Just waiting for me to show up?"

"I told all those patients you see up there on the board, 'If you want really good care, Dr. Randolph will be here about 9:00 AM.'"

They kept pouring in all morning and it was busy as hell. Late morning I got my expected call from Jack Schmidt.

"Hi, Jack"

"Hey, Doc, how ya doin'?" This had become my usual familiar greeting from Jack.

I got a little info for ya. You will be interested to know that there is no two thousand block of Northwood Drive. The owner of Social Security number 419-22-6843 is a little old lady in White Falls, Iowa. And Jawara Reynolds is an alias of a guy named William Reynolds who's got a rap sheet about a mile long. Done time for a variety of felonies including drug distribution, armed robbery, and assault. He *is* a Crip."

"What a surprise. Well, I guess the Crips have found us along with Mara Salvatrucha."

"Lookin' that way, Doc."

"I just hope they don't get competitive on our turf."

~

Fran Williams was the charge nurse again today. She slid a chart into the new patient rack and said, "An old friend back to see you."

"Yeah? Who's that?"

"Madeline Finney. You admitted her a couple of months ago with sepsis. She says you saved her life."

"Oh yeah!" I said, "I remember Mrs. Finney."

"She's back with shortness of breath. Her O_2 sat is only eighty-nine percent on room air. She's puffing away pretty good."

I walked into Bed Eight. Mr. Finney was there, standing beside his wife. I shook hands with him. April was starting an IV.

"Hi, Mrs. Finney," I said, leaning over her bedside rail.

"Hi, Dr. Randolph," she said warmly in short gasps, reaching out to grasp my hand with both of hers. "I didn't expect to see you again so soon. You saved my life last time," she smiled adoringly. Her hand was a little clammy. She had a non-rebreather oxygen mask on her face that muffled her voice.

"Saint Peter just didn't have your name on the list last time," I smiled. "Looks like you're a little short of breath." She nodded.

I looked up at the monitor and saw that her O_2 sat was up to ninety-three. Her blood pressure was considerably elevated at two hundred and ten over one hundred and fifteen.

"When did you start getting short of breath?"

"About ten o'clock this morning."

"Were you OK yesterday?"

"Fine."

I glanced at her neck and could see her external jugular veins distended like ropes almost to her jaw line. Reaching down, I pushed the tip of my thumb deep into the skin just above her ankle. It left a little dent indicating that she had peripheral edema—extra fluid on board. April was placing the last piece of tape on her IV.

"April, let's sit her up." We propped Mrs. Finney up into the sitting position and I listened to her lungs. Coarse, bubbly sounds ran about two thirds of the way up both sides of her chest along with some wheezes. We gently laid her back and I put my stethoscope to the front of her chest. Her heart sounded like a thoroughbred galloping around a mile-and-an-eighth track. This *S3 gallop*, as we call it, confirmed that Mrs. Finney was in congestive heart failure, with fluid backing up into her lungs behind her failing heart.

"April, let's get her started on a nitro drip and give her forty of Lasix. You can give her a nebulizer with albuterol. And let's give her twenty-five of captopril sublingually, too." April scurried off to get the drugs.

"Mrs. Finney, you've got a little bit of congestive heart failure. You give us just about an hour, and you're going to be feeling a whole lot better. Do you remember that you've had a little heart failure in the past?" She nodded.

"OK. So this is nothing too new. We're going to be able to take care of this." I patted her on the hand.

"OK, Doctor," she wheezed. Mr. Finney nodded and smiled, and I left the room.

It's interesting how people come to view you when you've treated them for a life-threatening illness. You may have done nothing special, and you may have just been doing your job, but the emotional bond that patients develop with you is deep and long lasting. The trust is almost child-like. There is an intimacy that is profound. I love it. It's one of the great rewards of medicine. When our old family doctor found out that I was going to medical school he used to tell me, *...the preacher gets into the parlor, but the doctor gets into the bedroom.*

~

About 3:30 I had finally had it and went back to the break room to get a cup of coffee before diving back into it. Cathy Rutledge was there in her usual civilian clothes and white clinic coat, pouring the last cup of coffee from the carafe of the Bunn machine. I hadn't seen Cathy since the party.

"Hi, Alex," she said brightly. "Sorry. Looks like I got the last *good to the last drop* drop."

"No worry. Making coffee is one of the few things I am really good at."

I gave her a hug.

"That was a great party on Saturday night," I said, emptying out the old grounds into a bulging trash can. "You should switch careers and be a party planner. You could make a fortune."

"The secret is in the guests," she said smiling. "Invite nice people and you have a nice party."

"But nobody does it like you, Cath."

I put two and three-quarters scoops of coffee into the basket and snapped it shut. Then I filled the carafe with cold water and used it to start pouring water into the machine.

"You'll never make it," said Cathy. "There'll be coffee spilling all over the place before you get that carafe back under the basket."

"Never happen."

I essentially turned the carafe upside down, rapidly pouring water into the inlet, a substantial portion of which overflowed down the outside of the machine. Then I quickly slid the carafe into place just as the first drop of coffee dripped from the basket. I turned to Cathy and smiled.

"Very impressive, Alex. I assume you're planning on mopping up all that water you've got all over the place."

"Of course," I said, tearing off a section of paper towels. "I'm well trained, after three years of being reminded that my mother doesn't work here."

"Elizabeth didn't stay very long on Saturday night. Looked to me like you two weren't hitting it off too well," said Cathy.

"Actually that was the first time I had seen her in over a month. We didn't spend a lot of time together, did we?"

"Is it over?"

"I think it probably is, Cathy."

"You spent a lot more time with Penny."

I looked at her for a long moment, then poured a fresh cup of coffee.

"Penny is a remarkable woman," I said finally, stirring in two creams and two sugars.

"Why don't you ask her out? You two obviously were enthralled with each other at the party."

I narrowly avoided spitting my coffee all over Cathy. I stood and stared at her.

"You're kidding."

"No."

"I don't do married women, Cath."

"Oh my God! You don't know, do you?"

"Know what?"

"Alex," said Cathy softly, "Penny is a widow. Her husband was killed in Afghanistan over a year and a half ago."

CHAPTER TWENTY-FOUR

I WOKE UP EARLY ON SATURDAY MORNING, HAD A cup of coffee, and headed to the barn to do my chores. Sally would no doubt be around today. Another week had passed by, and my guess was that this might be the last morning that I would be permitted to start out my day with General Lee and Abigail.

I felt about a hundred pounds lighter. Regardless of what may or may not ever happen between Penny and me, I felt enormous relief not to be dealing with powerful internal conflict. But there was no denying that I was enormously attracted to her. It was bizarre. In actuality, our contact had been rather minimal, yet I wasn't sure that I could remember another woman exciting me in quite this way. This wasn't sitting too well with my rational side. Lord knows, though, it was complex. How could I be thrilled that her husband and the father of her kids was killed?

I couldn't imagine the grief that Penny must have endured in the last year. She must have loved her husband deeply—she was still wearing his rings. He was the father of her children. I wondered if anyone could ever replace the man she had loved in her youth. And now he was gone and she was a single parent with two kids to raise. Yet, almost two years after his death, there was not a trace of self-pity that I could discern. She was a remarkable woman.

I ran my hand down Robert E. Lee's neck.

"I don't know about you, General, but so far, I have found women to be a huge pain in my ass. You'd think that I would learn, but, you know, I just keep going back for more. Maybe I'm a slow learner." The gelding tore a mouthful of hay out of the rack and tossed his head a couple of times. "But then again, maybe it makes it easier to forget 'em if they cut your balls off, huh?" That was a solution that didn't excite me.

~

I was running low on firewood, so I decided to fire up my log-splitter and get some more wood stacked up next to the mudroom door. I had a pile of cut logs on the north side of the barn that I had dragged out of the woods. I parked the New Holland next to the log-splitter and threw the logs into the front-end loader as they came off the splitter. Those little hydraulic log-splitters are wonderful devices, although perhaps without the glamour of those old photos of Ronald Reagan splitting wood with an axe.

Sally pulled into the driveway as the last log was coming off the splitter. I shut off the engine and watched her climb out of the truck. She didn't exactly hop out, but it was a much faster process than last week. And I was happy to see that those lovely tight jeans were back. She limped just slightly as she walked toward me, smiling.

"I can see that you must have had great medical care," I said. "You're making rapid progress."

"The best," she grinned. "And my physician is also a talented stable hand."

"Wow. I take that as a major compliment." Sally laughed.

"The General and his consort have already had their morning allotment of feed and hay," I said.

"And that was the last morning for that," replied Sally. "I'm back now. I can't thank you enough, Alex."

"Considering that the whole thing was my fault, I think I've gotten off lightly. Besides, I think it was of more value to me than to you. I'm going to feel lost without those chores and my daily conversation with the General and Abigail."

"Well, I can tell you that by the end of the first week, I was just one step short of the nuthouse door, so you can't have 'em. The chores are mine," she said emphatically. I laughed. Sally was feisty. I liked that.

"When I was sixteen I could never have imagined that I would be standing here arguing with a lovely woman over who got to get up at 5:30 in the morning to do barn chores."

"When I was sixteen, you couldn't have gotten me out of bed on Saturday mornings before noon," she said with a grin.

~

I went for a run about one o'clock. The truth is, I hate running. But if I'm not playing a lot of tennis, I will run maybe twice a week to keep from becoming a total slob. About a mile into my run along Shepherd Road, I vowed to join the indoor tennis club next winter.

It was two weeks before Christmas. I saw a couple of neighbors outdoors putting up Christmas lights and waved. I suddenly realized that I had a whole list of things that had to be done in the next two weeks, including one hundred percent of my Christmas shopping and getting candles put in the windows of my own house.

Ruth had lunch ready for me when I got back; a BLT on white toast and a bowl of French onion soup. I eat well for lunch on Saturdays. She wanted me to sit down and eat it immediately, but I couldn't stand to sit down in wet running clothes. So I went upstairs, took a shower as quickly as I could, and came back down, hoping that Ruth wasn't completely pissed that my sandwich was now cold.

"Your sandwich is cold," she said flatly.

"I'm sorry, Ruth. I just couldn't stand to eat in those wet clothes."

"Did you have a nice time at your party last week?" she asked.

"Well, Ruth, it was a great party. Lots of nice people."

"Brian and Susan were there?"

"Yes, they were. This is delicious," I said between bites, hoping to appease her.

"And your friend John and his pretty little wife—that French girl—what's her name?"

"Annick. They were there too."

"And she's going to have a baby?"

"Yep. She's about twelve weeks pregnant now."

"So," she said with satisfaction, "they're going to have kids..."

"I think that's the likely outcome of her pregnancy."

"Good. Well, I'm glad you had a good time. You deserve it. You work too hard. Did you meet any new nice girls?"

"Actually, Ruth, I met a very nice girl. She has two kids. Her name is Penny." Ruth raised her eyebrows, but said nothing more.

~

The holiday season was packed with social obligations. Tonight I was headed to my parents' house for their annual Christmas party. This has been a tradition since I was in my early teens. Apart from family, most of the guests are my parents' friends, but, of course, they also always invite close friends of their three kids too, so, in my case, that meant John, who had practically grown up in our house.

My mother has strong nesting instincts as well as an artistic streak, so she goes all out at Christmas with the decorating. It also makes it easier when you own a nursery. The front porch and railings were decked out in pine boughs, pine rope, and yards of red ribbon. Inside there were pineapples, pine cones, holly, and red apples. There were a lot of people there. Nat King Cole was playing on the stereo.

I gave my mother a kiss, clapped my dad on the back, and shook hands with many old family friends. Most of them mentioned their wonderful experience in the Mason-Dixon ER at sometime or another in the last year. I got a review of the complete medical history on several. I hadn't gotten any farther than the punch bowl when Anne spotted me across the room. She was on me right away.

"So who was that girl you were talking to on Saturday night?"

"What girl?" I asked, ladling out a glass of punch.

"The one whose eyes you were staring into."

"Well, I looked a lot of people in the eyes."

"Blond hair, white shirt, jeans, great body. Maybe that will stimulate your feeble memory."

"Penny Murray."

"Who is she?"

"She's an ER nurse." I paused. "Actually, she's many things."

"She excites you, doesn't she?" Anne generally likes to get right to the point. Questions like that make me nervous.

"It's very complicated," I replied.

"Why is that?"

"She's a widow with two kids who still wears her wedding rings."

"Wow. That's a new one for you. And how do you feel about that?"

"I don't know yet."

CHAPTER TWENTY-FIVE

IT'S USUALLY PRETTY SLOW AT 9:00 AM SUNDAY mornings. The conversation around the nursing station got steamy.

"My girlfriend told me that if you have sex and you do it with a shallow penetration, you're more likely to have a girl," said April.

"Yeah, but it has to be two days before you ovulate," Jen commented.

"I don't understand. The boys swim faster, don't they?" asked Rebecca. "So why don't you get a boy?"

"The boys swim faster, so if you do a shallow deposit of sperm the boys get to the tubes and die before an egg gets there, but the girls are slower, and by the time *they* get to the tubes there's an egg there. That's why it has to be two days *before* ovulation."

"My husband calls that *leavin' it on the rim*," said Lauren. "It worked for us."

"And you're supposed to be in the missionary position," added Jen. "The girl can't be on top."

"Sounds like it's all up to the guy," said Rebecca. "You gotta figure out how to get him to do it with just the head in."

ER nurses can make you blush. Maybe all women talk like this. I've never had this kind of conversation with a guy.

Today was the first day that I had seen Penny since the party. Our shifts just didn't cross in the past week. I knew she would be working today because I checked the nursing schedule, something I never do. I was a little apprehensive—an unaccustomed feeling. Despite my strong sense that we had connected, in truth I had no confirmation of Penny's feelings. Maybe it was wishful thinking.

Shortly after the beginning of the shift, she was walking past the nursing station when she looked up and saw me. I had already forgotten how lovely she was. Our eyes met for a moment and she gave me a broad smile. I liked that. So far so good.

~

I saw Viola McDonald, an elderly lady with a purplish cast to her white hair, who passed out in church—a common Sunday morning occurrence among folks of her generation. I'm never sure whether the root cause is fire and brimstone, or whether singing at the top of their lungs is a bit more exercise than they're prepared for, but it's usually a benign faint and most of them go home. Viola left feeling fine.

Jen slid a new chart into the rack in front of me.

"This kid looks sick," she said. "She's been vomiting for two days and she's dry as a bone. Rebecca and April are in there getting a line in her. She's not very responsive."

Shyanne Walker was four-years-old, I noted as I walked to Bed Twelve. She was afebrile—her temp was only ninety-seven point six. Her oxygen saturation was one hundred percent. But she was tachycardic—her pulse was one hundred and forty-four—and her blood pressure was in the high seventies; low, but not out of the possible range of normal for a four-year-old.

The room was crowded. Mom sat on a chair beside the stretcher in a stained, gray polyester sweatsuit, clutching a bottle of Pepsi. Long stringy hair fell over her shoulders. Dad was standing in the corner in jeans and a tee shirt that did little to cover his belly, holding a toddler with snot running out of his nose. Another toddler played on the floor with a toy.

On the exam table Shyanne lay in a pair of filthy pajamas with dirt caked under her fingernails. Her skin had clearly not seen soap and water for weeks. She lay there with her eyes closed, obviously breathing very rapidly. April held a skinny little arm while Rebecca searched for a vein. Shyanne wasn't moving. I introduced myself to the parents, then turned to Rebecca.

"Did she move when you stuck her?" I asked.

"She opened her eyes and cried for a second, then drifted off again."

I introduced myself, then looked over at mom. "When did Shyanne get sick?"

"Oh, she's been sick for a while," said mom.

"How long is a while?"

Mom looked over at her husband. "Well, she started complaining that her stomach hurt, what, three or four days ago?" Her husband nodded.

"Has she had any other symptoms?" Mom shrugged and looked at her husband again. *Maybe I need to rephrase that.*

"Has she seemed sick in any other way?

"Well, she's just been lying around—sleeping a lot."

"Has she been vomiting?"

"Well, *yeah*," said mom indignantly, as if I just didn't get it. "She can't keep anything down."

"When did she start vomiting?"

"I guess it was… Friday night."

"And how many times a day would you guess she has been vomiting?"

"She pukes up every time she drinks."

"But, if you had to guess, how many times a day? Five? Ten? Fifteen?"

"At least five."

"Has she had any diarrhea?" Mom shook her head no.

"Has she had any fever at any time since she's been sick?" Mom shifted in her seat.

"I don't know. Our thermometer's broken. But she didn't feel hot."

"Has she had a runny nose, or sore throat, or cough?"

"She had a cough."

"When was that?"

"I don't know. About two weeks ago." I looked over at Shyanne's frail-looking body, lying quietly on the table except for her rapid breathing. Her eyes looked sunken.

"Has Shyanne always been this skinny?"

"I think she's gotten skinnier in the last few weeks, but I feed her plenty," said mom defensively.

"Has she been wetting the bed?"

"Well, she was potty trained, but then she started wetting the bed again a couple of weeks ago. I had to put her back in diapers. I keep telling her, if she feels like she has to pee, she has to get up."

"Is she drinking a lot?"

"She's constantly got a sippy cup in her mouth."

The girls had the IV established now and were taping it to Shyanne's arm. They had drawn four tubes of blood in the process. Rebecca was stretching up to hang a bag of normal saline on the IV pole. Tall and slender, with long auburn hair tied back in a ponytail, Rebecca was a marathon runner who made the rest of us in the department feel fat, flabby, and guilty. On the other hand, watching her scrub pants stretch over her butt as she reached up, more than made up for my decline in self esteem.

"How fast do you want this going?" she asked. I pinched a fold of Shayanne's skin between my thumb and forefinger and let go. It stood up in a tent. It should have popped right back. She was very dry.

"Let's run four hundred in over thirty minutes for now."

I had a pretty good idea of what was going on here. I leaned down and smelled Shyanne's breath. It had a fruity odor. I quickly lifted her head and flexed her neck. It was easy to touch her chin to her chest. I rolled her onto her side and listened to her lungs. They were both crystal clear with loud breath sounds from her rapid, deep breathing. Apart from being fast, her heart exam was normal. I began to palpate her belly, apparently the site of the first symptoms of her acute illness. It was completely soft. I could feel no masses. No matter where I pushed, she didn't flinch or grimace with pain.

"Rebecca. Do a finger-stick sugar for me," I said.

"I can get a drop from one of these tubes."

"OK."

Rebecca left the room, and I continued the remaining items on my physical examination. They all came up normal except for her dry mucous membranes, a ton of dental cavities, and her nearly comatose mental status.

"Folks, I'm going to get some orders written for Shyanne, and as soon as I get that blood sugar result from Rebecca, I'll be right back and we'll talk." April started in asking the questions for her nursing assessment and I left the room.

Two minutes later Rebecca walked up to the nursing station.

"It's off the scale—her sugar's over five hundred," she said.

It all fit together. Shyanne was in diabetic coma—also called *ketoacidosis*. Poor little Shyanne's pancreas was producing no insulin. That was allowing her blood sugar to go sky high, and she was spilling tons of sugar—and calories—into her urine. That's why she'd been losing weight. It was also why she had started wetting the bed and was now dangerously dehydrated. The sugar in the urine pulls water out with it by osmosis, and then you begin to pee constantly—even as you're getting dehydrated. And, of course, all that water loss makes you thirsty as hell.

"OK. I need an accurate weight on her. Do you think you can get that?"

"Yeah. I'll just stand on a bedside scale, then hold her in my arms and do the subtraction."

"OK. Let me know what you weigh."

"No! I'll let you know what *she* weighs."

"OK. Also, Rebecca, I want you to straight cath her and get a urine. Do a quick check for ketones and let me know."

I knew what the result would be, but I needed the confirmation. Shyanne's blood was almost certainly highly acidic. Insulin is necessary for the body's metabolic factories to burn glucose. When there is no insulin, we start burning fat and protein instead, and the end result is production of ketones—powerful acids which can kill us.

Shyanne was using her respiratory system to try and compensate for the acidosis by breathing deeply and fast. This blows off more of the body's carbon dioxide, which, when dissolved in the blood, is itself an acid called *carbonic acid.* So by hyperventilating, we get rid of a lot of carbonic acid which helps to compensate for the accumulating ketones, if you can follow that. Vomiting and abdominal pain commonly accompany the acidosis. And, those nasty ketones have a fruity odor which I was able to smell. What Shyanne now desperately needed was insulin and rehydration.

I wrote some orders for laboratory work, handed them to Stacey, and began writing up my history and physical examination. Rebecca was back in a few minutes.

"She weighs about eighteen kilos."

"Alright. Let's give her one point eight units of regular insulin in a bolus, and then hang a drip of one point eight units per hour. And what was your weight?"

"Wouldn't you like to know?" she said smiling.

April appeared, cracking her gum.

"I dipped her urine. It's way positive for ketones," she said.

"Not surprising."

"Jeez, do those kids need a bath! Did you see their fingernails? That's disgusting."

"Mom and dad too, for that matter," I said. "Maybe we should just take a power washer in there and clean 'em all up."

"What do you want that saline running at when this first four hundred is in?" she asked.

"We'll cut it back to seventy-five cc's per hour after the four hundred. If we rehydrate her too fast she'll get cerebral edema. I'll make adjustments when we get the first lab results back."

It was time to let mom and dad know what was going on, assuming that mom and dad were really mom and dad. I walked back to the room.

"OK. Do we have mom and dad here?

"I'm her mother," answered the woman. This is my boyfriend."

OK. Well, I've got enough preliminary information now to know that Shyanne has diabetes." Mom and boyfriend showed no emotion at this statement. "Are you familiar with diabetes?"

"My mother has diabetes," said boyfriend.

"Well then you know that in diabetes our bodies don't manufacture enough insulin. In Shyanne's case, her body has almost completely stopped making insulin, and as a result she has drifted into what we call *diabetic coma.* Her blood sugar is very high, and she is very dehydrated." Mom's face remained expressionless.

"Shyanne is definitely very seriously ill," I said, "but, with a little luck, the odds are pretty good that we'll be able to get her over this crisis."

"How long will we be here?" asked mom. She was running low on Pepsi.

~

For the next twenty minutes I got a string of phone calls from the lab with critical values on Shyanne. Her blood pH was very low at six point nine five, and her potassium was quite high. Both results were not unexpected, but that's a really low pH, so I would be keeping my fingers crossed that this turned around in the next hour or so.

Two hours later her heart rate had dropped into the one-twenties, and she was actually beginning to stir a little. These were both good signs. A repeat pH was up to seven point one. We were turning the corner. Mortality in pediatric diabetic ketoacidosis is about five or ten percent. That puts the odds in our favor, but also means that one in ten is not going to be a pleasant experience.

Allison Taylor, the pediatrician on call, showed up a little after noon. I gave her the rundown on the case, and she walked to Shyanne's room. Two minutes later she was back at the nursing station.

"Have you seen the parents?" she asked.

"Mom and boyfriend," I corrected.

"They're not in the room."

"They're probably outside smoking a cigarette, or they may have made a Pepsi run."

"A Pepsi run?"

"Yeah. They were running low on Pepsi."

"Oh, God," she sighed.

"I'm afraid you've got a long row to hoe on this one, Ali."

Learning how to manage her daughter's insulin-dependent diabetes would require a huge investment of time, study, discipline, and patience on the part of Shyanne's mother. I was not optimistic about the outcome. I had the feeling we would be seeing a lot of little Shyanne in the ER.

~

We hit a little lull about 2:30. Rebecca was preparing for a marathon and sat at the nursing station talking with Penny about running.

"Well, I'm not in your class, Rebecca, but I *do* love to run," said Penny. "I only manage to squeeze it in once or twice a week though. I wish I had more time."

"Where do you run?"

"Usually on the old North Central Railroad Trail along the Gunpowder Falls," replied Penny. "There's a section just north of White Hall that's just so beautiful, with a small falls—maybe five feet high—about a half mile north of where you park."

"You want to run together one morning?"

"I'd love to. But I don't know if I'll be able to keep up."

"You look to me like you'll do just fine."

"How about you, Alex? You wanna run with us?" asked Rebecca with a smile and a hint of challenge in her voice.

I looked over at Rebecca. I felt an embarrassing little surge of excitement at the thought of being with Penny outside the hospital.

"You talking to me?" I asked. "You're obviously interested in embarrassing me."

"Penny, would Wednesday morning at 9:00 work for you?"

"I think I can arrange a babysitter."

"Alex, are you off on Wednesday?"

"I am."

"You want to run about 9:00 Wednesday morning?"

I hesitated. What the heck. "Sure. I'm in." *You're an idiot, Randolph. You hate running. These two are going to run your ass into the ground. And this is not a date with Penny.*

CHAPTER TWENTY-SIX

ALL THREE OF US PULLED INTO THE NORTH Central Railroad Trail parking area, in the once-bustling little railroad hamlet of White Hall, within a couple of minutes of each other on Wednesday morning. It was a good day for running—if there is such a thing—about forty degrees and sunny. Both girls jumped out of their cars in black running tights and started to stretch. It was a lovely sight. I began to feel that the morning might not be a total loss.

The old North Central Railroad was originally built as the Baltimore and Susquehanna railroad, just before the Civil War, and ran from Baltimore City to York, Pennsylvania and beyond. It ran for most of its route along the Gunpowder Falls through picturesque little hamlets like Monkton, White Hall, and Parkton, which became busy little centers of commerce by the turn of the century. Until 1959 you could actually hop on the Parkton Local in the rural northern part of the county, and go all the way to Calvert Street Station downtown in Baltimore.

Ironically, many northern county residents actually worked in the city at the turn of the century—riding the North Central—during a day when it would have taken four or five hours to get to Baltimore by horse and buggy. Now it takes almost as long to get to Baltimore on I-83 during morning rush hour traffic in your Mercedes, listening to your iPod. There's progress for you.

Hurricane Agnes changed things forever in 1972. Raging floods damaged bridges and track to the extent that trains never ran again on the North Central tracks. Ten or twelve years later, the county acquired all the rights and converted the rails to trails. Now you can walk or bike on a level, crushed gravel trail for twenty-one miles from Cockeysville to the Pennsylvania line. It's wonderful.

I know all this stuff because I grew up in Sparks, not a mile from the trail, and spent many boyhood hours with John and my buddies spying on hikers, and flying up and down the trail on BMX bikes.

"Are we going all the way to Pennsylvania this morning, or are you ladies going to take pity on me and maybe stop in Parkton?" I asked.

"Alex, for God's sake, stop whining," said Rebecca good-naturedly. "We understand the frailties of your gender and we're going to take good care of you." She turned to Penny. "I've actually never run on this northern section."

"Well, I was thinking of something on the order of maybe five miles," said Penny. My heart sank. "We're at the ten point five mile marker here, and if we run to the thirteen mile marker, just above Parkton, and then back, that would be about five miles. It's really pretty through that section."

"Five miles is good," said Rebecca. Both girls looked at me.

"Five miles I can do," I said.

"OK. Everybody ready?" said Rebecca. "Let's hit it."

~

Within less than five minutes we had passed the old bank—now a residence—and the antique shop, which used to be the community general store, and were out of town and into the hilly countryside. Just past Weisburg Road, the land began to rise steeply on either side. Huge rock outcroppings formed a narrow gorge rising a hundred feet high or more above the trail, cut by water eons ago. This was all forest, unlogged because of the formidable terrain.

"Wow, this is gorgeous!" Rebecca said loudly, her voice muffled by the constant babbling of water on rocks and the pounding of shoes on crushed gravel.

"Wait 'til you see the falls up ahead!" Penny shouted back.

The two girls ran side by side along the eight-foot-wide trail, ponytails bobbing. I took up a position about ten or twelve feet behind them. Of course, the black tights ahead of me did nothing to obscure the flexing of strong gluteal muscles. I had to laugh to myself. This was a little bit like the greyhound chasing the rabbit—just out of reach—at the dog track.

The white gravel trail beneath our feet was dappled with light shining through the trees from the weak December sun. It didn't take long for me to realize that although the trail appeared level, we were actually slowly climbing onto the Piedmont Plateau at maybe a two or three percent grade. The girls were setting a strong pace, and I was glad that I had invested a little time in running through the fall. They chatted intermittently about this and that. Occasionally I caught bits and pieces of Penny talking about her kids. Periodically when the trail widened a little I would pull up beside them.

About a half mile or so past Weisburg Road I began to hear a low roar, and soon the falls came into view with powerful plumes of water cascading perhaps five feet over rock outcroppings. Sunlight rippled on the frothing water below. A solitary Great Blue Heron majestically flapped his way beneath the tree canopy down the creek, legs trailing straight out behind him. We slowed and took in the magnificence of the scene, and then the girls picked up the pace again.

By two miles, we had crossed the York Road at Parkton. Rebecca appeared tireless as she effortlessly set the pace on the slow, shallow climb of the trail. I watched Penny's movements. She had the easy grace of an athlete. Despite her shorter stride, she, too, showed little evidence of tiring. The girl might not be in Rebecca's class, but she was in damned good shape.

I was pushing myself to keep up and was beginning to tire after two miles of a slow uphill climb. But there was no way I was going to give my lovely companions the satisfaction of seeing me with my tongue hanging out. Thank God there was a turnaround in another half mile. Then it would at least be a little downhill on the trip home.

Periodically Rebecca would turn her head and ask with a big smile,

"How're you doing, Alex? Are we going too slow for you?"

"Do they have wheelchairs at the thirteen mile mark?" I asked.

"Actually," yelled back Penny, "Medic 60's station is right up the road. I'll give A.J. Fortmann a call on my cell phone and the ambulance can come get you."

~

By the time White Hall came back into view, I was beat and soaked with sweat. I usually only run about two miles. Another three miles at Rebecca's pace was killing me. We slowed, then walked for a while to cool down. I plunked my butt down on the edge of the railroad tie retaining wall around the parking lot and stretched out my legs, my lungs sucking for air.

"Wow. Great suggestion, Penny," said Rebecca, still walking around. "That's a beautiful run."

"It is! And it's a lot more fun running with company. I'm glad you invited me."

"You're good. You can run with me anytime." Rebecca looked over at me and smiled. "OK, Alex, you, too. Not bad for an aging ER doc."

"Do you know a good psychiatrist?" I asked.

"Well, guys, I hate to run and run, as it were, but I've got an appointment to see a black lab with Peter at noon," said Rebecca. "Did I tell you we're getting a puppy? I'm so excited!"

"Life is going to change," I said.

"Good preparation for kids," said Penny.

"Let's not go there!" said Rebecca. She waved, jumped in her car, and was gone.

And so, there I sat, face to face with Penny. She sat down on the retainment wall beside me, a couple of feet away. Her pink cheeks glowed, and a fine sheen of sweat covered her face.

"You're in good shape," I said.

"You didn't do so badly yourself," she said smiling. There was an awkward pause and a long silence as we looked at each other.

"Penny… I… Cathy just told me the other day that your husband was killed. I'm sorry." *Wow. No transitions, Alex. You are very good at putting this woman on the spot.*

Penny looked down for a long moment, as if contemplating her reply, then raised her head.

"Yes," she said quietly, "he was." She paused again and searched my eyes, as if trying to decide whether to continue. Finally she spoke again.

"You want to know, don't you?"

I nodded.

"His name was Patrick," she began. "We met when he was at the Naval Academy. My dad was teaching there at the time, and I was a sophomore at Notre Dame. We fell in love and married the day after he graduated. I told you that he became a SEAL. You know about his wounds in Iraq. After that, they wanted to give him a desk job, but he insisted on returning to his unit. He was stateside for nearly four years, training new SEALs. A little over eighteen months ago he was reassigned to duty in Afghanistan.

"His job was to harass the Taliban at high elevation in the mountains—deny them sanctuary. His patrol got ambushed. Patrick was the leader. It was a long firefight. He was carrying a wounded buddy on his shoulders—trying to reach cover—when he was hit. Only two of them made it out."

I took a deep breath and sighed. What do you say to that? Our eyes remained in contact. I could see tiny flecks of black in her green eyes. The earliest hints of tiny, fine crows feet at the corner of her eyes etched her face with character. She continued.

"Both of them were at the funeral, and both spoke at the graveside. They credited their lives to Patrick. Their families were there with them. My only regret is that Jack was not old enough to remember what they had to say about his father. But I remembered every word. And I wrote it all down."

We sat in silence for a long time. It was no surprise that Penny still wore her wedding ring. She had just told me about a man who I could never hope to replace. Yet, strangely, I don't think I had ever had a more intimate moment with a woman in my life. For whatever reason, she had permitted me a small glimpse into her soul.

"And you have two children?"

"Yes," she replied with a smile, her face lighting up. "Catherine Anne is six. And Jack is three. They are my salvation."

CHAPTER TWENTY-SEVEN

BY THE WEEK OF CHRISTMAS, THE WEATHER had turned sharply colder. An Alberta Clipper blew through, bringing the first two or three inches of snow and, behind it, the first Arctic air of the season.

Christmas was on a Friday, and by Tuesday I had finished my shopping. Not that I had all that much: my parents, Brian and Susan, Anne, and Ruth—no girlfriend, kids, or nieces and nephews. Last year it took forever for me to find some things that seemed right for Elizabeth. Actually, when she opened them, they didn't seem all that right. But, in any case, that wasn't on this year's agenda. I did buy a nice ten-dollar bottle of wine for each of my docs.

Julie was the last one left on my list. It's always hard to decide what to buy for someone who means a lot to you, but who is a work colleague and happens to be a female. You can't just drop into Victoria's Secret and pick up a couple of nice little things. I finally decided on a gift certificate from Barnes & Noble.

Strangely, while cruising the stores on Tuesday evening, I kept seeing things that I thought would be nice for Penny. Each time I would bat myself in the head a couple of times, and by the end of the evening I had a headache.

I hadn't asked her out, despite Cathy's encouragement. It didn't feel right—at least not at this stage in Penny's life, knowing what I knew. I felt that it would be intrusive. She still wore her rings for a reason. She clearly needed time, and she needed privacy. That being said, I thought about her pretty much every day.

~

I had signed up for the day shift on Christmas Eve, and I also had myself scheduled for a half shift on Christmas Day. Lynn Saylor was working with me on both days because, besides Ben, we were the only single docs on the staff. Everybody else had kids, which made Christmas the most important holiday of the year for them. I guess we both figured that our turn might come someday, although at the moment that did not look like a very bright near-term prospect for either of us. Maybe we should hook up so we could have Christmas off.

Despite all of us having to work a holiday, everybody was in a pretty good mood on Christmas Eve morning. I carried in a nice, large, leftover poinsettia from the nursery that I had gotten from my parents at a very nice price. Actually, my mother gave it to me. It was early and slow, so everyone was sitting around the nursing station when I walked in. I noticed that Penny was among them. That brightened my day. I'd get to spend at least some of Christmas Eve with her.

"Oh, look!" said Fran Williams, glasses around her neck, "Alex brought us some Christmas cheer."

"This is not a bottle of Grey Goose," I said. "It's the wrong color."

"Ooooh, it's beautiful," cooed Rebecca. "I bet that's from Randolph Nursery,"

"Yes, it is."

"Well, we'd all rather drink our Christmas cheer, but, Alex, this is the next best thing. That was very sweet of you," added Fran. She took the poinsettia from me, gave me a kiss on the cheek, fluffed it a bit, and placed it in the middle of the center nursing station counter.

Julie walked into the nursing station all smiles. "Guess what, gang."

"Lisa had her baby!" yelled April.

"Yep. Last night about 10:30—just before Christmas Eve."

"Let me guess," I said, "Frank got his boy."

"Nope. Now he's got three little princesses. Six pounds, three ounces. Megan Frances Turano."

"Poor Frank," I said.

"You mean poor Lisa!" retorted Fran. "He'll probably make her try again for a boy."

"He must have been leavin' it on the rim," said Rebecca.

"She's going to hate her birthday," said April. "Everybody's going to try and combine birthday and Christmas presents."

~

The first predictable trickle of kids with fever and snotty noses started about 7:30. Moms had a lot of work to do today, and a sick kid was not going to help with the workload. They wanted to get here early and get this over with.

The tones on the monitor went off about 7:45 for the first ambulance call of the morning. Medic 60 was dispatched to Stottlemyer Road for a CVA—a *cerebrovascular accident*, better known as a stroke. Within ten or twelve minutes A.J. Fortmann was on the radio.

"Commander seven-oh-one, I've got a seventy-two-year-old white male with onset about 7:30, while eating breakfast, of left-sided weakness associated with drooping of the left side of his face. He was well prior to onset of symptoms. He has a past medical history of diabetes and hypertension."

"Upon physical examination this is a well developed, well nourished elderly male who is lethargic, but follows commands. He has garbled speech. Vital signs are pulse of seventy-eight, respirations of eighteen, blood pressure of one-ninety over one-oh-five. He has a left facial paresis and a dense left hemiparesis. Lungs are clear. Heart rhythm is regular. Abdomen is benign. There is no peripheral edema."

"Blood sugar is one-sixty. O_2 sat is one hundred percent on a non-rebreather. I have an IV established of normal saline. We're at your back door. Will give you more info at bedside."

"Mason-Dixon copies. Mason-Dixon out," Fran replied at the radio.

"OK, who's picking up this guy?" I said.

"I've got him," said April.

"Alright. The clock starting ticking at 7:30. Give CT a call. Tell 'em to warm up the machine. I want him to go directly to CT."

A.J.'s report was a pretty classic description of a stroke—a vascular disruption to the brain that leaves you paralyzed. There's two kinds of these nasty events: one produced by a clot that blocks an artery and cuts off the circulation to your brain, and the other caused by a blood vessel that ruptures with bleeding into your brain. If it's a clot, we can sometimes give you drugs that dissolve the clot and quickly re-establish blood flow, reversing the stroke. If it's a bleed into your brain, you've got a much tougher problem. A CT of the head tells us which of the two we're dealing with.

But we don't have a lot of time. Brain tissue that's not getting plenty of fresh oxygenated blood dies very fast—almost two million neurons a minute. Every minute that goes by without circulation means more dead brain cells.

I heard the sliding doors into the ER open and A.J. and his crew came into view, wheeling their stretcher down the hallway. April directed them to Bed Ten. I walked along.

"What's his name?" I asked A.J.

"Stanley Schwartz."

"Anything else in his past medical history?"

"He had a coronary artery stent placed in 'ninety-six. Had his gallbladder out. Otherwise pretty clean."

Four of us grabbed the sheet under Mr. Schwartz and slid him off the stretcher and over into the bed. Mr. Schwartz looked healthy as a horse, with shiny pink skin, a smooth, clean-shaven face, and carefully groomed, thinning hair, combed straight back. It wasn't until you spoke with him that it became clear that Mr. Schwartz had been struck with a devastating injury to his brain.

"Hi, Mr. Schwartz. I'm Dr. Randolph," I said leaning over his bed. "Can you tell me where you live?"

Mr. Schwartz slowly turned his head toward me and tried to speak. Gibberish came out, and his face became contorted as the muscles on the right side contracted while the left side just sat there unmoving. I grabbed both of Mr. Schwartz's hands.

"Mr. Schwartz, can you squeeze my hands?" I felt a firm grip from his right hand. Nothing from his left. I put my hands on the top of his right leg.

"Can you lift your leg for me against my hands?" His right leg pushed up vigorously against me with good strength.

"How about this leg?" I said, placing my hands over his left leg. I could feel the slightest pressure against my hand, but he was unable to lift his leg off the bed.

"CT is ready for him," announced April.

"Mr. Schwartz," I said, leaning over his bed again, "it looks like you're having a stroke." He looked up at me, his face expressionless. "We're gong to be doing everything we can to help you. Right now we're going to be sending you to x-ray for a CAT scan of your head, and then I'll be seeing you again." April unlocked his stretcher wheels, and she and Fran were off with Mr. Schwartz. We were racing the clock. My brief exam had taken about one minute. I'd have a CT report in about fifteen minutes. At that point we would be approximately fifty minutes into this life-changing event for Mr. Schwartz.

If the CT didn't show a bleed, it would mean that Mr. Schwartz's stroke was caused by a thrombosis, or blood clot. Then, if he was agreeable, we would immediately give him a drug called tPA that rapidly dissolves clots and restores circulation through the blocked artery. This is called *thrombolytic therapy*. It doesn't always work. About one in eight patients has full recovery at the ninety-day mark. The earlier you use it, the more likely you are to have full recovery. But other patients still show functional improvement, even if not full recovery. That beats lying around in diapers the rest of your life.

But, as is often the case with the treatment of disease, there's a downside—bleeding. About six or seven percent of patients who receive the drug bleed into their brain and have additional brain injury as a result. In fact, the bleed can kill you. That's about a one in seventeen chance of bleeding. Perhaps not bad odds, unless you're the one in seventeen.

Despite every major specialty society now endorsing thrombolytic therapy, it remains a very controversial issue because of the risks compared to the benefits. I haven't checked the statistics in the last year or so, but a few years ago you were likely to get sued either way. You got sued if you gave it and they bled. You got sued if you didn't give it and they were stuck with lifelong paralysis.

So this is a tricky decision that is, like end-of-life issues, as much philosophical as medical. It requires that a patient or family member really understand the implications of what is being proposed. Some people say, "I can't stand the thought of living this way. Either kill me or make me better." Others say, "We're talking about death here, if I bleed. That's way too high a risk. I don't want the medicine."

Ten or twelve minutes later, I saw April and Fran wheeling Mr. Schwartz back into Bed Ten. A couple of minutes after that, Stacey announced, "Dr. Randolph, I have Dr. Stathakis on the line for you." That would be George Stathakis, our congenial Greek radiologist with a razor-sharp mind and a taste for ouzo. I picked up the phone.

"Merry Christmas, George."

"And the same to you, Alex. I'm looking at Mr. Schwartz's CT here," said George in his deep baritone voice. "There's no bleed. And I really don't see any hypoattenuation to suggest edema or ischemia either. It must be an early thrombosis." I looked at my watch. It was 8:20.

"Well, onset of symptoms was about 7:30, so we're only about fifty minutes into it now."

"Are you going to thrombolyse him?"

"His blood pressure is up a little bit, but I can control that. He's got no other contraindications, so if he and the family are agreeable, I'll thrombolyse him. Thanks for the quick report, George."

"You bet."

April was standing on the other side of the counter, looking at me expectantly.

"No bleed," I said. "Get your tPA ready, but don't open it yet until I talk with the family." That stuff is three thousand bucks a pop, and we don't open it until we're sure we're going to use it.

"What's his blood pressure now?" I asked.

"About one ninety-five over one-oh-eight."

"OK. Give him ten milligrams of labetalol IV." I needed to get Mr. Schwartz's blood pressure below one eighty-five over one hundred and five to meet guidelines for using tPA. If the blood pressure is above that, there is increased risk of bleeding. Ten milligrams of labetalol would hopefully get me just below the number I needed without drastically lowering his blood pressure—also risky.

I pulled out my iPhone and reviewed the other contraindications to giving tPA. There's about eighteen of them, and you better not miss one or your opposing attorney will be tooling around in a new BMW. He was clear on all the contraindications.

"Is there any family here?"

"Mrs. Schwartz just arrived."

I walked to Bed Ten. An attractive, well-groomed woman in her early sixties stood by Mr. Schwartz's bed in faded jeans and a white sweater with red reindeer embroidered on the front. She was holding his hand.

I stuck out my hand. "Mrs. Schwartz?"

"Yes."

"I'm Dr. Randolph." She gripped my hand firmly. "I'm sure you've figured out by now, Mrs. Schwartz, that your husband has had a stroke. He's pretty well paralyzed on the left side." She looked at me apprehensively without replying.

"This stroke is caused by a clot in one of the arteries to his brain." I looked down at Mr. Schwartz. "Mr. Schwartz, are you with me here? Can you follow this?" He let out a garbled, but intelligible "yes."

"Well, we have a decision to make here, folks. We have a drug called tPA that can dissolve clots. Especially this early into your stroke, we have a reasonable opportunity of dissolving the clot and restoring the circulation to your brain. That would result in improvement of your paralysis.

"But there are also risks to this drug. It can cause you to bleed. And the worst place you could bleed is into your brain. There's a six or seven percent chance of that happening. That could worsen your stroke, Mr. Schwartz," I said, looking down at him again, "or even result in your death." Mr. Schwartz blinked, his face still impassive, but he attempted no speech.

"I'm sorry that I have to put this to you with so little time to think, but we have to move rapidly if we're going to do this. So, what do you folks think? Mr. Schwartz, would you like to have that drug, or would you prefer to go with standard treatment and rehabilitation of your stroke?" Actually, I needed to give Mr. Schwartz a yes or no question in view of his speech disability. I repeated the question. "Do you want to have that drug?"

Mrs. Schwartz leaned over the bed, close to her husband. "What do you think, honey? Do you want that medicine?" After a moment's hesitation he answered.

"Yossh," came the garbled reply from Mr. Schwartz.

"Are you sure?" she asked earnestly.

"Yossh," came the reply for a second time. Mrs. Schwartz looked up at me silently, her face awash with fear.

"OK, Mr. Schwartz. That's what we're going to do." Stanley Schwartz was going for it. Despite billions of cells in his brain sequentially shutting down and facing extinction, whatever center it was in his brain that contained the virtue of courage was still intact. I admired that.

"Mrs. Schwartz, do you know what your husband weighs?"

"About a hundred and eighty-five, I think."

I took my iPhone out of my pocket and did the quick calculations. I looked up at the monitor and saw that Mr. Schwartz's blood pressure was now one-eighty over a hundred and four. Ten milligrams of labetalol had done the trick. April and Fran were standing nearby, listening to the conversation.

"Alright, Ladies. Let's give him eight milligrams of tPA in a bolus, and then sixty seven milligrams over the next hour."

Fran repeated the doses back to me and started drawing up her meds. April pulled up a folding chair by Mr. Schwartz's bed for his wife and asked if she would like a cup of coffee, and, oh, did she need a phone to call any family members? I loved that. April was young, naïve, and a little rough around the edges, but what a great heart. While the girls worked, I completed my physical exam and asked Mrs. Schwartz a few more questions.

When I returned to the nursing station, Lynn was working at her terminal beside me. She had been watching events with Mr. Schwartz.

"So you decided to thrombolyse him, huh?" she said.

"Yep. He didn't do any agonizing. He went right for it. I have the feeling his wife was glad that she didn't have to make the decision."

"Give it to me when I come in," said Lynn.

~

I saw a wimpy twenty-two year old guy with a kidney stone who thought he was dying, and two more flu cases. I was briskly walking back to the nursing station when I passed Penny in the hall. We looked at each other without speaking or smiling as we passed, and I thought that Penny held eye contact with me for a couple of seconds longer than one might normally expect. It was a fleeting intimacy, and perhaps, after all, one that I imagined.

I sat down at my computer and Lynn had a deal ready for me.

"OK, Alex. There's a new guy with rectal bleeding in Bed Seven, and a vaginal discharge in Three. I'll give you your choice."

"I'll take the rectal bleed," I said.

I saw her check the status board to see which nurse had Bed Three, and then she turned to Fran standing over by the Omnicell medication dispenser. "Fran, get Bed Three ready for a crotch check," she commanded. In case you're not familiar with medical terminology, a *crotch check* is female physician-speak for a pelvic exam. This, of course, is a phrase that would never be tolerated out of the mouth of a male physician, but, hey, the world is full of discrimination and injustice.

~

Howard Goldstein, one of two neurologists on the staff at Mason-Dixon, appeared in the department to see Mr. Schwartz. Short, graying, and always impeccably dressed, Howard is one of those older physicians who effortlessly carries an aura of authority. He's gruff, blunt, and has no toleration for fools, but he is a superb neurologist. He's the kind of guy that Americus executives hate because he's utterly impervious to intimidation, and that means he's not within their control. More irritating to them, he's a private doc who's not on their payroll.

I walked into the room with Howard and introduced him to the family. Mr. Schwartz seemed more alert and he shook Howard's hand with his right hand.

"How are you feeling Mr. Schwartz?" Howard asked.

"I don't feel badly, but I've got an arm and a leg that are like lead," replied Mr. Schwartz. His speech was almost clear. He lifted his left arm a bit to show Dr. Goldstein that it wasn't working too well, but in truth, that was fabulous. Movement was returning on his left side. Now we'd keep our fingers crossed that his improvement continued and that he didn't bleed in the next twenty-four hours. If he made it for twenty-four hours without a bleed, we were likely to be home free. That would be a nice Christmas present for Mr. and Mrs. Schwartz.

~

Patient flow through the morning was very steady, but Lynn and I were able to keep up without getting too far behind. It had become very clear in the last several weeks that the changes to Samson were producing results. Our processing of patients was steadily becoming more efficient and our throughput of patients was improving.

Contrary to usual patterns, as five o'clock approached, patient volume slowed. Everyone must have been getting ready to go out to family gatherings or Christmas Eve services. I took advantage of the lull to grab a sandwich in *Le Petit Café*, the hospital coffee shop, which has not a French item on the menu except for french fries and a bottle of Grey Poupon mustard sitting on each table. I was paying the cashier when I heard someone call my name.

"Alex!" I turned and spotted Penny sitting in a nearby booth.

"Join me," she said, motioning with her arm. I slid into the booth across the table from her.

"Unusual occurrence," I said, "both to be able to get something to eat, as well as to eat it across the table from a beautiful woman."

"You should have either taken a job with the State Department, or maybe sold used cars," she replied. I liked this girl.

"So how are you spending Christmas Eve tonight?" I asked.

"Well, I took Catherine and Jack to my parents' house in Annapolis last night, so I'll drive there after work, have a glass of wine, and try to catch my breath. And then maybe—if Jack is still wide awake—we'll go to 10:00 PM services at church. If not, I put the kids to bed as early as I can and then have a quiet hour or two with my parents. It's likely to be an early morning tomorrow."

"And I take it that you'll spend the night?"

"Yep. Santa was notified by e-mail last week that Catherine and Jack would be at grandma and grandpa's house, so that's taken care of."

"So does that mean that Santa is dropping in on the official residence of the Superintendant?"

"Yes, it does." That would be Buchanan House—a comfy little thirty-four room Beaux Arts mansion that hosts more heads of state than any place in the country except the White House.

"He may have trouble deciding which chimney," I said.

"He might," she said, smiling broadly.

"How do you keep track of the kids in that place?"

"Oh," she moaned, "it's impossible!"

"Maybe you should put a little bracelet on them with a GPS transmitter so you can locate them. You could have the Navy track them with satellites."

Penny laughed, her lovely face lighting up the booth.

"I'll tell my dad that tonight," she giggled. "He'll love it."

As I watched her I felt a sudden surge of emotion wash over me. It was very pleasant.

~

I got out pretty much on time at seven, jumped in the jeep, and drove to my parents' house in Sparks. As usual, my sibs plus Susan were there, and we had soup and sandwiches with my parents before everyone headed out to a midnight Christmas Eve candlelight service.

By then my dad was pretty heavy into the Jack Daniels, and I suspected that everyone in his pew would figure that he had had his share of Christmas cheer. I skipped the service because I would have to be back at the hospital at 7:00 AM. Tomorrow my mother would serve Christmas dinner after I finished my half-shift.

The house was dark when I pulled into the farm about 11:30. I heard Robert E. Lee and Abigail whinny softly, and heard the clomp of hooves as they walked toward the fence. I walked over and let them nuzzle me for awhile, searching for carrots. I suddenly felt very alone.

"Sorry guys, no carrots tonight. But… what the heck. It's Christmas Eve." I walked to the house, grabbed a bag of carrots out of the refrigerator, and came back out.

"There you go, guys," I said, holding out my hand as their soft lips searched for the crunchy little treats. "Merry Christmas. When you're talking tonight at midnight, say nice things about me."

I climbed into bed just before midnight, my thoughts drifting, as they had all evening, toward Annapolis. I imagined the ritual that Penny was going through, perhaps putting the kids to sleep.

CHAPTER TWENTY-EIGHT

BY LATE MORNING WE STARTED TO SEE THE annual Christmas parade of psych patients. People think that they should be happy over the holidays. The media images of Christmas happiness surrounded by loved ones contrasts so starkly with the realities of their often barren and isolated existence that it throws them over the edge.

"I just want to die!" Andrea sobbed as she rolled over and propped herself up on one elbow. Her gown fell off her shoulders, exposing one small breast, and the monitor began to clang as her body pulled on the monitoring wires. The IV line stretched tight, the tape holding the catheter in place ripped, and the IV popped out, spreading blood all over the sheets.

"Andrea, you have to lie *down*!" yelled Jen as she grabbed a dressing and put pressure over the now former IV site to stop the bleeding.

"I have to puke!" said Andrea as she abruptly sat up. Jen got a basin under Andrea's face just in time as she retched, and a huge volume of stomach contents erupted like Mount Vesuvius. The smell of alcohol began to drift through the room. Andrea wretched a few more times and then collapsed back on the bed, moaning.

Andrea was thirty-three years old with a long history of chronic alcoholism and two previous psych admissions for suicide attempts. She also had a long history of opioid abuse. Percocet was her favorite candy—cocaine when she could get it. The staff knew her well. She had two children, custody of whom was long ago awarded to the grandparents. She was divorced in her early twenties, and since then there had been a long succession of boyfriends, most of whom periodically beat her up out of love.

I don't know what time the bars open, but by 11:30, when the ambulance call went out, Andrea had fallen off her bar stool.

I did a quick physical exam. Andrea was skin and bones. Most of her teeth were missing, and the ones that were left were mostly black stubs. She looked late-forties.

"Andrea, did you take anything else besides alcohol?"

"No. I just want to die. Leave me alone! Get out of my fucking face!"

"Alright Jen, if you can get a urine, let's do a toxicology screen on her as well as a blood alcohol. Start another IV, and hang normal saline with an amp of multi-vitamins. And, give her fifty of thiamine, too."

Andrea's psycho-social problems were so totally insoluble that there was virtually no hope for her. She's unemployable, single, without insurance, and has poly-substance addiction. Most of her immediate family have a raft of their own psycho-social problems and are only a step away from Andrea's level in purgatory. We would keep her here until she sobered up, have Crisis see her, and then she would likely be back on the streets again.

"So Jen, how did you end up working Christmas? You've got four kids at home," I said, as Jen started working on the new IV.

"Well, it's a long story, but I was off for Thanksgiving and off yesterday." Andrea let out a bloodcurdling scream. "Hang on, Andrea, I'm almost done. Anyhow, I haven't worked Christmas for two years, so it was my turn. We got a very early start this morning," she smiled. "The kids got up at four to see what Santa had delivered."

"Dan usually milks at four, doesn't he?"

"Yeah. He didn't start milking this morning until after 5:30. Our girls were not happy."

"You mean Teresa and Katelyn?"

"No, the cows," she laughed. "Milk them an hour or two late, and they're bursting at the seams. You could hear the mooing for miles."

~

The morning went fairly quickly, and before I knew it, it was one o'clock. I began to wish all my shifts went this fast. It felt like a vacation day. I signed out to Ben, who was doing the second half of the seven-to-seven shift, wished Lynn a Merry Christmas, and headed to my parents' house.

Everyone else was already there, except for Brian, who had to fly on Christmas. He had an early morning route, however, and would be getting in about 5:00—early enough to enjoy the evening and catch dessert.

The house was festive and fragrant with the smell of pine, not to mention sweet potato casserole with brown sugar and walnuts, and baking bread. As usual, on holidays, everyone was in the kitchen when I walked in. There were *Merry Christmases* all around. I saw that Susan had a beeper on her belt.

"You've got the duty today, huh?" I asked.

"Keep your fingers crossed," she said as she gave me a kiss. "I've got two that are due today, and one of them already called me with contractions five minutes apart. I'm afraid we're likely to have a Christmas baby."

Dad was carving a ham, and I saw he was wearing a red Santa cap with a little bell on the tip.

"Dad, you look really good in that cap. Keeps the light from glaring off your head. Easier on our eyes."

"You have a great sense of humor, son," he smiled. "Got that from your mother, I suppose, since I've already heard the same lame joke from her today."

"Did anybody open a bottle of wine yet?" I asked.

"That can be your job," said Anne, scrubbing a pot in the sink, "since that will probably be the maximal extent of your usefulness today." It's great to be among loving family during the holidays.

~

By the time Brian arrived at about 5:30, it was dark. Everyone was having coffee in the living room, illuminated by a dozen candles, a thousand tiny white lights on the Christmas tree, and an orange fire. It was a mellow time of day, and we slowly exchanged gifts, enjoying the intimacy of a group of people who are completely comfortable with one another.

My mother opened her last gift, then leaned back in her chair and let out a satisfied sigh. "The only thing missing here," she said, "is children. When are you guys going to get to work?"

Susan's beeper went off, and she looked at the number that popped up on the little screen. "Right now," she said.

~

I was only scheduled for two shifts between Christmas and New Year's Day. It turned out that Penny and I both worked the Tuesday day shift. At the end of the shift I ran into her walking down the hall, both of us headed toward the exit at the same time. It had been a busy day and I hadn't eaten.

"I am starved," I said. This was an inane, but common topic of conversation in ERs that provides many openings for conversation with women.

"Me too," said Penny. "I had a pack of Oreo cookies today, and that was it." Penny pulled the band off her ponytail and shook out her silky blond hair as we walked. It fell over a powder-blue ski parka, and the contrast was lovely. I began to feel very impulsive.

"Penny, would you like to stop by the Pioneer Pub and grab a burger on the way home?" *Uh-oh. Did I just ask her out?*

Penny looked at me for a long moment like she was asking, *Did he just ask me out?* I think she must have decided that this didn't actually qualify as a date, because finally she said, "Yes. I think a burger and a Corona would be perfect right now." *Wow. This might actually work out. So far, so good.* And so, off we headed to the Pioneer Pub in separate cars.

We slid into a booth below a neon Bud Light sign and shrugged off our parkas. Penny was still wearing her blue scrub suit, but I had changed into jeans and a sweater.

"So what's good here?" she asked, looking through a menu. Country was playing in the background on the jukebox. "Oooh… soft shell crabs on toast. I love soft shell crabs! That's what I'll have. And a Corona," she said emphatically.

Our waitress arrived in a low-cut black top with lots of cleavage.

"What can I get you guys?" she asked cheerfully, hands on hips. I ordered for both us, and stuck with my selection of a burger—rare. I needed some protein.

"So, you didn't have to get home to the kids tonight?" I asked.

"Nope. They're spending the whole of Christmas week at my parents."

"And I take it that Santa found his way to Buchanan House OK?"

"Yes, he did. Jack was very concerned on Christmas morning. He wondered if Santa had burned his feet in the fire." I laughed.

"And, I told dad about your GPS idea for the kids," she added. "He thought that was hilarious. He said he had old friends at NORAD who could track them." NORAD, if I recalled correctly, is the North American Aerospace Defense Command, which I knew to be buried within a mountain whose name I couldn't remember somewhere in Colorado.

"Was your dad at NORAD?"

"Yep. I went to high school in Colorado Springs. We were there for four years. I love Colorado."

"I thought NORAD was just Air Force."

"Actually, I think it's a joint command with representatives from all the services. They even have Canadians there."

Our food and Coronas arrived at the same time and we began to devour our sandwiches.

"So, let me guess," I said. "You ski, I bet."

"Uh-huh," she nodded, between bites. "I switch back and forth between skiing and 'boarding, but I'll probably just ski, now, with the kids. It's pretty hard to be holding up kids while you're on a snowboard."

"I can imagine." *This girl could probably ski circles around me. Running with her was hard enough on my ego.*

"Do you ski?" she asked.

"I love to ski. I really didn't get into it, though, until I was a resident and had a little bit more money. But in the last six years, I've gone to a medical conference somewhere out west for a week every winter. And then I usually try to take at least one long weekend a year in New England."

"Good!" she said beaming. She looked at me as if she was about to say something else, then reached down and picked up her sandwich. Little breaded legs with pincers were sticking out in all directions around the edge of the toast. She tucked one or two back in with a finger.

"OK, so it was junior high in Italy and high school in Colorado Springs. I guess that leaves being a toddler and elementary school."

"San Diego," she said. "I was born in San Diego when dad was at Miramar Naval Air Station."

"That was the Fighter Weapons School for the Navy?"

"Yep. He started out in F-14s. He spent four years at Miramar instructing. Then, I think, for the next eight years he was on carriers, and then we went to Naples."

"My brother, Brian, was Air Force. He flew KC-135's. Now he flies for Southwest."

"I've got a brother flying, too—Tim. But he's Navy, of course," she smiled. "F-18s. Actually, he's on the *Eisenhower* in the Persian Gulf now."

"I would love to fly. Someday I'm going to get my private license. Actually, I took a few lessons when I was in college, but it didn't take me long to run out of dough."

"Where did you go to college?"

"University of Pennsylvania. Then Duke for medical school."

"And you grew up around here, right?"

"My childhood was not nearly as exciting as yours. I grew up in Sparks. My dad has a nursery business there."

"I know. I saw that gorgeous poinsettia you brought in on Christmas Eve."

Miss Cleavage reappeared. "Can I get you guys another Corona?"

I looked at Penny. "Not for me, thanks," smiled Penny. "I've got an hour's drive." Miss Cleavage looked at me. "Yeah, I think I'll have one more."

"Probably wouldn't do for me to show up at my parents' house buzzed," she said. "Although, actually, after the last year or two, they might think that was a good thing." I thought that was a statement that I should leave untouched.

There was a pause in the conversation. Penny took a sip from her Corona. Then she put her elbow on the table and her chin in her hand and looked at me.

"So, you never married?" *Wow. She can get right to the point, too.* Miss Cleavage appeared with another Corona. I squeezed the lime in the bottle.

"No," I said looking back at her. "I never got to the point in a relationship where it felt right."

"I'm sure you've had no shortage of willing candidates," she said smiling.

"Tell me," I said, "what's it like to have kids?"

"You mean apart from endless diapers and sleepless nights?"

"Yes."

Penny looked down for a moment and then looked up at me again.

"It's incredible. Sometimes, when I'm holding Catherine or Jack in my arms, the intimacy is so powerful it leaves me almost breathless." She paused. "There's utterly no pretense. The innocence and the trust are complete. It restores my soul; makes me feel whole." I looked into her eyes and felt that well of emotion rise over me again. *Penny Murray, where have you been all my life?*

"I think I can imagine what it feels like," I said finally. "Sometimes when I'm examining a six or eight-month-old and they lay there staring directly into my eyes the whole time, I get a glimpse of that connection." Penny smiled. We sat there in silence for a moment.

As I watched her I thought I could detect a faint flush build around the base of her neck. Suddenly her expression changed. She looked down and started rummaging through her purse, laid down a twenty dollar bill, then stood and began to pull on her coat.

"Well, Alex, I can't believe how late it is. My parents will be wondering where the heck I am. I'd better call them and let them know I'm all right. The soft shell crab was delicious." I stood as she zipped up her parka.

"Thanks..." she said, and stuck out her hand. "Thanks for inviting me." *Well, I guess I'm going to have to get used to women abruptly leaving my dining table.*

CHAPTER TWENTY-NINE

THE SECOND TUESDAY OF EACH MONTH IS THE date for the evening dinner meeting of the Executive Committee of the Medical Staff. It is here that the work of all the medical staff committees is filtered and approved, making it the most powerful committee of the physician staff. All of the chiefs of the various services have an automatic seat on the committee, so my second Tuesday is always tied up.

Although hospital administrative personnel are not a part of the medical staff—and therefore have no vote—there are always three or four of the top administrators at executive committee meetings. They are there ostensibly to keep the medical staff informed about administrative matters, to answer questions, and to assist in carrying out medical staff decisions. But their presence at meetings also helps them to keep the medical staff in line and helps to prevent open rebellion by the docs.

Tonight, as usual, we had Stan Robinson, Jacquclyn Ford, and Ed Simpson, who took his seat a discrete three chairs away from Jackie. We were also graced with an unusual appearance by John F. Salzman himself, the CEO and Chairman of Americus, looking like he was doing a damned good impression of John Travolta in an Armani suit. Chairman Salzman doesn't usually come out to the country for our exec meetings, so I figured there must be some major announcement coming from him at tonight's meeting.

You might think that since hospitals are about healing, the physicians who do the healing would be among the top dogs in the organization. Ain't so. Over the last thirty or forty years, as the regulatory and legal environment have become like the forest of thorns around Sleeping Beauty's castle, the power of administrators has grown exponentially. Their control is now almost complete.

The final straw in the loss of physician control was the rapid demise of private practice. Reimbursement has been cut so deeply, and the administrative and regulatory costs of running an office are so high, that docs have been fleeing private practice like rats from a sinking ship. They're all salaried employees of big hospital corporations now. This means that the hospital is signing all of the paychecks, and, voila—the docs are just hired guns. The administrators are in control.

I looked around the room and mentally calculated how many of the twelve docs on the committee were Americus employees and how many were private guys. Counting myself, six of us were employees, and the other six were in private practice. Americus wasn't far away from owning a majority on the executive committee.

Harvey Mays was the current president of the medical staff, and he called the dinner meeting to order. Harvey would not have been the administration's first choice for president, I was sure, given his independent wealth and his enormous respect in the medical community. He was well beyond Americus' control. But the presidency is still an elected position on the medical staff, and the administrators don't yet control the elections.

After some housekeeping items, like approval of the last month's minutes, we reached "Administrative Reports" on the agenda. Harvey called upon our Vice President of Patient Services first. Jackie adjusted her black Gucci frames. I absently wondered if there was actually glass in them.

"First of all, as most of you are aware," she began, "Nursing Administration recently began an initiative to reduce our door-to-doctor times in the emergency department and to improve patient flow. One of the keys to achieving those goals was a modification of

Samson to reduce nursing documentation time and more efficiently process patients in triage.

"I am very pleased to report that our efforts have resulted in a sixteen minute reduction in door-to-doctor times year-to-date—an enormous accomplishment." There was a murmur of congratulations from everyone. "And I want to thank Dr. Randolph," she said, nodding toward me, "and our Emergency Department Unit Manager, Julie Talbot, for their cooperation in helping us to implement these changes."

The bitch was shameless.

"In fact," she continued, "our initiative here at Mason-Dixon has been so successful, that we will be implementing it across the board at all other Americus facilities." *Jackie, you are priceless.*

Next came Stan Robinson's report. He, of course, emphasized Americus' commitment to the safety of its employee family, and detailed the recent security changes in the hospital. "We are confident," he said, "that these expenditures will keep our employees safe and deter crime on our campus."

"Moreover," continued Stan, "I am also happy to report that due to Americus' influence as a major county employer, the Baltimore County Police Department has allocated an additional patrol car to the northern end of the county." This was news that I was sure Sergeant Schmidt would find to be of interest.

The Vice President of Medical Affairs was next on the agenda. Ed Simpson reported that the quality assurance staff would now be reviewing every admission to the hospital to ensure that *Interqual* criteria were clearly met. This was really good news. It meant that the final decision as to whether or not a patient got to be admitted to the hospital would be made not by a physician, but by a couple of nurses looking up criteria in the *Interqual* book, who themselves had never even seen the patient. This process, of course, had nothing to do with the patient's medical needs, and everything to do with whether or not the hospital would get paid by Medicare.

Since over two-thirds of admissions to Mason-Dixon came through the ER, we would be on the frontlines of this bureaucratic nightmare, fighting to get patients into the hospital who didn't neatly fit into this little book's algorithms.

Finally, Harvey got around to our corporate CEO. "We're pleased," he said, "to have John Salzman with us tonight. Mr. Salzman, what do you have for us?"

John was easy to spot because his was the only tanned face in a room full of mid-winter palefaces. He stood and smoothed back his graying hair, gold cufflinks glinting in the recessed lights of the elegant board room. "It's great to be here at Mason-Dixon tonight. I'm so pleased to hear of what Jackie and her team have accomplished," he said, gazing warmly over at Jackie. "You folks have set the standard for the other Americus emergency departments." *I think I'm going to puke.*

"My primary reason for being here tonight, however, is to announce that Americus has agreed to acquire two more practices to join our Physicians for Life subsidiary. The first is Hunt Valley Surgical Associates," he said, nodding across the big polished board table at Phil Timmons, "with Drs. Timmons and Matthews. Welcome, Phil." Phil smiled weakly. *Well, there goes the neighborhood. The Emperor has his majority.*

"The second is Sparks Internal Medicine, with Drs. Patterson, Jablonski, and McCleary. The addition of these practices will help further consolidate Americus' presence in the north county market." *...And its grip on the medical staff of Mason-Dixon Regional Medical Center.*

"Finally, we all know that patient satisfaction is one of the keys to establishing a dominant presence in the market for Americus, so we are rolling out a major new program in customer service, cultural awareness, and sensitivity training that will help Americus physicians better relate to our patients." *Oh, my God.*

"All Americus physicians will undergo this excellent four-hour interactive teaching program developed by our corporate office of patient advocacy in conjunction with the nationally recognized consulting firm, Joffrey Associates. I'm sure you'll find this program to be of enormous benefit to you in your patient encounters." *Wonderful! Finally, they've found a hot young MBA who can teach me what to say to the Kelly and John Butler's of this world.*

John gave a little jerk of his left arm to get his cufflinks clear of his coat sleeve, sat, and leaned back in his chair with arms folded and rings flashing. He had the confidant air of a man accustomed to command. I glanced over at Ed Simpson, who had not breathed a word to the medical staff that this atrocity was coming. He was looking down at the floor.

"Mr. Salzman," began Harvey Mays, speaking slowly and quietly, "I can't speak for all Americus physician employees—only for myself. However, I will not be participating in this training. When I feel the need for one of your corporate consultants to instruct me in how to communicate with my patients, I will let you know. Should that prove to be unsatisfactory to Americus, there is a vacant chair of endocrinology at University that needs filling."

Dead silence. You could hear the tick of Salzman's Rolex. I could see Harvey and Salzman holding eye contact. Harvey's departure would mean the loss of the crown jewel in Americus' physician stable. All eyes were on Salzman. He looked confused. I looked around the room. Phil Timmons' face reflected barely controlled terror. Ed Simpson looked like he was going to pee himself. Jackie's leg was jiggling.

In the background, Hyde had lost it. I hadn't seen him this stirred up in a long time. *Are you going to let these idiots treat you like children? They are out to dominate you! You can't leave Harvey Mays out there swinging in the breeze all by himself. Tell Salzman to go fuck himself! For God's sake, say something!*

Jekyll was trying very hard to keep this from spiraling out of control. *Look, you've got mortgage payments on your farm, and this is a very nice place to work. You need to simply calm down and quietly discuss these issues with the administration on a rational basis.* For once, I thought, Hyde had the more moral position.

"Mr. President," I said, addressing Harvey, "for the record, I would like to indicate that I, too, will not be participating in this training." Salzman looked at me. I stared back. His face had now transitioned to beet red as he glared malevolently. After a long moment, his face suddenly relaxed and he smiled, looking around the room.

"Very well, gentlemen. I can see that perhaps this program needs some additional discussion before we roll it out. I will have the Office of Patient Advocacy meet with Dr. Simpson, and we'll get back to you." He capped his fountain pen and stood, buttoning his Armani. "Thank you for permitting me to address you this evening," he said, glancing at his Rolex. "If you ladies and gentlemen will excuse me, I have another meeting I have to make in the city." And with that, he left the room.

~

An hour and a half later, with our business finished, I pulled up my collar and stepped through the sliding glass doors of the east exit into a frigid January evening. I heard someone call out my name as I walked toward my Jeep.

"Alex!" I turned and saw Harvey Mays in a long tweed dress coat twenty steps behind me. He walked up and stopped in front of me, his breath forming a luminescent cloud around his head.

"You didn't have to do that, Alex," he said. "You're young and have a long and, I suspect, distinguished career ahead of you. I've got nothing to lose at this stage. But they could make it rough on you."

"Harvey, we should all be thanking you. No one else has the balls or the stature to take on John Salzman, but it needed to be done. You were doing all of us a favor. The least I could do was stand behind you."

He reached up and squeezed my shoulder. "Good night, Alex," he said.

At that moment, on a cold Tuesday night, standing in the parking lot, I had no idea where all of this would ultimately lead. But of one thing I was certain: this was not the end of the confrontation.

CHAPTER THIRTY

THE COLD SNAP CONTINUED WITH NO January thaw in sight. The jet stream was locked into a pattern that dipped in the east deep down into Virginia. It was hitting close to zero at night and not breaking thirty-two during the day. I was dreading my next heating oil bill.

Everyone was wearing long-sleeved tee shirts or thermal underwear under their blue scrub suits. We all sat around the nursing station comparing thermometer readings at home when we rolled out of bed that morning.

"Dan said it was seven below when he got up to milk this morning," Jen said. Jen lives in Stewartstown, near York, Pennsylvania. Another twenty miles north actually makes a pretty big weather difference sometimes at this latitude. Interestingly, the rain-snow line usually ends up being just eight or ten miles to our south, somewhere between Cockeysville and Sparks.

"Mmmphh…," mumbled Fran through a mouthful of toasted bagel, "my outside faucet on the porch was frozen this morning, and I had to carry water out from the kitchen for the dogs. I'm going to have to get Andrew to take a propane torch to it tonight."

"It was two down on the farm at 6:00 AM," I said. I turned to Ben, sitting at the computer station next to me. "I bet you froze your ass off out on that boat last night."

"Actually, you know, the water keeps the local air temperature warmer, and I don't think it's been below about fifteen on the boat since this cold snap started. I go home and watch the Australian Open on TV and that keeps me warm. It's ninety-eight degrees down there," he chuckled. "The sweat's pouring off 'em!"

"Oh!" exclaimed Penny. "Did you watch that quarterfinal match last night between Radwanski and Popanova?"

"Ohhh, yes," said Ben, "that was one *hell* of a match."

"I couldn't believe it! It was fourteen all in a tiebreaker."

"And then when Radwanski dumped that forehand into the net, it was all over."

"Yeah. She doesn't hit with much topspin, and when she gets tight, she starts dumping her forehand," agreed Penny.

I looked over at her. This did not sound like novice talk. "Do you play tennis?" I asked.

"Not much anymore, but I used to play a lot." *My God, she plays tennis*! I could barely contain myself. This held all sorts of possibilities.

"Like, how much?"

"Like, all through high school."

"You played varsity tennis?"

"Uh huh," she said, nodding.

"What were you seeded?"

She smiled, with just a hint of challenge in her eyes. "Number one in singles," she said. I should have known. There was nothing this woman wasn't good at. At least not that I had discovered so far. But then again, I had developed a really substantial bias where Penny Murray was concerned, which bothered me not in the least.

~

A.J. and his crew burst through the trauma room doors with their loaded stretcher. All I could see in the blur of motion was a blotch of red above the sheets at the head of the stretcher.

"Alex, he's still breathing. I can hear him gurgling, but I could *not* get him intubated. I can't even be sure where his mouth is!"

Lying on a pillow—where I should have been seeing the features of a face—was a basketball-sized mass of pulverized flesh, oozing blood. There *was* no face—no jaw, no mouth, no nose, no eyes—all gone. Obscene gurgling sounds were bubbling up from somewhere in the middle of this unrecognizable mass of raw flesh. There was no way I was ever going to find an airway through this mess.

I could see ears laterally on both sides of the tissue mass, and the neck appeared intact from just below where it should have met the jaw, except that the jaw was now gone. The victim was black and, I assumed, male from the body habitus. A blood-soaked blue bandana was tied around his neck.

"A.J., this is the work of a shotgun under the chin, I presume?"

"A twelve gauge," replied A.J. It appeared that no vital structures were hit, unless, of course, you consider your face to be vital. With some really bad luck, this poor bastard might live.

I heard gagging and saw April rush to the trash can in the corner of the room and empty her guts. Danielle Jones and Penny were both still on their feet and functional. They were frantically working on stripping him and getting him attached to the monitor.

"Danielle, get me a number eleven blade and a number six endotracheal tube. A.J., he's got a line, right?"

"Yeah. He's got an eighteen in his right antecube."

"Penny, give him three hundred of fentanyl IV. What's his O_2 sat?"

"Sixty-nine," replied Danielle, handing me the scalpel. She knew what I was going to do and was already scrubbing the victim's neck with betadine antiseptic solution. Danielle used to be Navy, and had a lot of years in at Bethesda Naval Hospital, as well as field hospitals in Iraq. She had seen more than her share of gunshot wounds—lots of them from high-velocity weapons like Kalashnikovs.

Danielle was married to Charles Jones, the nicest retired Marine Master Sergeant you've ever met, and the one with whom you'd least like to be enemies. He worked for FedEx now, and coached Little League. They had two boys: thirteen and eleven. Needless to say, they were very polite kids.

When you can't get an airway any other way, and you've got a patient who can't breathe and is on death's door, the last resort is to slash their neck and stick a tube into their trachea through the neck.

I pressed the scalpel firmly into the skin just below John Doe's Adam's apple and could feel the blade scrape across his thyroid cartilage as I made a two centimeter vertical incision. His arms started to move. He was at least awake enough that he was feeling pain.

"Watch it! Hold his arms!" I yelled. A.J. leapt for one arm, and Danielle the other.

I spread the bleeding wound open with my thumb and index finger, then probed with the tip of the blade for a soft spot between the thyroid cartilage and the first tracheal ring. The sharp tip of the blade suddenly sank into what I knew had to be the cricothyroid membrane. A quick flick of the blade horizontally left and then right, and I was into his trachea.

I withdrew the knife, flipped it upside down, and roughly pushed the handle of the blade through the membrane, then rotated it to widen the hole. Danielle handed me the endotracheal tube and I slid it into the hole and down his trachea. I heard a gasp of air through the tube and saw mist appear. John Doe had an airway. The whole process had taken thirty seconds. I wasn't sure that I had done him any favor. In fact—if he lived—I was pretty certain that he would curse me for the rest of his life.

"OK, let's put him out." I wanted to make sure that John Doe was unconscious for a good long while before he awoke to this nightmare that would never end. "What's his BP?"

"One ten over seventy-eight," replied Penny.

"Give him one hundred and eighty of propofol and start a drip."

Jill Brown had connected John Doe's endotracheal tube to a bag and was now ventilating him. I watched his oxygen saturation rapidly climb on the monitor to one hundred percent.

"I need a helicopter to Shock Trauma, folks," I said to no one in particular, "and I want a gram of cefazolin IV. Let's get this tissue covered with wet saline dressings. And I need a tray so I can close the skin around this incision."

I watched Penny push the milky-white propofol through John Doe's IV line, personally relieved that, at least for the time being, there was a temporary end to his suffering.

~

I could hear the distant whine of the helicopter lifting off, even from inside the department, as Jack Schmidt spoke. He shifted his considerable weight uncomfortably as we stood in the hallway, leather gun belt creaking in protest as usual.

"He was gagged and tied to a chair inside an abandoned house on Bernoudy Road," continued Jack solemnly. "They had a twelve gauge shotgun strapped to his chest, with the barrel under his chin and a cord going from the trigger through a couple of pulleys to the door knob."

"Oh, my God!" said Julie. "He sat there—for how long—knowing that when somebody came through that door they were going to blow his head off?" Jack nodded silently

"Unfortunately for the officer, it was Corporal Baker that went through the door," said Jack. "Somebody called 911 and reported that the house was being used for drug deals. Calvin was the investigating officer. He said that when he entered the house he could hear a muffled voice from another room that sounded like somebody in distress—undoubtedly our gagged Crip friend trying to keep him from coming through the door. So, he called for backup, drew his gun, and when he kicked in the door to the room—BOOM! You should have seen it—blood and tissue all over the place; dripping off the ceiling. I think Calvin's a basket case right now."

"Ohhh, I think I'm going to be sick," shuddered Julie, leaning forward and putting her face in her hands.

Jack paused for a long moment. "The Crips can't match this kind of brutality," he said finally, shaking his head. "Almost makes you feel sorry for them. Julio—or whoever is calling the shots for Mara Salvatrucha—is sending the Crips a very loud message. Actually, us too. He wanted it to be the *cops* that killed him."

"Except it's worse than that," I said. "They didn't kill him. They just blew his face off."

"And," I continued, "I think I know who it was. When I checked his chest x-ray for tube placement, he had a healing fractured scapula. It was Jawara Reynolds."

~

April walked up to me with her head down.

"Alex, can I talk to you for a second?"

"You can have a couple."

"I'm really sorry about this morning," she blurted. "I feel like such a fool—like a student nurse seeing blood for the first time. I'm just so embarrassed. I was no help at all." Her eyes grew red and started to tear.

I put my hand on her shoulder. "You know what April? That will never happen again. This is part of the process. You know, you've been a nurse for not much more than a year, and you're making great progress. Already you're using your head; anticipating needs; taking action. If I've got a really sick patient, I want you in the room with me. Forget it."

CHAPTER THIRTY-ONE

THE SHOOTING OF WILLIAM REYNOLDS, A.K.A. Jawara Reynolds, was all over the media. The horrid fascination of the story line was irresistible to the public. We were inundated with reporters and camera crews crawling over the hospital, trying to find any involved staff member who would talk. Jackie Ford put out a stern memo warning that anyone violating HIPPA confidentiality rules and speaking with the media would suffer immediate castration, or oopherectomy—that's your balls or your ovaries.

Jawara was still alive at University Hospital. They had been able to confirm his identity. I was still able to conjure up his face in my mind, although it seemed much like a phantom of mist that was slowly dissipating. It occurred to me that he wouldn't be using the "F" or "C" word with Pat Cole anymore.

CNN picked it up, showing footage of the abandoned house on Bernoudy Road, surrounded by yellow police tape, and then the gleaming facade of the emergency entrance of Mason-Dixon Regional Medical Center.

Their graphics team put together an animation of Jawara tied to the chair, with details of the pulley system and cord tied to the door knob. It showed a cop kicking in the door, and then cut to an orange explosion with no view of the results. It was posted on YouTube immediately, of course, and by 7:00 PM that night had over two million hits. In an ironic twist, the Crips became something of local heroes in the media, arrayed against the brutality of Mara Salvatrucha, the foreign usurpers of our own narcotics trade. Buy American, as they say.

Ultimately, Americus couldn't resist the opportunities presented by this public relations bonanza, so they trotted out Stan Robinson before the media at a press conference. He related how the swift and certain actions of the Mason-Dixon emergency team had saved William Reynolds' life and enabled him to be transferred to Shock Trauma by helicopter. Stan didn't mention that the narcotics-peddling scumbag would likely be costing the taxpayer millions of dollars—if he lived long enough—in medical care costs over whatever remained of his lifetime.

The talk around the nursing station for the first couple of days was of nothing else, of course. But ultimately the staff tired of both the attention and the subject, and I started hearing people say that they would scream if they heard Jawara Reynolds' name one more time.

~

I punched John's cell phone number and he picked up right away.

"Hey John, are you in town in the next couple of weeks?"

"Yeah. I'm here 'til mid-February."

"Is Annick still playing tennis?"

"She's still playing in her Tuesday morning group. I think she's hoping to play until she's about six months."

"Would you like to play mixed doubles one night next week?"

"Mixed with you and who else?"

"You don't know her."

"Let me guess. Blond. About five-six. Maybe a hundred and twenty pounds. Very cute little butt. How am I doin' so far?"

"I don't know what she weighs."

"This is the girl you were slobbering over at Cathy's party?"

"C'mon. I wasn't slobbering over her!"

"Sure. We'll play. You'll be watching her butt at the net the whole time I'm serving. You won't even see the ball."

"OK. Suggest a night."

"How about Thursday at 7:30? Are you off?"

"That would be perfect. I just have to check her schedule first. I'll let you know for sure. Just pencil in the court time."

"Didn't I see a ring on her finger?"

"Yeah. You did."

~

My mission over the next couple of days was to find a way to invite Penny to play tennis so that it didn't look like a date. I watched highlights of the Australian Open every night on Tennis Channel so I could use that as a casual conversation opener if the opportunity arose.

A couple of days went by with zero tennis conversation at the nursing station. Time was running out, and so finally I casually put it to her at the coffee pot.

"Hey Penny, we have a mixed doubles group that plays tennis on Thursday nights, and we're short a player this Thursday. How would you like to fill in?" That was not exactly the truth, of course, but as lies go, it was a little one.

She looked at me for one of those long moments and frowned. *At least she looks like she's tempted.*

"Wow, I haven't played in a long time," she said finally.

"Yeah, but you were seeded number one in singles, remember?" I said smiling. "It'll come back fast."

"I don't know if I can get a babysitter."

"Try." Another pause.

"OK," she said finally, and maybe with just a little bit of enthusiasm. "If I can find a babysitter, I'll do it!"

"Awesome. Thursday night at 7:30 at Orchard Indoor Tennis Club. You want me to pick you up?" *Uh oh. That might have been pushing it, Alex.*

"Sure. Do you know where I live?" *Unbelievable. I am on a roll.*

"I don't have the slightest clue."

~

Needless to say, it took forever for Thursday night to roll around. I was early in front of Penny's townhouse in Padonia, so I drove around for ten minutes, just so I wouldn't appear too anxious to get this show on the road. I brought the Miata in case she didn't like rusty Jeeps.

She answered the door in a black nylon warm-up suit almost as soon as I pushed the doorbell.

"Hi," she said brightly. "Hang on just a sec, and I'll be right there." She went back into the house for about a minute, and I heard animated conversation that I assumed to be a round of good nights to the kids and last minute instructions to the babysitter.

"OK," she said, reappearing with a smile and a tennis bag over her shoulder. "Let's go. I'm looking forward to this." She wore a faded blue baseball cap with "NAVY" emblazoned in white across the front and her blond pony tail stuck out the back. The mindless part of me thinks that girls in baseball caps are very hot. We walked to the Miata parked at the curb, and I opened the door for her.

"Why didn't you bring the Jeep?" she asked. "I love Jeeps."

~

John and Annick were already at the club when we arrived, waiting for the buzzer to ring on the half hour so we could take the court. I did the introductions.

"Penny!" gushed Annick, standing on tiptoes to kiss her on both cheeks and holding her by the shoulders, "Look at you. You are so beautiful! I saw you at Cathy and Tim's party, but I didn't get a chance to say hello."

"I saw you guys at the party, too," smiled Penny, grasping Annick's hand. "Alex tells me that you are both wonderful tennis players, and now I'm afraid I feel a little intimidated."

"Nonsense! I am a woman with child and I can't move! And Alex will take care of John, so nothing to worry about."

~

I could tell instantly during warm-up that Penny had had good instruction. She was perhaps a little rusty, and her timing was off a little, but there was no disguising the fluid strokes and racquet-head acceleration. She hit with a nice, compact, two-handed backhand, but had a decent backhand slice as well. Her forehand was very clean with moderate topspin. She was moving well and always seemed to be in good position when she swung, without seeming rushed or expending a lot of effort.

Annick, for her part, I knew, was no slouch. She played club tennis in France when she was growing up, but made exponential progress under John's patient tutelage after they married. She was five months pregnant now, but watching her warm up, it didn't seem to me like that little parasite inside her was having much impact on her footwork. This would be a very interesting match.

We spun a racquet for the serve. Annick won. I asked Penny whether she preferred the ad or deuce court. She said that her net game was better than her baseline game, so I took the deuce side, and the match was on.

John was right. I saw Penny crouch at the net with widely spaced feet, her pink tennis skirt stretched tight over her buttocks, and my brain essentially lost control of my eyes. Above, she wore a matching tank top that rode up her back as she crouched, revealing a lovely little sliver of skin at the hip. The outline of her nipples was clearly visible through her sports bra. I needed a diversion, and began to recite baseball statistics to myself.

John likes to think that if his first serve explodes into the court at supersonic speed, his opponent will be intimidated. Well, he's right. He cranked out a first-serve bomb that skidded off the service line near the T, and I never even got a racquet on it. Fifteen-love. It would be interesting to see whether John showed any chivalry to Penny and eased up.

I expected Penny to stand deep outside the court after seeing the first bomb, but instead she stepped just inside the court, crouched, and slowly began to sway back and forth. John unleashed another bomb—so much for chivalry—which I thought would blow by her, but she simply stepped forward and blocked it without a swing. The ball had some backspin to it, so it slowly floated just over the net and dropped short in the court. John was taken by surprise, and by the time he sprinted forward, the ball was too low and he netted it. Fifteen-fifteen. *Whaddya know?*

John tried to put the next one to me wide, but this time it came too close to my hitting zone. I cracked a deep cross-court forehand that landed almost at his feet, and all he could do was dig out a floater back right toward Penny. I saw her toes leave the ground and her racquet move forward, and *BAM*, she sent a vicious volley straight down the middle of the court. "Don't trifle with me," it said. Fifteen-thirty. Things were looking up here.

John decided on a change-up and hit a high-bouncing topspin first serve. Penny was still standing just inside the court and took it early, but her forehand return got a little too close to the middle of the court, and Annick was all over it. She hit a forehand volley right at my feet, and we were thirty-all.

And so it went for two sets. John and Annick broke Penny's serve once in the seventh game, and we lost the first set six-four. Penny and I smacked hands after every point, my favorite part of the evening.

The next set went to a tie-breaker. John announced that since we were only playing two sets, the winner of the tie-breaker takes all.

It was six-seven on an Annick serve. Her first serve was down the middle, but was long. On her second try she hit a topspin serve to Penny's backhand. John was a little too close to the middle of the court. Penny rifled a wicked backhand passing shot straight down the line, and it was all over. John just stood there looking at it with his hands on his hips.

"Whoa! Look at that!," I yelled. Penny jogged over to me, her petite round breasts bobbing. I considered bumping chests like the Bryant brothers, but thought better of it. We smacked hands and gave each other a sort of half-hug, then shook hands across the net with our worthy opponents. Everybody started gathering up their stuff.

"OK, Penny, enjoy it. That's the last down-the-line shot you're going to get off me," said John, zipping up his tennis bag.

"I just *knew* you were going to try to poach on my return, so I got ya," she replied, jabbing him in the ribs with the end of her racquet.

To my delight, everyone seconded my suggestion for a post-match beer, so fifteen minutes later we were squeezing into a booth at Souris' Saloon on York Road. I could feel the warmth of Penny's leg beside me.

"Anybody hungry?" asked John. "I am starving."

"When are you not starving?" asked Annick.

"Well, let's see. We could split a pizza… or we could get a big platter of Nachos Grande with chili." I said, looking at a menu. Nachos Grande garnered the most votes, so we placed our order for nachos and a round of Coronas—all with limes.

OK, guys, when can we do this again?" asked Annick. "That was so much fun! Penny, you took care of my husband with that last shot. You are so *good*!"

"It was a lucky shot. He gave me just enough room to get by."

"Well, if you haven't played in a long time, I'd hate to see you after you get a few weeks of play under your belt," complained John.

"That little softball in your belly didn't slow you down much either, Annick," I said. "You were still pretty light on your feet."

"Just give him some time. Two more weeks and it will be a different story."

"Him?" I asked.

"That's right. Another John in the world," she said smiling. "We saw his little thing on the sonogram last week. It's so cute!" she squealed. Penny convulsed with laughter.

"A little Y chromosome." I said, grinning at John. "Now I get to be an honorary uncle!"

"So when is your due date?" asked Penny.

"Twelve June… we think. Fortunately that corresponds to the ten days when John was home in September," she smiled, elbowing John in the side. John grinned and shrugged his shoulders.

The ladies were sitting across from each other, and began chatting about pregnancy and babies. I overheard Penny tell Annick that she had two at home. John and I talked about the Australian Open.

Being a weeknight, another Corona later it was time to pack it up. John and I were both sitting on the outside edge of the bench and stood first. The girls slid out, and then kissed on both cheeks.

"Well, thanks so much for inviting me to fill in," said Penny. "It was great fun. If you ever need a sub again, just give me a buzz." John and Annick both gave her a slightly puzzled look. Finally John said,

"You will be the number one pick on our list." I gave a sigh of relief. This is what friends are for.

~

"Did you tell them about my… marital status?" asked Penny as the Miata descended the Padonia exit ramp.

"I told them that you were a widowed friend with two kids."

"Well, I didn't want them to—"

"It's OK. I think they understand the circumstances. This wasn't a date anyhow, was it?" I asked, looking over at her with a grin. I thought I could see the hint of a smile on her face in the reflected light of the dashboard instruments.

"No, of course not," she said definitively. "But I really like John and Annick. She is so *funny*!"

After a pause, she spoke again. "You're a very good tennis player, Alex. You didn't play in college?"

"No. I played intramural at Penn, and I played USTA tennis in high school, but I wasn't sure that I could handle both the premed program and tennis. John played, though, at Washington College."

"You guys are very evenly matched."

"Actually all four of us were. I loved it when you blew that backhand past him at the end of the match."

She giggled. "Yeah, I surprised myself. It's been a long time since I've hit a shot like that off my backhand." I swung the Miata into Penny's driveway.

"Well, Alex," Penny sighed, "I loved it! I had forgotten how much fun I have playing tennis." She paused, then looked over at me. "You're doing a good job of helping me get back into the swing of life. Thanks."

So far, so good.

CHAPTER THIRTY-TWO

THURSDAY, A WEEK LATER, WAS MY LAST SHIFT before I left on Saturday for my annual trip out west to an emergency medicine conference at Snowmass. I had actually not skied yet this winter and I was looking forward to this trip. I knew a couple of other ER docs scattered around the country who go to the same conference every year—without wives or girlfriends—and we usually end up skiing together. I was hoping that my twice a week runs along Shepherd Road had kept my legs in good enough shape for the mountain, because I hadn't done anything else to prepare physically.

I was working beside Rick Stapleton at the nursing station when April came in for her 3:00 PM to 3:00 AM shift.

She stood at the station for a moment with a smile on her face, and then placing both hands on the counter said, "Well, do you notice anything different?"

"Uhhh… you got a manicure," said Rick.

"No."

"Blond highlights in your hair," I said.

"No! My hair's already blond!"

"Oh, April! A ring! You got engaged!" squealed Jen from her computer, jumping up and striding over to give her a hug.

"Yep," smiled April, holding out her hand and making slight adjustments so that the light glinted off the small diamond.

"So tell me, how did he do it?" asked Jen enthusiastically.

"Well, when he suggested we go out to dinner last night at Red Lobster, I figured something was up. And when he ordered a live lobster from the tank, I said to myself, *This has to be it.* So right after the salad, he reaches into his pocket, pulls out this little box, and says, 'April, it's not as big as you deserve, but it's from my heart.'"

"Awwhhhh," crooned Jen. "That was so *sweet*!"

"So when's the big date?" I asked.

"Well, we're going to wait until spring of next year—maybe June. That way Brad will probably have gotten his promotion, and if we save our money we might be able to afford a down payment on a house."

"Damn!" said Rick. "I was hopin' you'd still be available when I get my divorce."

"Nope," she replied, lifting her nose and cocking her head to the side. "You're too late."

~

"He did pretty well for the first few days after his biopsy," said Mrs. Wells, leaning forward with one elbow on crossed legs, "but the last week he just had no pep." A pair of matched furrows between her eyebrows reflected the worry in her voice. "And the last two days I could hardly get him out of bed. He sleeps all the time. And I can't even get him to *drink*, Dr. Randolph!"

Kevin Wells—a fifty-five year old residential architect—lay quietly looking up at me as his wife spoke, content to have her doing the talking. His nostrils flared slightly as he breathed; his face was pale. He was now almost two weeks out from having a biopsy of a mass on his pancreas at Hopkins.

"Each day he complains more and more of pains in his stomach, and his belly is just getting *huge*," she added, placing her hand on the sheet that covered the mound of his abdomen. "I just don't know what's going on here."

"What did they tell you after his biopsy?" I asked.

"Well, they said that he had pancreatic cancer, and when he recovered from the biopsy we'd start chemotherapy." Not a good sign. The surgeons had apparently decided that the cancer was inoperable. I glanced at Kevin who showed no emotion.

"Did anyone say whether they thought the cancer had spread to any other organs?"

"He had a CAT scan before his biopsy that showed some sort of spots on his liver, but they weren't really sure what they were."

"Where did he have the CAT scan?"

"Here."

"Has he started chemo yet?"

"No. He's due for his first dose on Monday, here at the oncology clinic."

I glanced at the monitor and noted that Kevin was tachycardic—his heart rate was one hundred and fifteen. His blood pressure was on the low side—one hundred and two over sixty-eight.

I went through a detailed review of Kevin's body systems, made a last note on the chart and stood. "OK, Kevin, let's take a look at you." Despite the bulge of his belly under the sheet, Kevin's face looked gaunt. His forehead had a very fine sheen of sweat. I pulled down a lower eyelid and noted that the conjunctiva was very pale—none of its usual pink color. He was likely very anemic.

I pulled back the sheet and lifted Kevin's gown. He looked nine months pregnant and due at any minute. I placed one hand on the left side of his belly and with my other hand tapped the right side of his belly. I could feel the sloshing of a fluid wave against my left hand. Kevin's belly was tense with ascites—fluid that was collecting in his abdominal cavity, undoubtedly because of the growing cancer.

I did the rest of the physical exam and then stood staring again at the monitor, thinking. Kevin was dying. And he wasn't going to last for long. I wasn't sure that he and his wife understood that, although I suspected that deep down, Kevin knew it. I noted that he already had an IV. That meant that the nurses had already collected blood when they started the IV.

"Kevin," I said, "we've got some blood work cooking on you, and as soon as that's done, I'll be back. Are you reasonably comfortable for now? Do you need some pain medicine?" He looked at me silently for several seconds and then gave a brief nod of his head.

"You *do* want some pain medicine?" He nodded again. I had not yet heard Kevin speak. "OK," I said. "The nurse will be right back and give you some pain medicine through your veins."

I walked back to the nursing station and looked up at the patient tracker screen to see who was Kevin's nurse. "Rebecca F.," the screen said.

"Rebecca, can you please give Mr. Wells four milligrams of morphine IV?"

"Sure," she said. "Is he going to be admitted?"

"Don't know yet. He's got obviously terminal pancreatic cancer. Probably will depend on where he wants to die."

~

Kevin's blood work was a mess. He was, as I suspected, very anemic. His hemoglobin and hematocrit showed that he only had half the usual number of red blood cells in his circulation. I could tell that he hadn't been drinking—his kidney function studies were twice normal. The irony of this was that his body had maybe six or eight extra liters of water on board, but it was all in the fluid leaking into his belly and was not circulating inside his blood vessels. So as far as his kidneys were concerned, he was very dehydrated. He was like a thirsty man, adrift in an ocean. And as fast as I could give him water through his veins, it would leak right out into his belly.

Kevin's liver function studies were abnormal, too. And, not surprisingly, his pancreatic enzymes were elevated. I looked up his old CAT scan report, and there were two or three large densities in his liver that almost certainly were metastatic cancer lesions. Pancreatic cancer is almost always fatal. The median survival time is only four or five months. In Kevin's case, however, it was probably going to be more like four or five days—a week or two at the most—depending upon how aggressive he and his wife wanted to be with blood transfusions and IVs. We needed to have that discussion, but the immediacy of Kevin's death did not seem to be on Mrs. Wells' radar screen.

When I walked back into the room, Kevin's eyes were closed and he appeared to be sleeping. I motioned to Mrs. Wells, walked back into the hallway, and she followed. I led her to the family counseling room, and we sat down.

"Mrs. Wells, Kevin is not doing well. His heart is beating very fast, his blood pressure is low, and he's very anemic. Besides that, his kidneys are beginning to fail, and, as you can see, he's collecting a ton of fluid in his belly." She looked at me like I was from Mars.

"What's that from?" she asked.

"He has cancer cells that have spread into his abdominal cavity, and because they are very abnormal cells, they don't have much structural integrity. Fluid leaks out of them rapidly."

"So, what do we have to do?"

"I'm afraid that, in truth, we don't have a lot to offer at this point, Mrs. Wells, other than pain control and keeping Kevin comfortable."

"You mean you're just going to let him die?" she asked incredulously. It was getting pretty clear that no one had prepared Mrs. Wells for this moment. She had asked a direct question and she deserved a direct answer.

"I'm sorry. It's not a matter in which we have any choice, Mrs. Wells," I said quietly. "Pancreatic cancer at this stage is universally fatal. We could sustain him for a short period with blood transfusions, IVs, and maybe drain some of the fluid off his belly for comfort, but those measures will not save his life."

She looked randomly around the room for a few moments, bewildered. "Well, why… why didn't they tell us this before?" That was a good question. It's always easier to gloss over the hard facts and talk about treatment and hope. It's a lot harder to have this kind of conversation. It pisses me off when doctors don't level with patients and leave families bewildered and unprepared as the end draws near. I'm not an oncologist, and I don't have to deal with the volume of terminal patients they do, but on the whole, they often do a piss-poor job with this.

"I know this is very tough, but perhaps the most important question you and Kevin need to consider is whether you want Kevin to die at home, or in the hospital. If you want him to die at home, then we need to make some arrangements for Hospice to be there to help you care for him and to make sure that we are keeping him comfortable."

"I… I don't know. I have to think about this. I need to call the kids."

We walked back to Kevin's room. He awoke easily when I touched his leg. I reviewed the severe anemia and abnormal kidney function studies with him, and then moved on to the source of his pseudo-pregnancy.

"Kevin, the reason your belly is so big is because of fragile cancer cells in your abdomen that are leaking out fluid. The fluid leaking out of your blood vessels is also why your kidneys aren't getting enough fluid to function properly. How aggressive we get in treating these problems with blood transfusions, IV fluids, and maybe draining some of the fluid off your abdomen for comfort, is your decision."

Kevin held eye contact with me for a long silent moment and then finally spoke for the first time. "What good would all that do?"

"You'd have more energy with more red blood cells, and you might feel a little better with the IVs for a few days, as we improved your kidney function. That benefit would go away, however, when we stopped the IVs. If we drain some fluid off your belly with a needle, it would at least buy you some temporary comfort, but it *would* recur over a few days time."

"How long do I have?" There was the question. I hesitated for a moment.

"That always requires a crystal ball, and mine isn't working very well, Kevin. But if I had to guess, I would say days to a couple of weeks." He lay there quietly, never taking his eyes off me. Mrs. Wells looked at him with anguish in her eyes. Finally, he spoke again.

"I want to go home." Between Kevin's flat affect and terse verbal responses, I couldn't tell whether he was pissed off at me, or merely resigned to his fate, without the energy or will to engage in the niceties of conversation. I often find myself in this position during sentinel conversations with patients. I have learned over time to depersonalize it, because usually it's not about me. But in any case, it looked like Kevin had already made the decision that he wanted to die at home. That's what I'd want to do, too.

"Kevin, they could help you *feel* better," pleaded Mrs. Wells.

"I want to go home," repeated Kevin. Mrs. Wells looked up at me, took a deep breath, and sighed.

These are interesting moments, because usually in a patient encounter, I am pretty much in control. But when we get to the end of the road, the control often shifts—as it should—and I figure my job then is to be basically an expediter of patient wishes.

"OK, Kevin. I think I understand, and I will be supportive of your decision. I'm going to contact Hospice and have them come to your home today. And I'm going to give you some new prescriptions for pain control. We want to make sure that you're not in pain."

I turned to his wife. "Mrs. Wells, I'm going to have social services come down and outline for you all the services that are available." She looked up briefly, nodded her head, and then stared back down into her lap.

I walked back to the nursing station admiring Kevin Wells' realism. I wondered about the houses he had designed—my imagination extrapolating from my brief encounter with what I knew to be the distilled essence of his personality. I suspected that they were clean and uncluttered, without pretense, and elegant in their simplicity and functionality.

By the time you reach thirty-nine, you're just beginning to realize that you're not immortal. I hoped that when my time came I would be looking out my east bedroom window onto the pasture below with the solitary sycamore. And maybe, if I were lucky, there would be a couple of kids in the bedroom, and a woman I loved.

CHAPTER THIRTY-THREE

AT THE END OF A NICE LITTLE FOUR-INCH Friday night snowfall, the last few wisps of dissipating low clouds glowed a neon pink in the early morning sun. My 8:29 AM United flight to Denver accelerated down Aspen's runway 33 and lifted off to the north into an azure-blue sky. In fact, there was no other runway choice—north is the *only* route out of the Roaring Fork River Valley, surrounded as it is by rugged fourteen-thousand-foot peaks. It took a couple of minutes for the Bombardier CRJ-700 regional jet to clear the snow-capped Elk Mountain range visible from my left wing window seat. Then we turned east toward Denver and my connecting flight back to Baltimore.

The organizers of this annual emergency medicine conference are very smart because they schedule classes from 7:00 to 9:30 in the morning and 4:00 to 6:30 in the afternoon. That, of course leaves all day to ski, and no doubt accounts, in part, for the long-term success of this conference. Ironically, it's organized by the University of Miami School of Medicine.

Interestingly, most of the partying at ski areas is done from about 3:00 to 6:00 in the afternoon, rather than late at night. All the bars book their bands in the late afternoon because there's nothing worse than getting up to ski with a hangover, and everybody is there to ski. So conference attendees miss most of the partying, but we get out of the conference in plenty of time to have a couple of Grey Goose and tonics, a nice dinner, and then to bed in time to be up again at six. For docs who have a bit of a workaholic gene, like me, this is the perfect getaway, because with five hours of class a day, there's no guilt about slothfulness.

Counter intuitively, ski areas are actually a milieu fairly well permeated by sex. You might think that the beach wins out in this contest, but there are a lot of tight butts and sinewy legs on display at ski areas, despite the fully clothed dress style mandated by Mother Nature. In some ways it's sexier than the beach, perhaps because more is left to the imagination. The average age of skiers is pretty young, and the women are all in good shape. But in any case, it was enough to make me fully aware of the absence of female companionship.

I indulged myself with two private lessons during the week—one in the bumps and one in powder. I made some progress in the bumps and congratulated myself on getting reasonably comfortable on the widely-spaced moguls of intermediate terrain. But I was still in deep trouble on the closely-spaced moguls on steep terrain. I found skiing powder to be a whole lot of work. I was still leaning back too far—especially in deep powder. That being said, I loved every minute of the skiing, and at the end of the week, I wasn't ready to leave.

There's nothing quite like Colorado skiing. The weather is perfect, not to mention the spectacular vistas of the Rockies. If it's not snowing, the sun is shining. I always come home with an owl's eye tan from wearing goggles or sunglasses. The humidity is low, so even when it's cold, you don't feel cold. Unlike the east, at this altitude ice is non-existent—nothing but beautiful, soft snow that squeaks under your feet and lets you carve big GS turns without ever losing an edge on your skis.

So, as usual, I came back from Colorado psyched about skiing again. But it was also readily apparent to me that I could have had a *much* better time skiing and sleeping with Penny than with my four ski buddies, delightful chaps that they are.

I had been thinking all week about my self-imposed prohibition on asking her out. It was wearing a bit thin and I was getting impatient.

I had convinced myself that the chemistry between us was powerful—it was just an issue of when she was ready to admit it to herself. By the time of the flight home, I had decided it was time to give her a little nudge.

~

I was lucky to have Sunday off after my Saturday return, but was back in the ER on Monday morning. ER shifts have to be filled, and when you're away for a week other people have to work harder. So everyone expects you to be back in the saddle post-haste.

Somehow a week away from the department seems like an eternity, and I was anxious to find out if any crises had erupted while I was away. I got to work a little bit early and walked into Julie's office.

"You're back!" she said brightly.

"Not of my choosing."

"Well, sit down, and I'll fill you in on what ya' missed. Quite an eventful week." I didn't like the sound of that, because eventful weeks in my absence usually mean trouble.

"Lookin' for a new job?" she asked. I frowned.

"Tired of nights and weekends? You might want to apply for Vice President of Medical Affairs," she continued.

"Simpson's gone?" I asked.

"They fired his ass. The bastard's gone, but I'm not sure what really happened there," she said with a puzzled look on her face. "That makes me nervous." Julie's political antenna was up, and there was something about this that she didn't like, as happy as she was to see Simpson gone.

"I can tell you exactly what happened," I said. "John Salzman got humiliated at last month's medical staff meeting. He told the staff that we were all going to have to take some sort of half-ass corporate communication and cultural sensitivity training. Took everyone by surprise. We'd never heard a word of this from Ed Simpson. Harvey Mays basically told Salzman to shove it—he wasn't taking his damned course. And I opened my big mouth and seconded that. Salzman was royally pissed. No doubt he blamed the failure of the staff to accept this training on Simpson, and now Simpson's history."

"Terrific," said Julie. "Way to go. Now *you're* on Salzman's radar screen."

I shrugged. "He's an asshole," I said.

"Yeah, and that asshole signs your checks. If you get yourself fired, I swear I'll never speak to you again in my life."

"He can't fire all of us."

"Yeah, but he can fire *you*," she said emphatically. She was genuinely pissed at me.

"Well, I guess that's the end of my leverage over Jackie," I said.

"Yeah, and now you've got that bitch out for revenge, *and* Salzman determined to destroy you. You're in great shape."

It was great to be back.

~

Well, there was one bright note to that day: Lisa was back from maternity leave. She was sitting at a computer station when I walked into the ER after Julie's dressing down. Baby fat was melting away and she looked like she was almost back to her usual tiny self. I walked up to the station and put my hand on her shoulder.

"How's the queen and her three little princesses?" I asked.

She turned and looked up with a big smile, reaching up and squeezing my hand. "Alex! You're back! We're fine, but you know the king doesn't have a male successor yet. I offered him a slave girl to do the deed, but he graciously declined," she giggled. "Actually, he and little Megan have really bonded. He's even changing poopy diapers."

"I think I can understand that," I said.

~

I caught Penny at the coffee pot. I had only been away for a week, but, again, I had already forgotten how beautiful she was. My heart skipped a beat when I saw her, and I marveled at the emotion that she released in me.

"So," she asked brightly, "how was it?"

"Sunshine, pristine snow, and crisp clean air. Not to mention that those awe-inspiring peaks are still there."

"Ooohh, I'm so envious!"

"It would have been wonderful to have you there, Penny," I said, holding her gaze. She looked at me in silence for a moment, and then turned and picked up the coffee carafe. *Well, I think it's time.*

"Penny, I want you to have dinner with me. Friday night, if you're off. I'll tell you about everything you missed while you were here in the cold, gray east, and I was cruising in sunshine. Seven o'clock. I'll pick you up." *That's it. All out on the table now. No more pretending we're just friends.*

She looked back over her shoulder at me and bit her lip. I'd never seen her face look pained before.

"Alex… I just… I… I can't. I'm sorry." She set the carafe down and fled from the room.

CHAPTER THIRTY-FOUR

THERE'S A PRICE TO PAY FOR VACATIONS, OR vacation/conferences. The pile in my in-box was nearing the ceiling. My Tuesday shift wasn't until 7:00 PM, so I came in Tuesday morning to try and get caught up on my paperwork. I opened the next envelope on the pile and read the letter from Stan Robinson.

February 5, 2010

Alexander B. Randolph, MD
Mason-Dixon Regional Medical Center
1238 Middletown Road
Parkton, Maryland 21120

Dear Dr. Randolph:

Our records show that you have seven incomplete charts over twenty four hours old. If these charts are not completed by Wednesday, February 10, 2010, your medical privileges at Mason-Dixon Regional Medical Center will be suspended.

Sincerely,

Stanley W. Robinson
VP Americus Health Systems
COO Mason-Dixon Regional Medical Center

Hospitals have this thing about having all the little spots on a chart that require a signature being signed within twenty-four hours. If you don't think that it makes sense to send threatening letters to people who are still out of town at a conference, then you haven't worked in a hospital. This was a form letter that went out to everyone with overdue charts, but I nevertheless had a flash of paranoia after Julie's little tirade, and the thought crossed my mind for a brief moment that maybe this was the first step in getting rid of me. That, of course, was a ridiculous notion, my rational mind told me, and the thought was gone in a heartbeat.

The next envelope contained a letter from the principal of Hereford High School.

February 7, 2010

Alexander B. Randolph, MD
Mason-Dixon Regional Medical Center
1238 Middletown Road
Parkton, Maryland 21120

Dear Dr. Randolph:

Each month we have a school-wide student body assembly during which an invited speaker discusses a topic of current interest. As I am sure you are aware, in the last several years we have witnessed a dramatic increase in the number of children seduced by drugs, specifically heroin.

This has resulted in heartbreak for a number of extended families in our district.

You, perhaps more than anyone else, are uniquely qualified to discuss the devastating consequences of drug addiction, and perhaps communicate to impressionable young minds the peril brought by that first injection of heroin.

We would be very grateful if you would consider being the monthly speaker on Thursday, April 15, 2010 at 10:00 AM.

Very Truly Yours,

Bernard S. Kohler
Principal
Hereford High School

This was a speaking invitation that I would accept. I would have liked to have taken Jawara Reynolds with me as an object lesson, but I doubted that he would be free that day.

The next letter had a return address on the envelope from the county district attorney's office and contained an invitation—actually a subpoena—to appear in court as a witness in an assault case. I vaguely remembered the girl whose upper lip I had stitched after a little love tap from her boyfriend.

About 10:00 AM I had gotten about two-thirds of the way through the pile and I had had it. I put the pile aside for a while and turned to the complaint log. The next hour was spent on the phone with three patients who had filed complaints with administration about one aspect of their care or another. It's the one part of my job that I literally hate. I couldn't imagine how customer service reps that handle complaints, all day every day, avoid suicide.

These three complaints had accumulated over a couple of weeks. That might sound like a lot of complaints, but you should try seeing one hundred patients a day with whom you have no rapport or relationship, who don't want to be there, who are often scared to death, who didn't get to choose their doctor, who think that he'll probably kill them, and who know that the hospital is out to rob them blind. You'll get a few complaints.

Of course, some of those complaints turn into lawsuits, of which we currently had two pending. One of them was against me. They are usually "failure to diagnose" suits as opposed to errors of commission.

Mine involved an eight-year-old kid named Robert Kline with vomiting and abdominal pain. His belly was not very tender, and he had a normal white blood cell count and no fever when he presented to the ER. An ultrasound study was negative. I didn't feel that he had a high probability of appendicitis, so I tried to avoid the radiation and cost of a CAT scan. Instead, I opted to observe him for a little while longer and asked the family to bring him back for a re-examination and repeat white blood cell count in eight hours. If necessary, we could do a CT then.

Two days later he showed up in the ER of another hospital with a ruptured appendix. Robert recovered, but had a rocky course after surgery—an abdominal infection that required a ten-day stay in the hospital. The family—who had excellent insurance—wanted all of their bills paid, compensation for missed work, and two million bucks for pain and suffering for their child. The complaint said that I was guilty of gross negligence and had failed to deliver the community standard of care to my patient.

Naturally, the plaintiff's attorneys had secured a physician witness from a prestigious university who was struggling to put his kids through private school. He would testify that appendicitis was one of the most frequently missed diagnoses in the ER, that all physicians should know that they must maintain a high index of suspicion for appendicitis in children with abdominal pain, and that any reasonable physician would have ordered a CAT scan immediately on Robert.

Of course, filing the suit cost the Klines nothing, but with the contingency fee, would net their attorneys a little over six hundred thousand dollars if they were successful. If things were looking a little dicey for a win, they would settle out of court for maybe a hundred thousand, and the attorneys would net thirty-five. It's the great American lottery.

The suit had been dragging on for two years now, but the attorneys thought we were probably getting close to a trial date now. The outcome would hinge on whether the jury held me responsible or the parents responsible for the delay in diagnosis.

Most of the docs I know who have been through a couple of these suits eventually start ordering the million-dollar-workup on every patient that walks through the door—they never want to go through this again. Some of them begin to see each patient as a potential enemy rather than as a human being in need. I know my own docs spend tens of thousands of dollars a day covering their ass, and they're not a particularly paranoid bunch. It's a sick system.

The politicians will tell you very clearly, however, that defensive medicine and litigation are *not* significantly contributing to medical costs. This may not be surprising when one considers that in 2010, fifty-four out of one hundred Senators were lawyers. No conflict of interest there. I've often wondered how the American public would feel about fifty-four doctors passing legislation on health care.

Julie walked into my office and caught me next. The Department of Health & Mental Hygiene—the state agency responsible for regulating hospitals—was doing their biennial three-day inspection of Mason-Dixon next week. That is always an occasion for panic in the hospital because the DOH can shut you down.

She spent twenty minutes prepping me on how to answer their inane questions when they hit our department, and another couple of minutes warning me not to get mouthy. The team that would go over our hospital with a fine-tooth comb would include administrators, nurses, and at least one physician. It always seemed pretty obvious to me that these were people who either couldn't make it in the private sector, or didn't want to work that hard, so they spend their cushy lives telling other people what they can and can't do. OK, that's a bit of an overstatement, but they don't have to live by their rules, and their rules add hours of non-productivity to my work week.

By 11:45 I was wondering why I had ever chosen medicine as a career in the first place, and was thinking that it might be nice to inherit my father's landscaping business. I packed up and headed home for a nap before my night shift.

CHAPTER THIRTY-FIVE

ABOUT 10:30 PM, I LOOKED UP AND SAW JACK Schmidt ambling down the hall toward the nursing station. He was in uniform.

"Jack, how come a guy of your age, and with your seniority, is showing up here in my ER at 10:30 at night? You'd think that by now they'd at least give you a day shift."

"Hey, all the action's at night, Doc. Daytime is boring."

"So what's happening?" I asked.

"You like funerals?"

"Depends on whose funeral."

"Jawara Reynolds."

"The poor bastard finally gave it up?"

"Yeah. He died yesterday—a blessing. Nobody should have to die like that, even a piece of shit like Reynolds. So now we move on to murder charges."

"Against whom?"

"Funny you should ask. The state's attorney asked the same question."

"No physical evidence, huh?"

"Nothing. Prints wiped clean on the gun and all the doorknobs. And Jawara wasn't talking before his demise."

"I wouldn't think so."

"But I think the Crips got the message. Word on the street is that they're lying low and MS-13 has picked up most of the business."

"I think if I were a Crip I'd probably think twice about selling heroin these days."

~

The night shift wasn't so bad, and I drove home about 7:45 the next morning with bright sun in my windshield all the way out Monkton Road. I stripped, closed the blinds in my bedroom, and, with the talent common to most ER docs, fell asleep in several nanoseconds.

I was able to sleep until about 2:00. I stumbled into the bathroom to pee, then slowly descended the curving sneaky staircase into the kitchen and started coffee before I headed to the shower. I always forget to set the timer when I work night shift.

I had to think for a minute or two about what day it was because my days get all screwed up when I work night shifts. Sometimes, when I'm checking to see if a patient is oriented, I ask them what day it is and I don't know the answer myself. I remembered that tonight I was driving into the city to have dinner with Anne.

I sat on a stool at the island in front of my computer—Maggie licking my bare feet—drinking coffee and trying to lift the fog from my brain. Bouncing back and forth between day and night shifts is a little hard on your biorhythms. I didn't get very far before my thoughts turned to Penny. Our conversation had been a little short on rationale as to why she wasn't dying to go out with me. Most of the free moments in the last thirty-six hours had been spent wondering what it all meant.

Actually, I didn't spend much time anguishing over my decision to ask her out. None, more accurately. As my mother used to say, you can't change the past. I thought it was time to give her a nudge, and that's what I did.

But it didn't work. I couldn't forget the look of pain on her face, and didn't know how to interpret it. Maybe it was the reminder that the father of her children was dead. Maybe it was that she didn't want to hurt me, or perhaps feared losing my friendship. Or, maybe it was more straightforward than that—maybe Alex Randolph just wasn't who she was looking for.

I sighed. This was just so stupid. All of this emotion over a girl I had never even kissed, never mind taken to bed. I felt like an adolescent.

~

I picked up my sister shortly after 7:00 at her Federal Hill townhouse, and we drove the eight or ten blocks to Sabatino's in the Little Italy section of town.

The waiter, improbably an Italian-looking guy with an Italian name and an Italian accent, dropped off our drinks. We chatted about dad and his cancer—he was handling it much better than either of us had expected—our 401Ks, which weren't doing nearly as well as dad, and the hassle of politics at work. Finally I said, "So… how's your love life these days?"

"Actually," she smiled, "it's not so bad."

"New beau?"

"I don't know if I'd go that far, but we've had several nice evenings together."

"Who is he?"

"He's single, never married, and has a *very* good job."

"What's he do?"

"He's a physician."

"You're kidding."

"Nope."

"Where'd you meet him?"

"At a party. Mutual acquaintance."

"So what kind of doc is he? I assume he's practicing here in town?"

"He works for a hospital." *God, she's being evasive.*

"Doing what?"

"Actually he's an ER doc."

"No! I wonder if I know him?"

"Oh, I think you do," she said smiling.

Slowly it dawned on me. My mouth dropped open.

"No," I said. "You're not."

"Uh-huh."

"Ben?"

"Yep," she giggled.

"Wait 'til I see that bastard! I *told* you he was a predator. You never listen. He's got more girlfriends than you do!"

"Oh, but they can't compete with me," she said smiling.

~

I was still in shock when the antipasti arrived. Ben was taking out my little sister! I was about to launch into my lecture to Anne on the perils of charming, sophisticated, successful, and handsome doctors when she pre-empted my opportunity.

"So, did you take her out yet?" she asked, sipping her cabernet blanc.

"What?"

"Did you take her *out* yet?"

"Who?"

"Do I have to remind you again?"

"No."

"No what?"

"No, ma'am."

Anne drummed her fingers on the table.

"Why do I put up with you?"

"Because you can't divorce your brother."

"Did you, or did you *not* take her out?"

"I told her we needed a fourth person for our weekly mixed doubles league with John and Annick. It wasn't really a date. So… not exactly."

"You don't play in a mixed doubles league," she said accusingly.

"We just started it that night."

"Is she any good?"

"Actually, she's fabulous."

"So you really haven't asked her out yet?"

"Yes."

She threw up her hands in exasperation.

"How old are you?" she asked.

"Ten."

"That's an overstatement. I give up."

"OK. I asked her out and she said no."

She leaned back in her chair and looked at me for a moment. "Big brother's not used to that, is he?"

"I've been an abject failure with women for months."

"What happened?"

I gave Anne the rundown on Penny's life and the history of our quasi-relationship. My soliloquy ended with Penny fleeing the room after I formally asked her out.

"She's in love with you," Anne said flatly, "just like you're in love with her."

"What?"

"She's in love with you. It's perfectly obvious. You're a moron."

"Well, I don't see how you can say that."

"This is no high school girl, Alex. This is a woman. She's poised; she's capable; she's strong. And there's only one reason that she ran from the room in anguish—she's in love with you. If she didn't love you she would have smiled graciously and said, 'Oh, Alex, that's so very sweet of you, but it's just not the right time of life for me to start dating yet,' —end of conversation."

"I'd like to believe that, but even if it's true, I'm not sure it's a good sign."

"She's coming along, Alex. Just give her a little more time. She has to make peace with Patrick. She'll come to you when she's ready. She knows how you feel about her, even if you've never told her. And, believe me, she *wants* you."

I don't know how women can feel so confident about these things.

CHAPTER THIRTY-SIX

MONDAY MORNING STARTED OFF LIKE WE had posted a Washington's Birthday Clearance Sale sign in front of the hospital. By 9:30, all sixteen beds in the department were filled. Lynn Saylor had come on at 9:00 and she had three. I had the other thirteen. They were still pouring in and we were entering *Defcon Three—Barely Controlled Chaos*—territory.

I already had four admissions stacked up occupying ER beds because the day's discharges from the med-surg floors upstairs hadn't been processed yet, and there were no beds available. To make matters worse, the hospitalists were trying to get the inpatient discharges done upstairs and couldn't get down to the ER to pick up admitted cases. So I was managing a bunch of sick patients by myself, as well as trying to process the new arrivals.

"Dr. Randolph, I have Penny on five-three-one-three," called out Stacy.

"What?"

"Penny Murray is calling for you on one-three." My mind suddenly went blank. I picked out five-three-one-three among all the blinking lines on hold and lifted the receiver.

"Penny?"

"Alex, I'm so sorry to bother you. I know you're busy. Jack has been up all night crying with an ear ache and he's got a fever of a hundred and three. I can't get him into the pediatrician's office until tomorrow afternoon, and I just don't know what to do. I was wondering if you would see him?"

"Of course I'll see him. Why don't you just bring him in? Don't register him. Just come on into the ER."

"OK, Alex. I really appreciate it. It'll take me about a half hour to get there."

"That's fine, Penny. See you then." I put the receiver back in its cradle and sat there for a moment. *Huh.* I liked this. Penny had a family problem and she was calling me.

~

Forty-five minutes later Penny was standing by my computer station in her blue ski parka and black tights, with two of the most beautiful children I had ever seen—one on each side. Catherine, the taller of the two, stood there quietly, holding Penny's hand, in matching pink ski cap and gloves, with long platinum hair cascading to the middle of her back. She had her mother's green eyes.

Jack's arms were wrapped tightly around his mother's leg, and his face was buried in her thigh. She absently stroked his hair. His tear-stained face would turn to look at me periodically and then quickly turn back to her leg. He sobbed softly, trying mightily to control his fear.

"Wow," I said. "They're gorgeous."

"Thank you," smiled Penny. "I can see how busy you are today, Alex. I—"

I held up a hand. "It's OK. Don't even think about it." I looked up at the status board to see if there was an empty room in which I could examine Jack. They were all full.

"OK, I'll tell you what. Let me grab an otoscope, and we'll just go back to my office. I'll take a look at him there."

I grabbed a portable otoscope, and our little entourage went out through the secure doors and down the hall to my miniscule office. Penny started undressing Jack, and Catherine stood in the corner with her hands clasped in front of her.

"Any other symptoms, Penny?"

"Yes. He started with a runny nose two days ago, and last night he developed both the fever *and* a cough."

"OK. Sit him on your lap," I said, motioning to the chair beside my desk. I sat down in my chair and wheeled my way around the desk toward them.

"Jack," I said quietly and slowly, "we're going to listen to your chest first, and I promise that it won't hurt." Jack looked suspiciously at me as I put my stethoscope in my ears and Penny pulled up his shirt. I put one hand on his leg and placed the diaphragm of the stethoscope on his chest. He looked down at it but didn't pull away.

"OK. Let's turn him around." Penny turned him on her lap and pulled up his shirt in the back. Jack's head whipped around to keep an eye on me. I listened again. His chest was clear.

"Good boy, Jack. Next, I'm going to feel your neck." I slowly placed my fingers under his mandible and gently probed for swollen lymph nodes. There were none. The look on his face indicated that Jack found this barely tolerable.

I picked up the otoscope, placed the speculum in my own ear, and silently looked at Jack. He looked into my eyes, then at the otoscope, and back again.

"OK, Jack. I'm going to look at *your* ears now, and I promise you that this won't hurt either." Penny turned his head to the side with both hands, and Jack waited apprehensively, trying to see me out of the corner of his eye. I tugged upwards on his left earlobe to straighten the canal, and slowly inserted the scope.

"Which ear was it that hurts?" I asked.

"The other one," said Penny. Jack sat quietly, his left shoulder scrunched up slightly in anticipation of pain. His left eardrum was pearly gray and glistening, just as it should be. Penny turned Jack on her lap, grasped his head firmly, and rapidly turned it in the other direction. It's interesting how much information about people you can gather from observing little everyday actions, but from the way Penny whipped Jack's head around, this was a no-nonsense mom that was clearly and guiltlessly in charge of the parent-child relationship.

I tugged on Jack's right ear and inserted the scope. This time he pulled up his shoulder a little more and whimpered. His tympanic membrane glowed a fiery red.

"Ooohh, Jack, that looks like it hurts! He's clearly got an otitis media on this side, Penny." She turned Jack back around so he was facing me.

"Jack, one more thing, and then we're all done and you can go home." I pulled a tongue blade out of my pocket and showed it to Jack. He knew what it was and turned his head away.

"Jack, we need to look at your throat now. If you can open really wide, we might not have to use this," I said, holding up the tongue blade. "Let's see how wide you can open." Penny held his head and Jack struggled against his fear to open his mouth. I could barely see his tongue.

"Come on Jack, I know you can open wider than that, baby," I said. Jack tried again, then quickly clamped his mouth shut and started crying.

"Jack, you're a very big boy, and I know you can do this. Take your time, and then let's try it again." I paused for a moment.

"OK, Jack, one more time, now! Really wide this time!" Jack opened his mouth and started to gag as my hand approached with the tongue blade. But the gag was just what I needed and his tonsils flashed briefly into view—just long enough for me to see that his throat looked normal. Now he started crying in earnest. Penny turned him to her chest and he wrapped his arms around her neck while she patted his back.

"Sshhh, baby. It's all over now. You're OK. We're all done," she crooned.

"Well, Penny, I don't think the fever is from the otitis media. He's got a viral respiratory illness that's causing the fever, and the otitis media may or may not be a bacterial complication. But as red as that eardrum is, I guess we better put him on an antibiotic. Is he allergic to any drugs?" She shook her head no.

I grabbed a prescription pad off my desk and started to write a scrip for amoxicillin. I looked over at Catherine who was still standing quietly in the corner with her hands folded, and then leaned back in my chair.

"Catherine, I bet I know what your favorite color is." She smiled silently, then quickly shook her head "no".

"Green," I said. She shook her head again.

"Uhh, brown!" She giggled this time, with another shake.

"Pink!" This time her smile widened and she bobbed her head up and down.

"I knew that," I said.

I looked back over at Penny. Our eyes locked for a moment.

"Thank you, Alex," she said finally.

~

The volume of patients through the day was relentless. By five o'clock I was exhausted None of the staff had even had lunch. I was doing an exam in Room Five on Roger Parker, a fifty-year-old with abdominal pain, when Danielle Jones suddenly poked her head around the door.

"Alex, I've got a gunshot wound in Fourteen. He looks bad," she said quietly, her face immediately disappearing as she hurried back toward the trauma room. *Oh, Lord.* This was *not* what I needed. I didn't have time for this. We were already swamped.

Since Danielle had already seen more small arms wounds in Iraq than I was likely to see in a lifetime, I figured I'd best take her message as an order. I apologized to Mr. Parker and headed back toward Fourteen.

I spotted the blue bandana around the victim's neck the moment I walked into the room. He was maybe early twenties; wearing a gray sweatshirt which Danielle's scissors were rapidly filleting as she worked at undressing him. He was moaning through a non-rebreather oxygen mask, and was breathing very rapidly, twisting and turning on the stretcher with purposeless movements. His face was covered with sweat, and despite being black, he looked like a ghost.

Fran Williams and Rebecca were in the room. I called Fran over. "Fran," I said quietly, "get that button pushed under the triage desk, and tell Stacey that when the cops call, she should tell them that we've got a gunshot wound, and that the patient is probably a Crip. Have you seen anybody else with this guy?"

"No. He was dropped off by private vehicle and his friends split. They dragged him in with an arm over each shoulder, plunked him down in a wheelchair, and they were outta here."

"Nobody else in the lobby? No Hispanic-looking guys?""

"Not that I know of, but I'll check."

"And tell security to get all the officers in the building down here."

I turned back to Danielle and Rebecca, who were a blur of motion, stripping the victim and getting him connected to the various monitors. He was getting combative and making their job difficult. "What do we know about this guy, Ladies?"

"He's not talking—he's basically delirious—but he's got blood on the back of his sweatshirt and what looks like an entrance wound over his left flank," replied Danielle hurriedly.

I turned to the victim. "I'm Dr. Randolph. What's your name?" I asked loudly as my fingers slipped to his wrist. No reply. Nothing but moans between short, labored gasps through the mask.

His skin was wet under my fingers. I couldn't feel a radial pulse. *Not looking good.* He suddenly jerked and tried to sit up. I pushed him back down.

"Has he got a blood pressure, ladies?"

"The machine is trying to cycle now," replied Rebecca. I leaned on him to try to hold him still while the machine did its job, and watched the numbers count down on the monitor. Ten seconds later a question mark appeared where the blood pressure should have been on the monitor screen. That meant that his blood pressure was so low that the machine could not detect it.

"OK, Ladies, he's on his way out. I want four nurses in here, respiratory therapy, x-ray, and get me a surgeon. Danielle, I need four units of uncross-matched O-positive blood *now,* and four units of fresh-frozen plasma. And get a helicopter in the air. Tell Lynn that I need her in here. And get April in here, too." I needed to get April back into the thick of things—like climbing back on the horse that just bucked you off.

Fran returned. "No Hispanics in sight, Alex," she said breathlessly. I enlisted her help in leaning our new John Doe forward. He gave out a cry as we each grasped a shoulder and pulled. A small hole in his left lower back oozed a trickle of blood. It was lateral on his back, just over the costo-vertebral angle where the kidney lies. The rest of his back was unmarked.

"There's the entrance wound," I said. "Where the hell's the exit wound? Let me listen to his lungs before we lean him back."

I quickly listened to his right lung and it was clear with good loud breath sounds. But his breath sounds were much quieter on the left, and I couldn't hear them at all over the lower two-thirds of his lung.

We leaned him back again against the stretcher. I quickly inspected his chest and abdomen—no exit wound. John Doe was in respiratory distress and had absent breath sounds over his left lower lung field. That must mean that the trajectory of the bullet was north—he must have been lying horizontal when he was shot—the bullet traveling from his back, through his upper abdomen, and into his chest. Almost certainly blood was beginning to pool in his chest cavity, collapsing what remained of his left lung after a trip through it by a supersonic piece of metal. The slug apparently didn't have sufficient mass or velocity to exit.

I quickly listened to John Doe's heart and palpated his belly. He moaned louder when I pressed in the left upper quadrant through which the bullet had likely passed—perhaps through his kidney and probably his spleen on the way to his left lung. Most of his belly was already getting hard as a board. That probably meant free blood in his belly. The bullet mushrooms and tumbles after it enters the body, and I could just imagine the destruction to vital structures along this bullet's path. There must be bleeding everyplace.

I glanced at the monitor and saw that the oxygen saturation wasn't reading either, no doubt because the pulses in his fingers were too weak for the machine to pick up. He was going to need an intubation to try to get his oxygen levels up and a chest tube to suck out the blood in his left chest in order to re-expand his lung. And he was going to need a ton of blood, as well as both his chest cracked and his belly opened.

There was no way this was all going to happen in time. We were going to lose him.

"He's got nothing here in his arms," announced Rebecca, as she continued to search for a decent vein. "Track marks everywhere."

April walked into the room with an anxiety-ridden face.

"OK. Forget it. April, get me a femoral vein kit." We didn't have time to fool around looking for an IV site.

"He's got what looks like an entrance wound here on the back of his thigh," said Danielle, struggling to hold up his right leg for me to see. "And I think this is the exit wound laterally. Not much bleeding." He was probably shot in the leg first—as he was running—fell, and then caught a second slug in his back while horizontal on the ground.

"OK. Just dress those wounds for now."

Four people were now holding him down. I looked up at the monitor and saw a heart rate of one hundred and forty. I had competing immediate needs here for IV access, intubation, and a chest tube. The IV access had to come first. I needed to get sux into him and put him down so we could work on him. I also needed some help. *Where the hell is Lynn?*

I pulled on a pair of gloves, ripped open the sterile kit, and prepped his left groin for insertion of a triple lumen catheter into his femoral vein.

"Rebecca, as soon as I get this femoral line, we're going to intubate him. I'm going to need twenty-five milligrams of etomidate and a hundred and twenty-five of succinylcholine."

I thought I was able to faintly feel the pulsations of his femoral artery under my fingers wedged into his groin, but it was tough to be sure with all of John Doe's movement. The vein that I was searching for should be just to the inner side of the artery. I took my best guess, inserted the needle—inclining it at about a forty-five degree angle toward his head—and instantly a gush of blood surged into the syringe. I had lucked out, but luck trumps skill every time. I grasped the needle hub, unscrewed the syringe, and inserted my guide-wire through the needle. A minute later, the triple-lumen catheter was in place. Now we had IV access.

"OK. Let's get three bags of normal saline going wide open." Danielle started plugging IV lines into the catheter.

Mike Szymanski stuck his flat-topped head in through the doorway. "Everything looks secure in the lobby and waiting room, Doc, and I've got one guy posted in the parking lot. Police are en route. You OK in here?"

"I don't think our friend here is going to be too much of a problem, Mike." *This* John Doe was not going to constitute much of a danger to anybody for quite a while, and more likely, never again. Moreover, very shortly he would be literally paralyzed.

Lynn walked into the room and started to pull on a sterile gown. "Need some help in here, Alex?"

"Where have you been all my life, Lynn?"

"Just waiting for you, lover. Whaddya need?"

"Left flank gunshot wound. Looks like it went north into his chest. Diminished breath sounds left side. No blood pressure and no oh-two sat. He needs a chest tube. I'll be intubating him here shortly. You can go ahead and start your prep and I'll have him out for you in about one minute."

Rebecca walked back into the room with her drugs. I looked around the room and saw that April had already pulled out the intubation gear. Jill Brown from Respiratory Therapy was standing by with her ventilator. Everybody looked ready.

"Everybody ready?" Nods all around. "OK, Rebecca, etomidate first, then the sux."

Rebecca inserted the first syringe and announced, "Etomidate, twenty-five milligrams in." She quickly followed it with the succinylcholine—a drug not a whole lot different from the poison the South American Indians used to put on the end of their blowgun darts. Twenty seconds later John Doe's eyes closed and his cheeks puffed out. Another fifteen seconds later his muscles began to twitch as the succinylcholine took effect and began to paralyze him. The four people holding him tentatively backed off. He was still.

Jill Brown and I used the bag-valve-mask to ventilate him for about thirty seconds, but still couldn't get an oxygen saturation reading because his blood pressure was so low. I then quickly slid the laryngoscope into his throat, immediately saw the vocal cords, and slipped the endotracheal tube in without difficulty.

"OK, Lynn. You can put your chest tube in," I said. I saw her pick up her scalpel and rapidly make a two centimeter incision in the side of John Doe's chest between about his fifth and sixth rib. Lynn has good, confident hands. She always works fast and everything is neat as a pin.

"We've got a good CO_2 waveform," announced Jill. There was mist in the endotracheal tube and I could hear breath sounds on the right side of his chest. The tube was in good position.

There was a knock on the door and Mike Szymanski reappeared with a Baltimore County police officer in tow. "Police are here, Dr. Randolph," said Mike. "This is Officer Baker." I glanced at the big wall clock. Officer Baker was here about ten minutes after telling Fran to push the button. Not too bad. But ten minutes could also be an eternity if you had someone loose in your department with a gun.

"Officer Baker, we are pretty much under control at the present since our Crip friend here is asleep and paralyzed, and probably on his way to hell. There will be a helicopter here any minute, and he's going to be transferred to Shock Trauma—if he's still alive—so unfortunately, you're not going to get a chance to have a conversation with him here."

"OK, Doc. Well if you think it's OK, I'll just start interviewing witnesses here, then I may head downtown to University Hospital."

"Yep. That'll be fine. And thanks for the quick trip up here."

"You bet," said Officer Baker.

"Chest tube's in," announced Lynn, handing the end of the blood-filled tube to Fran to hook up to suction.

Betsy Stover from the blood bank strode in carrying four bags of O-positive blood and handed me a blood release form to sign, authorizing administration of blood without a cross-match.

I scribbled my initials on the release form. "April, let's get two of these units of blood started wide-open. And put a pressure bag on them."

"Do you want a propofol drip?" asked Rebecca.

"Let's use fentanyl to sedate him. That way we won't have to worry about him going into narcotics withdrawal, and it won't drop his blood pressure like propofol—that is, if he *had* a blood pressure to drop. Give him one hundred mics of fentanyl. Do we have a surgeon on the way?"

Julie was in the room now, and answered. "Dr. Matthews is finishing a case in the OR. He'll be here in about fifteen minutes. Same for the helicopter."

"Heart rate is starting to slow, Alex," reported Danielle. I looked up at the monitor and saw fifty-eight. I tried to feel for a carotid pulse—none. John Doe was dying.

"OK, let's get on his chest." Eli Harding, the day orderly, pushed a low stool to the bedside, stood on it, and began to deliver rapid compressions to John Doe's chest. Somebody started singing *Stayin' Alive* in the background, and Eli matched the beat.

After three minutes of compressions, sweat was dripping off Eli's nose. I told him to stop and we all stood silently and looked up at the monitor. The only sound was the whir and whoosh of the ventilator. John Doe's EKG complexes had now widened to twice their original width, and only one heartbeat crossed the screen about every ten seconds.

"OK, Eli, back on his chest. Give him a milligram of epi, Rebecca." This was the end. It wouldn't work. He was as good as dead. We were just going through the last-ditch motions now.

Ten minutes later I had them stop again. The monitor was flat line. The room grew quiet. Everyone stood silently looking at me. I watched the monitor a little longer—nothing but an ominous solid green line marching steadily across the screen. The alarm bell was clanging loudly.

"OK, guys, that's a wrap," I said finally. "The show's over. Good job everyone. What time have we got"

"Seven-oh-three," said Fran.

I stood and stared at the monitor as people slowly started to file out of the room, thinking about the volume of drug-related trauma we had seen in just the last few months. This particular John Doe was the fourth case—more than Mason-Dixon Regional Medical Center had seen the entire three years it had been open. And that didn't count Joyce Harbaugh. Our nice little civilized world out here in the country was collapsing.

~

"Wonderful!" said Stan Robinson. "Everything went smooth as silk, just like we planned. All of our systems worked and things couldn't have been more secure," he smiled. I was standing in the hallway with Stan, Mike, and Julie, anxious to get back to my chaotic and swamped ER. Stan wanted a little impromptu debriefing on the gunshot event—non-event, really—and was using this opportunity to pump us up and make sure we were all on board with Americus' wonderful security arrangements.

"You're right, Stan," I said. "Everything went great except for one thing."

"What's that?" said Stan, looking suddenly anxious.

"There *wasn't* any security problem today."

~

Toward the end of the shift-from-hell I saw April punching buttons on the Omnicell. I walked over and put my hand on her shoulder. "How'd it feel in there today?" I asked.

She turned her freckled face up to me, cocked her head to the side, and thought about it for a second. "Good," she said smiling. "Good."

CHAPTER THIRTY-SEVEN

TUESDAY MORNING I SAT ON THE STOOL AT MY computer in the kitchen with a cup of coffee and caught up on some e-mail. I read an e-mail from Julie to the nursing staff. She always cc'ed me on everything.

ED Team:

Just a reminder DOH will be visiting us tomorrow morning bright and early. Just a few simple reminders:

1. No loose medications on the counter at the nurses station by the Omnicell. Someone please help Ben with this.

2. No coffee or food at the nursing station. Someone please keep an eye on Alex.

3. Wash hands prior to going into room, and wash hands coming out of room.

4. Cabinets containing syringes and needles must be locked.

5. Wipe down all equipment in between patients. This includes stretchers, glucometers, any type of cables, BP

equipment, thermometers, IV poles and BSC. BSC should have a green clean sticker every time you clean it. They are kept in the old narc cupboard.

6. Keep computers minimized or logged-out.

7. Make sure to give your patients their call bells and document that. Don't be surprised if DOH reads your documentation that you gave the patient the call bell, and then walks back and checks if they have it. Also, since some of us like to just sit and listen to the call bells ring as a form of musical entertainment, don't be surprised if DOH doesn't ring the call bell and time how long it takes you to answer it. Call bells <u>must</u> be answered by <u>everyone</u>. It doesn't matter if it is your patient or not. This is for patient safety. This should happen <u>everyday</u>, not just the week DOH is here.

Thanks,

Julie

It was interesting that the only two people mentioned specifically by name as needing help in abiding by the rules were docs. Numbers one, two, four, and six of Julie's memo would go away the day after the Department of Health left. The hand washing, wiping down of equipment, and answering call bells would persist. Coffee would reappear at the nursing station, and people would start taking bites of a sandwich between patients again. It takes too long to open locked cabinets over a hundred times a day, so the locked cabinets would go. You have to survive.

But breaking these rules in front of the DOH would earn you a citation and could shut down your hospital. As is almost always the case, the inspecting agencies measure things that they know how to measure—like is there a coffee cup sitting at the nurses station? Things that they know how to measure usually don't matter much. The things that are important and impact quality of care—like can your nursing triage staff recognize a patient with heart failure, get them back, and start life-saving treatment before they are even seen by the doctor—they really don't have a clue how to measure.

~

Wednesday morning the January thaw finally appeared, only it was mid-February. The thermometer outside read thirty-seven degrees, although it seemed much colder because the humidity was high—one hundred percent, to be exact. Low clouds were disgorging torrents of water that were running off the frozen ground into the low areas. The gentle stream through my pasture was thirty feet wide and an angry red. General Lee and Abigail stood in the shelter of the loafing area of the barn, gazing out into the deluge with heads hung low as if they had missed a couple of doses of Prozac.

I drove to the hospital in the early gray light, the noisy wipers on my Jeep working furiously to clear the windshield to not much avail. A steady trickle of water poured through the seal between the canvas top and the windshield, past the rearview mirror, and onto the radio, which didn't work anyhow, probably because water had been dripping on it for years.

Early, as Julie had promised, but certainly not bright, the imperial forces from the DOH appeared at the nursing station. The entourage included Jackie Ford and Melissa Conklin, our regulatory compliance officer. Julie was escorting them. I took a quick sideways glance at my computer station as we shook hands to see if a coffee cup was in sight. None. So far, so good.

Ms. Bell, the stocky little nursing inspector who reminded me for all the world of Janet Napolitano, grabbed Julie, Jackie, and Melissa and started off down the hall, the click of her sensible low heels receding as she headed for Bed One.

Dr. Cook, the sallow-faced physician inspector who towered over his companion, turned to me and said, "Dr. Randolph and I will just chat in his office." *Oh-oh. Divide and conquer.* They were separating me from Julie. This was not good. He was going to ask me to show him a bunch of protocols, and I wasn't sure where we kept the damned three-ring binders. We stepped into my office, trying not to bump into each other, and there on my desk sat the protocol book. I said a silent prayer of thanks. Julie thinks of everything.

Thanks to Julie, I was able to wax eloquent about Mason-Dixon's progressive evidence-based emergency protocols. Dr. Cook, I discovered, was an ex-urologist, so I knew he didn't know a damn thing about what I was talking about. He would simply nod his head and say, "Very good… excellent" then turn to the next subject. So, I bull-shitted my way through our little *tête-à-tête* with flying colors—or at least I thought so.

Forty-five minutes later we all gathered back at the nursing station for the debrief. Predictably, Ms. Bell started off by telling us everything we had done right. *She's setting you up for the kill*, said Hyde. Dr. Cook chimed in about how pleased he was that a young, rural hospital had such sophisticated protocols.

Then the guillotine dropped. "Unfortunately," said Ms. Bell with a satisfied smile, "we *did* find a cabinet containing needles and syringes in the trauma room that was unlocked." I glanced over at Julie who looked livid.

"As I am sure you are aware," she continued, "this is a clear and important violation of Department of Health rules. I know I don't have to tell you how many substance abusers there are out there who would love to get their hands on those syringes. They *must* be kept under lock and key." That was true. Patients *did* steal stuff.

But this did not set well with Hyde, who immediately started going off. *What about our staff when it's a real emergency, you idiot! You think we have time to hunt around for keys to unlock those damned cabinets? Not to mention that most of our trauma victims are not exactly in shape to wander around the room opening cabinets and looking for goodies!* I tried to get him under control.

"Ms. Bell, I completely understand your concerns," I began sympathetically. "We have grave concerns, too, about the impact of drug abuse in our community. And I recognize that there are competing interests here. But don't you think that sometimes we let rules get in the way of good patient care? I know you are sympathetic to the fact that in the trauma room our mission is to keep severely injured people alive. That may mean that we sometimes have need for immediate access to life-saving equipment without having to hunt for keys."

"Dr. Randolph, that is a *most* readily solvable issue," she said in her most condescending and emphatic tone. "You simply have your trauma nurse carry the keys on her person at all times." *I'm such an idiot. Why didn't I think of that?*

"I'm sure you are quite right about that in hospitals that have dedicated trauma nurses, Ms. Bell. But, as you know, we're a small rural hospital, not a trauma center, and, in truth, it's very hard for us to come up with the resources to dedicate a nurse to trauma full time."

Mrs. Bell began to tap her foot. She was not accustomed to being challenged. Julie was giving me a look that said, "Zip it!" Jackie Ford's face was turning red. Dr. Cook began to shift his weight from one foot to the other.

"Dr. Randolph, you can take your argument to the Department of Health if you wish to change the rules," she said sternly. "In the interim, per DOH regulations, this emergency department will receive a citation. I thank you all for your time." With that she shook hands with everyone, and then clicked her way out of the department, Dr. Cook and the others trailing in her wake.

~

"You are an utter moron!" Julie fumed. That was the second time I had heard this from a woman in a couple of days. Pretty soon I was going to start believing it. In fact, I thought, it's probably true. Why couldn't I just leave it alone? At this point in my career, I was still trying to master the art of agreeing with idiots. I have this terrible libertarian streak that makes me resist taking orders from bureaucrats and administrators.

"Do you know what you just *did*?" she continued. "You just handed Jacquelyn Ford every weapon she needs to finish you off!" Julie slumped into her chair, looking depressed.

What could I say? She might be right. As my mother used to say, "The Lord gave you two ears and only one mouth for a reason."

"What happened?" I asked.

"They had a kid in the trauma room who fell off a horse," she said dejectedly. "They forgot to lock the cabinets when they shipped her up to the ICU."

CHAPTER THIRTY-EIGHT

I WAS STILL PAYING MY DUES FOR BEING AWAY out west for a week. Thursday was my fourth shift of the week. Thankfully, the deluge of patients this week had eased along with the departure of the rain into New England. I was actually able to get a lunch break, and headed off to *Le Petit Café*. I passed Jacquelyn Ford in the hallway who was striding in the opposite direction. She had a different click to her walk than Ms. Bell. Sensible low heels are not a part of Jackie's wardrobe, and Ms. Bell, no doubt, never practiced the Heidi Klum walk.

Jackie flashed me a wide smile, as we passed, and said brightly, "Good morning Dr. Randolph." Julie had put Hyde in a particularly paranoid mood, and he thought this bright greeting to be an ominous sign.

~

It seemed that time was flying by at warp speed in the last couple of months. I had last seen Elizabeth at Cathy and Tim's party just before Christmas, but it seemed like years ago. In truth, she rarely popped into my mind anymore, except occasionally when I woke up in the morning with most of my blood volume in my crotch. In my fog, I could see her walking across the room at the bottom of my bed in nothing but her pink thong panties, which, thanks to Ruth's uncertainty, were still in my underwear drawer.

John and I met at Souris' Saloon Thursday night after I got off work to have a beer together and catch up. We watched a Flyers game on ESPN as we talked. One of the nice things about being single is that I don't have to get permission from anybody to indulge in this sort of evening. John was a lucky bastard in that Annick seemed to see value in this, and encouraged him to go. As is the case with two boys who had grown up together since they were toddlers, there were few secrets between us.

"Have you seen Elizabeth since the party?" he asked between sips of a Sam Adams. I shook my head.

"Have *you*?" I asked.

"Saw her once at a party at Ashley and Todd's place."

"How'd she look?"

"Very hot, as usual."

"She didn't look depressed at my absence in her life?"

"*Au contraire*," he said between hamburger bites. "Vivacious. Charming"

"Always," I said.

"She had a date. Software developer, or something. Looked like the hormones were flowing between them. He looks older. Self-absorbed CEO type who thinks he lights up the room."

"Sounds to me like a good match," I said, suddenly realizing for the first time what a relief the breakup with Elizabeth had been.

"I heard they flew to St. Bart's together a couple of weeks ago on the corporate jet for a long weekend." He was watching me to see what my reaction would be.

"Perfect. Right up Elizabeth's alley."

"So, what happened between you two?" he asked. John had something of a vested interest in this relationship since his sister, Ashley, was married to Elizabeth's brother, Todd. He had been hoping for my company in the rarified air of Hamilton family events. I thought about his question for a second.

"I think we wanted different things from life. Different things were important to us. And the longer we went on, the more those differences came between us.

“Like what?”

“Believe it or not, some day I want children. And I like my farm, and I like my tractor, and I like my Jeep. And I can’t stand Elizabeth’s inane friends. Just *once*, I would have liked to have seen her with no makeup, in a pair of dirty jeans, forking horseshit.”

“I think the airplane probably trumps the Jeep for Elizabeth. And you’re not likely to see an *American Gothic* photo of her with a pitchfork in her hand.”

“But *Penny* likes my Jeep. You know, John, I don’t miss Elizabeth at all,” I said, “except for occasionally when I find her panties in my drawer.” John thought that was funny.

“Well, the way you were zeroed in on Penny Murray’s body at the tennis club, I’m surprised poor Elizabeth gets any fantasy time at all. Not that I can blame you.”

“C’mon, it wasn’t that obvious!”

“Oh, no? You know what Annick said on the way home?”

“What?”

“*Zat* boy needs to get laid.”

“That’s bullshit!” I yelled. John held himself, laughing. “Listen,” I said, “I was focused on the match. “You seem to have forgotten that you lost.”

“Your partner carried you.”

“That she did,” I grinned. “She does have a nice butt, though, doesn’t she?”

“Stellar. Although, if asked, I will deny that I ever said that. Did you conjure up any more lies to get her to go out with you?”

“In a moment of weakness, I actually directly asked her out last week.”

“And?”

“She ran from the room.”

“Wow, you’re a whiz with women.” The roar of the crowd suddenly welled from the TV. “OH! That hurt! Did you see that shot? I think he took the puck in his face mask.” We watched the replay and saw the goalie’s head snap back.

"So, she didn't say anything before she left the room?" John continued.

"Yeah. She said 'I can't.'"

"That was illuminating."

"*I* thought so."

"Maybe you need to go back to lies."

"Yeah, I've been thinking about that."

CHAPTER THIRTY-NINE

JULIE AND I MET FRIDAY MORNING AT 9:30, AS WE usually do once a month, to review numbers, talk about issues, and, in general, try to make sure that the staff is hearing the same thing from both of us. It was my day off, but the growing ER volume had made it virtually impossible for us to meet when I was working a scheduled shift.

"Almost three thousand visits last month," Julie said, tapping the computer printout.

"Holy shit, that's an annual volume of thirty-six thousand!" I said.

"Now you know why everybody's running ragged." Our staffing levels were designed to handle roughly twenty-five to twenty-eight thousand patients annually.

"For January, at least," said Julie, "we were forty-two percent over budgeted visits. Revenue was up forty-five percent."

We were being discovered. Patients from the northern Baltimore suburbs were beginning to head north to Mason-Dixon rather than south to the big city hospitals, lured, we suspected, by the shorter wait-times and a bunch of nice people that worked here. Our patient satisfaction scores were running very high. Obviously, the Crips and Mara Salvatrucha liked us, although the Crips weren't faring too well these days.

"That oughta make Hal Jellinik happy," I said. Jellinik was Mason-Dixon's Chief Financial Officer and had nearly as much power in the organization as Stan Robinson.

"Well, you wouldn't know it by the capital budget that just came out," sighed Julie.

"Why?"

"You know what we got?"

"What?"

"*Nada.* Nothing. Well, two IV pumps."

"You're kidding?" Julie shook her head.

"What's that—ten or twelve thousand bucks?" I asked.

Julie shrugged. "Maybe."

"How'd the other departments do?"

"Got pretty much everything they asked for," she said.

~

I was back in Saturday morning, working yet another weekend. Next Saturday would be my first full weekend off since my return from Colorado. After a while of working these chaotic schedules, it doesn't matter so much whether you're working a weekend or not. The days sort of just run into each other, and I tend to lose track sometimes of what day it is without the clear marker of weekends off.

It was early afternoon, and not a bad day so far. I picked up the next chart.

Allen Whitfield lay on the stretcher in Room Four, looking somehow dapper and aristocratic despite his rumpled barn clothes. He held a rather grungy-looking tracheostomy tube in his right hand. Trach tubes are supposed to be in a hole in your neck that goes into your trachea, not in your hand.

I knew Allen well. We had actually shared a drink together on several occasions. His big ruddy face broke into a wide grin when I walked into the room. He had the little red veins on his face and nose that betrayed a close kinship with an old Scottish distilling firm. He put a finger in the hole in his neck to plug it up so he could talk, stuck out his hand, and said in a raspy, but still booming voice, “How ya doin’, Doc?”.

We were neighbors of a sort. Allen was a retired sometime lawyer who was one of the last scions of old Manor money that was now running out. He still hung on to the decaying main house of the family estate on Hess Road—consoling himself with booze—but, bit by bit, he was selling off pieces of the once imperious *Chestnut Farms*.

Allen had a tracheostomy because he had obstructive sleep apnea. When you have OSA, your tongue and pharyngeal muscles relax so much during sleep that your upper airway just collapses, blocking airflow. Then, when you can’t breathe, you wake up. This cycle gets repeated over and over again, dozens of times a night. The solution—a hole in your neck into your trachea through which you can breathe when your upper airway collapses at night.

“Allen, what are you doing here with your trach in your hand?”

“I don’t think you have time to hear the answer to that question.”

“OK,” I said, looking at my watch, “since there’s no scotch here, you oughta be able to get it over with inside of fifteen minutes.”

Allen was nothing if not a sparkling conversationalist. And, he could not have cared less what you, or anyone else for that matter, thought of him, so you heard things out of his mouth that you didn’t hear from many other people. I could listen to him for hours.

“Sit down,” he ordered. I pulled up a folding chair.

“You know my dog, Daniel T. Boone, don’t you?”

“Yeah. He licks my scotch glass clean when it’s empty.”

“That’s one of the problems with empty scotch glasses. Well, anyhow, I was standing out on the stone terrace at the back of the house this morning—you know how the ground drops off there toward the creek, and the terrace is twelve or thirteen feet above ground level?” I nodded.

“Anyhow, I was standing on the terrace when I saw the farmer coming down the lane on his tractor, pulling a manure spreader. He was going to ford the creek, like he usually does. But with all this rain we had, there’s a low spot above the stream bank that I was afraid he’d get stuck in. So I started yelling, *STOP! STOP!*, so he could hear me above the engine noise."

"Well, that was a mistake. I yelled so loud that the pressure blew my trach right out of the hole, and it tumbled over the wall of the terrace. I'm peering over the wall at my trach, lying on the ground below, when who should come trotting around the corner but Daniel T. Boone." I could see it coming.

"Of course, it didn't take Daniel long to spot that trach, and he picks it up and starts trotting off again. All I could think of was, *a hundred and forty dollars*; *a hundred and forty dollars*—that's what those bloody things cost these days. So I raced down the stairs and started calling, 'Here Dan'l, here Dan'l'. But as soon as I got close to him he'd trot off again."

"So we went round and round the house, and finally I grab him by the collar. I'm holdin' him up in the air by his collar, but he doesn't wanna let go of the trach. So I put my fingers in his mouth and try to pry it open. Finally he lets go, and when I yank it out, my finger scrapes across a canine, and… here I am," he said, holding up a bloody finger. "Mary Beth made me come in to get a tetanus shot."

"So how come your trach tube is in your hand instead of your neck?" I asked.

"Well, sometime in all of this, that little plastic plug that goes in the trach got lost. So I went to the True Value store in Jacksonville, and I got this stainless steel bolt. Fits perfectly," he said, holding up his trach tube, "but it's a little heavy." I looked down at his trach tube and saw a gleaming hex head bolt sticking out of the end.

"Allen, that's a very sad story. Let me see your finger." It was just a superficial laceration—scratch, really—and *that* we would just clean and bandage.

I picked up his trach tube and started examining it. There were tooth marks and long linear scratches in the translucent plastic. "I applaud your engineering innovation," I said, turning the tube over in my hand, "but maybe we ought to get you a new trach tube. What do you think?"

"How much?"

"How much? Allen, I don't have the slightest idea."

"I think I'll just try this one a little longer," he said. "If it turns out to be too heavy, I'll get a new one from Hereford Pharmacy. You guys'll rob me blind."

CHAPTER FORTY

WHEN I CAME IN AT 7:00 ON TUESDAY morning, Scott signed out three patients to me in various stages of a workup, but there were no new charts in the to-be-seen rack. E-mail is both my salvation and the bane of my existence. It probably steals pretty close to an hour from my day. But, it also allows me to pick up the phone less and stay in touch with key people more easily. So during the lull I logged onto my Americus.com e-mail through the intranet, and began to scroll through the new e-mails. I always first mark the ones that I have no interest in reading, delete them, and then begin to work my way through the remaining e-mails.

I skipped over several containing agenda attachments for various meetings, read a reminder to the staff from Julie about keeping cabinets locked, and then spotted an e-mail from my attorney, or, at least, the attorney that the hospital had chosen to represent me.

> Dr. Randolph:
>
> I wanted to give you as much notice as possible, but we finally have a trial date for the Robert Kline case. It is currently scheduled to start on April 5th and will likely run for

two to three days. Keep in mind that this far ahead of time these dates often change, so you may want to try and arrange for some flexibility in your schedule in early April. Also remember that although Robert had a rocky course following his appendectomy, he did recover, and there is no evidence of lasting harm. I think we'll do all right with this case.

Regards,

Kathleen Stefanik, Esq.

Even though long ago I had decided that I wouldn't do anything differently if it were Groundhog Day and I got to re-live seeing Robert in the ER, I could still feel a subtle rise in tension as I read the e-mail. But I was beginning to learn from experience that in a few hours the tension would fade, and, within a day or two, I would have forgotten about it until the next reminder. Actually, at this point I was happy that in another six weeks or so, it would finally be coming to conclusion.

The next e-mail I read was from Gwen Reynolds. *Meeting with Dr. Myers*, the subject header said.

I clicked on the e-mail and opened it, wondering who the hell was Dr. Myers?

Hi Dr. Randolph:

Could you please give me a call at your convenience to give me a couple of dates when you could meet with Dr. Myers? Or, you can e-mail me some dates.

Gwen

I picked up the phone and dialed Gwen's extension in the administrative offices, but nobody was in yet. I made a mental note to try again later in the day.

Nine patients signed in between 7:53 and 8:12. It took ten processing minutes before the first chart hit the to-be-seen rack, and I finally started wading into the promise of a chaotic day.

Some of them were quick and easy, like a laceration suture removal and three twenty-somethings with flu. But about every third patient required some sort of workup, and by 9:00 AM, when Ben came on, we had ten beds filled.

"Looks like I scheduled myself for the wrong day," said Ben looking up at the status board."

"Yeah, we're not off to a great start," I said. "I think the flu is finally starting to hit. I've had three already this morning. They're all scared to death of H1N1 and think they're going to die."

In fact, the much-hyped H1N1 influenza virus was turning out to be no worse that the regular influenza strains. We needed an in-house shrink to handle all the anxiety.

"And by the way," I said accusingly, "I understand that you've been entertaining my sister."

"And a lovely young lady she is," he rumbled, "with a pretty good head on her shoulders, too."

"I used to think so until she told me she was going out with you."

"Hey, she recognizes quality in a man when she sees it."

"Do you think that you can remember her name?"

"Anne Merriman Randolph."

"You just remember that she's got a brother with a hair-trigger temper and a predilection for violence."

"Wait a minute," said Ben. "She's an investment counselor. What if she's just out for my money?"

I grinned. "Do you have a T. Rowe Price account yet?"

"No, but I will by tomorrow," he said laughing. "I just finished filling out the papers yesterday."

~

Mid-morning I saw Jack Schmidt ambling down the hallway, picking his way between wheelchairs and stretchers. It had been a week yesterday since the shooting death of John Doe, and I hadn't heard anything back from the police yet. Despite the horrible reasons for his appearances, I had come to look forward to his periodic visits.

"Morning, Jack."

"How ya doin', Doc?" he smiled, leaning on the corner of the nursing station counter.

"Well so far, Jack, every person in northern Baltimore County this morning has decided that they need emergent medical care, and, as you can see, we're spilling over into the hallways."

"Hey, good for keeping food on the table, huh?" Jack always managed to reduce complex issues to their simplest components.

"What have you learned of interest in the last week?"

"Well, I'm getting to know some of the boys in Baltimore City pretty well. Been workin' with a detective named George Ballantine. He works narcotics and knows the players in this little game. Your John Doe from a week ago was in the same Crip gang as Jawara Reynolds. His name was Milton Jones, aka Sonny Jones. Actually, he and Reynolds were second cousins, or something. Twenty-six years old. Long rap sheet."

"So, did you figure out what happened yet, or who shot him?"

"Well, we at least know where and when. There was a shootout down in the city on the corner of Jefferson and Patterson Park Avenue that day, maybe an hour before you got him. That's down behind Hopkins."

"Yeah, I know the area."

"That's right, you used to work at Hopkins," Jack said, waving his arm. "In any case, by the time the police got to the scene it was over. One dead Hispanic and a wounded black. But they found a blood trail close by the scene, running from an alley to the curb. It didn't seem to jive with the location of the two victims they found, so they took a blood sample and checked the DNA. We ran it against Jones' DNA, and it was a match."

"So, he was running away, took a hit in the leg, went down, and then took another shot in the back. Then he crawled away to a car."

"That's the way it looks. We're gonna turn you into a forensic pathologist yet, Doc," Jack said, giving a little groan as he straightened up and stretched his back.

You know, Jack, I was very happy just being an ER doc until you showed up. I assume the Hispanic was MS-13?"

"Probably. No direct confirmation, but they *did* find a match on his prints, and he *was* a Salvadoran national. He also entered on a student visa four years ago and disappeared. He apparently had managed to avoid arrest, because he's got no rap sheet."

"So, I wonder why Milton Jones' buddies brought him all the way up here?"

"Maybe he was the shooter of the Salvadoran and he didn't want a murder rap—was afraid he might get arrested if he went to Hopkins or Shock Trauma. We *did* get the bullet that lodged in his chest, by the way, and it's not in too bad a shape. We may be able to use that in the future for a ballistics match."

"Well, at least by driving all the way up here he saved the taxpayers a whole lot of dough," I said. "His *Golden Hour* was about up when he arrived." The *Golden Hour* is a term used by traumatologists to emphasize that if trauma victims are to be saved, you've usually got to get definitive care accomplished within the first hour, or the mortality skyrockets.

"Thoughtful of him," said Jack.

"Sounds like you're getting pretty good cooperation from Baltimore City."

"Those poor bastards are just swamped down there. Homicide is absolutely overwhelmed. I think the only reason they've spent the kind of time on this case they have is because we're an outside jurisdiction pumping them for information. They don't wanna look bad in front of Baltimore County. That, and George and I get along pretty well."

"You've been putting in a lot of time in the last couple of months, haven't you?"

"Well, this is a little more excitement than we usually have up here in Precinct Seven."

"So Jack, what do you do for rest and relaxation?"

Jack smiled. "I got me a little sailboat out on Middle River," he said, leaning forward on the counter again, "a twenty-six footer. She ain't fast, but she carries a lot of beer and the crabs are fresh. Me and the Mrs. get reacquainted out there sometimes."

"Not this time of year I bet."

"Nah. We don't generate that much heat anymore," he said laughing. "I save all my vacation time and personal days for the summer. You like steamed crabs?"

"Love 'em."

"You got a woman? I don't see any wedding ring."

"Uhh… not just now, although I'm trying to work on it."

Well, maybe we could eat a few crabs together and watch a sunset on the bay some evening this summer."

"Jack, I would really like that."

"Well, you land that woman before summer," he said grinning.

~

Just before noon I remembered to call Gwen and managed to squeeze in a quick call between patients.

"Hey Gwen, how are you today?"

"Hi, Dr. Randolph! I'm fine. Thanks for calling me."

"Who's this Dr. Myers?"

"Dr. Myers is our new Vice President for Medical Affairs."

"And he wants to see me?"

"Yes. He asked me to set up an appointment with you."

"Do you know what he wants?"

"I *don't*, Dr. Randolph."

"OK. You want some dates, right?" I looked for some dates in my Google calendar and gave them to Gwen.

"Thanks, Dr. Randolph. I'll check with Dr. Myers and e-mail you the date and time."

"OK, Gwen, thanks."

I didn't have a great feeling about this. Myers was hired awfully fast after Ed Simpson was fired. There was no time to do a search for someone of national stature who would bring credibility to Americus' physician community. I figured that this time, John Salzman had hired somebody close to him, whose loyalty was unquestioned, and who would do his absolute bidding. That might not bode well for me since the VP of Medical Affairs was ostensibly my boss. At least Ed Simpson had left me alone, asshole that he was.

~

Usually once the floodgates open on any given day, they never seem to close until the early morning hours. By late afternoon I was fading fast. We were up to sixty patients since 7:00 AM. Thank God, a lot of them were flu cases that we could get in and out fairly quickly. But there were enough abdominal pains, chest pains, and crashing old folks that Ben and I just couldn't catch up.

I ran my fingers through my hair, locked my fingers behind my head, and stretched. A young-looking female hand appeared in my field of vision and sat a cup of coffee down in front of my monitor screen. Steam wafted off the surface. It smelled wonderful. I looked up and saw Penny.

"You look like you could use that. It's fresh. Two sugars and two creams, if I remember correctly," she said smiling. Something different about her caught my attention, but I couldn't bring it into focus. I sat there blankly for a moment, then looked back down at her hand. She wasn't wearing any rings. I looked back up at her and for a few seconds our eyes locked. The last four hours of my shift went by in a blur.

CHAPTER FORTY-ONE

I FIGURED THAT MAYBE ANNE WAS RIGHT. AT least I *hoped* she was right. Maybe Penny had given me a message—a message that she was ready. I sure as hell was going to find out. Anyhow, I drove home feeling pretty good—actually it bordered a little more on euphoria—justified or not. It was possible that this was a fluke—that Penny had just taken off her rings to wash her hands or something, and forgotten to put them back on—but I didn't think so.

I pulled into the driveway, and walked over to the fence where Robert E. Lee and Abigail stood like shadows in the light of a full moon. Their necks were stretched out over the board fence, and both started immediately nuzzling me in their search for carrots. I didn't have any carrots, but I reached into my jacket pocket and found a couple of sugar cubes—even better.

"Here you go, guys," I said, as each horse slobbered over a flattened hand, greedily searching for cubes. Abigail whinnied. "Life is good, huh girl?" I said, rubbing her nose.

~

I slouched back in the chair in Julie's office and stretched my legs out in front of me, arms folded. I was ten minutes early for my 7:00 PM Wednesday night shift, and Julie was still in her office.

"How's life?" I asked brightly. Julie gave me a quizzical look.

"What are you so happy about? You're about to start a night shift."

"You know, life is short. You may as well enjoy it—even being here in your office, enjoying your sparkling conversation."

Julie smiled. "You need medication. Are you getting laid?"

"Unfortunately, not. So what do you know about this Myers guy?" I asked.

"Dr. Myers, the new VP of Medical Affairs?" she replied, looking up from her computer.

"Yeah."

"Nothing, except that he's a little nerdy looking," she said, returning to typing.

"You've met him?"

"No. I saw him walking down the hall near the administrative offices with Stan and Jackie."

"What's he look like?"

"He's young. Maybe your age. Has a crew cut and wears black frame glasses—like Jackie."

"Do you know where he came from or what kind of doc he is?"

"Nope."

"He wants to see me." She looked up again from her computer and thought about that for a few seconds.

"Your contract's up," she said quietly, her face growing a little pale.

"What?"

"Your contract's up in April. It'll be three years. He doesn't know you from Adam. What if he's the executioner? What if Salzman hired him to get rid of you?"

~

Roberta Flemming sat with her legs crossed on a folding chair in the corner of Bed 3, cracking gum. It was 2:00 AM. She wore a black shift top with fringes on the bottom, covering her black jeans to mid-thigh. Her fingernails were black, her lipstick was black, her eye shadow was black, and her short hair was black, except for the pink stripe bisecting her scalp.

I had the distinct impression that Roberta had been the victim of a voodoo party. She had metal sticking out all over her face: lower lip, nose, right eyebrow, and about five studs in each ear. I couldn't be sure about her tongue. She needed to be careful about going out into electrical storms.

"Hey, Roberta. I'm Dr. Randolph," I said, taking a seat on the exam table.

"Hi ya, Doc," she said, sticking out her hand. I shook it.

"What's the problem tonight?"

"I'm out of Geodon."

"You're out of Geodon?"

"Yeah. I'm schizo."

"Well, did you try asking your psychiatrist to write you a scrip?"

"Haven't seen him in two years. We don't get along."

"So you came in tonight just to get a prescription for Geodon?"

"Yep. Otherwise, feelin' fine," she said smiling.

"When did you run out of Geodon?"

"Tonight."

"Roberta, you realize, of course, that ER docs are not in the habit of trying to manage outpatient psychiatric disease?"

"Yep. I know that. But you wouldn't like me off Geodon. I'm a menace to society. You'll be doing the world a favor by writing me a scrip."

~

My Wednesday night was going pretty well—all except for Julie's paranoia regarding my imminent firing. Actually it made me feel good that she was so worried about me. And Julie, sadly, had real reason to be paranoid. Despite, in my opinion, being by far the best unit manager in the hospital—a Godsend to our department, really—the poor girl had consistently received below average performance ratings from Jacquelyn Ford, and three months ago had actually been placed on a formal action plan—the first step to kissing your ass goodbye. Julie thought outside the box a little too much, and was a little too creative in the way that she ran the department. She didn't always buy into the *Americus Way*. This did not set too well with Jacquelyn, who preferred obedience to innovation from her employees. I didn't think they would actually fire her. That would be a little risky, given her objectively stellar performance and the administration's recent crowing about how door-to-doctor times were falling in the ER. But they could make her life miserable and hope that she quit.

I supposed it was possible that they wanted to get rid of me, too, but, in truth, if you looked at the structural situation objectively, it was not likely.

Mason-Dixon's ER was thriving. We had the shortest door-to-doctor times in the state, were in the top couple of percent nationally in our patient satisfaction scores, and had a stable of really good docs. I was certain that we had the deep support of the medical staff. Our market share was taking off like a rocket, and our revenues were exploding. In the last year we had actually turned profitable—a rare and enviable case for an ER. So, what's to fix?

Penny was working the 3:00 PM to 3:00 AM shift, which had a decidedly positive impact on how well this night was going. Of course, the first thing I did when I came on at 7:00 was to check out her hand again. No rings. So yesterday probably wasn't a fluke. She'd come to some sort of decision. I had been looking all night for the right opportunity to pop the big question again, but hadn't yet found the right time.

It was nearing 3:00 AM when finally there came a moment when all the rest of the staff were busy in patient rooms, and I suddenly found myself sitting at the nursing station alone with Penny. We were both at our computers, two chairs apart. *Well, here goes.*

"Penny," I said, turning toward her, "I wonder if, by chance, you've had an opportunity to reconsider the advantages of having dinner with me?"

"And what might those be?" she smiled, brushing back a golden wisp of hair from her face.

"Well, the opportunity to spend an evening with a handsome and debonair young ER doc who thinks that you're the most beautiful woman he's ever met."

She looked at me for a long time without speaking.

"What took you so long?" she asked finally.

"What?"

"What took you so long? I've been waiting almost eight hours for you to ask me out."

"Does that mean that you'll have dinner with me?"

"Yes, Alex, I *will* have dinner with you," she said quietly. "We may have to take this in steps, and you may have to be a little patient with me, but I would like very much to have dinner with you." Her eyes never left mine. *Wow.*

"OK," I said finally. "Wonderful. Saturday night, if that's OK. I'll pick you up at 7:00 at your house. Uhh... do you need to check with a babysitter or something?"

"No. I've already arranged for that," she said smiling. *Unbelievable. I have to make sure that Anne never hears this story. I'll hear 'I told you so' for the rest of my life..*

"What should I wear?" she asked.

A little pink thong. "Uhh...I like the way you look in jeans."

She capped her pen and threw it at me. I could have sworn she knew what I was thinking.

CHAPTER FORTY-TWO

BY FRIDAY NIGHT, WHEN THE LEADING EDGE of a cold front came through, the January thaw in February was over. Forecast highs for Saturday were only in the mid-twenties. What's more, a low pressure area in Arkansas, with a lot of moisture, was riding up the cold front and was predicted to hit the mid-Atlantic with heavy snow by late Saturday afternoon.

I didn't care. I didn't have Penny's phone number to cancel the date for weather, and, furthermore, I had a Jeep with four-wheel-drive for whom the snow was its *raison d'être.* I would be in Padonia at seven o'clock. Obtaining a date with this woman was way too much work to let it go for a little snow.

I finished my shower and pounded down the sneaky staircase into the kitchen, whistling as I buttoned a flannel shirt. Ruth was mopping the floor. I could smell fresh-brewed coffee.

"Morning, Ruth."

"Alex!" she said like she hadn't been expecting me. "Good morning."

"Did you make the coffee this morning, Ruth? I think I forgot to put it on and set the timer last night."

"Yes I did. Three large scoops."

"Smells wonderful," I said, pouring a cup.

"What's on your schedule today?" she asked. "I don't have

anything on my calendar for you."

"Well, Ruth, I have nothing planned for today, so I will probably just piddle around the farm here. But I have to be out of here at probably about 6:15."

"You know there's a big snowstorm coming this afternoon?"

"Yep, I heard that."

"Do you really think you should try to go out in that?"

"Ruth, just like the U.S. Postal Service, nothing will keep me from my appointed rounds tonight." She was quiet for a moment. As usual, this was not quite enough information.

"Your must have a very important appointment."

"Ruth, this is not an appointment. I have a *date* tonight."

"Really?" She smiled.

I was feeling expansive this morning. "Remember that girl I told you about—the one I met at the Rutledge Christmas party?"

"The one with two children?" Ruth was not likely to forget that one.

"That's the one. She has finally consented to have dinner with me tonight." I could see Ruth's wheels turning.

"How old are her children?" The kids were obviously of at least as much interest to Ruth as the woman.

"Six and three. You should see them, Ruth. They're gorgeous."

"So she's divorced?"

"No. She's a widow. Her husband was killed in Afghanistan. He was in the military. She's a very remarkable woman."

Ruth thought about that for a moment, then seemed to reach a clear conclusion. "Do you need any food in the house or anything?" she said brightly.

"No, Ruth. We're going out. And, I've got everything clean that I need to wear."

"Do you have reservations?"

"Yes. Milton Inn at 7:30."

"Well, that's very nice," she said smiling. "The house will be clean, and I brought some fresh flowers for the family room. And I'll have lunch ready for you at noon." She walked toward the refrigerator, then stopped abruptly and looked back at me over her shoulder. "You don't have any toys in the house, do you?" It was a little bit early in this particular relationship to be bringing Penny and the kids home, but I certainly was able to appreciate Ruth's sentiment regarding having the house ready.

~

My mother always told me never to wish my life away, but, God, Saturday went by slowly. About mid-morning I put on jogging togs and went for a run. I pulled the snowblower out of the garage, gassed it up, and started it to make sure that it would run. Despite it being late in the winter, I still had the brush hog on the back of the New Holland, so I took it off and mounted the rear plow blade in anticipation of the snow. Pushing snow is interesting with a rear-mounted blade because you have to do it backwards, with the tractor in reverse.

Sally showed up about four o'clock. No sign anymore of a limp, thankfully. We cheerfully chatted for a few minutes, and then later I pushed out the week's manure onto the big pile. In retrospect, I was glad that things hadn't moved too far along with Sally. I enjoyed our relationship. This way it was uncomplicated. Sometimes things work out.

By five o'clock the first flakes were lazily drifting down from a densely overcast sky. It was cold. The flakes started laying instantly.

I had made reservations—without help from Ruth—for the Milton Inn on the York Road in Sparks at 7:30. It occurred to me that maybe I better check to make sure that the restaurant was still as enthusiastic about the evening's festivities in the snow as I was. The maître d' said, "Nope. We've still got thirty or forty reservations, so we're here until at least the last of those is served." They have a perishable product they need to get rid of.

It's interesting that the Milton Inn was the only restaurant within miles of my house when I was growing up on Sparks Road, but I never made it inside the place until I was in my early thirties. That's probably because the appetizers start at about fourteen dollars, and my father would have considered that a good price for dinner for two during the business-building/growing-the-family days.

But in any case, the inn is a magnificent two hundred and seventy-year-old stone structure. The food is expensive, but, in truth, superb, so I don't mind the money. Fortunately, the management isn't too pretentious—they're just happy to have your dough—so it's comfortable.

Under normal circumstances, it was only a twenty-five minute drive to Penny's Padonia Road townhouse. Tonight I would allow forty-five minutes—for the other drivers, of course, not for my Jeep. I love driving in the snow. When Brian and I were teenagers, my father used to get us up at two o'clock in the morning to go out and push snow for Randolph Nursery's corporate clients. It was always exhilarating to make the first run on unplowed roads.

I stepped out of the shower and looked in the mirror, feeling my face for stubble. It was probably OK. I decided not to shave again. I thought it unlikely, despite my fantasies, that there would be a lot of nuzzling tonight.

It was pretty interesting, though, the way that I imagined sex with Penny. It was a little difficult to visualize. Not that I couldn't visualize Penny naked. I spent a *lot* of time, in fact, visualizing her lovely little body naked. But, somehow in my brain, making love to her was much more of an extension of how I felt about her; my desire to get inside her—maybe somehow to merge with her. So, I guess it was as much emotional as visual. Still hot, but perhaps more powerful or moving than imagining sex with another hot woman that I didn't know, which was, without a doubt, pretty much an exclusively visual experience.

I threw on a sweater and jeans, grabbed a tweed sport coat, and pulled on my ski parka. By the time I stepped out the kitchen door about 6:15, the grass was completely covered with sparkling light powder. The air had that seductive stillness that only occurs during snowfalls, and the snow was so heavy that I could barely see the barn in the reflection of the lantern on the post at the end of the walk.

I took the Interstate, rather than driving down York Road, on the theory that I was less likely to get stuck behind a terrified ten-mile-per-hour driver who puts on his brakes when going around uphill curves. My timing was nearly perfect. I arrived just five minutes early.

I pushed the doorbell and waited. A long minute later, the door opened and Penny stood there with a big smile, looking like a grown-up version of Catherine. She wore a snug pair of jeans tucked into the top of fur-lined boots. A short sheepskin jacket ended at her waist, allowing me an unobscured view of her gorgeous little butt and hips. She had a long white knit scarf wound around her neck—one end dangling to the waist—and wore matching knit gloves and cap. Her wavy blond hair cascaded out from under the snug cap and down over her shoulders. I thought she looked like a poster model from Abercrombie & Fitch.

"You made it!" she enthused, and wrapped her arms around me in a hug, her head buried in my chest, then looked up. "I was so worried we'd get cancelled."

"You forget. You're on a date with a farm boy who's got his Jeep." Penny giggled, her eyes ablaze.

"You don't look like a farm boy to me."

"I'm in disguise as a debonair young ER doc."

"You forgot 'handsome,'" she giggled again. "C'mon, let's go!" she yelled, grabbing my hand and running, dragging me along with her through the snow to the Jeep.

~

By the time we reached Milton Inn, the setting was pretty spectacular. The big green English boxwoods surrounding the inn were topped with snow, glistening in the light from a huge gas lantern at the end of the brick walk. The windows were deep-set in the massive fieldstone walls and glowed softly with light. We walked hand in hand to the paneled black entrance door and stomped the snow off our feet, exhaling clouds of steam.

Penny looked around. "Oh, it's beautiful, Alex."

I knew John, the maître d', and he said, "Dr. Randolph, I see you made it through the snow tonight, and with a beautiful woman at your side, to boot." This was John's way of saying, "I haven't seen Elizabeth for a while. This is a new one."

He led us to a white-covered table for two by one of the tall, multi-paned windows. We could see the snow pouring down outside in the cone of light from a landscape spotlight. He pulled out a chair for Penny and she sat, shaking out her gleaming hair. She tucked it behind both ears, revealing big silver hoops that glinted in the light of the little oil lamp on the side of the table. She wore a thin coat of either lip gloss, or a light lipstick, that called attention to her wide mouth—the first that I had ever seen her with a trace of makeup. I was smitten, as usual.

"This is a gorgeous place," she said, casting her eyes around the red room with satin white woodwork. A fire burned quietly in a stone fireplace in the middle of the north wall. Surprisingly, three or four other tables were filled with stalwart patrons who had braved the storm.

John brought us drinks. A Grey Goose and a cosmo later, we dived into a plate of *Smoke Salmon Rose*, with creamed horseradish, capers, red onion and lemon.

"Mmm… this is divine," Penny said between bites. "So how *did* you swing buying the farm? You're so lucky. Property is so *expensive* up here!"

"I was *very* lucky. An elderly couple named Stuart and Emily Robinson owned it outright. They had lived there for fifty years, and both finally had to move into a nursing home. My dad knew their lawyer. So, I heard the property would be going up for sale and contacted them. They didn't need a big chunk of money—just steady income. So they said that if I would meet their price, they would take paper—hold the mortgage themselves. And voila. They didn't want a lot of money down, and I didn't even have to go through a bank. I'm not sure that I could have gotten a loan for that much money."

"Oh, that sounds so *sad*!" she said frowning. "After fifty years together there."

"Oh, it *was* sad. I actually felt terrible at the settlement—we had it at the nursing home. But, I think they were at least happy that it went to someone they knew—or at least knew *of*. Mrs. Robinson patted me on the hand at the end and said, 'Dr. Randolph, I hope you have as many happy years in that house as Stuart and I had there together.'"

Penny made a face. "I think I'm going to cry."

"It's the cycle of life."

"But I still can't wait to see the farm."

"Can you drive a tractor?"

"No."

"Do you ride horses?"

"No."

"Good. I've found two things that you can't do as well as me."

She smiled. "I bet there are lots of things that I can't do as well as you," she said, sipping the last of her cosmo.

"Penny, it's so awesome that you play tennis and ski so well. I've never dated a girl who could keep up with me like you can."

"How do you know? You've never seen me ski," she said smiling.

"I have no doubt that you will absolutely ski *circles* around me. You're such a natural athlete. Not to mention that you grew up skiing in Colorado, of course."

"You're very modest about your own gifts, Alex. I've never seen anyone play tennis so well who wasn't a college player. I think you could have played Division I tennis." We bathed in this mutual adoration for a few moments. So far I was liking the drift of this conversation.

The waitress arrived with wine—a nice old-vine zinfandel that, for Milton Inn, came cheap—thirty some bucks a bottle. A few minutes later she returned with salads—mescalun greens with raspberries, walnuts, and crumbled blue cheese, tossed with a raspberry vinaigrette. The greens were cold and crisp.

"So where are the kids tonight?" I asked.

Penny smiled. "Probably out on the lawn at Buchanan House, throwing snowballs with my dad."

"It's nice that your parents live so close-by."

"Oh, it's a *Godsend*! I don't know what I'd do without them. Two kids can run you pretty ragged."

"So do you have to make arrangements very far ahead of time with your parents, given your dad's entertaining duties and all?"

"Oh my God, my mother would keep them full-time if she could—doesn't matter who's coming to dinner. But, to answer your question, I try to give them as much notice as possible, but my mom will take them instantly if I need her in a pinch."

"So how much notice did she have for tonight?"

Penny smiled. "A week." I couldn't help but laugh.

"And how did you know that I was going to ask you out this weekend?"

"Women know these things," she said, still smiling.

"Did you tell your mom why you needed a babysitter?" Penny nodded.

"What did she say?"

"She was thrilled. She said, 'it's time.'" I took a bite of salad.

"Do you look like your mom?"

"I'm a composite. She's darker than I am, and taller. My father has blond hair and blue eyes. But she's a beautiful woman. My father adores her."

"I can imagine."

The service was prompt. A busboy, dressed in black, scooped up our salad plates. A minute later, our waitress and a male partner descended dramatically on the table, gripping the plates with towels—pan seared salmon with lime *crème fraiche* and avocado for Penny, and the twenty-five dollar special for me: a six-ounce filet and lobster tail, which I couldn't resist. I keep encouraging myself to break out of the red-meat-mold and live dangerously, but I often meet with limited success.

"Watch the plates—they're hot," she said, expertly sliding the plate in the exact center of my place setting. She gave a satisfied sigh, surveying the table with her hands on her hips. Spotting a stray drink straw, she scooped it up.

"Anything else I can get you?" she asked, refilling both wine glasses. Penny shook her head. I ordered an iced tea, and she was gone in a flash.

"It's so amazing to me how different two children can be, growing up in the same house," Penny said. "Catherine is so reserved and thoughtful. You can see her mind going constantly. It scares me sometimes when I think that she's only six years old. She'll say something unbelievably perceptive and I'll go, *Whoa! Where did that come from?*"

"Jack, on the other hand," she continued, "*that* boy's a disaster zone. He does the first thing that comes into his mind, and he's totally fearless. And tough? Oh, my! I see him crash and burn running down the sidewalk, landing on all fours, strawberries on both knees, and not a peep out of him." I smiled. *Probably like his father.*

I had been thinking all weekend about how to deal with the subject of Patrick Murray in our conversations. He was the unspoken giant presence in the room and the great unknown in this developing relationship. Did we talk about him, or ignore him?

In fact, Patrick would never go away, because he would be there every day in the faces of Jack and Catherine He and I would have to arrive at some sort of accommodation if this relationship progressed. I wasn't sure that it would be easy. Could I accept how deeply she had loved another man? Maybe. Probably. It hadn't stopped me from pursuing her yet. It occurred to me that maybe I would have to arrive at some sort of kinship with Patrick.

Could Penny ever really let go and give her heart to me? I didn't know that either, but there was no question that I wanted to take the risk, such as it was. In any case, ultimately I had concluded that the only way to deal with Patrick Murray was directly. There was no pretending that he never existed.

I wondered how Catherine had dealt with her father's death. She was old enough to remember him. So I decided to ask.

"I suppose Catherine's old enough to remember her father?"

Penny looked at me with a trace of anxiety, then nodded.

"How has she fared with his death?"

Penny took a deep breath, wiped her mouth with her napkin, then looked up. "It's been hard on her," she said quietly. "She was a daddy's girl. She would spend hours curled up on his lap, watching a movie, or reading books. She remembers little things like him tucking her in bed at night. I think it would have been harder if he had been home all the time, but she *did* get used to him being gone for long periods. When he was killed, he'd been gone for three months, so in a way, that was a blessing."

She looked at me, as if to ask, 'Is this going OK?'. She must have seen the answer she was looking for, because she continued.

"The concept of death is hard for a four year old. The questions are endless. When they ask questions, you learn to give uncomplicated answers. But, in any case, she was quiet and more withdrawn than usual for... actually, maybe the better part of a year. She still talks sometimes about Daddy being in heaven. My father has been really important, I think, in her recovery. She spends a lot of time in *his* lap, thank God. But you know, children are incredibly resilient, and in the last year, she started school, another year has passed, and she looks pretty lighthearted. I really think she's doing OK."

"I would bet that her *mother* had a lot to do with her recovery," I said. "I think she was an extraordinarily lucky girl to have Penny Murray for a mother. And I would guess that Jack has done fine?"

"Yes! He was only a little over a year old. He's perfect." There was a bit of an awkward pause in the conversation. Penny took a quick sip of wine, looking over at me. There was more that she wanted to say. Finally she spoke.

"Alex, you've been so patient with me. You deserve to know why I took off my rings." She hesitated, her face flushing slightly. "It's because...it's because I wanted to be with you."

I stared at her for a moment. That was the best answer she could have given me. She knew that Patrick was an issue. I thought that this was likely her way of letting me know that she had put him to rest. I reached out my hand across the table and she took it, our fingers entwining.

"And I know that you don't play in a mixed doubles league on Thursday nights," she continued.

"What?"

"I know that there's no Thursday night mixed doubles league."

"How do you know that?"

"Because you've worked three out of the last four Thursdays. You're not a very good actor, *or* liar," she continued, her eyes sparkling. I grinned.

"Then you knew that our doubles match was really a date?"

"Of course," she said. "When you asked me to play, I shocked myself. I couldn't believe that I said 'yes.'"

"So when I asked you in the car if this was a date, and you said 'of course not', you were lying, too?"

"Yes," she giggled.

~

I turned off the ignition key and we both sat in the Jeep in her driveway for a moment, looking at each other; neither of us, I think, quite knowing exactly how this evening was supposed to end. It was quiet. Fat snowflakes fell silently on the windshield, slowly melting.

Jeeps are small. Driver and front seat passenger are not far from each other.

"Alex…" said Penny.

I leaned forward and stopped an inch from her lips. She didn't move. Her warm, fragrant breath hit my face in short bursts. I moved again and slowly brushed my lips across hers, every nerve fiber exquisitely sensitive to the gentle contact; the rough dryness of my lips against her softness. Penny let out a soft moan. A wave of emotion swept over me. It was like I had waited my whole life to touch this woman's lips.

I could feel her breathing becoming more rapid. She rubbed both sides of her face roughly against my lips, then put her hands on my chest and pushed herself upright, her eyes wide; breathing deep. "Alex," she said, swallowing hard, "I think I need to go in now. I, ah, I think… I think I can find my way to the door."

She fumbled for the door latch, climbed out, then turned and stood in the snow, staring at me through the open door. Suddenly she leapt back into the Jeep on both knees, grabbed my face with both hands, and kissed me hungrily; her mouth open, devouring mine; her lips soft and compliant. I wrapped my arms around her hips and pulled her to me, greedily returning her kiss. Our tongues touched and fireworks went off in my brain. I could feel the warmth of her body through her jeans. My hand went involuntarily to her butt, and she pushed her pelvis against me. Blood surged.

Then she broke the kiss, still holding my face with both hands; her eyes blazing. "That was so you won't forget me before the next time," she breathed.

CHAPTER FORTY-THREE

AT 9:30 ON MONDAY MORNING, I HAD TIME TO see just one more patient before my 10:00 AM appointment with my new boss. I didn't like leaving my partners alone in the department for meetings, but Gwen had e-mailed me that Dr. Myers was insistent that we meet on Monday. The next case looked like an easy one, so I should have no trouble squeezing it in before my meeting.

Sixteen-year-old Shaniyah Bumbaugh sat in a patient gown on the edge of the exam table, swinging her legs and cracking gum. She still had her tank top and jeans on under her patient gown. A field of zits sprouted from her forehead and cheeks. Inside the chart that I carried into the room was a positive beta HCG pregnancy test.

An obese woman in a faded tee shirt and sweatpants sat in the corner chair with her arms folded on top of her belly. Her mouth had the sunken look that suggests the absence of teeth. She looked to be in her mid-thirties. This was probably mom.

I said, "Hi, Shaniyah, I'm Dr. Randolph," and stuck out my hand. Shaniyah looked down at it for a moment, and then back at me with a blank look on her face. A light bulb finally went off in her head, and she limply put her hand in mine with a shy grin. Mom had apparently shaken hands before, because she immediately stuck out her hand when I offered mine.

I sat down on a wheeled stool and opened the chart. "OK, Ladies, Shaniyah is apparently here today because she hasn't had a period in nine weeks. Is that right, Shaniyah?" I said, looking up at her. She nodded with a smile.

This is always a little bit of a tense moment because you never know how mom is going to react to the news that her teenage daughter is pregnant. But they were both here, and Shaniyah was under age, so there was no avoiding it—I had to make the announcement in front of mom.

"Well, Shaniyah," I said gently, "you are pregnant. Your blood test came back positive." She smiled again. I looked over toward mom to assess her reaction to this news.

"Well, you *are* OK," mom said, addressing Shaniyah. She turned back to me. "We were a little worried," she said.

"Worried?"

"Yeah. Shaniyah will be seventeen soon, and she hadn't gotten pregnant yet. We thought maybe there was a problem." I thought about this for a second. It was nice to hear that Shaniyah would be spared the time and expense of an infertility workup.

"Well, now Shaniyah is going to need some prenatal care," I said. "Do you need a referral to an OB-GYN?"

"No, we know how to do this. She's got an older sister with two kids. We'll go the clinic in York." She turned toward Shaniyah again. "We'll stop at the welfare office on the way home and get you signed up." I looked at the demographics sheet in the back of the chart and saw a Pennsylvania address.

The "signing up" would be for maternal benefits, no doubt. As soon as she delivered, Shaniyah would start getting a monthly check from public assistance as long as she didn't find a husband with a job, or get a job herself. Little risk of either, I thought. This would basically be Shaniyah's career. She would collect checks from the government as long as she could produce babies. We would pay her to do that.

If you happen to be looking for examples of the unintended consequencces of well-intentioned, but misguided, public policy, the ER's a wonderful place to do your research. And the long-term social and cultural consequences of some of those public policies are going to be profound.

~

I finished up the charting on Shaniyah and turned to Rick Stapleton, sitting beside me.

"Rick, I am sorry, but I have been summoned to the offices of Dr. Myers, and I'm going to have to skip out for a few minutes for a 10:00 AM appointment."

"Who the hell's Dr. Myers?" he drawled.

"Our new Vice President of Medical Affairs."

"Oh, that's right. They got rid of Simpson, didn't they?"

"I don't think he quite met with John Salzman's expectations."

"I was shocked that they fired his ass," he said. "Usually incompetence grants you tenure for life at Americus."

~

Despite a few misgivings about this meeting, nothing could shake my sunny disposition of the last two days. I walked down the hallway whistling.

I smiled at Gwen as I walked into the administrative offices.

"Hey, Gwen. How are you this morning?"

"Dr. Randolph!" she said brightly. "Hi. I'm just fine. Have a seat and I'll let Dr. Myers know you are here."

I took a seat in the elegant waiting area, and absently picked up a magazine.

I didn't get very far in the magazine. My mind turned immediately to Penny, as it had every unoccupied moment of the last thirty-six hours. I had relived Saturday night in my mind a hundred times—always with wonderment. I could hear her laughter, still feel her warm breath on my face, and could feel her pelvis pushing urgently into me.

The passion that Penny released in the front seat of my Jeep had not only left me in wonder, it had freed me completely from the ghost of Patrick Murray. The decks were cleared. Not that Patrick was gone. But I felt that he had been placed to rest for me as well as Penny.

Actually, in retrospect, a sense of kinship with Patrick ultimately *did* evolve in me over a period of time. I almost came to think of him as a brother, or a war buddy—some sort of compatriot—in a relationship that somehow bound us together. Maybe we were just two alpha males who loved the same woman, I don't know. But, in any case, he was a man of honor and strength and selflessness at a time when those traits did not appear with great regularity in our society, and I admired him.

All that being said, I had never felt such happiness. It almost didn't seem right. It wasn't edgy, contemporary, or hip. I felt as if my life were coming together in a way that I would never have anticipated. I was beginning to feel the first hints of a sense of completeness that I had never even really known was missing. And it all revolved around a woman who made my head spin. I thought of the old Frank Sinatra tune—*that old black magic has me in a spin… that old black magic called love*—and I laughed to myself. *I'm getting goofy in my old age.*

Dr. Myers burst through his closed office door and marched toward my chair with a sense of purpose. I gathered myself from my reverie and stood.

"Dr. Randolph," he said, extending his hand, "I'm Dr. Myers. Please come in." Dr. Myers' parents, I guessed, had neglected to bestow upon him a given name. Mr. Hyde noted the use of formal titles and said, *Batten down the hatches.*

He motioned to a chair in front of the clear desk. The shelves in the bookcase were empty, and the coffee table in front of the sofa was bare. Except for Dr. Myers, the room appeared uninhabited.

Julie's description was pretty accurate, although Myers looked more military to me than nerdy. He was at least young enough that his skin had that shine to it that comes with being young and in shape. He was wearing a tie and a white clinic jacket buttoned all the way to the top. People up here in the executive offices love clinic jackets.

"This is our first meeting, Dr. Randolph, but we may as well get directly to the point," he said impassively, taking his seat and laying a manila folder on the desk in front of him.

"Your three-year contract with Mason-Dixon automatically renews on May third of this year unless sixty days written notice not to renew is tendered by either party." He opened the manila folder, pulled out an envelope, and slid it across the desk. "You will find written notice enclosed in the envelope, dated today, March first. We are electing not to renew your contract.

"You will be permitted to work through the end of your contract period," he continued, voice steady and eye contact constant, "but your last day will be no later than May second.

"Sandra De Luca in Human Resources will assist you with out-processing. Your 401K, of course, is portable, and you will be permitted to purchase health insurance for up to a year under COBRA. Any questions?"

I thought about that for a second. Hyde, of course, had already launched and was ballistic. *Your fist will fit neatly right between the lenses of his glasses!,* he screamed.

"None," I said.

I stood and stuck out my hand, smiling. "Great job."

He looked down at my hand blankly, slowly grasped it, then looked back up. "What?"

"Great job. Crisp. Clean. To the point. In control. Sounded just like a lawyer. You'll go far with Americus."

CHAPTER FORTY-FOUR

YOU MIGHT THINK THAT AFTER HEARING THE news of one's own firing, a flood of fears would immediately overwhelm your central processor. Oddly enough, as I walked back to the department, I had only one real fear—facing Julie. She was going to kill me.

I felt terrible. We had fought a lot of battles together, but always with the knowledge that we had each other's back. She would be by herself, trying to survive in a hostile environment. I didn't think that she would make it—they'd either get rid of her, or she would resign. My serial verbal indiscretions had screwed up her life, probably a great deal more than my own.

My own future didn't worry me. I could have another job with a phone call, although maybe not my own department. Kit Owens, my old boss at Hopkins, would hire me back in a heartbeat if I wanted to go back to academia.

My docs would not be happy with me either. No doubt Salzman would find another loyal Dr. Myers to run the department, but whoever that was, they would certainly have their hands full. I was worried that the department might just fall apart. Maybe that was just my ego indulging in the thought that I was indispensable, but, in truth, at least half of the department were docs that were old friends that had followed me to Mason-Dixon, and this was not going to set well with them. *Wow. I've disrupted a lot of lives.*

I can't say that I was shocked at this outcome, but I hadn't really thought that Salzman would do it. This was going to be bad for the institution. As big as I knew his ego to be, I had underestimated his capacity to engage in personal vengeance at the expense of the organization. And there was no doubt in my mind that this was Salzman's decision. Jackie may have cheerfully thrown her little list of grievances into the laundry basket, but the driver and the power behind the decision was Salzman. I suspected that Stan Robinson was a silent participant, at most, in the process—just keeping a low profile and trying to stay off of Salzman's radar screen.

There were no legal issues here—no way to appeal or amend the outcome—because my relationship with Mason-Dixon was contractual. The language was very clear. They didn't need a reason not to renew the contract. No cause was necessary. This was a permanent and final end to the relationship.

I began to think about how to break the news to the staff. In point of fact, there was very little time—it would be beyond my control. The news would go viral within the hospital. No doubt Myers had immediately picked up the phone after our little interview and informed Human Resources. By now multiple secretaries knew. And by noon tomorrow, the only people who might not know that Alex Randolph had been fired would be the night shift at home asleep in their beds. Even they would have text messages awaiting their arising.

I decided that Rick was going to have to wait a little longer for my return to the department, and walked directly into Julie's office. Her neck cradled the telephone to her shoulder, and she was typing on her computer at the same time that she was talking. She looked up at me apprehensively when I walked in. I sat down in the chair beside her desk.

"OK, well, I'll talk to Alex, and maybe we can put together a little protocol that will solve everybody's problem." Pause. "OK. Bye." She put down the phone and turned to me.

"Well?" she asked.

"You were right," I said quietly. "They're not renewing my contract."

She was silent. I could see her chest rise and fall as her breathing got deeper. A moment later a tear trickled down her face. She took a deep breath with a little catch, and then finally she spoke.

"I'm so sorry, Alex... for both of us."

~

I decided that my primary responsibility in coming days was to leave the department in as good a shape as I could prior to my departure. People would be unsure how to react to my dismissal, and would take their cues from my behavior. Mason-Dixon was a good little hospital, and Mason-Dixon was *not* John Salzman. So I determined to be as upbeat as I could, and, to the extent that it was within my control, minimize staff anger at Americus so as not to destroy a great little department.

Remaining upbeat was actually not such a tall order, because my priorities in life were rapidly changing. Suddenly, where I worked and what was my position were not nearly as important as they used to be. I was astonished to find that I had just been fired, but almost didn't care. Penny Murray had radically altered my outlook on life.

My rational side told me that the euphoria surrounding Penny would not last, that the mundane aspects of life would return, and that it was, in fact, far too early in this relationship to even know where it might ultimately lead. And so, I tried to temper my outlook with a healthy dose of skepticism—quite unsuccessfully. I finally gave up and decided to just enjoy it while it lasted. The euphoria was part of life, too—a quite nice part.

That being said, I loved this department and I loved the people. The day would come when both would be missed.

I gave Rick the news shortly after I returned to the department. The air briefly turned blue and I had to quiet him down. He walked around the department fuming to himself—steam coming out of his ears—but on the whole, he was uncharacteristically quiet the rest of the shift. By late afternoon I periodically would catch someone staring at me, so I figured word was probably spreading. But no one approached me, which meant, I suspected, that they had not a clue what to say to me.

Penny was off on Monday. I thought it was important to let her hear the news from me first, but I was afraid that she would go to extraordinary lengths to be with me that night if I told her too early. She had other responsibilities that I should not impinge upon. I decided to call her, but only after I knew that she would have put the kids to bed. People were beginning to tumble to the fact that Penny and I had some sort of relationship, so I doubted that anyone else would call her. Besides, we already had plans to see each other Tuesday night, and then she could comfort me all she wanted.

~

I texted Anne.

r u busy tonite? need 2 talk. dinner? off at 7
charleston 7:45
who's paying?
u
ur expensive
good advice ain't cheap

This is what happens when you ask investment counselors to meet you for dinner to talk. I'd be lucky to get out of there for two hundred dollars.

~

I pulled up to Charleston restaurant on Lancaster Street about 7:40. Anne was already at the table sipping a martini.

"You're on time," she said smiling.

"I used to date a girl like you."

"Not like me."

"Well, let's just say we used to have similar conversations."

"So, you need investment advice?"

"No, but I understand you're making marketing inroads into the physician community."

She smiled. "Just helping a friend."

"Sure," I said sarcastically. "I was worried about you—trying to protect you from a predator—so I reminded Ben that you have a brother with a short fuse who's prone to violence."

"And, what did he say?"

"He said, 'Wait a minute. She's an investment counselor. What if she's just after my money?' So I said, 'Do you have a T. Rowe Price account yet?' And he said, 'No, but I will tomorrow. I just signed the papers yesterday.'"

Anne giggled. "He's really a very nice man, you know," she said.

"He's a great guy—just a little short on commitment so far."

"Maybe he hasn't met the right girl."

"Just take it a little slow, that's all."

"Like you?"

"Actually, we've picked up a little velocity," I said.

Anne sat up in her chair. "You asked her out again?"

"Yes."

"And she said yes?"

"Yes."

"What did I tell you!" she exclaimed.

"That's exactly what I knew you'd say."

"Tell me," she said, leaning forward on her elbow. "Tell me about it. I want to hear every detail." And so, I told her. Actually, I was dying to tell somebody.

~

Anne took a sip of her wine, still looking at me. I hadn't touched my one hundred dollar meal. Anne's plate was empty. "So how cool is that?" she smiled broadly, sitting back and folding her arms. "I think my brother's in love." *Actually, he's fallen off a cliff and he's stark raving madly in love.*

"He might be," I said. "He's just having a little trouble adjusting to the pace of events."

"My brother's a very competent person. I'm sure he'll manage," she said, still smiling.

I decided that I should taste my rack of lamb with pomegranate and eggplant caviar, with a substitution of mashed potatoes instead of saffron basmati rice. I stuck my fork in my mashed potatoes and it stood up straight. They were turning to concrete. The waitress came by and saw my fork standing proudly in the cold, untouched plate. She frowned. "Was everything OK?"

"It was fine. I just talk too much."

"You know, I think that plate needs a little help," she said scooping it up. "I'll be right back."

Draining my wine glass, I turned back to my sister. "Actually, Anne, there's another reason that I wanted to talk tonight."

"What else could possibly compete for your attention?"

"I got fired today."

CHAPTER FORTY-FIVE

WHEN THE DOOR TO PENNY'S TOWNHOUSE opened on Tuesday night, my breath was instantly snatched by a bear hug. This woman was strong.

"Oh, I'm so happy to see you! I wanted to be with you so much last night," she said looking up. "I felt terrible. I couldn't sleep all night."

I had known exactly how she would react to my call of last night, but I had thought that there was no way around it. She would have been deeply hurt to hear the news from someone else. But, Lord knows, with two kids and a full-time job, she needed all the sleep she could get.

"You know what, baby? I was just fine. In fact, I slept like a log. You know why?" I said, gripping her head in both my hands. "Because I knew I was going to see you tonight."

Her eyes gleamed. I had never called Penny "baby" before. It was completely spontaneous. I liked it.

I felt like I had loved this woman all my life—like I knew that she was out there, and I was just waiting for her. I marveled at the intimacy that had so quickly blossomed between us, and tried to figure out how that could be. I had only know her for what—a little over three months?

Penny had more character and strength than any woman—or

man, for that matter—that I had ever met. She had been tested in ways that I never had, and hoped to God never to be. Moreover, there were things that Penny obviously *believed* in—commitment; family; loyalty. She was all substance and authenticity. I think I was sick of social-ladder-climbing women. There wasn't a frivolous bone in this woman's body. And she obviously had the capacity of loving deeply and fiercely.

Perhaps it was respect, I thought, that made this relationship so different. I regarded Penny with awe. Maybe respect was the greater part of love—the factor that drew me so powerfully to her.

I was beginning to get the first glimpses of the constraints of life with kids. I was used to taking off when I felt like it, without consulting anyone, and without regard to school nights or baby sitters. Moreover, there were never any issues regarding open displays of affection, or a place in which to engage in intimate adult activities. A trail of clothes leading to the bedroom was no problem in my previous life. But not now.

"Come on in," she said, pulling on my hand, "I've got to say goodnight to the kids." She dragged me through the foyer and into an adjacent living room that opened to the rear into the kitchen. A college-aged girl sat on an overstuffed sofa, legs tucked under her, reading a book, and holding a yellow highlighter.

"Holly, this is Dr. Randolph," she said. "Holly is my nanny *par excellence* and my link to a life. I couldn't survive without her. She's going to graduate from Towson this year, and I'm trying hard to figure out how to arrange for a failure on her final exams. I don't want her leaving for graduate school."

Holly smiled, unfolded her legs, stood, and stuck out her hand. "Hi, Dr. Randolph." I looked at the title of the book in her left hand: *Cien años de soledad.*

"I think that looks like a Spanish title. You're a Spanish major?" I asked.

"Yes," she smiled. "It's nice. Penny and I get to speak together a little bit."

"Speak Spanish?"

"Yes," she said looking over at Penny. "She's pretty good."

I looked at Penny quizzically. She made a face. "I'm terrible! I had two years of Spanish in college, but I can't speak it. Holly's teaching me. I'm going to run upstairs," she said. "I'll be right back."

I stood with my hands in my pockets and looked around with more than casual interest. This room was a reflection of Penny.

It was a sparely furnished room with dark wood floors, bold colors, and subdued, recessed accent lighting. Two of the three walls were a light shade of taupe with a deep, rich red on the far wall. Several oriental rugs were scattered on the gleaming floors.

The furniture was an eclectic mixture—several very nice old pieces and a contemporary black ebony coffee table. A huge baroque oil of an ill child in bed, flanked by a worried mother and a person that I took to be a physician, hung over the sofa in an ornate, gilded frame.

I spotted a large, clear glass sculpture of a naked young boy sitting with his arms wrapped around his knees. I had seen glass sculptures like this before on a trip to Venice. They do it with molten glass and crude tools—metal tongs, to be exact—but the grace and exquisite detail are phenomenal.

"Wow. This is a stunning room," I said.

"Penny has great taste," said Holly from her perch on the couch. "She's an incredible designer."

"How long have you known Penny?"

"Four years. I've been babysitting since I was a freshman." *So, Holly knew Patrick.*

I walked over to an old pine hunt table with a collection of framed photographs and picked one up. It was a family photo taken in the late afternoon sun on the beach. Penny stood, cradling a baby in her arms. Beside her stood a tall, handsome man with crew-cut hair and steely gray eyes—one arm around Penny, and the other holding a beautiful blond girl of toddler age, her head resting shyly on his shoulder.

Penny strode briskly into the room. "OK. Finally!" she said smiling. "All set?" She saw me holding the photo and stopped. Our eyes met. There was a long moment of silence. Penny took a deep breath and then spoke.

"Virginia Beach," she said quietly, "two thousand and seven. Jack was two months old."

I looked at the photo again, carefully replaced it on the table, and turned back to Penny. "It's a beautiful family," I said.

~

"I don't understand. What did he have to gain?" she asked, her hair softly shimmering in the glow of the candle. I still hadn't gotten used to seeing Penny with her hair down. I wanted to stroke it. "It doesn't make any sense to me," she continued.

"I don't think there was *anything* to gain from the organizational perspective," I said. "Actually, it carried some risks. The medical staff knows it's a great little department, and they certainly won't be happy. They *love* the ER, in fact. We're the overflow relief valve for their offices, and we take good care of them.

"The Mason-Dixon Board of Trustees will want to know what this was all about," I continued, pushing my lime against the bottle neck, then plopping it into the golden liquid. "Hell, even the Americus Board knows that the Mason-Dixon ER was performing at a very high level. He'll take some heat—at least have to answer some pointed questions."

"Then why did he do it?" asked Penny, genuinely puzzled.

I shrugged. "He can't help himself. He's all about control. It's all about power. He's very narcissistic. I think he felt he needed to make an example of me with the medical staff. He couldn't fire Harvey Mays. Harvey is his showpiece—the equivalent of a trophy wife. Besides, Harvey's on the Americus Board, and it would get a little awkward to fire one of your bosses."

"Well, what will he tell them? He's got to come up with *some* justification."

"He'll tell them that Alex Randolph was a loose cannon. That he mouthed off to the Department of Health and earned the hospital a citation. That he gets complaints from pissed off patients. That he misses diagnoses and has a lawsuit pending that could cost the hospital a lot of money. That he's not supportive of Americus' strategic goals—

who knows what else?"

"He's an utter idiot," she said emphatically. "He has no clue what a great department you've built. I'd like to scratch his eyes out."

"I don't think he *cares* about the quality of the department. That's almost irrelevant to his calculations."

"You're really very calm about this, Alex. Wouldn't you like to strangle Salzman?"

"Cheerfully."

"So what will you do now? Will you go back to teaching?"

The waitress slid our pizza onto the table—half vegetarian and half with pepperoni and sausage. "OK with your drinks?" she asked. Penny nodded.

"You can bring me another Corona in about five minutes," I said.

"You bet," she said, and scurried off. I lifted the first veggie slice—cheese stringing out a foot long—and put it on Penny's side plate. I broke the string with my finger, then tried to get the cheese into my mouth—unsuccessfully.

"You've got cheese all over your chin," she said reprovingly, "not to mention your sweater."

I cleaned up with a napkin as best I could. "Did I get it all?"

Penny reached across and pulled a string of cheese off my sweater. "You're as much work to take out to eat as Jack."

"There you go… something Jack and I can bond over," I said, picking up another slice. "To answer your question, I don't know yet. I'm taking my time to think about it; at least for a week or two. I'm sure I could get my old position back at Hopkins, but I'm not sure that I want to do that. I have really enjoyed running a department, without all the academic politics and pressure to publish. Maybe I'll talk to some recruiters."

"Would you leave the farm and move?"

"Nope. I'm on the farm to stay."

"I still can't wait to see it."

"Well, I have a little introduction plan."

"Tell me!" she said, leaning forward against the table.

"I happen to know that you and I are both off this Saturday. There are also one or two dishes in my limited culinary repertoire at which I excel. Perhaps you would consider permitting me to cook for you on Saturday night?"

"There's a condition," she said.

"What's that?"

"You have to invite me early enough that it's still daylight. I want to see the farm."

"Madame, my entire Saturday will be devoted to you."

"Then it's a deal!"

"Actually, there was another part to my plan."

"What?" she said excitedly.

"I thought that maybe Jack and Catherine might be interested in climbing on the back of a horse Saturday afternoon. I… I don't how you might feel about that. I don't know if it's the right time to introduce a new man…"

Penny was quiet for a moment, holding my gaze, then she smiled. "That would be the second most wonderful day I've had in two years."

"Second?"

"The first was when I had dinner during the snow storm on Saturday night with a farm boy in a Jeep."

"You're my kind of woman."

"But we have to take them back home before dinner. I'll get a babysitter. I *won't* share dinner with them," she said with conviction. I very much liked the sound of that.

CHAPTER FORTY-SIX

ONE OF MY MAJOR CONSTRUCTION PROJECTS, when I bought the farm from the Robinsons, was converting two small adjoining bedrooms into a second upstairs bath, a hallway, and a laundry room. That way, of course, the laundry could be done upstairs, which, in fact, Ruth does every Wednesday afternoon, along with cleaning the bathrooms. Ruth was adding detergent to the washer when I walked into the laundry room and leaned against the door frame.

"Well, Ruth, your long-held dream is nearing fulfillment. There's going to be little voices in this house on Saturday."

Ruth stood up straight, and turned to me, measuring cap in one hand and liquid detergent in the other. "Little voices? You mean children?"

"Two of them, to be exact. I've invited Penny Murray to bring Catherine and Jack to ride the horses Saturday afternoon, and then I'm cooking dinner for Penny. You'll get to meet them all."

Slowly, something resembling a glow crossed Ruth's taciturn face. "Well, that's... that's marvelous! Catherine and Jack; Catherine and Jack," she repeated, memorizing the names as she began to pace around the laundry room. "You know they should have little plates and little sets of silverware... I'm sure I've got two sets at home someplace."

"Ruth, that is a very nice thought, but actually, we're taking the kids back home to the babysitter before dinner."

"Well, they should at least have some little snacks in the afternoon," she said emphatically. "Children get hungry. They have to eat. I'll take care of that."

~

Wednesday night was my first scheduled shift after my friendly little encounter with Dr. Myers. Over the last two days I had gotten three or four phone calls from very close friends—Cathy Rutledge, Lynn Saylor, Ben—all laced with spicy language to describe their warm feelings for Americus. That's not counting calls from family, of course. It is safe to say that my parents' stellar opinion of Mason-Dixon Regional Medical Center pretty well did a one-eighty.

I was grateful that a couple of days had gone by since my termination notice. Not that I want to wish my life away, but at least that meant that virtually everyone in the department would now know, and I wouldn't have to spend the whole night explaining to ten different people what had happened.

Everyone was unusually nice when I walked into the department—like maybe I had a terminal illness with only a few days left to live. Lisa Turano was the most direct in her approach. Sweet little Lisa walked up to me and said, "You know, Alex, Frank knows a lot of people. He has some acquaintances that are hungry for work, who would be more than happy to ensure that John Salzman met with a tragic and untimely end." This suggestion, of course, met with the vigorous approval of Mr. Hyde.

Over the course of the evening there was lots of bluster and talk like, "I'm outta here. I'm sendin' out my resume tomorrow." But in truth, these people all had mouths to feed, and most of them loved their jobs at Mason-Dixon.

I tried to explain that a contract like mine was just a business deal, and that Americus was perfectly free to try someone new as department head at the end of my three-year contract. "Yeah, whatever—they're still assholes," was the usual response I got to that line of reasoning.

I was quite discomfited by being the object of sympathy, so for most of the evening I busied myself seeing patients to the maximum extent possible. This worked to the distinct advantage of Lauren, the 5:00 to 1:00 AM doc, who noted that I was working at warp speed. She was having trouble picking up any patients at all, and finally said, "Did you have a half-dozen Red Bulls tonight before you came in?"

"No, I'm working on my legacy. After I'm gone, I want 'em to say, 'You know, that boy was a working fool.'"

"The 'fool' part they may remember," she said.

Rebecca slid a new chart into the rack. "Robert Peck. Left arm pain," she said. "You'll recognize him when you see him. He's been here a zillion times." I grabbed the chart like it was the last cookie on the plate, spent a little time perusing his old records in the computer, then headed into Bed Two. Lauren shook her head.

Thirty seven-year-old Robert stood in the corner of the room in a patient gown, supporting his large frame with one hand on the counter top. Two or three days of stubble covered his sour face—more hair than was present on top of his shaved head. A heavy, red-painted wooden hoop hung from his left ear.

Rebecca was right. I knew Robert. In fact, he was one of our best customers. Cynthia, his girlfriend—also a frequent flier whom I recognized—sat in a corner chair with her legs crossed, one knee poking through a tear in her jeans.

The computer had reminded me that Robert's last admission to Mason-Dixon was for a polysubstance overdose; in his case, a toxic mixture of alcohol and Percocet. His toxicology studies at that time also came back positive for cocaine and marijuana.

"Robert, what can I do for you tonight?" I asked.

"It's this shoulder again, Doc. I just couldn't stand the pain anymore. I've got all this numbness in my hand…" he said, rubbing his thumb across his fingers. "I need to get some sleep."

Robert had chronic pain syndrome, a term characterizing a group of patients with often vague chronic pain who have been worked up—usually endlessly—but for whom no clear etiology for their pain has been found. Robert had had more than his share of CT's, MRI's, and consults with a thousand specialists. No one had ever identified a clear explanation for his pain.

"Robert, I looked through your old records on the computer before I came in, and I think the last time you were here for this problem was, what… three weeks ago?"

"Yeah, somethin' like that."

"And didn't Dr. Foreman set up an appointment for you with the pain clinic?"

"Yeah, but Cynthia was sick that day, and I had to stay home to take care of her." Hyde was beginning to wake up. *Robert, that was so thoughtful of you.*

"I see that somebody along the way put you on nortriptylene to help with the pain. Have you been taking that?"

"I don't have the money. I can't afford it." *Unlike the cigarettes, cocaine, marijuana, Percocet, and alcohol.*

"You know you can get a month's supply at WalMart for ten dollars?"

"Hey, man, when you don't have the money, you don't have the money."

"You're not working anymore?"

"I lost my job when I was off with this pain. And those disability people have been putting me off for two years now. My lawyer says he hopes we'll get it in another six months," he said, getting more agitated. "You know, you suffer with pain like this, and there's just no one out there willing to help you. It's depressing. And I'm a veteran. I gave four years of my life to this country." *Oh, please… cut me a break.*

"What kind of work were you doing?"

"Construction. I couldn't do all that heavy lifting anymore. The bastards fired me." That did it for Hyde. *Look, this guy's a parasite on society. Don't give him a thing. Tell him to get his fat ass out of here, get a life, get a job, and don't come back.*

Jekyll was unusually quiet. This was a tough one for a humanist like Jekyll. Finally he was apparently overcome by a sense of moral obligation. *Alex, listen, I know he's a very unsympathetic figure. But he's got a character disorder—he's incapable at the present of accepting personal responsibility—you know that. Why don't you just do for him what you can and not aggravate the situation?*

The psychiatrists say that there are two kinds of mental illness relating to responsibility. The first is *neurosis*, in which the patient blames himself for everything bad that happens in life. They inappropriately accept personal responsibility for everything. The second is *character disorder*, in which the patient accepts no personal responsibility for his or her own choices in life, but rather see themselves as victims of the people, organizations, and society around them. I once read that the major difference between the two is that neurotics make themselves miserable, and those with character disorder make everybody else miserable. There's a ton of the latter out there these days.

"How about some work that's lighter; that doesn't involve a lot of physical labor?" I said. "Then you'd have some money to buy your medicines, you'd probably be less depressed, and perhaps you could get some health insurance again."

This was Cynthia's cue to join the conversation. "Robert doesn't sleep a lot," she said with authority. "He's up all night with this pain. It's hard for him to focus. I don't think he could put in eight hours. What he needs right now is some relief; something to get him over the hump." I heard Jekyll quietly mumble in the background, *You can't do that, Alex.* I was shocked.

I remembered hearing a speaker at a conference give us the six "D's" for chronic pain syndrome: dramatization of complaints, drug misuse, dysfunction, dependency, depression, and disability. Robert must have been in the audience. Unfortunately, Robert is not a rarity. If you don't think the U.S. has a problem with prescription drug abuse, you might be interested to know that ninety-nine percent of the world's hydrocodone production is consumed by Americans.

The worst of it is, the more you do for these folks, in general, the worse they seem to get; the greater their dependency. They develop a sense of entitlement. Perhaps that's why our well-intentioned government programs never seem to work.

"Robert, you know that you were told last time no more narcotics from the ER. That's why Dr. Foreman set up that appointment for you with the pain clinic."

Robert finally lost it. "You fuckin' doctors are all alike. Think you're high and mighty. Well I don't have to take this abuse. I'm gonna go to York," he said, ripping off his patient gown, "maybe I can get some help from somebody up there. And you can bet that this hospital's gonna hear about *your* fucking incompetence," he said, shaking his finger at me as he exited the room.

Robert was just what I needed to take my mind off things.

~

Just after midnight, we hit a lull. No more patients for me to see. It was nearly the end of Lauren's shift. She looked over at me from her computer and said, "You know, Alex, we've been talking."

"Who's been talking?"

"The docs."

"About what?"

"About the department. About you. Lynn's going to go talk to Harvey Myers for the group."

I stared at her. I didn't like the sound of this. "Lauren, look, I don't want a bunch of people putting their livelihoods on the line defending me."

Lauren ran her fingers through her hair for a moment, and then spoke. "I don't think they're in a mood to give Salzman a pass on this one, Alex. Take my advice. You need to just lie low and stay out of it. In the meantime, don't sign any contracts with anybody else."

CHAPTER FORTY-SEVEN

SATURDAY MORNING DAWNED WITH A CRYSTAL-clear sky and the first scents of spring in the air. Most of the snow from the previous week had melted except on shaded northern exposures like the north side of the barn.

The sun poured through my east bedroom window, the powerful golden light burning through my eyelids, until I finally opened them about 6:30. By 7:00, I had showered and shaved, and was sitting on a stool at the kitchen island, having a first cup of coffee, pencil in hand, going over my little checklist of tasks for the day.

I was scheduled to pick up Penny and the kids at 3:00. Horseback riding required no preparation on my part because Sally was going to handle that. However, my invitation to Penny had made reference to a limited culinary repertoire at which I excelled, but, in fact, that statement verged on an untruth. I was carrying a little anxiety about getting all the prepping done for dinner, and getting it all to come out together at the same time.

Somewhere along the line my mother had given me an old copy of *The Joy of Cooking* to ameliorate my culinary ignorance, in the hope, I think, that someday I might sufficiently impress a young woman with my skills to land a potential vehicle for grandchildren. I flipped through the pages, refreshing my memory on the dishes I had selected for the evening.

In truth, my menu did not incorporate a great deal of complexity. You might even think that it was a little pedestrian—a Caesar salad, followed by filet mignon with a mushroom sauce, potatoes sautéed in olive oil with oregano, and steamed asparagus. I decided to purchase the bread and dessert.

I jotted down all the ingredients for the mushroom sauce, turned to the salad section, and then added to my list the ingredients for Caesar salad. This would be my shopping list, together, of course, with bread, dessert, meat, potatoes, and asparagus. I already had the wine.

I thought about the anchovies in the Caesar. Was that a good idea? What if Penny didn't like anchovies? What if I ate them and she didn't? The anchovies would clearly have to be on the side.

Finally, about eight thirty, I gathered up all my papers, climbed into the Jeep, and headed out to Graul's Supermarket in Hereford.

~

Ruth was already at the house when I kicked open the door and carried my two armfuls of groceries into the kitchen. "Morning, Ruth," I called out. "What's in the oven? It smells wonderful."

"It's bread," she yelled back from the dining room. "Sourdough. You need fresh bread for dinner." I plunked my groceries down on the countertop, carefully avoiding a fresh unbaked pie of some sort that was obviously Ruth's creation, and a box of brownie mix. *So much for my French baguette and strawberry pie from Graul's.*

I looked around the room, and there were flowers everywhere—on the granite countertop, on the kitchen table, and a vase on one of the end-tables in the family room. Actually, it was beautiful, although the thought occurred to me that perhaps it too greatly resembled a funeral parlor. Ruth had developed an obvious interest in the outcome of this dinner date. A fleeting panic flitted through my brain. What if she decided that her help was required through dinner? *We'll deal with that when the time comes.*

It was already ten o'clock. I spent the late morning working on the Caesar dressing, sautéing croutons, and washing lettuce.

Ruth watched with bemused interest, periodically offering gentle advice, as she retrieved her bread from the oven, baked her pie, and then moved on to the brownie mix. "You know," she said with a rare smile, "you're going to make some woman a good wife one day." This was as close to a joke as I had ever heard from Ruth.

We chatted as we worked, and it was actually a very nice time. I had never spent a day with Ruth in the kitchen. I learned a lot. I knew that she was a widow and was childless. What I didn't know is that she *did* have one pregnancy—a baby girl named Lily. Lily developed leukemia when she was three years old. Chemotherapy was in its infancy in those days, and little Lily lasted only four days after her diagnosis.

Ruth's husband, Bill, was a supermarket manager who died suddenly of a heart attack about ten years ago—two weeks before his retirement. She had one younger sister in California, and that was it. It finally dawned on me that I was Ruth's remaining family.

She asked a few discrete questions about Penny, and, for once, I answered them forthrightly. In fact, I opened up to her like I never had before. It was somehow very satisfying.

Ruth fixed us both a ham sandwich about one o'clock, and then for the next hour, I assembled all the ingredients for the mushroom sauce on the countertop, assembled all the appropriate pots and pans, and tried to figure out in what order I had to do all the steps, and at what time. When I finished, I had just enough time to set the little walnut table in the kitchen for dinner, and then hop in the shower again.

~

Penny pulled me through the door, gave me a brief hug and a kiss on the cheek, her eyes bright, and called out, "OK, kids, Dr. Randolph's here. Let's go. Get your coats on. We're going horseback riding!" Jack came running in from the kitchen, threw his arms around Penny's leg, and said, "He doesn't have one of those sticks, does he?"

"No baby, you're not sick. He doesn't need to look at your throat." She opened the closet door in the foyer and began pulling out coats, hats, and gloves. "Catherine!" she yelled up the stairs, "come on, we're ready to go." Catherine eventually appeared at the top of the stairs with a shy smile, and slowly began her descent as Penny struggled to get Jack to put his arms into his little jacket.

When the packaging of kids was complete, she shooed them out the door. I followed and started heading toward the Jeep.

"Alex," said Penny, "you forgot. We have to take my car. You don't have any car seats."

"Oh… of course."

"You'll have to move your Jeep. Here, you can drive," she said, throwing me a set of keys.

I repositioned the Jeep in the driveway, while Penny started loading the kids in the back of her SUV. I climbed into the front seat and looked back. Catherine expertly clicked her buckles together, pulled the little strap tight, then sat back and looked up at me with a smile. Jack was zooming a jet fighter around the back seat as Penny struggled to get his arms inside the seat belts. Finally she succeeded, climbed into the front passenger seat, and exhaled. "OK," she said smiling, "we're ready to go."

This was my very first experience with a car full of kids. The chatter was incessant, interspersed with the zoom of Jack's fighter. "Mommy," said Catherine, "are we going to ride a boy horse or a girl horse?"

"I don't know, honey. You'll have to ask Dr. Randolph."

"No, you ask him."

"Honey, he's not going to bite you. Ask him."

Catherine contemplated the risks for a moment, and then apparently decided that they were tolerable. "Dr. Randolph, are we going to ride a boy horse or a girl horse?"

"We are going to ride Abigail, Catherine. She's a girl horse," I said.

"How can you tell?"

I had to think about this one. Penny looked at me with an expectant grin. I was entering risky terrain. I took a guess that Catherine was used to seeing Jack naked.

"Well, Catherine, you know how Jack has a—"

"A penis?" she yelled.

"Yes. Yes, a penis. Well, Abigail doesn't have one of those."

"Do you have a boy horse?"

"Yes. His name is General Robert E. Lee."

"Does his look like Jack's?" At this point I was becoming concerned about my driving. Penny was holding herself, convulsing with laughter, and the noise in the car was deafening.

"They're similar, Catherine, but slightly different in size," I yelled back.

Sally's blue truck was in the driveway when we pulled in, and she was standing by the paddock fence with Abigail already saddled. General Lee, grazing in mid-pasture, looked up briefly with indifference, and then put his nose back to the grass. Penny climbed out, put her hands in the back pockets of her jeans, and looked around. "Alex, it's just beautiful!" *Good. She likes it.*

Catherine and Jack immediately made a beeline for the paddock at warp speed. Penny took off after them, grabbing the hood on the back of Jack's parka, and yelling for Catherine to stop.

"You guys have to stand right here by me, and don't move until I tell you!"

Sally slowly walked forward, smiling, and I did the introductions, unexpectedly slightly discomfited by the proximity of Penny and Sally on the same real estate. They warmly shook hands, Sally telling Penny how beautiful were her children, and Penny thanking her for allowing the kids the pleasure of their first horseback ride.

Sally crouched down on her haunches at eye level with Catherine and Jack, and said quietly "OK, guys, we have just a couple of little rules to talk about. The horses are very big, but believe it or not, they are scared of you, so when we get near them we have to walk very slowly and quietly."

"They're afraid we'll hurt them, right?" asked Catherine.

"You're right, Catherine. And there's one more rule. Never walk up behind them where they can't see you or they might kick you. Always walk up to their face. OK?" Catherine nodded, and Jack buried his face in Penny's leg.

"OK, we're going to ride Abigail today. Do you want to walk over and pet her first before we ride?" she asked cheerfully. Sally offered Catherine her hand, which Catherine, surprisingly, willingly grasped. Jack put his arms up in front of his mother and jumped up and down. Penny pulled him up and slung him on her gorgeous little hip.

"Abigail's a girl horse, right?" asked Catherine. *Oh my. Look out, Sally.*

"She is, Catherine. We call a girl horse a mare."

"And you call a boy horse a stallion, right?"

"Very good, Catherine. You know a lot about horses already."

"I *love* horses," she smiled, revealing a wide gap where two front teeth had taken a leave of absence.

Abigail put her head over the fence as we approached, no doubt hoping for a treat. Sally rubbed her nose, and said, "OK, Catherine, do you want to pet her?"

Catherine reached up tentatively and touched the side of Abigail's face, quickly pulling back her hand. When nothing catastrophic happened, she reached up again and slowly ran her small hand back and forth over the side of Abigail's nose.

"She's soft!"

Penny walked slowly closer with Jack in her arms until she was close enough for Jack to reach out to Abigail. "Do you want to pet her, Jack?" she crooned. Jack reached out and smacked Abigail across the nose. Abigail gave a start and jerked her nose back, straining against the halter rope.

"Jack! No!" Penny said, whipping him back beyond reach. "Oh, Sally, I'm so sorry. Jack! You must not hit! If you do that again you're not going to ride her. That was very naughty!" Jack buried his face on Penny's shoulder.

~

By the second circuit around the paddock—Sally leading with a halter rope—it was clear that Catherine was smitten. The smile was permanently affixed to her face. She sat up straight in the saddle, looking all around, and periodically reached down to pat Abigail's mane.

Jack, on the other hand, initially clung to Penny like Spiderman on the side of the Empire State Building. She tried to lift him into the saddle without success. Finally she looked over at me and said, "Do you want to try?"

"Jack," I said, "you and I are boys, and boys are good at riding horses." Penny rolled her eyes. "Can I lift you up, and then I'll hold your hand while we walk around? What do you think?" Jack stared at me for a long time, his head lying on Penny's shoulder. Finally he nodded. I reached out my arms and he came forward.

Jack's legs were so short, and Abigail's back so broad, that perched on the saddle it looked like he was doing the split. He latched onto my thumb with one hand, and with the other gripped the saddle horn. Sally slowly coaxed Abigail forward. By the end of the first circuit around the paddock, Jack was tired of holding hands. Midway through the second circuit, he grasped the horn of the saddle with both hands and started rocking back and forth, going 'vroom, vroom'. Abigail walked around the paddock with her head low, wondering when this was going to be over.

After a second turn for Catherine, who jumped up and down begging for another ride, we watched Sally unsaddle Abigail, and then let Catherine take a turn at brushing her down as high as her little arms could reach.

Ultimately, Jack was more interested in Maggie than Abigail. They bonded. He yanked on her tail, pulled her ears, and occasionally smacked her on the nose when she wasn't fast enough to avoid his little roundhouse. Maggie loved every minute of it. She barked and bounded and they rolled around in the grass together. By the end of the afternoon Jack was covered in mud and dead winter grass.

I looked up toward the house. Ruth stood motionless in the distance on the patio with her arms folded, watching. I waved and she waved back.

"Does anybody here like brownies?" I asked.

"I *love* brownies," said Jack exuberantly. "But I don't like nuts," he said, making a yuck face.

I crouched down on my haunches. "Do you see that lady standing up there?" I said, pointing toward the solitary figure on the patio.

"That's Mrs. Hollens. She's very nice. And this afternoon I think that she baked some fresh brownies, and I don't think they have any nuts, Jack. But if they do, we'll just pick them out."

"Is that your wife?" asked Catherine.

~

I boosted Jack up onto the stool at the granite countertop. Catherine insisted on climbing onto her stool under her own power. Arrayed in front of each of them was a warm square of brownie on a little paper plate with mouse ears, a napkin imprinted with Cinderella in a pink gown, a small pink plastic glass for Catherine, and a blue sippy cup for Jack—both filled with milk. I had never seen any of this stuff before.

Penny and Ruth stood in the kitchen on the other side of the counter, comfortably chatting; Penny sipping on a cup of hot mulled cider, and Ruth leaning back against the counter with her arms folded.

"Can I have another brownie?" yelled Jack.

"What's the magic word, Jack?" replied Penny.

"Pleeeeaaaase."

Ruth opened the oven door, pulled out a pan, and used a spatula to slide another brownie onto Jack's plate. "There you go, Jack. There's plenty more where that came from," she said.

CHAPTER FORTY-EIGHT

WE TOOK THE JEEP BACK TO THE FARM THIS time, after placing the kids in Holly's safekeeping. It was past dusk by the time we reached the house. I turned into the stone driveway with my fingers crossed and watched as my headlights swept across the parking area. Ruth's car was gone. Incredibly, it was the first time that Penny and I had ever been alone—well, alone in a place where things could happen.

The air had cooled rapidly after the sun went down, and frost was already beginning to gather on the grass. The brightest first stars of the evening had made their appearance in the darkening sky.

I hung our coats on the pegs in the mudroom, pushed open the red paneled door to the kitchen, and flicked on the recessed lights over the island.

"Welcome to *Casa Alex,* Madame" I said. "Can I offer you a drink?"

"In fact, I'm dying for a drink. Do you have a good house cabernet?"

"Madame, we offer only the finest in ten dollar wines here at *Casa Alex*—that's by the bottle, not by the glass." I stifled a chuckle at my own lame humor. "My name is Alex, and I'm the owner, chef, maître d', server, and busboy. So if there's anything we can do to make your stay more pleasant, you know who to ask for."

"Actually there *is* something that would make my stay more pleasant," she said, slowly walking over and placing her hands on my waist. Her scent began to make its way into my brain.

"Who am I addressing at the moment?" she asked imperiously, her hands slowly running up and over my chest.

"Uhh… I'm just the busboy. I think I better go get the owner."

"You'll do just fine," she murmured, standing on her tiptoes and softly kissing my cheek. "I've always liked busboys and farm boys." And with that her lips met mine; gently at first, then fiercely.

~

We made it as far as the family room, and fell into the big leather recliner in front of the fireplace, Penny lying in my lap, her lips plying my neck and face with kisses. My hand found its way under her sweater, kneading her spine and the ridges of muscle in her back, then slowly made its way around her lower ribs until it caressed a breast through her bra.

She gave a soft moan into my mouth and then leaned back. For a long moment, she looked deep into my eyes, as if to consider the impact of what she was about to do; as if to never forget the moment.

Slowly, she grasped the bottom of her sweater with both hands, pulled it over her head and dropped it to the floor, her hair cascading in a jumble around her face. Never taking her eyes off mine, she reached behind her back with both hands, unsnapped the neon-pink bra, and tossed it aside. Then, sitting up straight in my lap, naked from the waist up, arms at her side, she waited while my eyes roamed over her body. I was awestruck by the gesture.

In the dim light I soaked in the delicacy of her shoulders; the graceful curves and shadows of her breasts; the suppleness of her belly; the gentle flare of her hips.

Placing her hands on my thighs, she leaned forward, allowing her small breasts to fall free from her chest. I reached out with both hands and gently cupped them, savoring their silky softness and taking the measure of their weight. Her eyes closed and she let out a soft sigh as my thumbs brushed her nipples and they stiffened at my touch.

Leaning closer, she softly placed her mouth over mine, brushing my lips and kissing the corners of my mouth.

Abruptly breaking the kiss, she sat up again, unbuttoned my shirt, and roughly pulled it open wide, her eyes unblinking as slowly she ran her hands over my chest. She flicked one nipple with an index finger, looked up, and smiled. Emotion poured over me like a tsunami. I grabbed her head with both hands and roughly pulled her to me, her naked breasts pressed to my chest, our mouths crushed together.

My hand ran slowly down her belly, fumbled to open her low jeans, and then gently slipped under the waistband of her panties. Penny gave a little involuntary shudder, her legs opening slightly wider. I passed a narrow patch of soft hair, paused to briefly stroke it, and moved lower into her slippery folds. She held my face with both hands and groaned into my mouth, her tongue searching. "Love me, Alex, love me," she breathed.

Penny stood and I knelt in front of her, sliding the open jeans over her hips to the floor, watching intently as first the front of her pink panties came into view, and then the smoothness of her thighs. I rubbed my face across the soft expanse of her belly, inhaling her scent, then pulled away and slowly slid the panties down until she was naked. God, she was beautiful. Placing my hands on both hips, I gently turned her, watching muscles flex as she shifted her weight. Her buttocks were round and smooth with a little hollow near the hip. I ran my hands over them lovingly and gently kissed each cheek.

Turning again, Penny lowered herself to the carpet. With her eyes glued to mine, she slowly let her legs fall apart until they were resting wide on the carpet. Little explosions went off in my brain. She watched as I tore off the rest of my clothes and crawled toward her, the desire overpowering.

"Wait," she whispered. "I want to touch you first." She pulled me forward until I was straddling her breasts, my rigid member bobbing in the air with each heartbeat. Gently she ran one finger up and down its length, her eyes watching intently, then, wrapping one little hand around the base, she slowly milked it.

A single drop of clear fluid appeared at the tip. She reverently touched it with her index finger and slowly spread the fluid around in ever widening circles until I was afraid that I would lose it. She lifted her head and gently kissed the sensitive part underneath, then murmured, "Now, Alex. I'm ready for you."

With one hand under her raised legs, she guided me to her slick opening. I gently pushed until the resistance gave way and I slid smoothly into her, my body throbbing violently. Penny gave a soft gasp. I held still for a long moment, our eyes locked together, savoring the sensation; the heat; the powerful emotion of being buried deep inside her. And as I stared deep into those animated green eyes, I thought that I could see into her soul.

~

I watched Penny pull the short camisole over her head, and then wriggle into her tiny jeans with the two-inch zipper, leaving exposed a lovely expanse of hip. To my immense pleasure, her bra and panties remained strewn across the family room floor. As she walked to me, her breasts swayed gently with the movement of her hips. I began to have serious doubts about my ability to pull off this dinner.

"Uhh… let's see," I said. "Where were we? I think when we left off, I was about to serve you with a glass of house cabernet."

"Does the owner of this inn know that you behave like this with female customers?" she asked accusingly.

"That was the first time." I said.

Penny laughed, and wrapped her arms around my waist, laying her head on my chest. She looked up at me, her liquid green eyes glistening. "That was *so* incredible, Alex," she said quietly. I kissed her forehead and squeezed her to me, every fiber in my body madly in love with this wonderful woman.

~

We cooked together, Penny gently offering little culinary hints here and there. Nothing came out on time, of course, but it didn't matter. We cheerfully ate in courses, sitting across from each other at the little walnut table with a candle burning in the center, pots and pans piling up in the sink.

"Mmmm... this bread is heavenly," Penny said, leaning over her plate and ripping off the corner of a slice with her teeth.

"That's Ruth's work. She thought that I should have fresh-baked bread tonight—an important part of the courting process."

"That was so *sweet* of her to bring all those little things for the kids today," she said.

"Ruth is determined that one way or another there will be children in this house. My mother's not far behind her."

"You were wonderful with Jack today," she said, leaning on an elbow, fork in hand.

"Not much concern about him not being an alpha male, despite living in a house filled with females."

"Oh! I know! I could have killed him when he smacked Abigail."

"I believe that was just after the lecture about how horses are afraid of people," I said smiling.

"It must be in his genes. It's got to be instinctual—although his grandfather and his uncle keep him in no short supply of fighters, aircraft carriers, and tanks. I try to civilize him, but it's a long process."

"What's your father like?"

"Like an admiral. All honor and principle. He can be brusque, or charming, depending on the circumstances. He's actually very scholarly. He and I butted heads constantly when I was in my early teens. I think I got my stubbornness from him," she said smiling. "But underneath there's a very, very soft side. He's mellowed over the years. Catherine and Jack adore him. So do I."

"I'm anxious to meet your parents someday. I want to see what kind of man and woman produced you."

"I told my mother I was going to make love to you tonight," she said looking up.

I stopped in mid-chew. A stalk of asparagus encountered a malfunction on its trip down my esophagus. I choked and reached for my water glass. Penny smiled, her eyes sparkling mischievously. This was an unanticipated revelation. *Oh, my. These two women are far too close.*

"Does that surprise you?" she asked.

"I'm just a little unsure now what to say the first time we meet."

"How about, 'Madam, your daughter is a *marvelous* fuck!'" Penny said with a deep voice. I slowly grinned widely, then collapsed with laughter at the thought.

~

"It's a little late, Alex, and I'm not sure how you go about this—what the rules are these days—but I guess there are a couple of things that we should talk about," Penny said, drying a sauce pan with a hand towel.

"What's that?" I asked, looking over at her as I stacked plates in the dishwasher.

She dropped the towel and looked at me. "I started back on birth control pills with my period a week ago," she said simply, "and I don't have any diseases." I thought about that.

"You're a nurse with a couple of different degrees, and I'm a doctor, right? You'd think that that's a demographic group that might have these discussions *before* sex. And we wonder why teenagers get pregnant." I put my arms around her waist and pulled her to me.

"For the record, I'm *not* on birth control pills, I have *not* had a vasectomy, and I *don't* have any diseases… at least none that I know about," I said smiling.

~

The second time it was more urgent; faster; primal. Penny was naked, poised on her knees above me on the bed. She crawled forward and pressed her sex to my face, my hands cupping her little buttocks. Her fingers caressed my head as I gently explored her with my tongue, enthralled at having my face buried in her most intimate places. Her hips gave little involuntary jerks. Little satisfied sighs emanated from her throat.

She lifted one leg over my head, pivoted, and crawled toward the bottom of the bed on all fours. She stopped, knees wide apart, and dropped her spine into a deep curve, presenting me with her lovely round buttocks and her open sex. She looked back at me over her shoulder—her hair wild; her eyes blazing. It was the most erotic sight I had ever witnessed.

I kneeled behind her, grasped her flaring hips with both hands, and pulled her onto me. She groaned and lowered her shoulders to the bed. As the waves built, her tiny fingers reached under her, stroked me, and suddenly we were soaring over the edge together for the second time tonight.

~

I brushed a wisp of hair off her eyes and watched her face as her breathing became deeper and she slipped into slumber. One arm was draped across my chest; her head tucked into my shoulder. The corner of her mouth gave a little twitch, and I gently placed two fingers on her lips. I pulled her tightly to me, never wanting to let go of this marvelous creature who had so completely and utterly captured my heart.

I took Penny home and returned to the farm about 2:30 AM. As I locked up the place before turning in, I noticed a pink bra and wispy thong still strewn across the family room floor. I smiled. These would have to take their place on top of my boxers in my underwear drawer, although first, I supposed, I should dispose of another pink item. I picked them up and smelled them, picking up a trace of her scent, carried them upstairs with me, and fell into a deep and dreamless sleep.

CHAPTER FORTY-NINE

I WHISTLED AS I WALKED DOWN THE HALL AND past Julie's office on my way to my 7:00 AM shift. I heard Julie call out through her open door, "What are you so happy about this morning?"

I stuck my head in the door and smiled, "Life is good."

Stan Robinson walked through the ER about eight thirty, doing his daily rounds to ensure that the administration was visible to its valued employees. This was the first time that I had seen Stan since my visit with Dr. Myers.

"Good morning, Dr. Randolph," he said, walking up to my computer station, silk yellow bow tie gleaming.

"Hi, Stan."

"Uhh… Alex, do you have a minute?" he asked without his characteristic bravado.

"Sure." I stood and led Stan out of the department to the staff lounge. It was empty. A half-carafe of coffee remained. I picked it up and sniffed it. I'd smelled worse. "Coffee, Stan?"

"No, thanks. I've already had my quota." I fished a styrofoam cup out of the cupboard and poured for myself.

"Alex, I wanted to tell you that… I'm sorry," he said simply. "There wasn't much that I could do about this." I looked over at Stan. There was genuine anguish on his face.

"Stan, I appreciate very much you telling me that. In truth, I never thought that this came from you, and I suspected that it was out of your hands. You don't need to say any more. Don't take any risks."

"If there's anything you need—a letter of recommendation—anything… I'll do it."

I shook his hand. "Thank you, Stan."

~

Penny came in for her shift about 2:30, caught my eye and smiled softly. The little shared intimacy was intoxicating.

The tones on the fire/EMS dispatch radio went off shortly after 3:00 PM. They caught my ear because there were a lot of them—usually signifying a major incident. I stopped to listen to the dispatch.

"Alert medical box forty-four-dash-fifteen in the area of Bunker Hill Road and York Road. Engine four-forty-one, Brush four-forty-three, ATV forty-four, Medic sixty, and EMS seven, for a shooting in the area of Bunker Hill Road approximately three-quarters of a mile west of York Road in the Gunpowder State Forest. Units to stage at the intersection of York Road and Bunker Hill Road and operate on talk group two, time fifteen-ten."

"Four-forty-one enroute."

"Sixty's on the call."

"Four-forty-three with crew of three."

"ATV forty-four's rolling."

"EMS seven enroute."

They were staging the units—holding them back from the scene until it was secured by the cops. It was a miserable afternoon to be staging in the state forest—low clouds, rain, and cold. I looked up at the status board and saw that there was a patient in Fifteen, the trauma room.

"OK, folks, it doesn't sound good out there," I said to no one in particular. "We better make some room in here for a gunshot wound. They're not going to get a helicopter up today in this rain. Can we move that patient in Fifteen to another room?"

"Lisa Turano piped up. "Yeah, he's stable. I'll move him to

Twelve. And I've got a new one in Thirteen that just walked in with what looks like a shoulder dislocation and some facial lacerations. Said he fell through a window, although I'm not sure that I buy that. I sent him straight to x-ray. He might be back by now."

"OK. We'll need to do a conscious sedation on him. Get set up for that."

Penny was at the nursing station. "I can do that," she said.

"What's the guy's name in Thirteen?"

"Martinez, Louis Martinez."

I walked over to the PAC system screen and pulled up Martinez's x-ray films. As Lisa suspected, his right shoulder was dislocated—out of socket. We would need to put him to sleep with propofol to get that shoulder back in place.

Ben was walking down the hall back toward the nursing station. "Ben, we've got some sort of shooting incident going on in the state forest near Hereford. They're staging EMS. We're cleaning out Fifteen. I'm gonna do a shoulder dislocation in Thirteen."

"Gotcha'," said Ben.

I walked into Thirteen with its two massive surgical lights hovering over the patient stretcher like a pair of alien spaceships. A wide rectangular column rose to the ceiling at the head of the stretcher, bristling with equipment and capped by a large color monitor.

Penny was taping her IV in place on a Hispanic male who was lying fairly calmly for a shoulder dislocation—typically a very painful injury. He lay in a patient gown with his eyes closed, perhaps the only evidence that he was in pain. A gold chain was just visible around his neck under a full beard. A bloody dressing was taped in place over a presumed laceration above his right eyebrow, and much of the rest of his face was covered with linear scratches.

I touched his right arm. "Louis?" He opened his eyes and looked at me. They were black and cold as death. I would never forget them. It was Julio.

"Louis, I'm Dr. Randolph. I understand that you fell through a window." *Nice and relaxed, Alex. Just pretend he's any other patient—a high school football player. Don't rush it.* Julio nodded.

"Louis, I've looked at your x-rays. Unfortunately you have dislocated your shoulder. The ball is out of its socket. We're going to need to put the ball back in the socket, but to do that, we have to give you some medicine that relaxes the muscles in your shoulder. Otherwise it's very hard and very painful to try to get it back in. It will also make you sleepy, but it's a very short acting medicine and you'll wake up in about five minutes. Did you understand that? Do you have any questions?" Julio stared at me for a moment, then shook his head 'no'. I decided that in this particular situation we could probably afford to dispense with written informed consent.

Lisa walked in the room with a syringe filled with propofol. *With a little luck, this could work out.* I could put him to sleep, get the shoulder back in place, and simply keep him asleep until the police arrived. *First you've gotta get rid of Lisa.* I had promised Frank that I would keep her out of the room if any Crips or MS-13 showed up, and I intended to keep my promise.

"Lisa, I'll take the propofol," I said, plucking the syringe out of her hand, "and I'm going to have you get Bed Fifteen ready. They just dispatched a couple of ambulances, and we may be getting a trauma."

Lisa shot me a strange look. I put my hand firmly on her shoulder and started walking her out of the room. "I want you to get a chest tube tray set up, and get me two units of O-positive blood from the lab..."

When we cleared the doorway, I whispered a set of rapid-fire instructions. "That's Julio in there. Push the button for the cops, and don't come back into the room yourself. Send one of the other nurses in. And alert security, but have them stay out of the room until I get him asleep."

I was back in the room in ten seconds. Penny was placing oxygen and a sidestream carbon dioxide monitor on Julio. She reached up and touched a couple of icons on the monitor screen to bring up the tracing. Julio stared at me as I walked back to the bedside. I hoped to God that he couldn't tell that I had recognized him, or we would have a big problem. I had to assume that he was armed. *At least he seems to be here alone.*

April walked into the room and coolly walked to the head of the bed. She wordlessly began to assemble suction tubing and a bag-valve-mask in the event that Julio had to be ventilated after the propofol injection. I guessed that she knew this was Julio. If she did, her stock just went up in my book a thousand percent. I was sure that Penny *didn't* know.

"OK, Ladies, are we all set?" *Stay relaxed, Julio. You're going to be in a very sweet sleep in just another minute, and then you're going to be prosecuted for murder.*

"Do you want respiratory therapy here?" asked Penny. I was afraid that this was coming. Penny knew that it was standard protocol for respiratory therapy to be present during a conscious sedation. I didn't want any delays to give Julio time to get nervous.

"She's going to be tied up in Bed Fifteen," I said. "I think we'll be fine with just the two of you." *Don't ask any more questions, lover... please.* We exchanged glances and Penny remained silent.

"OK, Louis, here we go." I inserted the syringe into the port in Julio's IV and began to rapidly push in twenty cc's of propofol. "When you wake up, that shoulder will be back where it belongs." He gazed up at me malevolently, then slowly his face softened.

"Sweet dreams... Julio," I said. I thought I saw a brief flicker of recognition cross his face. He seemed to struggle briefly to raise himself to consciousness, but it was too late. Five seconds later his cheeks puffed out, and I gave a huge sigh of relief.

It happened in slow motion. A powerful explosion ripped the air as a fine mist of red suddenly appeared like a halo around Julio's head. The right side of his skull exploded outward and splattered against the adjacent blue wall cabinets and ceiling tiles.

I recoiled and turned toward the source of the explosion. An extended arm holding a semi-automatic pistol came into my field of vision and slowly lowered as its owner turned and began to sprint for the door. Screaming registered someplace in my brain and my eyes began to search for the source. I followed the sound to April's open mouth and contorted face. And then suddenly it was over. He was gone. Only the echo of April's screams remained.

My face felt sticky. I wiped my cheek with my fingers and looked down to see blood. Penny stood staring at Julio, motionless, her hands covering her mouth. Instinctively I looked to Julio, assessing the damage, but there was nothing to be done.

I jumped, as two more deafening cracks abruptly echoed through the door from outside the room. *Shit! He shot somebody else!* My mind was beginning to work again, and I sprinted toward the door. As I reached the doorway a black hand appeared and hit my chest like a sledgehammer. I could feel myself become airborne as my feet left the floor. Pain ascended my peripheral nerves and exploded into my brain as first my elbows and then my spine hit the floor, followed by a deafening crack and a constellation of stars as my skull smashed into the composite-covered concrete.

The next few moments are somewhat vague in my memory, but I recall hearing Penny's voice first. I remember it being quiet and composed. "He's been hurt. His head is bleeding. At least let me put a dressing on it."

"You stay in that corner and shut up, bitch, or you will be one dead white woman. You, too," he yelled, waving the gun at April, "over there." Her bottom lip quivering, and without ever taking her eyes off him, April put her hands out behind her, backed into the wall, and cautiously began to feel her way around the equipment in the room toward Penny. "Down on the floor, both of you," he barked. The two girls slowly slid down the wall and sat with legs stretched out in front of them on the floor.

I was up on my elbows now. My vision was coming back into focus, and I could see that the owner of the hand that had decked me was a very tall, broad, black male who looked vaguely familiar. His hair was covered with a stocking and he had a scar on his left cheek. My computer was slowly processing this image without results, and then bingo—I hit on it. He was one of Jawara Reynolds bodyguards—the big one at the bedside. I was having a little trouble making sense of this. He shot Julio. He had escaped. Why had he come back into the room?

He was peering nervously around the curtains that covered the room's window to the nursing station, when he turned and saw me on my elbows. He wordlessly walked toward me with his arm extended and his gun pointed directly at my head. When the distance was right, he unleashed a powerful kick into my left ribs. I could hear cracking and crunching sounds as the pain once again exploded into my brain. I was curled into a ball, moaning, when the second kick caught my left flank.

"Crawl over to that corner, prick, and don't make a move, or those two bitches over there will be trash. Do you hear me? Trash! Dead!"

I guess that was a rhetorical question, because without waiting for an answer, he walked over to the closed door, opened it slightly, and standing behind it began to yell into the hallway.

"Listen up, you motherfuckers. I know the cops are out there. You try anything—anything at all—and I got me three people in here who are dead. You hear me? The bitches go first, and then the doctor. You know I'll do it, 'cause I got nothin' to lose. I already killed one cop.

"You want them to live, you gonna get me outta here. And one of them bitches is goin' with me, so you try anything and she'll be dead!" Sweat dripped off his face like a fountain. He whirled, looking around the room in a frenzy, and spotted a phone on the wall where Penny and April sat.

"There's a phone in here," he continued. "I want the cops on that phone in five minutes, and I'm gonna tell you what to do if you want these white people to live. Five minutes. You hear me? You got five minutes." He slammed the door shut, and began to pace aimlessly around the room. The big black and white clock on the far wall read 3:17.

CHAPTER FIFTY

THE PAIN WITH EACH BREATH WAS excruciating. My head throbbed with every heartbeat. I lay among bits of brain matter on the floor in the corner as I watched the big second hand on the clock move relentlessly around the face.

Julio's body still lay on the stretcher, blood slowly dripping from the gaping hole in the side of his head and pooling on the floor beside me. I could see Penny and April through the open space below Julio's bier, sitting motionless. Penny stared at me, her face a collage of anguish and fear. We made eye contact. A single tear streamed down her cheek. For the moment, April's soft sobs were the only sound in the room, excepting the constant footsteps of our captor as he paced, pistol in hand at his side.

Periodically he would risk a quick glance with one eye along the edge of the curtain through the glass window out into the nursing station. I wondered when the first sharpshooter would arrive, training his scope on that window, patiently waiting for his opportunity. It seemed quiet in the hallway beyond the door. I could hear nothing. The clock read 3:20. Two minutes remained until the deadline.

I tried to force myself to move beyond the pain and to focus—to envision what was happening beyond the closed door, and to anticipate what was to be a likely sequence of events. I frantically searched my brain for what meager knowledge it held regarding hostage situations. The next few minutes were crucial. The first deadline was dangerous, I knew that. The only thing I could think of was to try and establish a relationship—anything that would make it more difficult for our captor to act against one of us.

I heard a zipper fly and watched him struggle out of his ski parka, keeping one hand with the gun trained on me as he switched hands and shed the coat. He violently threw it in the corner. Under the parka he wore only a black tee shirt. It was soaked. The PA system overhead announced "Code Brown, ER" three times.

He kept looking at the door. It must have finally sunk into his head that the door had no lock, because he grabbed Julio's stretcher and, without seeming to notice that the wheels were locked, his powerful body drug it across the floor, rubber tires squealing. Angrily, he slammed it feet-first against the door. The frantic pacing resumed.

"You must have hated him," I said, "after what he did to your brother." He stopped in mid-pace and shot me a fierce look, breathing hard. I wasn't sure whether the brother part was figurative or literal.

"What do you know? You don't know shit."

"I took care of your brother when they brought him in here. Actually, all three of us took care of him. Nobody should have to die like that." He hesitated, as if unsure what to say. "He was still awake when he got here," I continued. "I put him to sleep. We stabilized him and flew him to Shock Trauma."

"I wish I could have cut his balls off and stuffed 'em down his fuckin' throat, like he did to P-Loc," he spat, looking over at Julio's lifeless body. *P-Loc must have been the one that went over the spillway without his balls.* I glanced at the clock—3:21. The deadline would be up in one minute. *OK. Just keep him talking until they call.*

"Well, you didn't get to cut his balls off, but Julio got what was comin' to him."

"Yeah, I blew his fuckin' brains out," he echoed venomously.

"Poor P-Loc didn't stand a chance. Julio shot him in both knee caps first." He looked at me, like something wasn't making sense to him, but he wasn't sure what.

"Did you know that he was still alive when he went over the dam?" I asked.

"How do you know all this shit?" he asked suspiciously.

"Julio was in here a couple of months ago with a stab wound. The cops were here and got his blood samples. They found the same blood on the wall above the dam. That's how they figured out it was Julio who killed P-Loc. They told me that the coroner said he died by drowning. So they knew he was still alive when he hit the water." I checked the clock—3:22. *Shit! What are they doing out there?*

"They've been lookin' for Julio ever since, but *you* found him first," I said with a hint of admiration. He glared at me silently. I continued. "I figure you saved the cops a lotta time and trouble."

The phone rang. My body gave a jerk at the sound, searing pain setting off a thousand tiny explosions of light in my throbbing brain. He turned toward the sound, and stood for a moment with his mouth open, looking at the phone. Finally he realized that Penny and April were seated directly under it.

"You two," he said waving his gun, "over there; over in that other corner. And stay on the floor!" Penny and April scurried on their hands and knees to the other corner of the room, staying close to the wall. The ringing continued. He walked to the phone, reached for it, hesitated, and then picked up the receiver.

"Who is this?" he yelled into the phone. He listened for a moment, then, apparently realizing that he wasn't watching me, whipped around in a panic. Not that I was a big threat to anybody at the moment.

"You listen to me," he yelled again. "I don't give a shit who you are. You have a helicopter here in thirty minutes. One pilot. And he better not be a cop, or I'll put a bullet in the back of his head. Thirty minutes. Do you hear me?" He glanced over at Penny and April. "If there's not a helicopter here in thirty minutes, the skinny bitch with short hair goes first. She's dead." And with that he slammed down the receiver. The clock read 3:26. April's body shook uncontrollably.

CHAPTER FIFTY-ONE

I DID ALL THE TIME CALCULATIONS IN MY HEAD A dozen times. I knew from my experience with emergency medical services that nothing was going to happen of substance until the arrival of a hostage negotiator, and probably, an incident commander. Thirty minutes was going to be cutting it close before either of them could be on the scene. I didn't think that they would make it. It would likely be closer to an hour.

I couldn't tell from the one-sided conversation to whom our captor was speaking, but I figured it had to be an entry-level patrolman—what Baltimore County calls an "Officer." He had no authority, and had apparently tried to explain that, but our captor had told him that he didn't care. I hoped to God that whoever he was, he had a good head on his shoulders. He would likely have to deal with the next deadline himself, and there sure as hell wouldn't be a helicopter here in thirty minutes. Nobody would even be flying today. The deadline would be unmet.

What I couldn't figure out is what the police were doing here at the time our captor tried to make good his escape after shooting Julio. It was too early for them to be arriving solely because of Lisa's push of the panic button. Was it related to the shooting incident in the state forest? Had Julio been involved and escaped? Were the police following him here? Or maybe there was a big shoot-out in the forest that was over by the time the cops arrived, and they were just checking the hospital for victims.

In any case, a cop had been shot and apparently killed—at least our captor thought so. I wondered who took the bullet. I hoped to hell it wasn't Jack Schmidt. There must have been more than one cop, or our captor would have just continued his escape.

My ribs were killing me. Each breath was torture. I lay on my right side trying to breathe as shallowly as possible. My shoulder was now beginning to ache from carrying the weight of my upper body against the unyielding floor. I shifted my weight slightly and winced as another round of pain shot to my brain.

He was still pacing, staring at the floor; obviously lost in thought. Periodically he would look at me for a second or two, as if considering what to do with me, then resume his pacing. Every two or three minutes he would look at the clock again. Wearing just his tee shirt, I could see that he was a powerfully built man with massive shoulders and biceps that stretched the sleeves of his shirt. I, myself, could barely move. There was no contest here—I would be no match for him physically. I had never felt so helpless.

From my position on the floor, I could see a TV on the wall near the door, installed to make the long waiting times in the ER a little more pleasant for patients. Soon the local stations, and maybe the networks, would be covering this hostage crisis live. I weighed the pros and cons of suggesting to our captor that he turn on the TV. Perhaps I could make the case that it would be an independent source of information that would help him to make decisions. The real reason would be that it would give me more information about what was happening on the outside.

But ultimately I decided that I would only suggest this if he became agitated about a helicopter not arriving. The TV could prove that the weather was bad and no one was flying. On the other hand, if some enterprising independent helicopter operator with a profit motive managed to make his way up here—skimming low under the clouds to feed live video—we'd all be screwed. I hoped that the cops would think about that.

He walked over to the wall-mounted sink and put his mouth under the faucet, keeping an eye on me as he drank deeply. Wiping his mouth with his forearm, he resumed the pacing. I looked up at the clock: 3:46. A total of only twenty-one minutes had passed, but it felt like I had been a hostage for a lifetime. Fourteen minutes remained until the next deadline.

No one had spoken in the room for the last fifteen minutes. I looked over at April, hoping to make eye contact and in some way offer some comfort, but her face was still buried in her hands, and her body still intermittently gave a violent shudder.

There was no doubt that our captor was going to get bad news about the helicopter. If he followed through on his threat, April had fourteen minutes left to live. Could I prepare him in some way for the bad news? Would his reaction be less violent if he had had some time to think about it? Would he become immediately violent if I raised the issue?

"You know, maybe we should start to think about some other way to get you out of here."

He stopped and glared at me. "What the fuck do you mean?"

"You came in from outside. It's raining. The clouds are low. There are no helicopters flying today," I said quietly.

He stood, staring at me for a long time, as the words sank in. He turned toward the wall behind him, saw a trashcan and kicked it violently, spewing trash across the room. "Fuuucck!" he roared, raising both hands to the ceiling and tilting back his head. He whirled towards Julio's stretcher, raised his gun, then smashed the butt into Julio's face again and again, bones crunching, until nothing of the dead face remained but a bloodless pulp, and the raging fires of emotion within him died down. He slid his back down the wall by the door and sat for the first time.

~

The phone rang. I glanced at the clock: 3:49—seven minutes before the deadline. He slowly rose to his feet, staring at it, then walked to the phone and picked it up.

"Yeah," he said loudly. This time he listened—for maybe a minute—then said "Ronnie". Turning, he cast his gaze around the room at the three of us, studied the phone console for a few seconds, punched a button, and hung up. "OK," he said with what I thought was resignation, "you're on the speakerphone."

A warm and friendly voice came across the phone, radiating calm. "Dr. Randolph, April, Penny, this is Tom. I'm going to be talking with Ronnie about how to resolve this without anybody getting hurt. But first, I need to know that all of you are OK. Can each of you please say your name for me and let me know that you're OK?" I breathed a huge sigh of relief. This was a professional hostage negotiator. He made it in incredible time.

~

"Ronnie, my job is to help; to make sure that no harm comes to anybody in that room, including you. I think you probably know that there is a SWAT team here. And you know how hard they train—they're good. But I don't want to see a single shot fired. I want to see you walk out of there unharmed. I can promise you that if you slide your weapon through that door out into the hall, and then come out with your hands on your head, that no one will hurt you."

Ronnie was silent for a long time. He leaned against the wall by the phone and tilted back his head. Finally, he spoke. "You must be fuckin' crazy. Nobody gets out of here alive unless I get a helicopter."

"I will look into that, Ronnie. I'm going to have to check with my boss, and I think you know that we've got a weather problem. It's raining outside and the clouds are very low. I don't think that anybody can fly at the moment. I'll talk to the National Weather Service and get a forecast. You just stay calm there, and I promise that I'll get back to you. In the meantime, if you need anything, or need to talk to me, you can reach me by dialing five-five-three-seven. Remember, Ronnie, our goal is to not see any of you hurt. Do you want to write that number down? Five-five-three-seven." Ronnie was silent, and after no replies to his questions, Tom eventually hung up.

The deadline passed, and Ronnie took no action against April.

CHAPTER FIFTY-TWO

RONNIE DISCOVERED THE TELEVISION ABOUT fifteen minutes after Tom hung up. He punched the power button and three commentators appeared on the screen previewing Monday night football. He flipped through the channels until a woman dressed in a yellow rain slicker appeared, holding a microphone and standing under an umbrella. Mason-Dixon's gleaming emergency façade was visible in the distant background.

"...few details are available, Chuck, but we do know that a gunman is holed up in the emergency department here at Mason-Dixon Regional Medical Center off Middletown Road in Baltimore County, and that he is apparently holding hostages. We *do* have reports that shots were fired, and that at least one person is known to be dead, but we can't confirm that, and we have no information on who the deceased might be.

"As you can see, Baltimore County Police have cordoned off the area, and in the background to the far left you can see the Baltimore County mobile command post with its antennas and satellite dishes in that far parking lot." The camera swung and zoomed in on what looked like a huge motor home, bristling with electronic devices.

"We *have* seen some evidence that the Baltimore County SWAT team has arrived, but the police are keeping everyone back, and we have not been able to confirm that either.

"And, Chuck, the hospital administration has asked us to inform the public that, of course, the Mason-Dixon ER is closed until further notice, and that patients with emergency problems should proceed to their next closest hospital. Also, of course, the hospital is closed to visitors, and we are told that hospital employees should *not* report for work unless you have been contacted by your supervisor. We'll keep you posted as further details emerge. Back to you, Chuck."

Thank God—an umbrella. In truth, I doubted that the police would ever let Ronnie take off in a helicopter, regardless of the weather. But at least the weather was helping to buy time, and buying time was probably a good thing.

By now every family connected to the emergency department staff would be frantically trying to reach their loved ones. Anne would have called and texted me a dozen times, but my cell phone was lying at my computer station and there would be no answer.

With the passage of the deadline, April now appeared a little more in control. Her body was no longer wracked with spasms, and her face was no longer in her hands. But she looked ten years older; her eyes huge red circles. I caught her eye and smiled. She looked at me imploringly, tears once again trickling down her cheeks. I cringed at my helplessness.

Penny sat close by April. Our eyes locked. I silently mouthed "I love you." She breathed deeply for a few seconds, then silently returned the words, crossing her hands over her heart. It was the first such expression between us.

~

I hadn't seen a weather forecast, and I didn't know if this rain was the product of a quick cold front or a slow moving low pressure area. It had already been raining for five or six hours, so I suspected that it was a low pressure area. If so, it might be around for another ten or twelve hours.

In time, Ronnie would start running up against some real physiologic realities—emotional exhaustion, sleep deprivation, and hunger. As those pressures accumulated, would they lead to outbursts of violent behavior, or would they wear down his will to resist? I didn't know. I decided that now was a good time for sleep. I wanted to be awake and alert when exhaustion overtook Ronnie. I, myself, was exhausted from the pain, and, like any good ER doc, I had little trouble falling asleep.

~

I jolted awake, thinking my alarm had gone off, but it was the telephone. The pain hit my brain instantly. I glanced at the clock: 4:40. I had slept for less than an hour. It seemed like the middle of the night. A drop of something trickled into my eye and I wiped my forehead with my hand. It was wet. I was sweating.

Ronnie didn't push the speaker button this time. He picked up the phone and remained silent, listening. After about two minutes he slowly returned the receiver to its cradle and hung up. Not good—no dialogue.

He walked over to the TV and started flipping the channel until a weather radar image popped up on the screen. I recognized the mid-Atlantic.

"As you can see, wide bands of showers are streaming toward the northeast, being fed by this low pressure system sitting off the Outer Banks, which is supplying lots of moisture to this storm. We're going to be seeing an inch—maybe even an inch and a half—of rain in the big cities of the mid-Atlantic; Baltimore, Washington, Philadelphia, and then up the I-95 corridor throughout the evening and well into the early morning hours. But by rush hour tomorrow morning, with a little bit of luck, we may be seeing the first few rays of sunshine in the Baltimore-Washington area. That's it for—" Ronnie flipped the channel back to the local station covering the hostage crisis.

He must have gotten some news relating to the helicopter. No doubt he was told that the weather made it impossible for some period of time—until the storm cleared. He had checked the information against the TV weather. Remarkably, at the moment, Ronnie seemed very calm—maybe even fatalistic. He sat on the floor with his back against the wall next to the door where he could see all three of us. This was a change in demeanor, and I wondered if it meant that Ronnie had reached some sort of decision. But despite his apparent calm, he still had a sheen of sweat on his forehead and his tee shirt remained soaked.

April had begun to quietly sob again. After about ten minutes, she abruptly buried her face in her hands and blurted out, "I have to pee!"

Ronnie looked at her for a moment with disdain. "Piss yourself, bitch," he said finally. Thirty seconds later, April began to sob in earnest, the crotch and thighs of her blue scrub suit slowly darkening as her bladder emptied.

~

As the minutes ticked away, my thoughts gradually began to focus on two themes. The first was what would happen if the cops decided to launch an assault, and who would get hurt in the process? I tried to visualize how that would happen to prepare myself. I figured that they would probably cut the power first so that we were in darkness. Then they would likely force open the door and toss in those noise and light grenades to temporarily blind Ronnie, followed by the assault.

It would help that the three of us were lying on the floor. Maybe in the darkness and confusion it would be hard for Ronnie to execute hostages, but I worried just as much about one of us catching friendly fire from the SWAT team, particularly since Ronnie might be on the floor too, and it might be hard for them to distinguish him from one of us. But at the end of the day, there was, in fact, nothing that I could do about this. It would happen or it wouldn't.

The second recurring thread in my thoughts was whether there were enough kernels of humanity left in Ronnie's hate-wracked soul to talk him into letting one or both of the girls go. I kept thinking of Catherine and Jack who had already lost a father to a fanatic's bullet. The tragedy of losing their mother, too, was unthinkable. As for me, I couldn't bear the thought.

I hadn't spoken to Ronnie in over an hour. I didn't think that enough rapport had yet been established to make the suggestion of releasing one of the girls. We had all maintained a respectful silence. It was time to try and engage him. He was up and pacing again. Periodically he would wince, slow his pace, and grab his belly. I wondered if he was an addict himself, beginning to go through narcotics withdrawal.

"Was Jawara your full brother?" I asked. He glanced at me, but didn't stop pacing this time.

"Yeah."

"It must have been hard on your mother—him dying the way he did."

"My mother's dead. It was my grandmother that cried." *Good! A little glimmer of humanity*. I remained silent for a time.

"I hope she doesn't lose two grandsons."

"What do you care?" he shot back.

"In truth, I didn't like your brother. You were there. You saw that he didn't treat my nurses with respect the first time that he was here. But even I felt pity for him the second time. I can't imagine how horrible it must have been for your grandmother." Ronnie was silent, and I decided to leave it there.

At 5:35 the phone rang again. They were checking in with Ronnie at least once an hour. This time when he answered he spoke.

"I want you to listen carefully to me. This is the last time I am answering this phone. I am watching the weather. When I see that the rain has stopped, I'm going to call you. You will have thirty minutes to have that helicopter here before I kill the bitch. Don't call me again. I will call you." And he hung up. *That's it. With Ronnie not talking, they won't think they have any choice. They're going to launch an assault.*

CHAPTER FIFTY-THREE

I WAS BEGINNING TO FEEL EXHAUSTED; depleted. I must have dozed off again, because when I next looked at the clock it was 7:03. Ronnie had the sound on the TV turned down—I guessed so that he could hear any sounds in the hallway beyond. He seemed tireless, because he was still up and pacing, but now he appeared to me more anxious, his head turning in all directions as if searching for something.

Periodically he would grab at his belly, then clasp his arms around his chest, holding himself. His biceps gleamed with sweat. I waited for him to walk nearer to where I lay so I could get a look at his pupils. It was twenty minutes before he finally walked to the paper towel dispenser on the wall above me, yanked one out, and blew his nose, keeping his gun trained on me throughout. His eyes were dark and bloodshot. It was hard for me to distinguish brown from black at this distance, but I thought that I could see dilated pupils. I was becoming more and more convinced that Ronnie was going through withdrawal.

A screen change on the TV caught my eye and a full headshot of a policeman in uniform popped up. I recognized him immediately. My heart sank. The caption read "Sergeant Jack Schmidt, dead at 56." *Jack… who had done his best to protect us.* I looked over at Penny and April—the two of them representing everything good in this crumbling world—now sitting trembling with fear; both now soaked in their own urine. My eyes shifted to Ronnie as he paced. A burning rage and venomous hate welled up within me. Had I the power, I would have killed him, but my body was incapable of responding to my violent emotions.

I turned back to the TV as a grainy photo appeared of a smiling Jack in tee shirt and shorts with his arm around a short, stocky woman at some sort of family gathering. It was followed by fresh video of a modest row house.

From somewhere overhead my attention was distracted by a scraping sound, followed by a soft metallic clunk. Ronnie immediately stopped pacing and listened, his wide eyes roaming over the ceiling. Pistol raised, he quietly and slowly walked toward an air vent in the middle of the tiled ceiling. A pair of explosions ricocheted around the room, assaulting my eardrums, as he fired two quick shots into the air vent, and then all was quiet again except the tinkling of a few pieces of plastic falling from the shattered vent. I kept waiting for a body to fall through the ceiling tiles or blood to start dripping from the vent, but neither appeared. Maybe a camera or listening device was being threaded through the air vents.

The telephone rang. Ronnie looked at it, started toward it, and then stopped. The ringing continued for about a minute and then ended. I could imagine the fear and panic in the command post. They didn't know whether he had killed two more people or not. An assault could not be long in coming.

I raised my head to look at the clock and had a little difficulty focusing: 8:02. Just lifting my head made me whoozy. The pain in my lower left ribs, if anything, was worse. I was getting very thirsty. My hand ran over my forehead and came back wet again. For the first time it occurred to me that maybe my injuries were more than just fractured ribs.

I put my fingers over my wrist and searched for a pulse. I couldn't find it. I held my breath to better feel, and slowly moved my fingers up and down the little groove until finally a faint rapid pulsation pushed against my fingertips. I counted out thirty seconds of pulse: fifty nine. My heart rate was a hundred and eighteen. *Shit.* I was tachycardic with only a faint peripheral pulse.

I reached under my scrub suit top, slowly ran my hand up to the left upper quadrant of my belly, and pressed. The muscles in my abdomen immediately clenched, and a wave of pain again skyrocketed to my brain. The pain didn't feel like broken ribs. It had to be my spleen—Ronnie's kick had ruptured my spleen. I was slipping into shock. My sense of helplessness was near complete. I wasn't sure that I would make it until the rain stopped.

I looked up and saw Penny watching me, her face awash with fear. "Are you OK?" she mouthed with exaggerated lip movements.

I hesitated. I didn't know how to answer. I was afraid that if I was truthful with Penny she would take some sort of action that was an unaffordable risk. Jack and Catherine had only one parent left. But deceiving the woman with whom I had experienced the greatest intimacy of my life was a painful alternative.

"I'm OK," I mouthed back. She stared at me for a few moments, biting her lower lip. A solitary tear slowly dribbled down her cheek to the crease of her nose.

Ronnie was more agitated than ever now. His pacing was faster. Sweat was dripping from his forehead and he was holding his abdomen almost continuously. Suddenly he bolted for the hopper on the far wall by the phone—the one in which we empty bedpans—and violently wretched over and over again until there was nothing left.

He stood leaning over the hopper for a long time, one hand on the porcelain bowl supporting his weight, the other gripping the pistol; his breathing deep and rapid. Ronnie hadn't thought about missing a heroin dose. He was in full-fledged withdrawal.

The silence was broken by a quiet voice. "I can help that." Fear sliced through the pit of my stomach. *No!*

Ronnie slowly stood up straight and turned toward Penny, still sitting with her back to the wall, maybe ten feet away. The pistol in his hand trembled slightly.

"Help what?" he said with a raspy voice.

"You're going through withdrawal. I can help that." *What is she doing?*

He glared at her for a long moment, thinking through this offer.

"How?" he said.

"There's a medication dispenser at the nursing station, just outside the door. I know all the codes. There's morphine in the machine. You'll feel better with the morphine."

Ronnie continued to stare at Penny, his chest rising and falling rapidly, sweat dripping into his eyes. Finally he reached over, picked up the phone, and punched four buttons. He turned again to Penny and made eye contact before he spoke.

"The blonde is coming out to get morphine. I'll have my gun at the head of the skinny one the whole time, and I'll be watching the clock. If the blonde isn't back in exactly two minutes, or if anybody tries anything, I'll pull the trigger."

Ronnie hung up and slowly walked to the girls, placing the barrel of the pistol against April's temple. Her body shuddered. "Bring me the bottle. Don't draw it up. You've got two minutes. After that, your little friend will look like Julio."

"I can't bring you a bottle," Penny said softly, her voice composed. "We don't have any. The morphine comes in pre-filled syringes, but they're labeled." Ronnie thought about this.

"Get 'em," he said.

"I need more time. The electronic process to get into the machine is complicated. I need two and a half minutes."

He studied her face. "Go."

Penny rose to her feet, sprinted to Julio's gurney, unlocked the wheels, pushed it to the side, and disappeared through the door. Ronnie looked up at the clock.

CHAPTER FIFTY-FOUR

I WATCHED THE SECONDS TICK BY, THE BIG second hand relentless in its advance; April's pitiful whimpering the only sound in the room. Every ten or fifteen seconds, Ronnie would look up at the wall behind him to check the time, the cold steel barrel of his gun buried in the wispy copper hair covering April's temple. If Penny didn't return I was certain that he would kill her.

Two and a half minutes was not a lot of time to get in and out of the Omnicell medication dispenser. Penny would have to type in a user name, then password, select a patient, select the morphine, push all the buttons in the right sequence, and then physically remove the drugs. Any error would kick her out of the process, the machine would start squawking, and she would never make the deadline.

The hostage rescue team was in a huge bind. They would not want Ronnie to get morphine. His withdrawal symptoms gave them leverage. Moreover, they would not want to give him *anything* without getting something in return—namely the release of at least one hostage.

Would they hold Penny and take the risk that Ronnie would not follow through on his threat to kill April? If they tried that, they'd have a wild woman on their hands. They'd have to handcuff Penny. The only option was to let her come back. I prayed to God that their command structure was streamlined enough to make such a decision that fast.

The second hand passed two minutes, and still there was no sound of Penny outside. My breathing stopped. At two minutes and twenty-three seconds I heard a voice outside the door.

"It's me, Penny. I'm coming in now." Ronnie didn't move. Slowly the door opened. Penny's head appeared around the door, and then she entered, closing the door behind her.

"Push the gurney back against the door," Ronnie barked. Penny pushed Julio on his makeshift barricade against the door and locked the wheels. I breathed a huge sigh of relief, my heart pounding through my chest.

The barrel left April's temple, and she began to sob uncontrollably. Ronnie walked toward Penny. "Let me see the syringes," he commanded, holding out his hand. Penny reached into her scrub suit pocket and pulled out two pre-filled morphine syringes. Turning them over in his hand several times, he read the labels twice. Finally, apparently satisfied, he handed one of them back to Penny.

"Use this one," he said. He slid down the wall on my side of the room until he was seated, perhaps eight feet from my position on the floor where I lay against the same wall. Making a fist, he held out his left arm. His right hand still gripped the gun.

"Do it," he said.

Penny knelt before him, reached into her pocket, and pulled out a rubber tourniquet. She tied it around his biceps and began to feel with her fingers at the crease of his arm for a vein.

"There's nothing there," said Ronnie. "You'll have to use the hand."

She grasped Ronnie's huge hand and turned it over, searching on the back side for a vein that wasn't scarred by repeated heroin injections. Slowly she shook her head. "I can't find anything here. Let me see the other hand," she said, pulling the tourniquet. Ronnie switched his gun to his left hand and Penny re-tied the tourniquet around his right arm. I looked at the gun. It was almost within my reach. But in this body, I would never make it.

Penny apparently found a vein that satisfied her, because she wiped the back of his hand with an alcohol swab and reached into her pocket for the syringe. She pulled the rubber cap off the needle and, with trembling hands, slowly pushed the needle through Ronnie's skin. I watched as she pulled back on the plunger, searching for a return of blood to be certain that she was in the vein. I was close enough that I could see the dark red blood gush into the syringe.

With her left hand she reached up and unsnapped the tourniquet, then slowly began to push in on the plunger.

"Only half of it," Ronnie said. Penny could barely control the tremor in her hands. She pushed the plunger in halfway and stopped, looking up at him. I watched his face. His eyes closed. Ten or fifteen seconds passed, and he said, "OK, the rest of it." Penny pushed the plunger in all the way, pulled the syringe from his hand, and stood, slowly backing away, her eyes never leaving Ronnie.

Ronnie's face began to twitch. His eyes popped open. Something was wrong. He tried to sit up, but fell back against the wall. He looked up at Penny. Slowly the barrel of the gun began to rise toward her chest, wobbling and waving in the air. I could hear the screaming of my own voice as I lurched to my knees, my body on fire, the light rapidly fading, and lunged for the gun. As I floated through space, a distant explosion roared, and, after a brief dazzling light, all became darkness.

~

I swam slowly toward the light above, my limbs leaden. As I neared the surface, a lovely feminine face hovered above, wavering and shimmering in the soft swells, watching me. Finally, as I broke the surface, Lynn Saylor's face slowly came into focus. "Where do you hurt, Alex?" she asked softly.

I could hear voices all around me. I was in a chaotic room, packed with people; soldiers with automatic weapons everywhere. An oppressive fear consumed me and I lifted my head, searching for Penny. As the light gradually faded again, I saw Ben effortlessly lift a limp body in blue. He carried it in slow motion as he stepped over my body, golden hair swaying from the head he cradled in his arms, and then darkness returned.

EPILOGUE

CATHERINE RAN UP THE HILL THROUGH THE lush, emerald-green grass to the patio as fast as her legs could carry her, her hair backlit by the warm May sun, forming a shifting golden halo around her head.

"Mommy, Mommy!" she yelled. "Abigail *loves* apples!"

Penny yelled back, "Catherine, if you feed her too many of them, she'll get a belly ache."

Jack rolled in the grass nearby with Maggie, both of them growling ferociously. "Come on, now—both of you. It's time for dinner." Jack struggled to his feet, and then ran full bore into Penny, hitting her in the legs and wrapping his arms around her. Penny reached down for him and winced, "Oooph! I have to be careful about that."

They had four operating rooms fully staffed—with a surgeon gowned and gloved—all afternoon and evening of the hostage crisis, waiting for the unthinkable. Art Sherman, the chest and vascular surgeon was one of them. Penny was the first of us to reach an OR suite. The bullet had entered just below her left breast and blasted out the back through her scapula. It just missed the apex of her left ventricle. Art had her chest open in minutes. They worked on her for an hour and forty-five minutes. She got ten units of blood. She would have died had it not been for that preparation.

Bob Broddick, the bastard whose privileges at Mason-Dixon I had threatened, was one of the other surgeons standing by that night. Ironically, he got me. He took out my spleen, and I got eight units of blood during the procedure. I was certain that he had relished every slice of the surgery, smiling to himself at the thought of the pain I would have when I awoke. Another hour and I probably would not have made it. "You cut it a little close," he smiled after the surgery.

Penny and I spent the next two days sort of together in adjacent rooms in the ICU. They discharged me to a floor room first. Penny was in the ICU for two more days. My kidneys shut down briefly the second post-operative day from lying around in shock for a couple of hours before my surgery, but they soon opened up again, and my recovery was otherwise uncomplicated.

Penny shooed the kids through the mudroom door and into the kitchen. Ruth had been happily working through the afternoon, baking bread and simmering a pot roast. She moved into one of the spare bedrooms when I was discharged from the hospital and had been living here ever since. It was a very satisfactory arrangement. Ruth's personality seemed to have changed. She was constantly chatty, and when Penny was here, they behaved much like mother and daughter.

Catherine and Jack noisily took their places at the table—Jack on his knees reaching across the table for a roll, dragging the tablecloth with him; a little fork and spoon tinkling to the floor.

"Jack! Sit down! Look what you're doing," his mother admonished.

I was uncertain in those first days about what had happened in the final second or two before I lost consciousness. I was haunted by my failure to reach the gun before Ronnie's shot into Penny's chest. Worst of all, I feared that perhaps my lunge for the gun had somehow contributed to the shot that nearly ended her life.

April visited me in the ICU on the second day after my splenectomy. She leaned over my bed and cried in my arms, as best as I could hold her, for a full fifteen minutes. "You never made it," she sobbed. "Your body just collapsed."

"Can I have another roll?" asked Catherine.

"Catherine, you haven't touched your pot roast," said her mother. "No more rolls until you eat some of your meat. And you have to eat at least two of your green beans."

I don't know how Penny managed to empty the morphine syringe, fill it with succinylcholine, and get back to the room in two and a half minutes. It was a huge risk. She told me that the other syringe contained only morphine. There had only been time to fill one syringe with the paralytic drug. Ronnie had chosen the syringe with the succinylcholine.

Lieutenant Tom O'Brien, the hostage negotiator, visited me in the ICU and told me that they had given Penny the option of not returning to the room, which, of course, she had steadfastly refused. To his credit, Lieutenant O'Brien had the courage to make a decision on the spot, and the police stayed out of her way. An assault had been planned for 8:45 PM.

The ER staff, who had waited poised throughout the crisis, worked on Ronnie, of course, just as hard as Penny and me, but he was paralyzed and unable to breathe for too long before they got to him. His oxygen-deprived brain was fried. He ended up traveling the same path as Andrew Price, and they harvested his organs on the fifth day. This outcome spared me the burden of killing him.

Ten days later, the Baltimore County State's Attorney called a press conference and announced to a media-packed room, amidst hundreds of camera flashes, that no charges would be filed against Penny Murray.

"So you gave your mom the weekend off?" I asked.

"Yes, poor woman," said Penny. "I sent her home. I told her, 'That's enough. I'm well enough now to manage. All I have to do is get Jack to day-care and Catherine on the bus.' She needs some recovery time. My poor father hasn't seen her in a month."

"Well," said Ruth, "I can help anytime. I just need to do laundry on Wednesday afternoons and clean on Saturdays. Otherwise, I'm free."

The Crips' attack on the Mara Salvatruca safe house had taken MS-13 by surprise. Julio survived by diving through a first floor window, dislocating his shoulder in the process. Ronnie followed him to Mason-Dixon. When the dispatches for the shoot-out hit the airwaves, Jack Schmidt grabbed another officer from precinct headquarters, hopped into his car, and, on a hunch, headed straight for Mason-Dixon to his death.

Ronnie's first shot felled Jack, and his second shot seriously wounded Officer John Svoboda. Ironically, Ronnie could probably have escaped—they were the only two cops on the scene at the time. Officer Svoboda refused to be evacuated to the operating room until additional officers arrived. It was he who made the call from his stretcher—ER staff working on him—just before Ronnie's first five-minute deadline.

"Mommy, can we ride Abigail again after dinner?" asked Catherine.

"No, baby. Only when Sally's here."

"Can you call her? Pleeeaase!" Catherine pleaded, hopping up and down on her chair.

"Honey, I'm sure Sally is having dinner herself right now, and has other things to do tonight. You've already ridden once today. Maybe next Saturday."

I had signed out of the hospital against medical advice on the fifth day to attend Jack Schmidt's funeral at St. Rita's Catholic Church in Parkville. Ben drove. The street in front of the decaying church was clogged with communications trucks from the TV stations. Ben dropped me off as close as he could get, and I slowly walked the last block to the granite steps.

The church was overflowing with Baltimore County police officers and media camera crews. I found Mrs. Schmidt and briefly thanked her for her husband's sacrifice. I didn't mention our plans for a summer evening eating crabs on the Chesapeake. The bagpipes wailed, and the service began.

Overnight Penny Murray became a household name. This was an unanticipated nightmare. The public's appetite to see more of the beautiful young widow whose intelligence and courage saved the lives of her fellow hostages—at the cost of nearly losing her own life—was utterly insatiable. By the end of the week her face was on the cover of every national celebrity magazine, and her voice mail overflowed with offers from journalists, TV producers, and publicists.

Carloads of paparazzi appeared as if out of thin air whenever it was rumored that Penny was on the move. They whisked her out of the hospital in the middle of the night in the back of an ambulance to Buchanan House, where she took refuge for the next month with her parents. The U.S. Navy proved to be a fairly formidable obstacle for the circling paparazzi.

I leaned back in my chair, stuffed, and watched the animated conversation and periodic admonishments around me. Catherine sat beside me, my arm draped over the back of her chair, my hand absently playing with her hair. Jack and Penny sat on the other side of the walnut table. Ruth sat at the head.

"Mommy, can I be excused?" asked Catherine.

Penny looked at Catherine's plate and, apparently deciding that the remaining pile of green beans looked small enough, said "Yes, baby."

"Me, too," said Jack.

Catherine hopped off her chair and ran off. Jack climbed out of his booster seat, taking the tablecloth with him and tipping over the milk remaining in Catherine's glass.

"Jack! Watch it!" Penny folded up the tablecloth before the milk hit the floor, and Ruth grabbed a dishcloth from the sink. The kitchen rang with the voices and laughter of children. Penny caught my eye and smiled, her green eyes gleaming.

ABOUT THE AUTHOR

D. Bruce Foster is a native of northern Baltimore County, Maryland, the location of the novel *Kiss Tomorrow Goodbye*, where he grew up observing the cultural milieu of My Lady's Manor steeplechase country. For twenty-five years he has been chief of emergency medicine at a Pennsylvania hospital, and is the medical director of an aero-medical helicopter service.

He has two published medical textbooks: *Twelve Lead Electrocardiography for ACLS Providers* published in 1996 by W. B. Saunders (Harcourt Brace), and *Twelve Lead Electrocardiography- Theory and Interpretation* published in 2007 by Springer. The former, now out of print, sold seven thousand copies, a significant performance for a medical textbook, and the latter earned a four star "Outstanding" rating from Doody's Book Review, a review service for the medical publishing industry.

Kiss Tomorrow Goodbye is Foster's first work of fiction. He lives with his wife on a farm in southern Pennsylvania in a lovingly restored pre-Civil-War brick farmhouse. You can learn more about Bruce Foster at www.dbrucefoster.com.

Made in the USA
Charleston, SC
21 February 2012